THE
DUKE
& THE
PIRATE
QUEEN

THE DUKE & THE PIRATE QUEEN

VICTORIA JANSSEN

Spice

Spice

THE DUKE & THE PIRATE QUEEN

ISBN-13: 978-0-373-60550-7

Copyright © 2010 by Victoria Janssen

Recycling programs
for this product may
not exist in your area.

For questions and comments about the quality of this book please contact us at Customer_eCare@Harlequin.ca.

www.Spice-Books.com

Printed in U.S.A.

For the Nameless Workshop, then and now, near and far.

CHAPTER ONE

"MY LADY," MAXIME SAID, "I UNDERSTAND YOU'RE disappointed—"

Lady Diamanta Picot threw a gold-and-ruby pomegranate at Maxime's head. He ducked, but it still clipped the top edge of his coronet and rebounded into the wall of the receiving room before hitting the floor and spinning to a stop.

A handblown goblet whizzed by his ear; he flung up his hand and caught it before it could shatter against the ducal throne behind him. "Now, wait," he said. "That was a particular token of my esteem—look at all these beautiful cloud fish etched into the bowl—"

"Fuck you!" Lady Diamanta screamed.

"I'm afraid not," Maxime said. "I did not agree to this marriage. Therefore I will not marry you."

Diamanta vibrated with rage, her slender fingers clenched upon the next gift, a handful of ebony hair sticks topped with gold knobs, the rich coppery-red gold of the far south, seldom seen in the duchies. She snarled, "You have no choice in the matter."

"On the contrary," Maxime said. "I am a duke of the realm. I may marry whom I please. My charter clearly states—"

"You will marry at the king's command," Diamanta said, her voice going cold. She set the hair sticks back on the table, but continued to fondle them, as an archer might fondle arrows. "If you refuse me, my life will be ruined."

"No, it won't," Maxime said. "You hate me. You've hated me since we were both fourteen." He set the goblet down on another table, out of her reach.

Diamanta licked her lips. They were plump and pink and inviting. Her fingers trailed along the table and lightly caressed the marquetry lid of a box of caraway comfits before returning to the hair sticks. She said, "My feelings don't enter into it, nor do yours. I am wealthy."

"So am I."

"That's why we belong together. That's why I am to be a duchess. My father's wealth will provide a substantial dowry for the crown, and for your duchy, as well. I've been trained from birth to manage a duchy and its interests."

"You won't be my duchess," Maxime said. He clasped his hands behind his back. The elaborate rings he'd worn, hoping she'd see them as the respect he intended for her, dug painfully into his fingers. "My refusal has nothing to do with your management skills. I am despondent you traveled all this way. I informed the king weeks ago I would not marry you, or anyone of his choosing. Perhaps you could convey this to him directly."

"You are a fool," she spat. "Our marriage could be a mutually beneficial arrangement. I would increase your wealth beyond anything you can imagine. You may have two heirs of me, or even three. And I would not restrain you from your…interests outside the marriage bed, if you would extend me the same courtesy."

She'd just stated his worst nightmare. Slowly, he shook his head.

He held her gaze. She held his. Slowly, she released her grip on the hair sticks and trailed her fingers up her rib cage and over her bosom, perfectly displayed in her low-cut purple gown. It was one of the finest bosoms in all the duchies. She lifted a brow. Maxime shook his head.

Diamanta took one of the hair sticks and briskly used it to tidy dislodged strands of her platinum-pale hair. She remarked, "You would have been lucky to have me. You're not such a prize, you know. No matter what the women of the court say of your…endowments."

"I'd rather not be a prize in a contest," Maxime said. "You will of course accept my gifts, which express my regret in refusing our betrothal?"

Diamanta cast a glance over the tables spanning the room, each one laden with silks, jewels, sweetmeats and exquisite handicrafts. Thirty matched tourmalines were arrayed on black velvet and surrounded by twists of intricate lace. Whole pears, glittering with an armor of sugar crystals, spilled from a brightly polished silver bowl, and a mixture of saffron pastilles and candied violets adorned a perfect marzipan replica of the king's castle. A tiny yellow bird with an orange beak warbled sweetly in its bamboo cage, and an albino monkey watched them from atop a tree carved from jade.

Diamanta fondled a distinctive enameled sweets box, this one the most valuable item of the lot, containing as it did candied lumps of a balsam imported from the other side of the world, which Maxime had not yet released to a general market. Feigning reluctance, she picked up the palm-size box. "I suppose they will have to do." She gestured to her silently waiting maid, whirled in a swirl of silks and exited.

After the door closed, Maxime sank into a chair and scrubbed his hands over his cropped dark beard. He'd barely escaped a fate that made him shudder inside—a lifetime of brittle politeness and brittle, obligatory sex with someone with whom he never wanted to converse. Being threatened with such a marriage was one of the things he'd managed to avoid while still merely Lord Maxime of the Coastal Protectorate.

He was lucky the king hadn't had him drugged and forced to speak vows. He cast a glance at his wineglass, remembered Diamanta had passed near it and poured its contents into a potted tree.

The monkey ate another grape.

He'd thought he had more time.

Until five months ago, he and his duchy had been treated as a client state in all that mattered. As the son of a duke murdered for unspecified acts of treason, Maxime's position had been precarious. One false move, or even a whim on the part of the king, and he would have been swept from power, perhaps even executed. For that reason, he had never married, and made certain never to sire an heir or indeed any child. He'd been left orphaned when his own parents were killed. He wouldn't wish that fate on anyone, either the initial pain or the subsequent subjugation to another.

He'd wanted to be his own man when he proposed marriage, free to ask because it was what he wanted, not because it was required of him. He'd wanted to marry a woman of his own choosing, who would share in ruling the duchy with him, as his parents had shared. He wanted a lover and a confidante, and he wanted those things with legal status that no one could take away. He'd waited years for the privilege of marrying as he wished.

This business of being a duke was not all that he'd hoped it would be. It was more of a prison than a privilege.

When he was still merely a lord, his unmarried status had been allowed, and even encouraged. Now, though, the dukedom was restored to him. His marriage had become a matter of concern to the new king, a concern that grew steadily more pressing. Letters and messengers had been succeeded by the actual appearance of Diamanta as a potential bride, and he didn't doubt other "choices" would soon arrive at his castle gates. He needed to marry soon, before the king took stronger action.

He would have to approach Captain Imena Leung.

For the thousandth time, he cursed himself for employing her soon after they'd met. If he'd known she would be so scrupulous about separating pleasure from her business relationships, he could have tried some other method to get to know her. It was too late now. He had to work with what he had, and if he wished to escape being married off like a virgin princess, he needed to work quickly.

He hadn't wanted to rush something so important. Again and again he'd delayed, out of fear he'd make a mistake and lose any chance at her forever. Now he had no choice, and for that, he cursed King Julien as well as his own cowardice.

Captain Leung was due back in the duchy this week, after a visit to her parents in the Horizon Empire. He would speak to her then.

Captain Leung seized one end of her trunk and hauled it noisily across the bamboo decking. "I'll visit in the spring," she said.

Her father stopped her with a hand on her shoulder. "Let me call a servant to carry your trunk."

"Quickly," she said. She didn't actually want to man-handle her trunk all the way across the palatial houseboat, up the stairs to the main deck and then down to the waiting cargo skip. She lowered it to the deck.

Her father smiled and gently stroked her arm with his large, callused hand. To most, his dark-skinned, elaborately tattooed face with its odd pale eyes was frightening; to her, impossibly dear. "Imena, you don't have to leave just yet. Your mother and I—"

Imena crossed her arms over her chest. "It was her idea to marry me off."

"Well, you *are* past thirty now, and—"

"*Your* marriage wasn't arranged for you," she pointed out. In fact, her father had been a prisoner of the imperial navy; his love match with her mother, his former captor, was still a scandal, decades later.

"That was different," he said. "Utterly different. We want to do the right thing for you. We don't want you to grow old alone."

"I'd rather marry one of Mother's lapdogs than one of that crew of—"

"Imena!" Her mother stood in the doorway, dressed in full regalia as an admiral of the fleet, looking much larger than she actually was; the immense pile of hair atop her head added to the illusion of size, but not as much as her posture and air of command. Three snub-faced dogs with silky black-and-white hair snuffled at the hem of her deck-length robe. The fourth flung itself onto a pillow on the deck, resting its head on its paws. "They are all respectable men," she said. "You won't have to suffer for your choice as I did. I had them investigated very carefully. Any one of them would make a fine husband for you."

"I don't want—"

"I spoke to all of them first, as well, and made sure to impress upon them how closely I'll keep my eye on them," her father said. He stroked the long knife he wore at his hip. "I've seen that these arranged marriages often work out well, much better than you would think at first. Most of the marriages in this port came about that way. If you would only reconsider—"

"I don't want—"

Her mother interrupted. "You'll never find a husband at sea, or among the foreigners. Be reasonable. Let us find a suitable man for you."

Apparently, her mother's own husband didn't count as a *foreigner*. "I don't want you to find a suitable man for me."

Admiral Leung's cheeks colored with anger. "Imena! I am your mother. It's your duty to obey me in this."

"As you obeyed *your* parents?" Imena asked. "I'll see you both in the spring." She bowed to her parents, stepped over her trunk, pushed past her mother and climbed up to the deck. She'd catch a ride in the cargo skip rather than wait for more formal transport.

At least on her ship people listened to her.

Three weeks later

Imena straightened her embroidered turquoise dress coat and brushed off the matching silk trousers as she emerged onto the deck of her ship, *Seaflower*. Her feet were bare, displaying their swirling wavelike tattoos, and she wore a long, jeweled dagger at her waist, a gift from her employer, Duke Maxime. She smiled. It felt good to be back in the duchy, where she was free of parental dictates. If only her mind could be free of them, as well. Her visit to Maxime should help. She always looked forward to seeing him. He was pleasant to look upon, and he wasn't difficult to talk to, either. Under other circumstances, she might have tried to seduce him.

No, she *would* have tried. And knowing him as she did, she would easily have succeeded.

Imena's handpicked sailors, both male and female, filled *Seaflower*'s narrow deck, chanting while they passed crates of mangosteens from hand to hand and thus onto the

dock. She gave them a nod in appreciation of their efficiency, and went to the railing where her first mate
waited.

Chetri smiled at her. His long, wavy hair was loose,
rippling in the breeze, a sure sign of upcoming shore
leave; normally he wore it tightly coiled at the back of
his neck. "We'll finish the offloading by this afternoon,"
he said.

"Shore leave is port watch first, this trip."

"Aye, Captain." He grinned at her. "And may I say the
captain looks…very clean and tidy?"

She laughed. "You may." She ran her hand over her
bare head. At sea, she rarely bothered to use a razor, but
in port she made a point to expose the intricate blue, red
and white designs tattooed on her scalp, each hard won
in her youth as an imperial privateer. Like Chetri, she'd
outlined her eyes with kohl.

Chetri wore tightly fitting trousers and a silver-
embroidered vest that showed his muscular form and the
black tattoos on his pectorals, circles within circles within
circles, to good advantage. Silver rings cascaded along
his earlobes; his neck was hung with bright silver chains,
one of them suspending a medallion engraved with birds,
another a cluster of black pearls. Another tattoo, this of
a snarling monster's face with a tongue of flame, marked
out his hard-muscled belly. He needn't worry that advanc-
ing middle age would deter anyone's glances. She said,
"May I offer the hope that my first mate is…lucky…on
his shore leave?"

"You most certainly may. Now, be off with you, Imena,

and do the pretty with His Grace. And may you be lucky, too. What's his name again? Sanji?"

Her stern glare only made him laugh. Chetri knew very well that Sanji had been her only lover for almost a year. There was a saying, that making the tide on land didn't count. For her, that had never been true.

She was lucky the potential husbands her mother had introduced to her hadn't permanently put her off sex. She'd never seen a more tightly laced bunch, draped in layers of fine silk robes and ballasted with necklaces and belts enough to festoon an entire fishing village, all of them eyeing her as if she were a trinket they wanted to buy, if they could only overcome their distaste at her profession.

She would have to face them again the next time she visited, or worse, she would have to confront her mother and make plain that she would not marry a man of the Horizon Empire, and forever be considered his accessory. After that, it would be almost trivial to convince her father that he could never threaten such a man into loving her. For a couple who swore they'd fallen in love at first sight, their opinions on marriage for their daughter seemed decidedly odd. Perhaps they'd finally realized the truth of the matter, as Imena had.

Her good mood was spoiling rapidly. Imena concentrated on the wooden pier beneath her bare feet, and the warmth of the sun on her scalp. Slowly, her mood improved. She missed the sea, as always when a voyage had ended, but shore had its own charms.

Here in port, the briny sea air mingled with the bite of boiling tar from the shipyard and tantalizing whiffs of sugary fried dough, overlaid with the scents of ripe fruits and steaming mint tea served hot and honeyed, of sticky rice balls and steamed fresh fish and hot spices. Her mouth watered; she would snack on a fish cake before she reported to Maxime.

Perhaps she would ask his advice on what to do about her parents' demands. He was past forty and unmarried, though his position was much different from hers; he could pick and choose his potential spouses. She shook her head. Doubtless, he had no time for personal conversations of that nature. Or if he made time…she didn't want his pity. She wanted…she didn't know what she wanted from him.

She stopped at the harbormaster's office to drop off the necessary paperwork from her last voyage. She made a brief call at the shipyard to deliver a list of supplies she and Chetri had prepared, bought a fish cake and a sugared dumpling for good measure, then waved over a donkey cart to carry her up the long hill to Maxime's castle.

The ride was the first time she'd had entirely to herself in months. She savored each bite of her fish cake as she watched the traffic around them, mostly traders, but a few locals, as well, who divided their work between the castle and the nearby town. One day, she planned to be one of those locals. She thought the duchy would be a better home to her than the land of her birth, where her position suffered from her mixed race. Her mother might be an admiral in the empress's navy, but even now her father was considered barely higher in rank than a concubine, despite all her mother's efforts to the contrary.

If Imena lived in the empire, with them, she would

have to endure low status. Privateers were considered far inferior to sailors in the navy, and in the company of her mother's people, her darker skin and paler eyes marked her out to even casual view. If she married here, however, she would be a citizen. Mixed race was less of a sin here, and she would be far from the only person of foreign birth, as well.

However, her past as an imperial privateer would still be against her. It was emblazoned forever on her skin. Even here, in a coastal town that knew the difference between pirates and privateers, she was often looked at askance, and sometimes worse. After all, she hadn't been a privateer for the duchy, but for a country that was only nominally an ally. Her motives would always be suspect.

She imagined presenting a list of her failings to a potential husband in the duchies. She could write each problem in a different color of ink: foreigner, mixed-race daughter of a not-entirely-respectable potentially-enemy naval officer and her exotic barbarian husband (acquired in dubious circumstances), and had she mentioned she was a suspected pirate?

Of course, she needn't marry. She could bear a child to a citizen of the duchy and gain citizenship through that route, but she didn't plan to go through the rigors of childbearing unless she was married already. Owning land in the duchy was another path to citizenship, except she was always at sea and wouldn't be able to oversee the land properly; also, even if she met all the other legal conditions, she would need to steward the land for a period of ten years before her petition would be heard. Marriage was the most direct path, and the most appealing to her.

An ox-drawn wagon trundled by, loaded with vegetables. Two children rode on the tail, their bare legs dangling over the edge. They whooped when they saw her; she waved a casual salute and they bounced with excitement until her donkey cart passed them. She glanced at her driver. "You'd think I was the duke."

He grinned. "His Grace they can see any day. It's not often they get to see Captain Leung."

Imena rubbed her hand over her scalp. "No, I suppose not." Sometimes it still took her by surprise that people she'd never met might be impressed with her; she was more used to wariness or outright fear from those who'd heard about her past and linked her with piracy and other crimes. Being viewed with admiration had never happened in her previous postings; but then, before her employment with the duchy she'd worked for and around the empire, where she would always be her mother's daughter, who could not inherit her mother's position as was proper. Where her appearance would always set her apart.

She could make her own position, here.

The duke's castle was built of local stone, green alternating with white in striped layers, the whole topped with crenellations and spiky observation towers, lending a resemblance to fish she'd seen when swimming among tropical reefs. The donkey cart crested the hill, passed the castle's first low wall and approached the bronze gates, heavily ornamented from top to bottom with representations of octopuses and different species of fish. The gates stood open on a path made of crushed white shells leading to the castle's ceremonial main doors, used for occasions such as when Maxime had been made duke.

Imena paid off her driver and approached a side entrance. Two guards with pikes checked her credentials and the handwritten note that allowed her to carry weapons into the castle, then a boy in livery swung open the door and waved her through. The temperature dropped inside, the deep green floor tiles cool against her bare soles. Imena was led down a corridor where oil lamps flung colored light on the white walls. Near the corridor's branching, she entered a chamber full of clerks, all busy calculating the duchy's wealth. Her own cargo would soon be written in the long books, minus her own share, and that of Chetri and her sailors.

The duke's aunt, Lady Gisele, was seated on a high stool near the door, reviewing columns of figures while a senior clerk stood by attentively. The pen Gisele held looked more incongruous in her scarred hand than the sword that hung at her hip. She looked up when Imena entered. "Captain! How very good to see you back. Will you have time for an evening of cards while you're here?"

Imena was always surprised that Lady Gisele welcomed her personally. She'd seen the older woman stand on much more ceremony with other captains in Maxime's employ. She replied, "I'll find out shortly, from His Grace. Chetri is arranging for your special shipment to be carried to the castle." Imena usually obtained some of Gisele's favorite teas on each voyage, along with new types for her to try. She reached into her pocket and withdrew a tin box. "I've also brought you more of the balsam ointment."

"Thank you!" Gisele beamed. "I used the last pot you brought me on an old scar. It's much better, look." She swung her arm in a full circle and added, "Sylvie is visiting. Perhaps she will join us for cards later. Maxime is in the baths. He asked that you be sent to him whenever you should arrive."

Imena had last seen Sylvie, the duchess Camille's bodyguard and lady's maid, at Maxime's accession. Sylvie had lost to her at cards, but, Imena later learned, had seduced Imena's card partner, a wealthy merchant. And the wealthy merchant's male paramour, an acrobat. And the acrobat's female performance partner, a contortionist. All at the same time. Imena was not in the mood for hearing about such adventures today. She resolved to avoid seeing Sylvie this trip.

She said, "I'll find His Grace in the baths."

Maxime often welcomed his guests in the extensive system of steam baths in the castle's lowest level. Sometimes sexual pleasures were offered, as well. Imena wasn't often entertained there, and she wondered at it now. Though they'd never spoken of it, Duke Maxime clearly found her attractive, and she just as clearly never encouraged him in the least. He was her employer, and off-limits.

She'd made *that* mistake once before. Never again. One unmitigated disaster was enough for any lifetime.

If Maxime *hadn't* been her employer, though, he might have been a candidate for a shore-leave affair, except that now he was also a duke, and clearly out of her reach. He definitely wasn't husband material. Dukes couldn't afford companionate marriage, and she refused to be merely a concubine or occasional lover.

She tried not to regret his accession to the dukedom. He'd been denied it his entire life; she ought to be happier that he'd achieved his goal. She never could have married him. Dukes or even almost-dukes didn't marry politically difficult foreign sailors of ambiguous social rank.

And Maxime…she didn't think he was made for marriage. Not the sort she would want. He had too many sexual partners, both his social equals and his servants alike. She wouldn't share. She couldn't see how he could forswear all others.

It was her parents' fault she'd suddenly become obsessed with marriage. Perhaps Maxime had planned on a bath anyway, and had no ulterior motives. It wasn't as if he had summoned her to his bedroom. She could use a soak in hot, mineralized water, and perhaps a massage from one of Maxime's highly trained servants.

Her muscles had been knotted for weeks, ever since she'd arrived home and been ushered aboard her parents' houseboat. The decks had been crammed with wealthy bureaucrats, swilling her parents' liquor and estimating the value of the furnishings. One of them in particular, a provincial tax collector, had offended her with his oily grins and the way he took every opportunity to offer her food and drink, as if he were the host and not her parents. He'd touched her arm without asking, pretending fascination with the muscles of a woman who worked on a ship. She'd had to resist planting her knee in his crotch.

She really must stop stewing over it. Her mother meant well. Her father went along because he trusted her mother's opinions when it came to imperial society, and planned to make the best of it in his own way. That didn't mean Imena had to go along, as well. She would tell her parents so, as soon as she saw them again. Or, better, she would simply marry here and tell them afterward. She didn't want to marry for convenience, but offered the alternative of an imperial, she would do it... wouldn't she? If it didn't work out, there was always the sea.

The corridor leading to the baths was utterly silent except for the faint rippling sound of lantern flames behind colored glass.

A heavy door, decorated with octopuses, opened and a man stepped out. He was naked, but in the area of the baths that was unremarkable. They exchanged polite nods, and he headed in the opposite direction, toward a row of guest chambers.

Was the man one of Maxime's lovers? He'd partnered with almost as many men as women. She knew firsthand from two different ship captains that they'd shared liaisons with him.

It shouldn't matter to her. Maxime was no worse than many a sailor, except he had more opportunity for affairs. She wasn't sure why it bothered her. She had no business being jealous of his attentions.

She dragged open the door and slipped in, remembering to say, "Your Grace?" rather than "my lord." She had not seen Maxime since soon after his accession.

He'd looked grand that day, his shoulder-length hair bound back in a sheath of gold filigree, emeralds glinting from his earlobes, encrusting his white gloves and shining from the buttons of his white silk coat, embroidered all over with waving kelp and heraldic octopuses.

Just now, all the panoply was gone; he was naked, and pouring a pail of water over his head. Soap bubbles sped down his muscular back, rear and thighs along with the water, leaving a damp sheen on his pale skin that begged for touch. Also, for her tongue.

Imena shook herself and repeated, "Your Grace?"

Maxime whirled. The pail in his hand did not block her view of his dark chest hair, flat belly and impressive cock. Hastily, she shifted her gaze to his face. Nudity was normal in the baths, but it wasn't polite to stare.

He didn't look as if he'd been engaging in sex, and the bathing room did not hold any scent of such activities.

His voice was low and pleasant as usual. "Captain Leung. I hadn't expected you so soon. It's good to see you. How was your visit home?"

He turned away quickly and scooped up a towel from a nearby bench, wrapping it around his waist. He wasn't usually modest at all, so the towel surprised her, but perhaps he was chilled. Perhaps he'd dunked himself in cold water, but if so, surely his genitals... She stopped the thought, and an urge to laugh.

No doubt the towel was intended to let her know he wasn't trying to seduce her. She hadn't expected to find him alone, without even a servant. It was the unexpected intimacy that led to such thoughts about him, forgetting he was her employer. She hadn't ogled him before, in similar situations. Well, not very much.

"I can return later, if you wish," she said.

He used another towel to rub at his dark hair, then

twisted it back from his face with a ribbon. "No, no." He gave her a closer look, and grinned. His smiles could be stunning, white teeth slowly revealed in his dark beard, and Imena was momentarily dazed. "Perhaps I shouldn't have asked about your visit home. You look as if you could use a nice soak. Here, I'll scrub you down while you report."

Men and women were usually segregated in public baths, but in private ones standards were relaxed. She'd more than once visited the castle baths to see servants ministering to guests of opposite gender, or guests doing so themselves. However, she hadn't thought a duke would take on such a task.

She was being foolish. This was Maxime. Duke or not, he was a very physical man. He wouldn't change his bathing habits because of a title. And she…would like to have someone else bathe her. She was more tired than she had any right to be, her body tight with stress and unresolved anger. Maxime's strong hands would feel good on her skin. A little indulgence wouldn't kill her. This was only a bath.

"That would be welcome, Your Grace."

She was already sweating in her silk coat and trousers, and it felt good to slip them off and hang them on hooks next to Maxime's elaborate coat. Her dagger and belt knife went on a shelf next to his. The gold hoops from her ears went into a wooden bowl that already held his lacquered finger sheaths, an official-looking medallion and a pair of immense ruby earrings. Normally, he didn't adorn himself quite so much. She asked, "Who visited today?"

He grimaced. "An envoy of the king." Imena glanced around, and he gestured to a wooden bench. "Sit. I'll carry the water."

The bench was warm and polished to a sheen with age and scrubbing. Oil lamps in niches lit the stone chamber in sunset shades of red, orange, pink and gold; portions of the stone floor had been mosaicked in similar colors. Steam curled gently from the soaking pools; she inhaled and felt her breathing ease. It felt good to be nude. She could already feel the warmth easing into her as she laid a towel over the bench and sat. She listened to Maxime pour water. As he approached, she asked, "Why did the king send an envoy? Does he want his taxes? Have you been holding back, Maxime? Your Grace," she added.

He didn't appear to notice how she'd addressed him. "Close your eyes." He smoothed a warmed cream around her eyes and gently wiped it away, removing the kohl from her skin. She could feel his breath on her face as he worked, more intimate than his hand's touch. He cleaned the rest of her face with more lotion and a new cloth, then scrubbed her ears and finally her scalp. Shivers passed down her back with each touch. She was hard put not to shove her head against his hand like a petted cat.

"Why an envoy?" she asked again.

The soapy cloth touched her shoulder blade and he scrubbed vigorously. She bit back a moan of pleasure and closed her eyes. Maxime didn't answer her until the delightful scrubbing paused and she heard him rinsing the cloth in the bucket. "His Highness sent the lord Odell, whom you might remember is the chief steward of the Duke's Council. His Highness King Julien the

Seventh, Master of the Eastern Passes, Sovereign of the Eight Duchies—which includes mine, he made sure to remind me—requires me to marry. He is weary of waiting for me to accomplish this on my own recognizance, and has ordered I marry immediately." He returned to scrubbing her back, more vigorously than before.

She sighed and rested her elbows on her thighs so he could scrub harder. "I suppose since he can't bear your heir himself, someone under his thumb is the next best thing."

A moment's silence, then Maxime laughed. "Julien *is* an attractive man, but I don't think his tastes run to partners who are bearded."

Fighting down an unexpected sharp disappointment, she asked, "When's the wedding?"

"I refused."

Imena peered over her shoulder at him, awkwardly because he was scrubbing her arm, shoulder to fingers. He wasn't smiling. "You're a duke of his realm," she said.

"So I am. With all the rights and powers given thereunto. I'm a tad annoyed it took blackmail for that to happen, given that I was born to the position. Julien likely has another envoy on the way. I've already begun preparing a legal defense if he should try anything dubious."

"Do you have an heir already?"

"I wouldn't be so careless!" he said harshly. Immediately, he released his grip on her. "I'm sorry. Did I hurt you?"

His fingers had tightened on her, but only for a moment. "No. Will you scrub the other arm?" She'd never seen him show anger, not like this; not helpless anger, like the kind she felt herself. The rush of empathy she felt for him startled her, and she barely resisted laying her hand on his shoulder.

Maxime was much gentler with her left arm. "You didn't come here to listen to me complain," he said. "I have nothing to complain of." He rinsed the cloth and added more soap; he swept the cloth over her breasts and belly with cool detachment. "Did the mangosteens travel well?"

Imena tried to ignore the warmth of his hands through the cloth. "Exceptionally so. We'll be stowing them that way next time, as well. The custard fruit also. Chetri will be sending up a crate for you."

She detailed the rest of the cargo, its cost and the expected profit, grateful for the distraction. As he swept the cloth over her thighs, Maxime said absently, "I like this one." His fingers outlined an octopus tattoo, concealed within swirling tracery.

She shivered; this touch felt more intimate than the others. She didn't mention she'd been thinking of him as she chose the design, and seen him in her mind as the needles had punctured her skin. The memory mixed oddly with the gentle pleasure of his touch.

He moved on to the rest of her leg without further comment. He asked other questions, his usual ones involving local conditions at the ports she'd visited, occasionally inquiring after a port official or shipyard master whom he knew. She gave him all the bits of information she'd gathered, no matter how small, including reports she'd had from Chetri, various of her sailors and her cabin girl, Norris.

Maxime listened to it all, an abstracted look on his face, but she knew from past experience he would forget nothing. When she'd finished speaking, he tossed a towel on the floor, knelt and began washing her feet.

He wasn't massaging, or stroking more than he needed to stroke, but she couldn't deny the erotic thrill racing up her legs. Imena stared down at the nape of his neck and thought about resting her hand there, or pressing her lips where his hair was pulled aside. She needed to say something, anything to distract her from his fingers sliding soap between her toes. She imagined his tongue sliding delicately between her toes and shivered with desire. Desperately, she said, "My parents want me to marry."

CHAPTER TWO

MAXIME'S HANDS STOPPED MOVING, AND IMENA
slowly let out her breath. He would stop touching her
now, and she could relax. He was to marry a courtier's
daughter because his king commanded. She was to marry
someone who wasn't a duke; therefore even the thought
of…this…was impossible.

There was no *this*. Maxime was performing a servant's
duty for her, that was all. One of his odd notions of diplomacy. She was a little overcome by his touch because
she'd been at sea for months and was sadly deprived of
sex.

She needed to shake off inappropriate arousal, leave
here and find Sanji, who was always glad to see her on
her infrequent visits to his chandler's shop. Sanji would
take care of her need in his sunny bedroom, and then
they'd have a lovely dinner and she would play with his
two sons out in his garden, and she might spend the night.

He'd be happy to have her spend the night. He always said he'd like to see more of her.

She was having a difficult time remembering why mild, steady Sanji was preferable to Maxime.

After a pregnant pause, Maxime placed her soapy foot on the towel covering his thigh and began washing her calf, his strokes slower than before. She flexed her callused toes involuntarily against hard muscle; his shoulders tightened. She looked away. She would not think of it. She would not. He said, "Did your parents offer you any choice of husbands?"

Never had she been so grateful for conversation. "Nearly a dozen," she said.

"Were any of them suitable?"

"They were all…very monied. Very eager to marry into the family of Admiral Leung. She chose them, though my father had final say."

Maxime moved to her other calf. "They were eager to join with her family, but not with you? They object to your father?" When she didn't answer, he said, "You told me about him, remember? I know he was a foreign captive."

She'd forgotten that drunken evening, which he'd referred to as her interview for a position as his trusted captain. "Did I tell you what else that means?"

"You can't inherit a position in the imperial navy," he said in a detached tone. "Nor can your children. They can't work for the imperium, at least not for payment, though their children's children will be allowed to do so, so long as they pass the appropriate examinations. And provided all their other ancestry is imperial. You *are,* however, permitted to work as a privateer, risking death for the imperium's glory." As he spoke, he stood and dropped the cloth in the bucket. His hands closed over her tight shoulders and massaged.

Despite the bitter truth of his words, Imena drooped forward, sighing with pleasure. His thumbs were digging unerringly into the worst knot, just at the base of her neck. She hadn't realized how much her head was aching until the gnarled muscle released. As if he knew, Maxime smoothed his palm over her scalp before returning to the massage. He said, "So what is the advantage, if you marry one of these men?"

Imena considered, though it was hard to think while his hands squeezed the tension from her shoulders and neck. "Position," she said. "I'd be absorbed into his family, and would thus be considered trustworthy, at least to a certain extent. My husband would be responsible for me." She tried to keep the anger from her tone, but couldn't manage it.

"You're not going to do that."

"I might have to." She slumped on the bench as his hands traveled down either side of her spine, pressing out tension as they went. "I'd have money of my own, to dispose of as I wanted. I would have to give up *Seaflower,* though. The wives of wealthy men don't go to sea."

He said, "It won't come to that, if you'd accept sanctuary in the duchy."

She smiled. "Thank you for the offer, but I don't think King Julien would be happy to have the daughter of an imperial admiral living in his kingdom."

"What if you married someone here? Your loyalty

would be assumed more readily, and your children could do whatever they wished."

She closed her eyes. "I've...considered it."

"Have you?" Maxime clapped his hand against her shoulder. "Let's have that soak."

Imena chose cool water to douse herself and disperse her arousal before she slid into one of the smaller pools, across from Maxime. The stone bench beneath the water was slippery, and she had to brace herself with her toes. A moment later, she realized she'd braced herself against Maxime's leg.

"I *am* sorry!" she said, splashing as she hitched herself higher on the bench.

Maxime laughed. He reached out and snagged her arm, drawing her to sit next to him. "If you sit here, you can see the new sculptures."

Imena eyed him and tried not to grin. "Your Grace, are you trying to seduce me?"

"Only a little," he said, and slung his arm over her shoulders. "Have pity," he said. "I've had a difficult day, too." He leered in a patently false way, and she laughed. Perhaps it would be all right. She could indulge, just a little, and harm nothing.

"Just this once, I will sit with you," she said, and settled back against him. A velvety thrill chased over her skin as their bodies met. She shifted so their shoulders overlapped. His muscular bulk was as solid and comforting as it looked; the hair on his chest was softer than she'd expected. She wanted to rub herself against him, all over, just for the sensual pleasure of it, a reaction she didn't even have to Sanji.

Such a pity Maxime was a duke, a pity for her and for him. She, at least, could flee the men her parents had chosen for her. She didn't think Maxime would elude his king's choices for very long. His arm tightened around her shoulders. It was more difficult to fight her body's desire when she was this close to him. She slid lower in the water and rested her cheek on his firm pectoral, her nose tantalizingly close to his nipple. He smelled of cedar-scented soap. She could lick him with no effort at all, if she wanted.

Maxime said, "You're not dozing off, are you? You haven't admired the sculptures. Over there, in the grotto."

Imena looked. The grotto had been hollowed out of the bathing chamber's far corner to reveal stalactites; they'd been embedded with crystals that glowed softly in the lamplight. The new sculptures were small glass octopuses in every color of the rainbow, attached in different positions as if they swam among a forest of stone.

"They're lovely," she said.

"I'm glad you like them," he said. He rubbed his hand over her upper arm. "Captain Leung, what if you married me?"

Imena laughed. "That's the worst possible solution to both our problems. I would be a terrible liability to you."

"Not necessarily," Maxime said. He leaned a fraction to the side and kissed her ear, then the bare sensitive skin above it; the touch resonated down to her toes. Imena shivered and thought about edging away, but her body didn't want to move. His nearness sang along her nerves. He said, "You have many valuable qualities. I also have many admirable traits that I would like you to consider."

"Such as?" He was nuzzling behind her ear now, and at the back of her neck, and she really ought to stop him, but just those small touches felt amazingly sweet. She reached out to steady herself and found she'd grabbed his thigh.

"I would make your mother angry," he suggested. His fingers trailed along her forearm, more gently than she would have expected. "You didn't say you wanted that, exactly, but—"

"You're entirely too good at this," Imena said. Still she didn't move away from him. She should do it. She should. But his touch felt so good, and she felt...close to him. Close from their talking, not from his body against hers. She wanted more closeness, however she could get it. Just a little. A little while longer.

She could be casual with him. She could keep her emotions under control. She was in no danger from him, nor he from her. She always worried too much. Perhaps she should give that up, and just once take what she wanted when she wanted it.

He said, "I'm too good at enticing you, or at guessing what you want?"

"Either. Both. I don't know." His breath was warm on her skin. It was making her flush more than the heat of the water. What if he kissed her? What could it hurt if she kissed him? She'd hardly be the first and would certainly not be the last.

"If you married me, you'd be a citizen of this duchy,

and your children would even have diplomatic protection if they wanted to visit their grandparents."

She said, "I never said I wanted children." Maxime kissed the nape of her neck and, retaliating, Imena squeezed his thigh.

"You wouldn't have to give up your ship."

"Stop it," she said. She twisted around, grabbed his hair and said, "If you're trying to seduce me, I'd rather you didn't talk about impossibilities." She kissed him, firmly, and had to take a sharp breath at the taste of him. "Your seduction has worked. You don't have to discuss this anymore."

"But what if I want to—"

Imena kissed him again. "I don't want to talk about it anymore. I have had a very trying few weeks. Do you want to fuck, or not?"

"An interesting question." Maxime slid off the bench and stood in the pool before her. "I've tried that, in these pools, and it really wasn't as exciting as you'd think. Inconveniently placed lumps of stone, for example, and of course there's the mineral residue. But if you would just lean back and relax—" He smoothed his hands over her arms, then cupped her breasts. He could cover each one entirely with a hand; she felt her nipples tighten and press into his palms. "Stop scowling."

His touch felt wonderful, but wasn't distracting her from her problems. "I'm not scowling."

"You think this is a bad idea."

"Not entirely," she admitted. "I do want you."

"I suppose my being a cure for a terrible mood is better than some of the alternatives. I won't be offended if you refuse me. Do you want me to stop?" When she shook her head, Maxime smiled and touched her face. His thumb brushed her cheek like a kiss. "Then perhaps if you come screaming a few times, it will help."

Startled at his bluntness, Imena laughed. His mouth closed over hers, his tongue searching. She grasped his shoulders, then tangled her fingers in his hair. Wet, it dragged between her fingers. She burrowed down to his scalp and scratched. He moaned into her mouth and pulled back.

"No, no, you're the one who's supposed to be moaning," he said. He rubbed his palms over her bare scalp, sending tingles down her torso. He didn't stop, and she shuddered, arching up toward his body. "I wonder if I could make you come like this? You just shaved it, didn't you? Your skin is so smooth. It feels like honey looks." He leaned forward and licked. "You taste better than honey," he said, his voice lowering.

He bent and suckled her nipples, one after the other, just enough to tantalize, not enough to satisfy. "Round and firm as grapes," he murmured, and pressed them with the flat of his tongue, as a tongue might press her clitoris. She spread her knees, using her thighs to grab his hips; he made a needy sound and nestled between her legs. His cock thumped against her belly, enormous and hard and hot as the water, and she squeezed his length with her hand while he rubbed against her. His cock filled her palm, heavy and growing heavier. She wanted to put her mouth on it.

"That feels exquisite," he murmured in her ear.

"Stop, stop. You've got to stop that, or I won't be able to—here."

He slid his hands beneath her buttocks and lifted her out of the water, planting her firmly on the pool's edge. "Strong," she gasped. She caressed his shoulders, his skin satiny from its recent scrubbing, his muscles like carved jade beneath.

Maxime rubbed her thighs, then pressed her legs apart and teased her cunt with his forefinger, sliding down the seam of her outer lips, leaving heat in his wake. She stopped breathing. He said, "You're all gorgeous muscle with this glorious softness in the center. Have you ever sucked the sweetness from an orange? I'm going to peel you open, hold you captive against my mouth and suck your flesh until your juice runs down my chin."

Imena grabbed his head and tugged him forward. She saw his teeth glint in a grin before he pressed a kiss to her inner thigh, on her octopus tattoo, his damp beard rasping softly against her skin as he nuzzled the line where her torso met her thigh. "Your skin is like silk, soft as water, soft as water on my skin," he murmured. One cheek brushed her cunt, his beard tangling in her hair, pulling with a thousand tiny flashes of pleasure. She dragged his head to her cunt and growled wordlessly, knowing he would allow it, sensing he would even like her forcefulness.

Maxime's breath steamed over her flesh. Delicately, he opened her lower lips with his thumbs. "Did you know all women look different inside? But you're all so tender, and slick, and you smell so delicious—" He rubbed her with his nose, then pressed his tongue to her flesh, a sensation soft and wet above and faintly rasping with beard below. "You taste like the ocean."

Imena panted and dug her fingers into his hair. She might be hurting him. She tried to relax her grip, but couldn't manage it at first. When she did, she couldn't drag her hands away from his head, couldn't stop stroking his hair.

He was suckling at her now, and teasing inside her with a fingertip. She wound tighter, tighter, then shuddered in a brief climax. "More?" he said. He scraped her clit with his teeth, soothed with his tongue, then did it again, and again until she gasped and writhed up against his mouth. Still he continued with the sequence of hard and soft until all at once she came forcefully, for a few moments losing control of her limbs.

Maxime brushed her softly with his tongue as ripples of feeling passed through her, easing her down. When she'd caught her breath again, she released her grip on his hair. Her arms felt loose and relaxed now, at least more so than they had been; she still wanted to bury her fingers in his hair, stroke his scalp and tickle her fingers with his beard. Perhaps it was the way he smiled at her, openly delighted that he'd made her come.

Her chest tightened at the sight, tightened enough to hurt. For long moments, she couldn't breathe, couldn't look away from his eyes, creased at the corners with his smile. He was sweet, as sweet as Sanji. She hadn't expected that. She wanted to curl up against him and lie quietly for a time; she wanted to close her eyes so the sight of his smile wouldn't hurt her anymore. Instead, she said, "My thanks."

"You didn't scream," he said, stroking her thighs. Her muscles were still trembling, just on the edge of perception. "I think you need another or three."

He rose higher on his knees and kissed her; she tasted the sea on his lips, and belatedly realized she was tasting herself. She shuddered, deep in her belly, and Maxime caught her to him with one arm. Her breasts rubbed his chest and she abruptly wanted to be lying down, with his weight pinning her. Wanted to hook her thighs around his hips and burrow her heels into his muscular buttocks. Another few moments and her desire would be fulfilled.

She couldn't do this. It would hurt too much.

She couldn't make the tide with her employer. She shouldn't even have glimpsed the merest flicker of a possibility of fucking her employer. Who was a duke. It was a terrible idea, and she'd even warned herself against it before arriving here. It didn't matter that Maxime was a trustworthy man whom she liked. She had learned her lesson about mixing business with pleasure years ago. She should never have taken her clothes off in the first place.

"Thank you," she said again. "That was lovely. I'll send the manifests over as soon as I've received them from the harbormaster. Goodbye, Your Grace."

She was nearly out the door before he called to her. She whirled; he'd scrambled out of the pool and stood dripping on the floor. "What's wrong?" he asked.

"Nothing," she said. "It was fun. Thank you. I'll see you later on—"

He glanced down at the floor. "You might want to put

on a robe first," he said. "No, why don't I leave? You can stay here, and have your soak. I'm sorry I upset you."

"You didn't." Useless words, when he could see her knees trembling.

Maxime grimaced. "Of course not. If you need me, I'll be in my rooms." Imena barely remembered to move out of the doorway so he could leave. He snagged a robe from a hook, wrapped it around himself and exited.

Imena stared around the empty bathing chamber. "That went well," she muttered.

She ought to have stayed at sea.

CHAPTER THREE

THE WALK BACK TO HIS QUARTERS DID NOTHING to ease Maxime's agitation. He hadn't been so maladroit since he was a boy. Imena had enjoyed his seduction, it was clear, but it was also clear to him he'd misjudged how to ease her mind about marriage. Or misjudged something else entirely. Or—

He stopped in the middle of the staircase and glared down at his erection until it subsided somewhat. He might have done better to remain distant, but such a thing was impossible when he was faced with her. He had never wanted anyone so much in his entire life. At least not since he'd been a young man ruled entirely by his genitals.

Resuming his climb, he muttered, "I seem to be ruled by them even now." Next time—if there was a next time—he would plan. He would make sure to take himself in hand before he saw her, to be able to ignore his own desires for long enough to convince her of his sincerity. Even if he had to take himself in hand several times.

He flung open the door to his rooms, strode in and stopped. Sylvie, a trusted courier of the adjacent duchy, sat cross-legged on a padded hassock, idly selecting from a tray of grapes and other dainties. Her blond hair hung loose to her waist, contrast to the snug riding leathers and matching jacket she wore, which clung to every sleek curve of her body; that lushness balanced nicely with her sharp features and the sarcastic intensity of her expression. He wondered if she was about to cut another swath through his staff. Her visits usually resulted in a string of besotted glances.

Sylvie never had problems with her unending stream of lovers. He should take a lesson from her, and not let a physical act affect his emotions in this way.

"The reports are on your desk, Your Grace," she said, looking up at his entrance. She popped a marzipan starfish into her mouth. After she'd swallowed, she added, in a more formal tone, "Her Grace the Duchess Camille and her consort, Henri, send greetings." She took a sip of wine. "Henri said Aimée sends her greetings, as well, though I think this is unlikely, since the child doesn't yet speak intelligibly, and I doubt she remembers you at all. It has been so many months since any of us have seen you. If you recall, she fell asleep during the ceremony when you were made duke."

"Have you done putting me in my place?" Maxime asked. "Was there anything specific Camille wished from me, that you couldn't leave with my aunt or one of the secretaries?" Camille was enough his friend—they'd once been lovers—that she likely would have sent him a detailed document if she'd needed anything from him personally. And Sylvie would have told him before now if she'd carried any queries that could not be committed to paper.

Sylvie sampled a few aniseed comfits, uncurled and rose effortlessly to her feet. "I think you have a sea urchin shoved in a delicate place," she said. "Has the exquisite captain refused you?"

Maxime swallowed outrage. Sometimes he liked Sylvie's impertinence. Today was not one of those times. Rather than answer, he passed through a doorway into his office and opened the diplomatic pouch. He spilled letters, reports and other dispatches onto the desk's marquetry surface. Camille had sent a drawing of her plump baby daughter: her lover, Henri, held the child atop a sleek pony. Maxime reflected that the child might be his if things had been different. In the normal way of things, one duke might marry his daughter to the son of his neighbor, forming local alliances. Instead, Camille's father had slain both Maxime's parents, taken their duchy as his own protectorate and kept Maxime as a political hostage. Camille's father had let Maxime know, in more ways than one, that he would not be permitted to marry his captor's daughter or even to think himself worthy of her.

Perhaps it was for the best. He and Camille were far too much alike. Maxime was happy and relieved she'd displaced her insane husband in order to rule her own duchy, and found love in the process, however much she might deny how she felt about Henri.

His mind snapped back to the present when Sylvie said, "I don't think you normally walk about your castle clad only in a robe. And the lady Gisele told me Captain Leung had gone to speak with you. Are your bollocks still in a clench over her?"

He grabbed his own diplomatic pouch and thrust it into Sylvie's hands. "I am going to marry her."

"Madame tells me the king says different."

"Julien can go and suck a splintery arse-dildo," Maxime snarled.

Sylvie laughed. She tossed the diplomatic pouch onto a latticed chair. "The exquisite captain is a fool, refusing both me and you."

"She has no interest in women," Maxime said. "She's interested in me. I know it."

Sylvie stepped closer, and closer still. She laid her small hands inside the open neck of Maxime's robe. "Quiet," she said.

"I'm running out of time," Maxime said. He hadn't intended to say it, but her soft touch had bypassed his control.

Sylvie slid her hands down, parting his robe as they went. "This will help," she said. "You needn't fear. I do this merely as a favor given out of pity for your sad state, and will have forgotten it by tomorrow. Let me help."

"I can—"

"Oh, be quiet. It will help me, at least. I've been want-ing to get my hands on your cock." True to her words, she grasped him firmly in both hands. She pricked him briefly with her nails, and he gasped. "Pay attention."

He'd been aroused for a considerable time already, and

her touch had made his painful erection rigid again. He closed his eyes as her hands stroked him firmly. "Sylvie, you really don't have to—"

"I have never heard any man protest as much as you! Not even Henri!" Her grip changed, and when he looked, she'd dropped to her knees in front of him. Thoughtfully, she said, "You have the biggest cock I have ever seen."

"I've heard that before," Maxime said glumly. "I've thought of giving it its own title and lands, a signet cock ring, maybe commissioning a special song from the ducal musicians."

She wasn't listening to his attempt at humor. She said, her tone still speculative, "I'm sure I can swallow it."

"Sylvie!" Maxime tried to step back, but gently, afraid she wouldn't loosen her grip. Or perhaps afraid she would loosen it. "Don't you have business elsewhere?"

"You look very uncomfortable. Do you want me to suck your cock?"

Her touch felt wonderful. She wasn't Imena, but... "Yes?"

Keeping a firm grip on him, one hand over the other, Sylvie licked the ridge beneath his cock, end to end. "I need a better answer than that," she prompted. She licked him again.

"All right! Go on!"

"That's the answer I wanted," she noted approvingly, and nestled her mouth over his cock's head. Her tongue dipped into the slit and he grasped her slender shoulders, leather crumpling softly beneath his fingers. Sylvie smelled overwhelmingly of leather, with hints of aniseed and marzipan. Nothing like Imena.

If she'd only given him another chance, it might be Imena's mouth on him now, her full lips grasping and pulling at his cock's head, her soft tongue swirling beneath his foreskin. She'd liked it when he'd caressed her scalp. He would do that for her, caress her with palms and hard fingertips and the gentlest of scratches.

Sylvie. This was Sylvie, not Imena. He was letting Sylvie suck his cock because it was less lonely than bringing himself off, alone in his rooms. He needed to tell her how much he appreciated this, but she was so skilled it was difficult for him to form words. A groan fell from his lips, and she rubbed his hip approvingly.

"Sylvie—" he said.

"Yes, Your Grace?"

She nibbled at his foreskin, fondling him with both hands. This wasn't as encompassing as her steady suction, and he breathed easier. He said, "I'll never be able to watch you eat anything again without remembering this."

"I know." She reached around and slapped his buttock. "I think you would like this to be fast and hard."

"I would prefer that, yes." Fast and hard would blank his mind, stop him yearning for the woman he could not have.

Sylvie let go of his erection and dug her fingers into his buttocks. "You are pathetically in love with her, aren't you?"

"Just get on with it, Sylvie. Are you going to swallow that or not?"

Sylvie pinched him sharply, an exquisite thrill down the length of his cock, and sucked him into her mouth, unmercifully torturing his tenderest spots. Seconds later, all his thoughts were gone, whited out with rapidly climbing, painful need.

He came hard, his spine unkinking with each spasm. Gasping for breath, he threw out a hand and caught himself on the desk. Warmth shuddered over his skin, leaving relaxation in its wake, but also burgeoning despair. "Thank you," he said to Sylvie, who still crouched on the carpet. She was smirking with arrogant satisfaction. At least she had enjoyed herself. "And you?" he asked.

Sylvie rose to her feet, wiping her mouth on the back of her hand. "You're already wishing you hadn't let me, aren't you?"

"Of course not!" Maxime said. "You're amazing, Sylvie. What would you like from me? The same? Or would you like to take your pleasure with me otherwise?"

She laughed. "*Pah!* I can see it in your eyes. Guilt. You don't want me right now. The captain hasn't given you anything, and still you feel loyalty to her." She dug a handkerchief from the pocket of her jacket and wiped Maxime's softened cock, a little more roughly than he would have liked. "You are like a girl in the first throes of infatuation." She tugged him down to her and kissed his mouth, quick and hard. "I already had to endure endless sighs of longing from Henri and Madame as they discovered romance. From you, it is even more pitiful."

Wonderful. He couldn't even manage an uncomplicated fuck to console himself. "I see. I'm dismissed, am I?"

"You are, Your Grace," Sylvie said. She patted his hip. "If you will excuse me, a pair of your largest footmen await me in my chambers. And the little one, too, Volker. The one who does the thing with his tongue."

Maxime winced. "I'd prefer not to know what you're doing to my staff."

Sylvie poked out her tongue at him. "You may come to me again when the delicious captain abandons you barefoot on the docks of a foreign port, and I will consider—consider only—tying you to a bed for my pleasure."

CHAPTER FOUR

IMENA WASN'T ABLE TO ENJOY HER SOAK IN THE baths. As soon as she was sure Maxime had truly departed, she dried herself, dressed and returned to *Seaflower,* heaving a sigh of relief as soon as she felt the deck shifting beneath her feet. Chetri was gone, as was half of her crew, all of them no doubt carousing throughout the town's shops, brothels and bathhouses, having perfectly licentious shore leave. She would do the same. She stormed into her cabin and swiftly divested herself of her turquoise finery, tossing it onto her wide bunk.

"No, sir! You'll crush it!"

Imena's cabin girl, Norris, darted into the cabin, hands outthrust as if to prevent wrinkles by force of will. She darted beneath Imena's arm and seized the jacket and trousers to her flat chest. Small and slim-hipped, she wore her long ginger hair pinned up with myriad lacquered clips, and her face made up with a careful selection of cosmetics. Though she was, in fact, male, she had dressed as a girl since a young age, and as a result was usually better turned out than her captain. Her tailored green jacket and loose trousers were considerably more elegant and stylish than most of Imena's garments. Also, she was very skilled at making the most of Imena's minimal bosom.

Imena scooped up a faded linen singlet and yanked it over her head. "Fine. Pack it away. I won't need it for a while."

Norris took the silk garments to the wide table Imena used for charts and spread them carefully atop the glass surface. "I've packed a trunk for you, to take to the castle."

"I'm not going back to the castle."

"But Chetri said—"

"I've already seen His Grace. I'm going to visit Sanji." Imena snatched a pair of linen trousers from atop a trunk and yanked them on over her knee-length drawers. "Where's my jacket?"

"Hanging in the wardrobe," Norris said. "I pressed it. You can't go ashore all crumpled. You're the captain."

Imena slid open the wardrobe's bamboo door and found her plain black jacket, now crisply tidy and scented with lavender. She grabbed a brimmed cap from the top shelf and crammed it onto her head to shade her eyes. "His Grace did not hire me for my sartorial elegance," she said wryly.

"No, I don't think he did," Norris said, winking. Imena threw her discarded undershirt at her.

A few minutes later, Imena ventured back into the streets of the town. Past the dock area, she was much more conspicuous, and as usual, she steeled herself against stares, most of them curious, a few hostile, and all of them wary. As soon as she could, she hailed a pony-cab and gave Sanji's address. She leaned back in the padded seat and closed her eyes, forcing herself to replace Maxime's image in her mind with Sanji's. It was more difficult than she'd thought. She'd seen Sanji's body dozens of times, Maxime's rarely, but she had recent sense memory of Maxime's heavy muscularity and the scent and texture of his hair and skin. Remembering how his hands had felt on her body made her belly melt. If only he was not the duke. If only.

Sanji's home adjoined his chandler's shop. For once, his two young sons were not playing in the grassy back garden where Sanji kept a milch goat; with a twinge, she remembered this was their week to visit with their aunt who lived inland. She had been looking forward to playing with the boys. Imena went into the shop, saw Sanji's assistant minding the counter and ducked outside again.

She found Sanji in his workshop, mounting a compass into a new protective casing crafted from slender strips of varicolored woods. The navigator in her appreciated his craftsmanship; as apprentice to a starmaster in her teens and early twenties, on *Sea Tiger,* she'd learned the basics of building instruments, and had a healthy respect for the difficulty of the task.

She leaned against the open doorway for a time, watching him work. He was a tallish man, as dark a brown as Chetri, with narrow stooped shoulders and lush black hair he wore in a messy tail down his back. Wide, thick black eyebrows gave his eyes a severe look at odds with his mild personality. Imena found him soothing. His hands at work were as gentle as his hands would be on her skin.

She waited until he'd set aside the compass before clearing her throat. Sanji looked up and smiled. "Imena. I heard *Seaflower* was in."

"Yes." She swallowed. She opened her mouth to ask if he could spare an evening for her, but instead said, "Sanji, I'm not sure I can see you anymore."

His welcoming expression changed to mild dismay. "That's unfortunate for me, but…have you met someone else?"

"Yes," she said. She might as well admit the truth. Just because she couldn't have Maxime didn't mean he wasn't there, in her thoughts, seemingly inside her very skin. "I'm very fond of you, Sanji," she admitted. "You and the boys, too. But—"

"I understand," he said. He rose from his stool and took her hand, kissing her fingers. "I must confess, I've been wanting to, well, marry. Give my sons a new mother. And I wasn't sure what you would say."

A few weeks ago, she might have said yes. "They need someone who will be here with them," she said. "You and I, we're good together, but…" She took his hand in hers and drew it to her mouth, placing a kiss in his palm. "You need someone who will be here always. Don't you? You just haven't said so."

"Yes," Sanji said, his cheeks flushing. He caressed her cheek. "Will you stay for the evening meal, at least?"

"I can't," she said. "I need to find Chetri. A business matter." She paused, and slipped her hand into her jacket pocket, withdrawing a small canvas bag. "I brought shark's teeth for the boys. Remind them the teeth are sharp."

"I will," he said. When he took the bag from her, their fingers did not touch. He said, "They'll miss you. You'll visit now and again?"

Throat tight, she nodded. She said, "There is a pearl in there for you, the purple-black such as you like so well."

"Thank you," Sanji said. "I'll think of you when I wear it." He slipped the bag into his trousers pocket. He added, "You're always welcome in my home, you know. For whatever reason."

"And you are always welcome on *Seaflower*," she said. She took a deep breath. "Goodbye, Sanji."

"Fair sailing, Imena," he said, and kissed her gently. They shared a long, close embrace of farewell. She walked away, her regret mingled with relief.

Imena refused to admit she'd failed at shore leave by returning to her ship. She left Sanji's shop and wandered the streets until darkness fell. She spotted Seretse, the ship's carpenter, at an open-air stall buying clusters of fine steel needles for the tattooing he practiced. Twice, she saw groups of her crew amusing themselves. Her purser, Arionrhod, rambled through the night market in company with One-Eye, the cook, their apprentice mates and several of the other youngsters. Later she saw a cheerful group of sailors led by Nabhi, the armsmaster, and her unofficial master's mate, Kuan, chatting and laughing beneath the awning of a crowded coffeehouse. The opulent smell of roasting beans and honeyed pastries emanating from the latter almost enticed her to stop, but she walked on, not caring that even her callused feet were beginning to hurt from cobblestoned streets and stone pavements.

Her feet led her to the cluster of tavern-boats anchored off the far end of the docks. The licenses for such taverns cost less than those on shore, and customers could enter by boat as well as from the docks, creating privacy for business deals. Imena routinely visited offshore taverns and brothels in every port to obtain information for Maxime, but she'd never been to these. She assumed Maxime's local staff kept their ears open here.

The carved and painted wooden sign for the Squirting Squid depicted a squid whose tentacles closely resembled long, stiff cocks, each given a distinct shape that might have come from nature. Noise spilled out from the tavern, heavy with male voices and the *thwacking* of leather tankards on wood; she could smell bread fried in lard and sour wine. The next tavern along looked more welcoming. Glass lanterns in bright colors hung from its railings. She could go there, if she wanted to be welcomed.

She chose the Squid, stooping through its low doorway, brushing aside the curtain of shells that served as a door. The decking was tacky with spilled wine and pine tar, and she regretted not wearing shoes. She halted in the doorway and took in the single narrow room. Its sole purpose appeared to be drinking, though trenchers of fried bread were available to soak up the alcohol if one desired. A plank propped on barrels ran the length of the space. A young man stood behind the plank, splashing wine from a skin flask directly into a row of tankards. The drinkers crowded on the other side of the plank, jostling for position. Most of them wore padded harnesses of one kind or another, with leather gloves or gauntlets shoved through their belts, the garb of porters and cargo handlers. Two men at the far end wore no shirts at all and were shaved as bald as she was; she recognized their large shoulder tattoos as those of divers, who were often employed to cut free trapped anchors, scrape hulls or retrieve items lost off the docks. She didn't see any of Maxime's spies whom she could identify. After a moment, she also realized she saw no women at all. Given the sign outside, she decided it had to be a men's den, intended for quick pickups of a sexual partner for the night, or perhaps just for a few moments. Good. No one would look for her here.

Most of the noise she'd heard came through a second doorway, which led into a larger room crowded with tall tables, each just large enough for two or three tankards. A boy wiggled between the tables while carrying a tray atop his head. Imena stopped him with a click of her fingers. When she didn't promptly hand over a tankard, he muttered, "Cup rental's extra," and held out his grimy hand.

Imena handed over three coppers. The boy said, "Four coppers for a bunk down below, no sleeping allowed." She shook her head; she had no need to rent a private space. The boy pocketed the coins, unhooked a tankard from his belt and expertly aimed a stream of wine into it before ducking behind the bar for a new flask. She sniffed discreetly at the wine—awful—and pretended to take a sip as she shouldered her way into the rear cabin.

No one took notice of her. Her cap hid her distinctive face and scalp tattooing; her loose clothing hid the shape of her body. No one was looking at the floor to see her tattooed feet. She was tall and slender enough to pass as a man at a casual glance. The anonymity relaxed her. She eased between patrons clustered around the tables, heading for the end of the cabin, where one bulkhead was propped on poles, leaving that side open to the outside air.

One of the cargo handlers leaned against the outside bulkhead, another kneeling before him, apparently just having completed a brief encounter, as the kneeling man was licking his partner clean. They ignored her as they tucked away their cocks and went back inside. She glanced around but saw no others concealed in the shadows cast by the deck lamps.

If she'd been thinking logically, she would have headed inland for her solitude. Few traveled even the main road up to the castle at night. She might have sat beneath a tree in complete comfort, and forgone this tankard of wine more suited to stripping paint than drinking. But then she would not be listening to the slow lapping of the water against the sides of the boat and feeling the easy rocking beneath her feet.

She set her tankard on the deck and dangled her feet over the side, hooking one arm around a post and resting her feet on one of the ropes that traversed the side. She inhaled the sea air and tried not to think of Maxime. She need stay ashore only tonight. Tomorrow, perhaps she would hire a light boat and go out alone, or take Norris and give her a lesson or two in handling small craft. Also, there was the business of visiting the enclave of naturalists down the coast; she had samples to show them, of resins and dried flowers, dried leaves and seeds. Some were probably useless except for the sake of study, but others might have monetary value. She had particular hope for one of the resins; not only would it bring in considerable coin, of which she and her crew would receive the largest share, but the trade itself provided a useful excuse for information gathering, among peoples who'd had little contact with the duchies thus far. The new resin might be as valuable, or more so, as the balsam she'd found on her last trip; it was reputed to have medicinal value.

The boat's motion and her own exhaustion lulled her to a doze. She dreamed Maxime was there, settling in behind her on the deck, and insisting she call him by his name; then she came awake and realized she had heard his name, and more than once.

Voices carried by the breeze to her ears. A man's voice with a sleek accent was saying, "Julien will reward me well if I bring Maxime to heel."

Julien the king? Referred to so informally? The king had sent a man here recently, Maxime had told her. Was this the messenger Maxime had spoken of, or someone else?

The other man's voice was also accented, and more indistinct. Imena heard only fragments of his reply: "Your business—she won't—I could—" An indistinct murmur, then she clearly heard, "An accident."

Imena stiffened. Men speaking softly of *accidents* did not bode well. And who was *she?* What wouldn't she do? Cause an accident? Pay for an accident to happen? Or something else entirely?

Imena couldn't identify the exact source of the voices. The men could be concealed behind a heap of cable opposite from where she sat, or they could even be on one of the adjoining craft. Until she had a hint of which direction to move, she didn't dare risk alerting them to her position.

The first man said, "I will arrange everything. You may return, and report back to me if there is any news."

"—king asks?"

They did refer to Julien, then.

"You know nothing. I will take care of that rutting tomcat Maxime. He won't trouble Julien any further. And when I'm rewarded with this duchy, I will reward you beyond your wildest dreams."

The clink of coins carried even better than the sound of voices. It was clear Maxime was in danger. Imena didn't wait to hear more. She eased soundlessly over the boat's side and slithered down ropes until her foot touched water. She took a series of deep breaths as silently as she could, then slid beneath the cold water, keeping one hand on the boat's hull as her guide.

She had to go to Maxime, and quickly. But first, she would need to find Chetri.

CHAPTER FIVE

AFTER SYLVIE LEFT HIM, MAXIME CALLED FOR A bath in his quarters, but it did not make him sleepy as he'd hoped. He sent the servants away and spent several hours at his desk, reading the accounting for the past couple of days and then placing his seal on various permissions, customs documents and requisitions to supply the castle. All had been meticulously prepared by his aunt, Lady Gisele, and two of her children, whom she was presently training in the fine art of bureaucracy. He tried not to think about how little he was actually needed here; no longer was he necessary to distract Julien's attention from the business of the duchy, because now everything was legal, open to inspection.

Being a duke felt more like extra bonds than the freedom he'd thought the position would represent. He was tempted, sometimes, to run. To head down to the docks and take ship for elsewhere.

He moved to a tray of letters already opened and ready

for him to peruse. As he'd feared, Julien hadn't waited for his formal refusal of Diamanta; another envoy was on the way.

Maxime glanced at the piles of legal texts he'd assembled. He would need to shift a few of his secretaries to that duty, for copying documents if nothing else. Because no one was watching, he put his head in his hands for a few moments and allowed himself to curse at length. He didn't want to do it, but he would start in on the legal tomes tomorrow. For now, he composed replies to some of Camille's letters, and to a personal one from Henri, whom he was beginning to consider a friend, as well. He briefly considered sharing his worries about marriage with Henri, but what could the boy tell him in return? Henri was barely twenty, and though acknowledged as legal consort to Camille, his situation was vastly different from Maxime's.

When he'd finished, he wiped off his signet ring and laid it in its dish along with the carved stamp that bore the same design, an octopus curling around the initial letter of his name. He blew out the lamp, tossed his robe over the back of his chair and walked naked into his bedroom. The floor, heated by piped water from the hot springs, soothed his feet. Sometimes he stretched out upon the warm tile, with a pillow to prop his head, and reviewed the day's work in his mind. Today, though, he planned to go straight to bed. Perhaps sleep would organize his thoughts on Imena Leung and how he could entice her to listen to his point of view.

His bed, with its intricately carved wooden canopy, loomed in the dim light of a single yellow lamp. The servants had carefully tidied the heaps of goose-down-filled bedding and pillows and attempted to straighten the mountain of leather-bound books and encased scrolls stacked near the bed's head. Despite their efforts, the pile leaned dangerously and soon would create a landslide of reading material in five languages.

It didn't matter if the room was a mess. He rarely entertained anyone in here. He preferred the baths and the adjacent chambers; it was safer that way, easier to keep his partners at a distance. The only woman he'd fucked in his own bed was Camille, and he didn't count her, exactly; they'd known each other for such a long time that she didn't seem like a mere sexual partner, and besides that, he'd known she was in love with her stable boy, Henri. It had been safe to have her here, safe to let her see his things spread about. He'd known she wouldn't ask more of him than he was willing and able to provide for her.

Strangely, after he'd shared this room with her, and they'd finally consummated their relationship, he'd known they were finished as lovers. It was as if a string, pulled tight for decades, had finally snapped, and his burning desire for her had flown away with it. He was grateful they'd had other commonalities between them, and remained friends.

He ignored all the books, even a half-finished legal treatise on marriage laws and the manual he'd lately been reading on stellar navigation. It was written in the court language of the Horizon Empire, and though like all the aristocracy of his duchy, he'd studied the language since boyhood, it was rough going, with technical vocabulary that wasn't usually required for normal trade relations.

He was still trapped in the introduction. He had hoped to ask Imena to help him; she'd been trained in stellar navigation and he suspected she would have a gift for teaching it.

He blew out the lamp before sliding wearily between soft cotton sheets. He'd been awake since the dawn, waiting for Imena's visit. He closed his eyes and the world tilted into sleep.

He woke to a familiar touch and scent—Imena. Groggily, he smiled. He didn't mind her in his rooms. He didn't mind her here in the least. Her callused hand clamped over his mouth. "Get his feet, Seretse," she said.

Maxime struggled to blink awake. A sailor had a firm grip on his ankles, and another grabbed his shoulders as Imena removed her hand from his face. "Quiet," she said in a low voice. "Don't struggle."

He hadn't thought she played these sorts of games, but he was willing to go along, even when the two sailors laid him on a cinnamon-scented wool carpet and proceeded to thoroughly wrap him within its folds. He tried to lift a hand to clear fabric away from his face only to find it trapped. "Imena—" In the other room, he heard his door open.

"Quiet! Chetri, did you find the courier?"

"Aye, Captain. Here she is."

Maxime heard a laugh, quickly muffled, then Sylvie's voice. "Well, well, Captain. You want him after all. I never would have thought you'd have your muscled crewmen carry him off."

"Listen carefully, Sylvie," Imena said. "Chetri, go with Seretse and Kuan."

Maxime relaxed. Imena clearly intended to tell Sylvie her plans for him. She might play games, but she didn't plan to put his entire castle into an uproar. He remembered the envoy from King Julien that would be arriving in the next day or so and began to struggle. Someone, probably Imena, kicked the carpet with a bare foot and said, "Get him out of here!"

He realized even a complicated game like this one would be unlikely to last more than a day and a night, and if the envoy arrived during that time, someone would send him a message. He had quite a lot of work to do, but courting his future wife was work, as well. He relaxed into the spice-scented carpet—the sensation of soft wool all over his bare skin reminded him of pleasurable encounters of the past—and let the crewmen carry him from his rooms and out into the corridor. They exited, he thought, through one of the side entrances and loaded him, still wrapped in the carpet, onto a cart. He heard a pony snort. Two men climbed onto the bench seat, shifting the cart's weight, while the remaining man, probably Chetri, stayed in the rear with him. Maxime could just sense the weight of Chetri's hand on the outside of the roll of carpet; the hand rested just over his genitals. Maxime grinned, wondering if Chetri was intended to be part of the evening's entertainment, as well. If Imena had no objections, he certainly wouldn't raise a protest.

Soon he smelled the sea. Chetri and the two crewmen slid his carpet from the cart and carried him down the dock, their feet slapping hollowly on the boards. He almost protested when he felt a cargo sling being adjusted around his carpet, but closed his mouth when he remembered his role. She'd told him to be quiet, so quiet he would be.

It was rather exhilarating, being swung into the air and into a boat, rowed for a distance, then lifted much higher and swung across to what he assumed was *Seaflower*'s deck, more exhilarating because he couldn't see, move his limbs or balance himself in any way. He had to give over control completely. Imena was delightfully devious. He'd chosen even better than he'd imagined.

The sailors manhandled his carpet down a set of shallow stairs, which told him they were beneath the captain's cabin. He remembered the low-ceilinged space there. Temporary bulkheads could be erected at different intervals. It was sometimes used for passengers, sometimes for cargo, and at present smelled strongly of mangosteens and farm animals, who were kept below. His carpet was carried into a space that felt smaller, a temporary cabin perhaps, and set on the deck. The sailors departed in a hurry. The door shut and a chain rattled. They did not leave a light.

He wondered how long Imena would be, and if waiting was part of the game. He didn't think he was intended to remain rolled in a carpet until her return; or if he was, he didn't intend to behave, as the pressure of fabric against his face was beginning to irritate him. He shifted his weight, struggled and rolled to one side then the other. The folds of the carpet loosened. He persevered, and was soon free.

The cabin was small, only just long enough for his outstretched body, the ceiling too low for him to stand without stooping. There was no bunk or chair, but someone had provided a pair of loose trousers, a blanket and a spread towel that held a large jug of water, a loaf of bread, several oranges and a waxed-paper package of soft cheese, which he identified by smell and by the faint light filtering through tiny cracks between the boards of the temporary bulkhead. His searching fingers soon found an enameled box, as well: candied balsam, probably from the same shipment as the box he'd given to Diamanta. The food indicated his wait might be lengthy, and they didn't intend to stint on him while he was aboard. He was grateful someone had thought to leave a chamber pot, as well.

It was a good thing Imena had told Sylvie where he was. He pushed the towel with the food into the corner and spread the carpet as far as it would go, folding the edges under so one end made a sort of pillow. He leaned back against it, pulled the blanket over himself and in moments was asleep.

Imena shoved her hastily scribbled transcript of the conversation she'd heard into Sylvie's hands. "So there is a woman involved, but I wasn't able to tell how, or what, her intentions might be."

Sylvie made a face. "Where His Grace is concerned, she might be any one of dozens. Including you, Captain Leung."

"It is *not* me," Imena said sternly. "You will take care of this? At least until it's safe for us to return?"

Solemn and cold, Sylvie nodded. "You may take refuge with Madame Camille if needed."

"Aye, Captain." She scampered up the rigging, barely touching the ropes with her feet.

Chetri said, for her ears alone, "Looks like one of the king's cutters."

"Fuck him with a bowsprit," she said. "I don't think it's a courtesy visit."

"Do you think they'd take His Grace by force?"

Imena took a deep breath and concentrated on the clean salty breeze that brushed her face and scalp. As always, sea air calmed her. She was in command here, not just of the ship, but of herself. "The duchess Camille told me that King Julien is a reasonable man, but I don't know what her definition of *reasonable* might be, after she lived with that insane husband of hers for so many years, while he wreaked havoc on the duchy." She added, "I would have thought a reasonable king would have removed the man from power himself, not left it to Camille to take care of."

"Who knows how royalty thinks?" Chetri asked. "Her Grace Camille seems a woman of good judgment in many ways, so perhaps she's right about her king."

"I believe she trusts him, but…whether this cutter is the king's doing, or that of the men I heard at the Squid, or just coincidence, I can't take the risk."

"There won't be any accidents on *Seaflower*," Chetri said. He touched the long knife at his side.

"It's best if they're not allowed to board."

Norris slid down the ropes and landed almost at Imena's feet. "A royal cutter," she said. "No signals flying."

Chetri said, "They'll have seen us by now, and it's no secret you're His Grace's captain."

Flee or bluff? Fleeing was more suspicious. The fewer suspicions about Maxime's whereabouts, the safer he would be.

"We let them approach, and we bluff," she said. "On no account does anyone from that cutter go below."

"Captain," Norris said. "I could stow His Grace more safely."

"Where?" Imena asked. "No, don't tell me. I don't want to betray his hiding place. Very well, Norris. Do it now, then hop back up top as quickly as you can."

Maxime waited impatiently as someone fussed with the chain and padlock on his door. When the door was flung open, he was startled to see Norris, Imena's cabin girl. "What's going on?" he demanded.

"This way," she said. When he didn't move, she hesitantly reached out and grabbed his wrist.

"Where are we going?"

"I have orders to hurry."

"Whose? Captain Leung's? I pay her salary, you know. And that means I also pay yours, Norris."

She heaved at his arm, but he braced his weight and didn't budge. He said, "There's no real rush, is there? Given that she left me here for half the night."

"Please, Your Grace." Norris released his wrist.

Maxime didn't think Imena would blame Norris for his lack of cooperation, but the girl seemed distressed, so he sighed and said, "All right."

He regretted acquiescing when he saw the narrow deck cubby into which he was expected to squeeze himself. "Is this your cabin?" he asked. Little more than the size of a small wardrobe, the enclosed space held only a hammock and a large trunk. "Have you been smuggling? Does the captain know? Of course she must—"

"Just climb in!" Norris struggled with the weight of the trapdoor as she wrestled it to the side.

"Is there air?"

"Enough. It won't be long, I promise."

Another test? Was Imena testing his sincerity? He was willing to do a great deal more than pretend to be smuggled goods, if he could have her in the end. He managed to cram himself into the cubby, which smelled sweetly but strongly of the valuable balsam resin that had been stored within. Norris yanked the trapdoor over him and hammered it down with the heels of her hands. Maxime was left in warm, perfumed darkness.

Imena did her best to appear bored as the royal cutter's first officer examined the papers Arionrhod, the purser, had handed over. Chetri stood at her side, chewing mastic, hands clasped behind his back. He looked casual but was ready, she knew, to draw his knife at a moment's notice. Several of her crew handled inconsequential tasks within easy distance; she'd been careful to order most of the younger sailors to stay below on the lower cargo deck. At the first sign of trouble, the cutter's first officer and his boat crew would become hostages. If worse came to worst, she might also claim diplomatic immunity; anything to gain time.

She might also accidentally knock the officer down for looking at her as if he'd like to pay for her services. A knife pressed to his genitals might give him more respect for women.

The officer peeled off the second sheet and returned it to her. Imena slid the page into its case. "As you can see, we're in the employ of the duke Maxime."

"You were scheduled to remain in port for another week. Why did you depart early? Without a full cargo?"

He wasn't looking at her face, but at her bosom, despite its being bound into a bodice and concealed beneath a loose shirt. She was careful to show no hint of emotion as she said, "Personal matters."

"Personal matters that caused you to recall your crew from shore leave and vanish from the docks in the wee hours of the morning?"

"I wanted to catch the tide," she said blandly. "Are we finished here?"

"I'm curious as to the nature of these personal matters." He glanced up at her face now, and smiled. He was a young man with bright teeth, symmetrical features and glossy hair. He wouldn't be used to being refused.

"You will remain curious, then," she said. "Chetri, will you escort the officer to his boat? I need to speak with Bonnevie." She turned toward the wheelhouse.

"Oh, come now," the officer said, looking annoyed. "You could at least offer me a drink."

Imena frowned. "That's not required by law."

The officer's back stiffened. "I wasn't aware you particularly cared for laws, Captain Leung."

"I have no idea what you mean." She felt Chetri ease closer to her.

"Everyone knows why His Grace hired you. You're a pirate."

Chetri's blade whistled from its sheath, and he spat the mastic gum at the man's feet. Imena blocked his arm without breaking the officer's gaze. She heard movement, then settling, as the sailors realized there would be no fighting. "I was a privateer, in the service of my government."

"It's all the same to us. We've been keeping an eye on you."

"Have you." She pushed on Chetri's arm until it lowered and he stepped back to sheathe his blade. "Unless you are accusing me of piracy now, you will leave my ship."

CHAPTER SIX

MAXIME HAD NEVER FEARED ENCLOSED SPACES,
but as time passed, he felt more and more confined in his
narrow cubby. The bottom wasn't padded, and though he
didn't feel any splinters, it wasn't comfortable, either. The
trapdoor pressed entirely too close to the end of his nose,
now numbed to the smell of balsam; his breath returned
to him, forcing him to tell himself that he was not suf-
focating. It only felt as if there was no air. He could feel
air: warmish, stale air, flowing across the soles of his feet.
He could also feel the trapdoor against his chest if he took
too deep a breath. Perhaps he was lucky he wore only
trousers; if he'd been wearing his usual layers of clothing,
this cubby would be considerably more stifling.

He opened his eyes. That was a little better. There
was no light in the cubby, but it made him feel better
anyway.

He'd heard quite a lot of noise from above: pounding
feet in large numbers, a wooden thumping as of something

heavy rocking into *Seaflower*'s hull, more feet. Then silence, until he heard more steps, closer, and the welcome sounds of someone wrenching open the trapdoor above his head.

As soon as the door was opened, he said, "I've had about enough of this game."

Chetri stared down at him without answering, brown face studiously blank, light playing on his necklaces and array of silver earrings, many more than any courtier would wear. Despite all his adornments, he clearly had no fear of anyone's branding him a dandy. He extended a hand, layered in calluses, to pull Maxime up.

Maxime was impressed there seemed to be no effort involved, despite the fact that he was considerably larger than Imena's first mate. He eyed Chetri's muscular chest, decorated across the pectorals with dense black tattooing. He wondered how much Imena liked looking at such a fine specimen of a man, day in and day out. "How far out to sea have we gone?"

Chetri looked him up and down slowly, without answering. "Come along," he said. When Maxime didn't follow, he grabbed his hand and tugged him.

Maxime soon discerned they were returning to his belowdecks cell. He said, "I shouldn't be away for this long. Much as I'd prefer to stay, I'm expecting a royal envoy any day now."

"I'll fetch you out later on," Chetri said, gently pushing him into his cell with a hand on his back.

Maxime grasped Chetri's shoulder to stop him from closing the door. Imena would be displeased if Maxime seduced him. At the moment, he was in the mood to cause her displeasure. "You don't need to lock me in here."

"I suspect I *do* have to lock you in here," Chetri said with a wry twist to his mouth.

Maxime tightened his hand on Chetri's shoulder, squeezing gently and sensually. "Perhaps we could both be locked in here."

Chetri turned his head and nipped at Maxime's fingers. "I don't trust myself, and I don't trust you further than I could throw you, Your Grace."

"You wouldn't be sorry. I suspect you have no aversion to men. Wise of you."

Chetri grinned. "And I'm sure you'd make it worth my while, is that it?" Gently, he dislodged Maxime's hand and stepped back. "You'll be a handful for the captain, that you will." Easily fending off Maxime's lunge, he slammed the door closed, calling through it, "I'll bring you something to read later. A nice philosophical volume." A moment later, Maxime heard the noise of the lock and chain.

It hadn't been polite to try to seduce her second-in-command when he was hoping to convince her that she ought to marry him, but did she really expect him to play the innocent virgin and wait patiently for her attentions? Otherwise, why make him wait so long?

Unless she knew what he'd done with Sylvie. Maxime sighed. That had been a mistake, too. It wouldn't do him any good to explain that it had been nothing to Sylvie, and that he'd been thinking of Imena throughout most of it. Despite knowing Sylvie, and what Sylvie was like,

Imena wouldn't be pleased with him for giving in, not at all.

Yes, that could be the reason for his current imprisonment. Imena knew about his brief encounter with Sylvie, and she planned to make him pay. But couldn't she have chosen a more…pleasant revenge?

He refused to consider that Imena might not care at all.

Maxime grimaced, sat on the blanket and tore off a hunk of bread.

This bit of ocean was far too crowded for Imena's liking. It made sense that every courier cutter and fishing trawler would be taking advantage of the wind, but that also meant every one of them would spot *Seaflower* with her distinctive imperial rigging and duchy profile. While Chetri sent the crew through a series of complex maneuvers designed to get them out of the most trafficked sea lanes, Imena sat in her cabin and labored over her charts, deliberately putting off talking to Maxime. He would be furious that she'd swept him away out of danger without telling him. She didn't want to face that right now. She didn't want to face him, after what they'd done in the baths, and what she'd briefly felt there.

Here, she could work in peace for a while. She had the largest cabin on *Seaflower,* furnished with a spacious wooden bunk projecting from one wall, two trunks to serve as seats, and her worktable and chair. One bulkhead was lined with a row of glassed-in windows, the others decorated with painted screens of historical battles. Several books and a new length of hempen rope, which Norris would use for drying clothes, were piled in a basket near the door, waiting to be stowed, distracting her from the charts spread in front of her.

The problem was, she had no idea how long Maxime would be in danger. He was safe belowdecks, but he would be wild with curiosity about the situation right now, and angry. Rightly so. Angry with her.

Sylvie would pass on the vital information about the plot to Lady Gisele, and hopefully Gisele would be able to stall any royal envoys who traveled to the castle, but Maxime himself was still in the dark.

Doubtless he'd figured out something had happened. He was no fool, and would know she only had his best interests at heart. He wouldn't be angry for long. He could wait.

Imena returned her thoughts to navigation. Remaining on the open sea seemed the safest option, but just to be safe, she reminded herself of available ports, official or otherwise, on the heading she planned. She scribbled down her preferred course, then two options, with some side notes to Chetri, then fastened the paper firmly onto the corner of a table. Carefully, she rolled and stowed her charts in their waterproof casings. She couldn't put off talking to Maxime for much longer. She would go and speak to him immediately after she'd been up to pass on her orders.

Chetri said, "We're not fully provisioned. We got the extra spars loaded last night, but we're lacking some of the supplies I'd like to have, if we're to stay out for as long as you fear."

"You think I'm being too cautious?" she asked.

He considered, stroking his fingers over the hilt of his dagger. "No," he said finally. "I don't trust royalty, especially not when money's involved. And that's what it's really about—His Highness wants control of His Grace because then he'll have control of a duchy stuffed with coin."

"If it is King Julien."

"If not him, then his flunky," he said. "They're all corrupt—well, aside from His Grace. He's fair and honest in his dealings. Will we be getting word from that Sylvie girl? Will she really be able to uncover this plot? She puked the whole time she was aboard that one time."

"Her Grace the Duchess Camille relies upon Sylvie," Imena reminded him. "She's an experienced courier and spy. She'll know to send us news through the usual channels. We'll just have to be careful where we dock."

"Aye, Captain," Chetri said. "By the way—you might want to speak to His Grace soon. He's...anxious...to be released from durance vile."

Chetri's sly grin arrested her attention. "Anxious?"

"He offered me delights of the flesh if I'd set him free."

"He did *what?*" She paused. "Was he joking?"

"Possibly. Possibly not." Chetri licked his lips. "He *is* a fine figure of a man, your duke. Plenty to hold on to, a bitable arse, and I hear reports he's skilled as any whore with that cock of his *and* otherwise. Making the tide with him would be no hardship, no, not at all. I almost took him up on it."

Through a red haze, Imena said, "You will not bite his arse nor hold on to any part of him."

Chetri laughed. "Of course not. I know he's yours."

"He is not—"

He patted her shoulder. "Of course not, Captain, sir. That's why you scooped him up, naked as the day he was born, and tossed him into your hold."

"I was in a hurry." She was aware she sounded surly, but could not help herself. Sometimes, Chetri considered himself entirely too much like her father. Only worse.

Chetri continued, "You had time to let him put his trousers on before you rolled him up in a carpet. Nice cock like that, you ought to wrap it up safe." He lifted his eyebrow, the silver ring through it glinting in the sun.

"Enough." She thrust the orders into his hand. "Get us out of here. Every scrap of canvas we have. Spring a topmast if you have to. I'm going below."

Imena had intended to invite Maxime up to her cabin, now that the chance of discovery was so much less, but that was before he'd tried to seduce Chetri. As she unlocked the door to his refuge, she considered simply leaving him in the hold. The accommodations might not be to his liking. She was no longer in a mood to please him. However, if she left him down here, who knew how many more of her crew he would try to subvert? Or seduce? Or both? Who would be next? No doubt Maxime would like a challenge. Seretse? Leggy Roxanne, the second mate?

It was a pity they needed to shift the cargo, poorly stowed thanks to their precipitous departure. Maxime would be in the way belowdecks. The needs of her ship were more important than a small act of revenge.

She shouldn't have expected better of him, anyway. She

knew what he was like. She knew far too much about what he liked.

But he'd made a fool of her on her own ship. It would serve him right if she treated him as a prisoner for a little while. Did she dare? She thought she might be angry enough to dare. And perhaps jealous enough, even though she had no right to *be* jealous.

She swung the door open a bit too hard, and it slammed against the temporary bulkhead. Maxime sat cross-legged on the deck, eating an orange. The tart scent perfumed the cabin. His lips and fingers were shiny with the sticky juice, forcibly reminding her of how he'd looked, smiling at her with *her* juices on his mouth.

"Keep your hands off my crew," she said.

"Even if they ask nicely?" He rose slowly, effortlessly, and held out a crescent of fruit. "Orange?"

"Chetri didn't ask."

"He was certainly looking. I know that's mostly frowned upon in the empire, but surely you—"

"I should leave you locked in here."

"That won't be much fun," Maxime said, and popped the slice of orange into his mouth. Hypnotized, she watched him chew and swallow.

She said, "I *would* leave you down here, but we need to shift the cargo. We stowed it hastily, and— Never mind. Get your things. I'll put you in my cabin."

Maxime smiled and bowed. "Thank you. I'm at your command." Nearly naked and smeared all over with sweaty streaks of grime from the smuggling cubby, he nevertheless made her want to straighten her spine. Belatedly, she realized he had that in common with her mother, and winced.

"Hurry up, I have things to do."

As they ascended the stairs, Imena first, Maxime said, "You really didn't need to go to all this trouble. I was willing to fuck you yesterday. But if you enjoy games—"

Outraged, she exclaimed, "Is that what you think?" She'd left port with her ship barely provisioned and still bristling with barnacles, for his sake, to save him from potential murder, and all he could think about was making the tide. She bit back a longer retort.

"I must admit, the carpet was novel. Being carried off by two muscular young men—I assume they must have been muscular—the solitary confinement to think it over—"

She whirled on him. "I never realized you could be so utterly infuriating." She would not fight with him now. She would not.

"It's a talent I spent my entire childhood honing. If I had to live with Camille's father after he'd killed my parents, I wasn't about to make it easy for him." He paused. "So, did I make you jealous? With Chetri? I'd be willing to go further with him, if he'd consent, if that would make you jealous. Or if you'd like it."

If he didn't shut his mouth, she was going to have to kill him. Perhaps she'd better shut it for him. "In," she said, swinging wide her cabin door.

"I'm to be a prisoner in your cabin now, am I?" He grinned and swept through the doorway. "I feel a flutter of virginal apprehension. I've always wondered what went on in the cabins of privateers. Though I did fuck in a hammock once. That was terribly awkward, but it came out all right in the end."

"Sit." She pointed at one of her two trunks that doubled as seats; they were spread with folded layerings of cloth, to pad the hardware fittings. Maxime did her bidding, but he sat straddle-legged, his cock and bollocks lewdly on display through the cloth of his trousers. Idly, he stroked the length of his cock, which was considerable.

"Stop that," she said. "I need to speak with you."

"Oh, I can speak and do this at the same time," he said, grinning at her. "You've really made me wait quite a long time. I'm not sure I can wait much longer. I might have to ask Chetri to ease my pain—"

Imena's hand closed over the coil of line Norris had left behind. It was fairly soft, chosen so it wouldn't snag silk clothing. "You were less asinine before I let you bathe me," she said.

His grin faded. "That was before you locked me up and left me, then sailed me out into the ocean without so much as a please or thank-you. I think that entitles me to be as asinine as I like."

Imena strode over to him. "Give me your hands," she said.

"Oh, no, you don't," he said. His irritation sounded genuine, and she felt a glimmer of triumph.

She said, "You won't fight me."

"Won't I?"

Imena grabbed his wrists and, in a few swift movements, lashed them together with a series of hurricane knots.

Maxime stared down at his forearms, now wrapped in hempen line. "I didn't think you truly would do it."

Imena grinned at him. Suddenly, she felt much better. She sliced through the long end of the line with her belt knife, knelt and snugly hitched his ankles to the trunk's deck braces, which were loops of iron embedded in the planking. To do so, she drew his legs even farther apart. As she sat up, her mouth nearly brushed his knee, and she saw his thigh muscle twitch.

"Tying my hands was enough to make your displeasure clear," he pointed out.

"Not for me," she said. Her eyes were nearly on a level with his genitals; quickly, she shoved herself to her feet before he could get the wrong idea. "I'll return in a while, and then I will talk and you will listen."

"Wait!" Maxime said. "We're not finished. Why are you leaving me again?"

Imena grabbed a piece of candied lemon peel and popped it into his mouth before she escaped. She didn't trust herself not to truss him head to foot, just for the pleasure of seeing him at her mercy.

CHAPTER SEVEN

MAXIME HEARD THE SHIP'S BELL RING TWO QUARTER hours before the cabin's door opened again. Norris poked her head in, then slid around the door and shut it behind her, reaching for a basket on the deck. When she saw Maxime, she stopped and looked at him incredulously.

"Is this your rope?" Maxime asked mildly.

Her mouth opened, then closed.

"You can have it back if you like. Though I'm afraid you'll have to untie it yourself."

Norris clutched the basket to her flat chest. "I... The captain borrowed it? My line?"

"She did."

"You'll have to ask her about untying it, then." Norris grinned and slipped out again, this time with the basket.

Maxime cursed, but without much vigor. He returned to trying to lift his feet. The deck braces to which he was hitched showed no hint of movement and the sturdy decking didn't even creak, no matter how hard he pulled. The knots on his wrists, he'd quickly learned, drew tighter if he struggled, and there was no accessible end for him to attack with his teeth.

"Being kidnapped," he said, "is much more dull than I would have expected." Perhaps things would improve once the ravishing began. If it began. He was beginning to have his doubts.

When another quarter-bell rang, he began to sing, loudly. "Oh, the army had no courage in them! But then came La Rose, the whore! She swore she'd put the courage in them! And give them something mo-o-ore!" He paused, and swallowed, wishing for another orange.

"La Rose, she had a dainty hand! And lips as red as blood! She took the captain first in hand! And soon, upright he stoo-oo-ood!"

The door slammed open. "My ship is not a bawdy house!"

"They're called licensed brothels in my duchy," he said. He looked at her hopefully. "All that singing made me thirsty, and I recall there are seventeen more verses. Twenty-three, if you count the extras my aunt taught me. Those are even worse. There's one where her dog licks—"

Imena stalked over to stand in front of him. Anger had brought a high color to her cheeks, and he was forcibly reminded of how she'd looked as he'd pleasured her in the castle baths. He lifted his hand to touch her before remembering his wrists were bound together. She glared at him, then looked away, visibly collecting herself. She said, "I'll get you a drink. Did I tie you too tightly?"

She didn't betray me. Until relief at that realization washed over him, Maxime hadn't realized he'd been doubting her loyalty. He lifted his bound hands. "You could loosen these. I won't be much good to you if my hands are numbed."

She propped her foot on the trunk beside him and placed his hands on her knee, unfortunately palm up, so he couldn't sneak in a squeeze of her leg. She bent over his wrists, tugging at the knots. The faint rasp of hemp against his skin wasn't entirely unpleasant. When coupled with the warmth from her hands, it was intriguing. Maxime leaned forward and nuzzled her bare scalp, letting the warmth of his breath caress her skin. A shudder rippled across her before she said, "Stop that."

"Why?" He bent closer, investigating the soft skin behind her ear. "You smell good," he said.

"Now is not the time. Occupy your thoughts with something else if you can." With a final tug at the rope, she straightened and stepped back, out of his reach. She poured water from a stoppered jug and held the wooden cup to his mouth while he drank. After two cups, he refused more, and she said, "I'm busy up top. I promise, I'll be back later to speak with you."

"You could untie me, then."

"I don't think so," she said. "You're too unpredictable." She smiled at him. "I hear tales of how creative you are. Surely you can amuse yourself for a little while."

Before he could ask her to untie his hands and provide him with pen and paper, she was gone. "Agh!" he growled.

The cabin, he realized, smelled of her. Even pine tar

and lemon oil could not conceal from him that she lived in this space, worked and ate and slept here. She would sleep nude on the spacious bunk across from him; the flat, cotton-stuffed mattress would smell of her skin even more strongly. He closed his eyes and inhaled. Her trunks were lined with cedar, whose scent impregnated all her clothing; sitting atop one of the trunks was like being close to her.

He opened his eyes. "You are just as pathetic as Sylvie said," he noted to himself. Smelling her furniture. He was behaving worse than the soggiest hero of a provincial melodrama.

He'd wasted enough time with patience, waiting for her to speak of her interest in him, or at the least demonstrate she *had* an interest in him beyond her immediate needs. His seduction of her in the baths had gone well, much better than he'd expected, at least until she'd rejected him. That was the first advance he'd made since he met her. He needed to continue in that way, as talking didn't seem to be doing any good. He could sway her with touch. A little sway, as a way into her thoughts and feelings, was all he needed.

Therefore, he had to touch her again. That would be difficult at the moment, given that she'd knotted his hands together.

His singing had brought her into the cabin. He would draw her into the room again, and then he would talk. Talking had served him well over the years. It was a lucky thing he'd honed the skill, because he needed it now.

He stared at her bunk, unfocused his eyes and meditated on what he would say.

* * *

Norris spotted another royal cutter from the upper nest, necessitating another alteration in *Seaflower*'s course and subsequent tacking to accommodate both the new heading and the change in wind. Chetri might have handled it all on his own, but Imena was reluctant to enter her cabin again, at least not yet.

She couldn't leave Maxime tied there indefinitely. Sooner or later, she would have to be close enough to him to untie him so he could put on the rest of his clothes. Then she would have to fight the urge to taste him again, mouth or throat or the muscle atop his shoulder, she didn't care.

Lust was ridiculous. And inconvenient, as well. She shouldn't have let him bathe her, shouldn't have let him kiss her, shouldn't have let his mouth anywhere near her cunt. By the Great Whales of the Deep, she knew what he was. She knew he would fuck anything that moved, and she knew herself well enough to know she wasn't strong enough to bear that, not for long.

But she couldn't think of anything else but having him. She wanted to grab him and shake him for enslaving her thoughts, but even that thought led, soon after, to her atop him, or him atop her, joined as tightly as tongue-in-groove decking.

She could still feel his skin against hers, and the soft scratch of his beard against her inner thighs.

She should just fuck him and be done with it. That was what some of her sailors did. A different partner in every port, met by chance, pleasured for a day and a night, then left behind with a kiss and a lingering smile, and perhaps a scratch mark or love bite.

Sanji had been that to her, she realized. No matter how much she looked forward to seeing him upon sailing into port, or how she'd enjoyed their lazy afternoons together, once she was out to sea again he was forgotten. She'd thought more about his two sons than about him, knowing that if they ever married, those boys would be hers, as well; she'd wondered what it would be like to have children, and if she really wanted that at all. All those thoughts had trailed off before she could explore the idea too deeply. She tried not to wonder why, but her conclusion was inevitable: she had never seriously entertained the idea of marrying Sanji. He was simply too dull to marry.

"I'm going below," she said.

She didn't knock at her cabin door, since it was hers; also, despite knowing why he'd done it, she was still angry with Maxime for trying to seduce Chetri. She took perverse pleasure in denying him the small courtesy of a knock. She swung the door open without a pause and strode in.

Maxime was still hitched to the deck braces. He was also, however, demonstrating an impressive erection. He rubbed his bound hands, or rather his rope-covered forearm, against one of his nipples while gazing fixedly at her bunk.

Imena stared at his eyes, dark with passion, and the flexing of his shoulder and arm. Her mouth went dry, her cunt moist. She could almost see what he saw: the two of them, together in her bunk, bare skinned, undulating against each other like sea creatures. Or, better, Maxime still bound while she had her way with him.

She needn't be in a hurry to talk to him. Maxime was safe for now; she'd made him safe. Knowing about the threat to his life wouldn't change anything in the next few hours.

She could have him. He wouldn't protest. He would be pleased, and she would be pleasured, and if that was all there was to be, she would be pleased, as well. She knew he'd had many partners; she'd watched some of them arrive and depart. She'd never heard any of them speak badly of him, which was impressive. Or was it because he said what his lovers wanted most to hear? She'd noticed he always made a special effort to remain on good terms with people. It seemed logical that this desire to please would extend to his sexual partners.

Except she hadn't wanted to hear about marriage. Not from him.

She was being ridiculous, she thought. Maxime had said she ought to marry him, but he hadn't really meant it. He needed to make a politically advantageous marriage. Even if he rejected all of King Julien's candidates, he would have to marry someone of their ilk. Therefore, he could not be serious about her. Therefore, she could have him. Right now, if she chose.

In fact, it was better if she had him now, because soon she would have to return him to his duchy, and there was no guarantee he'd ever approach her again. She felt better once she'd accepted both that she wanted him and that this would be short. She would be able to extricate herself without pain. He would allow her to do so. He might even make it easy for her. She said, "Maxime."

His gaze snapped to her face, and she realized he'd been so lost in fantasy that he hadn't been aware she'd entered. "Come to set me loose, have you?" Very slowly, he licked his lips.

Imena wiped her damp palms on her trousers. "If I unfasten your feet, will you promise to stay in my cabin?"

"If that means you want to fuck, then yes."

Imena swallowed. The way he said it, direct but caressing, with a raw edge of wanting, made her knees tremble. If making the tide on land didn't count, why did it count at sea? She swallowed again and said, "I think we'd better fuck and get it over with."

"I don't think this will be over with quite so easily as that," he said quietly. "I want a great deal more than a quick fuck." He grinned fleetingly. "At the moment, though, *quick* is what you'll get."

"Twice, then," she said, falling easily into negotiation. "Once now, once later when I'm feeling a bit more reasonable."

Maxime dropped his bound hands into his lap, using his wrist to nudge his cock through his trousers. His eyelids fluttered at his own touch; he quickly withdrew, lifting his hands against his chest. "Twice isn't reasonable. I'll never be able to demonstrate my talents as extensively as you deserve if you only give me two chances. I think we should decide on a length of time."

Imena caught herself before she swayed closer to him. She'd been watching him touch himself, and hadn't followed everything he'd just said, only the last sentence.

After a moment's mental fumbling, she said, "I won't know how long to offer until I've had you."

He grinned. "After you've had me, you won't be in any state to negotiate."

"You probably say that to everyone who crosses your path," she said. "I've never witnessed the truth of it."

"You didn't give me enough of a chance earlier. Untie me, and I'll demonstrate."

Imena pondered for a few moments. "Maybe I won't."

His dark eyes narrowed. "You're angry."

"I am not angry."

"I did nothing to you—nothing you didn't ask me to continue—so…are you still angry at your parents?"

"I wasn't angry with them," Imena said, even though she knew she lied badly.

"Are you angry with me? Because of what we did in the baths?"

"I told you, I'm not angry."

"I think you are," Maxime said. "It's all right, you know. It's only me."

"You're my employer, Your Grace."

"Oh, it's *Your Grace* now, is it? You can't put that distance between us, Imena, not when you've brought me aboard your ship naked and tied me up in your cabin." He smiled slowly.

Imena took a deep breath, trying to calm herself. "One night," she said.

"A week," he countered. "Days *and* nights. Shipboard emergencies don't count against the time. You're entirely too good at finding those."

Reluctantly, she said, "I accept your conditions. But for three days."

"Five. And if I was a whore, that would cost you my bollocks' weight in silver. You'll get me for free."

Not free. Not free in the least. "Four days is as high as I'll go," she said.

He nodded slowly. "All right. Four days with an option of a fifth."

"I said nothing about an option."

"Who's the diplomat here?" he asked. "You'll want that option later."

She sighed. "Fine." It didn't really matter what she agreed to, after all. He hadn't been very careful in setting his terms. She'd never said he'd have unlimited access to her during the four days, just as he'd never specified what he would demonstrate to her. And it didn't matter, anyway. They could never be together for any extended period. He would have to marry in the near future.

Maxime grinned. "*Now* will you untie me?" He wriggled a bit. "And I need some help getting these trousers off."

Images rushed through her head and her mouth went dry. She loosened his waistband and peeled the trousers down to his knees. She studied the muscles in his splayed thighs, the weight of his bollocks, his cock thrusting up from a tangle of dark curls, its rosiness a sharp contrast to the pale skin on his belly. She remembered his solid flesh thumping against her hip, and contemplated how the soft warm weight of his scrotum would spill over her hand, how his cock might feel throbbing against the roof of her mouth while her tongue dipped and tasted and swirled.

He could move his legs a little, but not enough to control his movements if she sat astride him, not properly. His bound hands would be in the way, though, and she wanted them on her. She wanted him to touch her as he had before, except this time she would be in control. She would take what she wanted from him. Though she had no claim on him at all, he'd said he would give her what she wanted.

She said, "I've never bound a man in my cabin before."

She glanced up at his face, and he was watching her solemnly. He leaned closer to her, looking up into her face. "I provoked you. Take it out on me," he said in a low voice. "Whatever it is. I don't mind."

She couldn't look away from his eyes. She'd never realized before that they weren't entirely dark brown—there was a lighter, amber ring around the pupil that vanished as his eyes darkened with arousal. "Take—"

"Take me," he said.

She fell forward, gripping his shoulders in her hands, and kissed him. Unable to tempt and tease, she sucked hard on his tongue while her fingers dug into his muscles. She felt his groan inside her mouth, the futile struggles of his hands against her chest. His forearm pressed hard against her breast, and she whimpered from the rope's soft friction.

She yanked back, panting.

"Untie my fucking hands," he growled. "I want to hold you."

Too much, she felt too much, but she wouldn't run away. This was just making the tide. Well, a storm tide.

She couldn't pretend this was a mere mild, satisfactory pleasure.

Like a storm, the only way out was through. She straddled his left leg and leaned in close, trapping his arms between them. His cock lay along her hip, hot and hard. She kissed him again, deeply, while her fingers found her knot at his wrist and released it with a few swift tugs.

He didn't seem to notice at first that his hands were free. She unwound the line from his arms, stopping only when his mouth slid down her throat. He sucked lightly at her neck and abraded her skin with the edges of his teeth. She tipped her head back, sighing with pleasure, and squirmed against his thigh.

His arms snaked around her waist, supporting her before she slid to the deck in sensual abandon. "That's better," he murmured, nipping his way along her throat. "I can taste sea salt on your skin."

She shifted, struggling to free herself from her jacket. Maxime shoved it aside with his chin and nuzzled his way beneath her loose linen singlet. She fought free of her jacket, letting it fall to the deck. She rose off him and yanked off her loose trousers, then her drawers.

Imena felt drunk, but not so drunk she couldn't sit astride him again and reach behind his back, feeding out the doubled line as she went. Maxime covered her breasts with his hands and kneaded gently, murmuring something about how soft she was. Another moment and she'd wrapped herself in the rope, as well, binding them loosely together around the waist the same way they'd been bound by his arms' embrace. She kissed him while her fingers fashioned a sheet bend, strong enough to hold when she leaned away from him to change position.

"I'm not going anywhere," Maxime said when he discovered the rope. "Why did you—"

Imena swung her leg over his other thigh and braced herself above his erection. "Later," she said. There might have been no interval between this moment and their encounter in the baths. She brushed her cunt against him, savoring the lightest brush of her outer lips against his straining cock.

"Oh, Imena," he said. "Do that again."

She brushed against him again and winced and shuddered, already on the edge of orgasm. She moved up, then down, gradually pressing harder, testing herself against his full length and breadth. He was big and solid, and would stretch her deliciously once they were joined.

Maxime's fingers dug into her hips, but he didn't try to control her movements. He said, his voice tight, "I hope you're willing for me to fall dead on your deck, because you are killing me."

Imena struggled to catch her breath. "What happened to *take me?*"

"I didn't want you to torture me first." She pressed against him a little harder and he said, "You can torture me later. Just fuck me now." His voice lingered over the word *fuck* and his eyes met hers. She could see her face reflected, in miniature, in his eyes before he shuddered and closed them. "Please," he said, shifting his hips. He grasped the hem of her singlet and lifted it over her head, tossing it aside before leaning down and sucking one of her nipples into his mouth.

She slipped her fingers inside her cunt, gathering moisture, then grasped his erection, using her other hand to balance on his shoulder. She could almost feel his heart beating, could see his pulse in his throat and feel its quick beat beneath her fingers. She stroked the head of his cock gently, spreading fluid around the cap, and he moaned, releasing her nipple and tipping his head against her. He panted hot breaths into her shoulder.

Imena breathed out and pressed down on his cock, letting her downward movement spread the lips of her cunt over the head of his cock, slowly and exquisitely. Maxime's groan vibrated against her skin. She couldn't stop a moan from her own throat as she took him into her, rocking slightly, taking him a little deeper with each breath.

Maxime murmured into her neck, "Imena, sweeting, you're so sleek inside. So hot. I could catch fire and we'd burn together and it would be glorious."

"The ship would catch fire," she gasped, taking another inch of him and stopping for a moment to revel in the sensation. "Then we'd have to stop so I could kill you."

"Metaphor, sweeting."

"Do not quote poetry to me," she said, squeezing her inner muscles on him. A shudder raced over her skin, and he made a choked sound.

"Fine. Then I want to fuck you hard up against the mast."

"Obsessed with masts, are you?" She took more of his cock inside her and sighed. The initial joining was her favorite part of fucking, at least while it was happening:

she loved that each time, even with the same partner, it felt new and intimate.

Maxime laughed, his hips surging up. "Masts, spars, long smooth prows—"

She was laughing, too, jolting her down onto his cock until, with a bump, she could go no farther and all her air rushed out of her on a moan. After a moment of being unable to draw breath, she rocked cautiously. Her nipples rubbed against the hair on his chest, and she gasped at the spikes of sensation.

Maxime said, slurring the words together, "Oh fuck oh fuck oh fuck, you are killing me."

Imena grasped his shoulders in her hands while her hips pressed and pressed against him, as if independent of her will. "You," she said, "have the biggest cock I have ever had inside me."

"That's what they all say," he said, his tone both wry and desperate. "I want you flat on your back, with your legs around my neck, and then you'd feel just how big I am."

"You'd only last three heartbeats," she said.

"I'd have my sanity back," he pointed out. He shifted his weight, then froze. "Sorry. I'm trying to…to let you… but…"

Imena kissed the side of his neck, openmouthed, nipping skin between her teeth and sucking hard on it as she ground down, rubbing her clitoris hard against him, tightening and relaxing her inner passage rhythmically. Small shudders chased up her thighs and into her belly, precursors of the greater climax that rapidly approached. They weren't going to be able to make much tide before it was all over. Maxime's arms tightened convulsively around her waist and he pressed his mouth to the bare skin behind her ear, sending a cascade of warmth down to her toes. His hands kneaded and spread her buttocks, one finger teasing the tender skin between.

That tiniest of touches was enough to spark the first convulsive wave of her climax. She groaned, lifting off him for the first time and driving down, as his hips pounded upward. Maxime lasted barely longer than she did and only, she thought, because their position was so awkward.

As her spine fell limp, she was glad for the rope that bound them together. If only their emotions could be bound as tightly as her knots.

Maxime woke abruptly from his doze when he felt soft rope brushing his skin. Imena no longer straddled him. She stood nearby, coiling the rope around her hand and elbow. Her face looked dazed and satiated, and when she noticed him watching her, she bent and pressed her open mouth to his. He lost himself for a moment in the kiss. When she began to draw back, he pressed one more kiss next to her mouth. Lovesick, he thought. Definitely, hopelessly lovesick.

"That was wonderful," she said, and swiftly turned away.

"You're not leaving again, are you?"

She knotted the two ends of the rope together and tossed it onto her bunk. She handed him a damp towel with which to clean himself, then helped him pull his trousers back up. "There, now I can think."

He couldn't help smiling. "Is thinking necessary just now?"

"Your Grace—"

"Don't be ridiculous," he said, stung. "You have always had permission to use my name."

"Your Grace, I think you have a mistaken impression from my lack of control. I did not sail with you as part of a sexual game. You're in danger."

CHAPTER EIGHT

SYLVIE REFUSED TO FEEL TREPIDATION AS HER carriage rumbled along the royal palace's long, cobbled drive.

She'd planned carefully for this mission. She carried a letter of introduction under Maxime's seal, sufficient to grant her lodging at court as she awaited a royal audience regarding an unspecified business matter. After consulting with Lady Gisele, who would conceal Maxime's absence for as long as she could and rule in his stead, Sylvie had borrowed one of Maxime's trusted couriers to carry the regular diplomatic pouch as well as coded word of her new mission to Madame. She could count on support from Duchess Camille, if such was ultimately needed.

For now, she needed to concentrate on finding the person who meant harm to Maxime, and either eliminate him or suborn him. In addition, she needed to find his confederates and hired help—she was sure there *would* be hired help whom she or one of her many contacts would be able to locate. Few aristocrats dirtied their hands with the mundane details of conspiracy. Finally, she needed to discover who the woman they spoke of might be, and if her intentions ran parallel, opposite or otherwise to those of the male culprit.

She shifted on the lavishly padded carriage seat and rearranged her layers of whisper-thin skirts. The fine cloth would have clung to the outlines of a pistol, but the knives strapped flat to her thighs and calves, beneath layers of petticoats, could not be detected except by touch. The busk of her snugly fitted bodice was sheath for another blade, and she had concealed a number of useful burglary tools made from fine wire within the hem of her lightweight silk cape. Finally, the decorative sticks in her piled hair were useful for stabbing, but any woman could make use of those. Hers were merely sharper than most.

The carriage rumbled to a stop. Grateful for the years she'd had to closely observe Madame, Sylvie gathered her skirts and scooted to the edge of the seat, ready to emerge with grace and dignity as Lady Sylvia, who'd supposedly gained her wealth as a proprietress of fine brothels on the peninsula, just far enough away that no one at the king's court would expect to recognize her. For the rest, who might have seen her in company with Duchess Camille, would any of them expect to see a humble maid in the garb of a lady? She'd made judicious use of cosmetics and tinted her hair to a darker shade, just to make sure she would remain anonymous.

The carriage jolted as her footman, borrowed from Lady Gisele, sprang off the back and came around to lower the steps and open her door with a suitable flourish. Careful of whoever might be watching, Sylvie gathered her pastel skirts in her beringed hands and swept down the carriage stairs, spine erect and head held high. She saw a man watching her from where he leaned indolently against the palace wall, smoking a cigar.

She had to look away as she descended the last step, to avoid stumbling on the cobbles, and when next she glanced up, he'd moved; he was strolling toward her. He wore a sword at his hip. Beneath the brim of his hat she saw dark skin and a close-cropped beard. Possibly a peninsular native, or more likely, from the Southern Kingdoms that abutted the peninsula; the heeled, narrow-toed boots he wore were more common there. The embossed silver foil on his heels and toes, and the cutaway leather patterns on his calves, were less common. However, she doubted he was an envoy; his clothing was nowhere near as elaborate as a diplomat would wear.

Either a merchant or a gossip or a spy, Sylvie decided. He pretended to loiter so he could inspect the new arrivals to the palace, in any case. She would be glad to let him inspect her. Well, at least until she discovered the name of his employer.

She released her grip on her skirts with a flourish, to shake them back into place, and awaited his arrival.

He stopped a polite distance from her, took the cigar from his mouth and thoroughly crushed its glowing end between his gloved forefinger and thumb. He bowed to her, but did not remove his hat. It had a broad brim, carefully curled, and was banded and trimmed in embossed leather. She wondered if he either had some purpose for concealing his face, or simply wished her to admire his headgear.

"Sir," she said, offering a slight tip of her own head in return. Her footman appeared at her elbow, ready for her defense, should it prove necessary. She could adequately defend herself, but shouldn't appear to be capable of doing so in her guise.

"Madame, I see from your beautiful gown that you come from the peninsula," the foreigner said.

Sylvie nodded.

"My people trade with yours," he said. "Though I must confess, I have never seen a trader so beautiful as you, or one so graceful."

She nodded again, rather enjoying forcing him to speak by her reticence, even if he spoke mostly non-sense. Though his hat still blocked most of his features, she could see his lush lips whose beauty was enhanced by their slightly asymmetrical shape. At her scrutiny, the corners of his mouth lifted, and his finely carved nostrils flared. "I see you admire me as I admire you," he said. "Is it not a lovely thing, to be admired? Is it not what we are to spend our time discussing, here at King Julien's court?" He turned slightly in one direction, then in another. "I do not entirely agree with the fashions of this land, but you will note that they seem to agree with me." He stretched out one boot. "The cut of the trousers, for example." Fabric stretched over his muscled thigh, and clearly delineated his endowments.

He went much too far. Either he was completely shameless, he was joking with her or he was a prostitute.

"Are you in search of employment?" she asked, resisting laughter.

"Employment?" he said. "Do you require a swordsman, madame? Or merely an ornament?"

Sylvie looked down the length of his body, slowly. "You have a fine sword?"

"The finest southern steel," he said with relish, laying one black-gloved hand on the hilt of the blade he wore. "Decorative but sharp. You would be surprised how long it holds an edge."

She smiled, enjoying the verbal play, but she had no time for it this evening. "That is not the sort of sword we employ in my establishment. I am Lady Sylvia. Perhaps you have heard of me?"

"I fear not," he said. "But since you have offered your name, mine is Raoul."

"And what is your role here, Monsieur Raoul?"

"Why, I am a guest of the royal palace, just as you are. An ornament, as it were."

"Not a courtier?" Or a paid concubine? He was lying about something. He was terrible at it. Or wished to appear so.

"No, madame. A mere visitor."

"A merchant, perhaps."

She caught the hint of white teeth gleaming beneath the brim of his hat. He said, "Must something always be bought and sold?"

Sylvie didn't need to consider that for long. "In my experience, yes."

Raoul sighed. "Then you will not believe that I came to this land only out of interest. I traveled overland for many weeks, then took a barge down the great river. Did you know the river, and the islands of the river, change shape every season?"

He demonstrated with his gloved hands, delineating an ovoid shape that thinned and disappeared as water curved and split around it. The gesture was sensual, graceful, a thousand times more so than his previous posturing. Sylvie blinked, for a moment sure she had seen exactly what he meant. He said, more briskly, "You have come on business?"

She recovered quickly. "I am always considering business," she said. "I must be about it now." She gestured to her footman. "Bring the baggage."

King Julien, Sylvie learned with relief, was not in residence today or tomorrow. He was visiting a hunting lodge with various of his cabinet; she wondered if the retreat was due to Duke Maxime's recalcitrance in the matter of his marriage. To her, it seemed likely the conspiracy against Maxime did not have its origin with the king himself. Julien was more efficient than that, she had always thought.

If that was true, and if Sylvie could capture the conspirator or conspirators, then surely the king would take her side. He wouldn't like, couldn't allow, action against one of his dukes by the hands of an underling, no matter his own feelings in the matter. Also, if Sylvie succeeded in this matter, it would please Her Grace Camille as well as His Grace Maxime. Pleasing the aristocracy was not a bad thing in general, and Sylvie lived to please Her Grace Camille.

After washing the dust of the journey from her face, hands and bare arms, and changing her dress with the aid of a palace maid, Sylvie took up her silk fan, left her guest chamber and descended a staircase to the main audience hall.

The hall filled the center of the palace, and was in turn filled to the walls with people. Its ceiling rose through all three stories; balconies with carved wooden balustrades projected from each level, large enough to hold musicians for balls and, on other occasions, either crowds of on-lookers or companies of royal bowmen. The stone walls were concealed by paneling that had been plastered over in elaborate floral designs, painted while still wet and then glossed with purple lacquer. The designs gleamed like metal in the light of hundreds of fat beeswax candles, each shielded behind the finest clear glass. The smooth wood floor was today covered by layers of plush carpets in shades of lavender, gray, mauve and plum. Sylvie re-membered how Captain Leung had bundled Maxime into such a carpet, and smothered a snicker.

She found Raoul idling near a fireplace, swirling wine in his glass. He was hatless, his curly hair cropped short above small, well-placed ears, emphasizing his deeply set dark eyes. He still, she noted, wore leather gloves. She wasn't sure if this was affectation or merely the custom of his country, but she definitely liked it. She loved the feel of leather on her bare skin. If he touched her with his gloved hands, he would leave the aroma of leather behind. She might nip the tips of his gloves and drag them free of his hands before laving each finger with her tongue, tasting leather with each lick. Yes, she liked his gloves very much.

The snug fit of his leather trousers over his high, tight rear was no hardship to her eyes, either. She pondered the lacings down the sides of his legs, and then how easily she might be able to unlace them, either with her hands or with her teeth.

She gathered the skirts of her lavish afternoon gown in one hand and swept down the staircase, fanning herself idly. Various women of the court, in dresses almost identical to hers but for color and fabric, cast sidelong glances at her. The men, as one, stared, and she had to resist a smile at how easy it was to impress them. If only they knew she was merely a maid. Then they might realize how foolish they were, to be so impressed merely by a woman's appearance.

She recognized three lords who had visited the ducal palace in the past few months. She had escorted all of them at least once from one room to another. None of them showed a flicker of recognition. All the better. If any of them conspired against Maxime, it was best they didn't recognize her. Several women, in dresses even more elaborate than hers, were gathered along the wall, chatting with each other and ignoring the delicacies laid out on silver trays. Sylvie's eye was drawn to a woman with a truly magnificent bosom. She wore a golden dress that emphasized her charms, and her masses of hair, pale blond, were dressed with a forest of hair sticks. She recognized the ruddy-gold knobs—they were a less artful version of hair sticks that Duke Maxime had given to Her Grace the Duchess Camille. Sylvie shifted slightly, just enough to glimpse the woman's face. They'd never met before, but if she wasn't Lady Diamanta Picot, to whom Maxime had recently refused marriage, Sylvie would eat the hair sticks in a sauce of garlic oil.

In a moment, Diamanta might notice she was being watched. Sylvie took an aniseed sweetmeat from a tray and began walking, as if without purpose. Raoul was not looking at her, but into his goblet. She approached him at an angle, accepting a goblet of wine from a servant on her way. He looked up when she came within arm's reach. He was just as handsome close up as she had expected, his cheekbones slanting like wings and his eyes arresting.

"Madame Sylvia." He smiled, a flirtatious smile without apparent pretense. Could he really be so naive as to reveal himself so clearly? "You remain beautiful. The passage of time has, in fact, only improved you. I cannot imagine how beautiful you will become on longer acquaintance."

"Monsieur Raoul." She inclined her head, then took her time looking at him on her way back up to his face. She asked, "With whom are you seated this evening for supper?"

"I am the guest of Lord Odell," he said, "privy to the Duke's Council. We visitors are not presumed to be loyal to any one duke, of course, so he acts as our docent while we learn the ways of the royal court."

How convenient for me, she thought. Lord Odell was one of her chief suspects, mainly due to the fact that Duchess Camille did not like him very much. When Madame's opinions could be pried loose from her, they were often very insightful into a man's character. Second, Odell held much power in relation to the Duke's Council and might have hopes of being elevated to duke himself. Third, he had been a messenger sent to Maxime's duchy with the king's demands; therefore, he might even have been the man Captain Leung had overhead conspiring. She asked, "Why is he not with you now?"

Raoul wrinkled his nose. "Lord Odell is attempting to speak with Lady Diamanta. See him, over there? He schedules his appointments with her near mealtimes, in the hope she will accompany him."

"And is he successful?" Her surreptitious glance at the pair told her little, as courtiers were skilled at concealing emotions at public gatherings.

"I am sure she's begun to consider him an annoyance." He paused. "But she is very beautiful. I can hardly disparage his persistence, though I myself am a more practical man." He smiled at her.

Sylvie favored Raoul with a smile in return. "Perhaps I may join you at table later this evening?"

He studied her for a few seconds, then said, "I would be most pleased, but I wonder how I can possibly afford you."

He had gone to the trouble of learning about her, or whom she pretended to be. "In this matter, I am not for sale," she said sharply. "I do as I like."

"And you will request nothing of me after supper? How sad." He took a sip of his wine. He flicked his gaze to hers, then coyly lowered his long lashes. He tilted his goblet and drank again, more deeply.

Sylvie watched his throat move, and licked her lips. "I

did not say that," she said. "If I did such a thing, however, I would make sure you regretted nothing."

"Nothing at all, ever?" he asked, lifting his brows. "I wonder that I am the only one seeking you out, if that's the case."

Sylvie snapped her fan closed. "Do you imply I am less than desirable?" she said.

"No, only that I am lucky to have seen you first," he said. "I have much to regret." Then he smiled and bowed, with a graceful flutter of his gloved hand. It was a smile bright and stunning as lightning, and struck her in the chest with bittersweet pain.

I will have him, Sylvie decided then.

When she met his eyes, his smile broadened. He offered her his arm.

Taking the part of Sylvie's lady's maid was Gisele's fourteen-year-old granddaughter, Alys. Alys had never before been to court, but was well practiced in dressing hair, thanks to her own long tresses and those of her sisters. She'd arrived after Sylvie, with the extensive luggage and an additional footman who would, if needed, serve as bodyguard. No one would think it strange that a rich woman such as Lady Sylvia would bring three retainers with her; in fact, they might be surprised she did not have more.

As Alys unpinned Sylvie's hair from the day's coiffure, she whispered into her ear, "Will you find the traitor tonight? Will you shoot him?"

Sylvie gave her a quelling glance. "Your grandmother informed me that your discretion was impressive," she said loudly enough for any eavesdroppers to hear. "I don't wish to hear your gossip."

Alys sighed. "I had thought this would be more fun."

"We did not come here for your benefit," Sylvie pointed out. With satisfaction, she added, "I will need to wash my hair tomorrow, and I would like a proper bath each day. Perhaps you could obtain the necessary servants? I would prefer a bath here in my chambers."

"Of course, madame. I will find rose oil for madame's hair." Sighing, Alys removed the last of the pins from Sylvie's hair and let them fall into a lacquered dish.

Sylvie closed her eyes as Alys began to brush out her hair. She didn't often have someone to perform that service for her. She'd forgotten how decadent it felt. She determined to enjoy every minute of the pampering.

When Alys began to separate out locks of hair for decorative braiding, Sylvie tipped her head to the side. Very softly, she said, "There is a man named Raoul. He puzzles me. Find out what his servants say of him."

Alys's hands froze, then resumed. Breathlessly, she said, "Yes, madame."

"Also," Sylvie said, "the lady Diamanta."

CHAPTER NINE

IMENA'S CABIN WAS SILENT EXCEPT FOR THEIR breathing, and the omnipresent sounds of the sea. She was retreating from their intimacy. Again. Maxime said, "I'm in no danger of accepting a proposal from any of Julien's candidates. Nor from anyone, except for you."

Imena looked at him incredulously. "I said this had nothing to do with sex."

"Oh, so we weren't just fucking to glorious completion? That had nothing to do with anything? I can still taste you."

She had the grace to color slightly. "That was my fault," she said. "I couldn't concentrate—"

He felt cold. "So you fucked me so you could tell me this had nothing to do with sex," Maxime said very slowly. "Or perhaps it does have to do with sex. It has to do with you needing a fuck, and me being besotted enough to offer one."

"You aren't—"

"I was playing a game, it's true, but I thought you were playing the game, as well. Lovers play games. They pretend to make bargains, but those bargains don't change what those lovers are to each other."

"You're my employer."

"And now I'm your lover. I've had my cock inside your cunt, Imena. I've had my tongue in your cunt. Do you think I do that with just anyone?" Her face betrayed her, and suddenly instead of being cold he was hot with rage. "You do! You think I'd fuck anyone off the street at first glance!"

She crossed her arms across her chest. "You wouldn't?"

"No!"

"What about merchant captains whom you barely know?"

He gritted his teeth for a moment, then said, "I know certain merchant captains better than you'd think. My spies give me thorough reports. You should know, you're my spy, too."

"So now I'm your spy, not your lover, is that it?"

"*You* said you weren't my lover," he observed.

"I did not say that!" Imena hissed. "I only said this wasn't about sex. By the Great Whales of the Deep, if you would let me finish speaking, then I would tell you what it was about! I cannot believe you are being such a fool. You're a duke, not a ten-copper lay!"

He *was* being a fool. He sucked in a deep breath, then another. He wanted to leap to his feet and pace the room, but his ankles were still hitched to deck bolts. On any other day he would have laughed at the indignity of it; just now, he couldn't summon his sense of humor. He crossed his arms across his chest, mirroring her position, and inhaled again, deliberately slowing his breathing to calm himself. After a few moments, his pulse quieted, as well.

"I do not understand you," he said at last.

"I don't understand you, either," she said. "I respect you, Maxime. Don't think I feel nothing for you." She lowered her hands as if to plunge them into her pockets, then appeared to realize she wasn't wearing any clothing. She scooped her trousers off the deck and tugged them on, then put on her singlet, as well.

It was easier for him to be calm once she was no longer naked. He wasn't sure what to say, but an apology never went amiss. "I'm sorry," he said.

This time, Imena did plunge her hands into her pockets. "I shouldn't have left you so long alone, but we were pursued, and I was required on deck."

Maxime blinked. "Pursued by whom? My aunt?"

"No. A royal cutter, perhaps two. I feared for you."

That explained a great deal. He said, "Julien will not truly harm me," he said. "Too much money flows from my duchy into the royal coffers. He will be unpleasant if I refuse to marry as he suggests, but in the end—"

"No. There is a plot of some kind. I don't know its extent, but from what I overheard, you were in imminent danger. Perhaps in danger of death. I couldn't think what else to do."

He'd never before known her to act so rashly. Perhaps she did care about him. He said, "Thank you."

"Don't say the rest," she said. "I know it was foolish to drag you off the way I did. I should have told you what was happening, you and Lady Gisele. But if I hadn't hurried, we would have missed the tide." She paused and looked at the deck before looking into his eyes. "I'm sorry I didn't tell you immediately. I was angry."

"Because I approached Chetri?"

"Yes."

Maxime drew a deep breath and let it out. It wasn't as if knowing sooner would have done him any good. He still would be trapped on this ship. "Does my aunt know now?"

"I gave Sylvie all the information I had to pass on to your aunt and to Her Grace Camille. It wasn't much. Sylvie will investigate. When it's safe, we'll return you to your duchy." She went to her desk, unhooked the chair from it and sat down. She drew paper from a drawer and began to make notes.

"That's all? You know nothing else?" He could feel his muscles tensing again. He strongly disliked helplessness, particularly when helplessness went along with lack of knowledge. "Did you arrange drop points?"

"I wasn't planning to visit any drop points with you on board," she said. "That would defeat my purpose in keeping you safe. There's no guarantee your drop points would be safe."

He threw up his hands. "You might as well seal me into that cubby under the deck, then. What's the use of having mercenary captains if they won't try to obtain information?"

"This conspiracy originates at court, you may wager on it," she said. She dipped more ink onto her pen. He noted it was the steel-nibbed pen with inlaid lacquer designs he'd given her after her previous voyage.

"And we're at sea." Nowhere near court, or anywhere else they might obtain information.

She smiled. "I suggest you set your mind to enjoying your idyll," she said. "I know you'd rather investigate the danger yourself, but I refuse to allow you to get yourself killed. You pay me, after all."

"Too generously, I'm thinking," he said. "Or—" he grinned "—perhaps not generously enough, for such services as rolling me naked into a carpet and carrying me off to your lair."

He could tell from her voice that she was fighting a smile even as she said, "This is a serious matter."

"So it is," he said. "All the more reason not to worry overmuch. You can be frozen with worry."

"Are you attempting to lull me?" Imena asked. "I won't have you plotting anything aboard my ship."

"You said yourself that I was your employer."

She thought for a moment, then said, "My services as a bodyguard come for free."

"You can't forbid me to deal with a problem that concerns me most of all," Maxime noted. "I also remind you that I am the person aboard this ship who knows the court most intimately. I've swum with those sharks since I was a child."

"So long as you swear to me that you will not attempt to leave *Seaflower*." She took a cloth and blotted her ink. He could see the muscles flex in her arm with the motions.

"I can hardly leave the ship while we're in the middle of the ocean," Maxime pointed out.

"When we reach port," she said patiently.

"There might be extenuating circumstances."

Imena sighed explosively. "You can never agree to anything straight out, can you?"

"Of course I can. I hired *you*."

"That wasn't immediate." She meant that he'd treated her to a long and elaborate dinner, over which he'd questioned her about her qualifications, followed by an increasingly more drunken evening that had included a tour of the local taverns.

He said, "Actually, it *was* immediate. I knew as soon as we met. I just didn't tell you until later on." He'd decided he wanted to marry her almost as quickly, but now was definitely not the time to bring that up.

She looked dubious. She said, "You should allow me to protect you. I don't think you give the threat against you enough credence."

"Well, we haven't much information, have we?" he asked in as reasonable a tone as he could muster. "I've never known you to be so cautious."

"We're on the defensive," she pointed out.

"We don't know from where attack will come," he countered. "Imena, it is your profession to gather information. I pay you to gather information. So why aren't you finding out all you can, instead of merely delegating to Sylvie?"

She turned in her chair, straddling it and resting her arms on its back. She'd straddled him that way and—He looked away, thinking cold thoughts. She said, "You forget, Maxime. I am hardly inconspicuous in your country. Even if I grew my hair to cover my tattoos—and there was no time for that—I am a foreigner. Clearly a foreigner, even in my own land. And I doubt there's a single person at the king's court who wouldn't be able to figure out who I am."

"There are ways to obtain information quite openly," he said. "Or for one person to draw attention while another is more discreet. We could still return to shore and pursue this together, separate from Sylvie's inquiries."

Imena closed her eyes, and Maxime inwardly smiled. She hated being idle as much as he did, or even more. She would see the sense of his words and sail them back to the duchies, and then he would find out who was trying to rule his life. Aside from the king, that was. The sooner this was taken care of, the sooner he could resume persuading her to marry him.

Imena met his gaze and said, "I don't think we should take the risk. I can't risk your life."

"You? Speak of *risk?* After a youth spent chasing pirates?"

She half rose from her chair, then subsided. "You are the duke now, Maxime. You have a responsibility to your people."

"*You* have a responsibility to *me*."

"It doesn't involve me getting you killed. I can't allow it, not when there's an alternative. Besides, Her Grace Camille would never speak to me again if I allowed you to be killed."

"If that happened, I wouldn't be speaking to you,

either," he pointed out, again striving to calm himself. "All right, for now I'll accept your recommendation."

"For now," she said, looking unconvinced.

He grinned at her. "We have other things to do. You gave me four days, with an option on a fifth. Perhaps you might untie me now?"

Imena looked down at the deck. Her hands twisted on the chair's back. "We can't do this, Your Grace," she said. "It's foolish to pretend you're persuading me of anything. You know I want you. I know you want me. That's all there can be—wanting but never really having."

"I seem to recall having you quite recently," Maxime said.

"You did. But I'm afraid I can't go through with it again."

CHAPTER TEN

TWO DAYS LATER, IMENA SWAM ALONG THE SIDE
of *Seaflower*. "Roxanne! I'll need a hull scraper!" She
plunged beneath a cold wave then let herself bob to the
surface, shaking droplets from her head and vigorously
treading water. Her hair had grown out to a soft stubble,
but it wasn't enough to keep her warm unless she kept
moving.

Roxanne leaned out of the shoreboat and tossed a rope
with the scraper and a small buoy knotted onto the end.
Imena retrieved the tool, filled her lungs, then dived
underwater to clear the troublesome barnacles from the
rudder's housing that impeded its bite into the water.
She hadn't performed such a menial task since her first
year at sea, but just now she needed physical activity.
Her free hand followed a rope they'd stretched, which
would hopefully prevent her from being smashed into
the rough hull by the waves. She would have preferred a

more thorough cleaning of the ship's bottom. Until they could sail into port, this would have to do.

She'd spent entirely too many of her free moments lately mooning over Maxime and his fine body. If she'd been as busy as she ought to be, she wouldn't have had time for such foolishness. She scraped more vigorously, until her arm throbbed.

When she surfaced for the final time, some of the youngsters, Deena and Kiesha and Ailf, were clambering into the shoreboat, and Roxanne had extended her hand to Maxime, who'd also taken the opportunity for a swim. Roxanne's hook, which replaced her lost left hand, was secured by an oarlock, but even so, Maxime's muscular form rocked the boat as he half fell over the side, laughing. Roxanne didn't give his near nudity a second glance—she was a lover of women, and partnered with *Seaflower*'s surgeon—but Deena and Kiesha glanced at each other and giggled, and Imena felt a surge of jealousy at how friendly he'd become with her crew.

There was such a thing as being too charming. Her crew was hers, hard-won over a decade at sea. She didn't want—

She was being ridiculous. Her crew were not her possessions. Tying the scraper to her belt, she used the rope to walk up the side of the ship. She inhaled brine and tar, warmed wood scented with a distant echo of the forests from which it had come, paint; as she grew closer to the rail, she smelled the paste her crew used to polish the brightwork, and cinnamon-pineapple-pork dumplings steaming in the galley. Home.

Standing on deck again, she wrung most of the water

from her singlet and drawers as best she could before padding to her cabin. First she would rinse off the salt, then put on fresh clothing. They could spare the water for at least a catbath. She knew of a discreet island with more than one source of fresh water, and planned to make a stop there within the next few days. She hadn't yet mentioned this to Maxime. She suspected he would argue for a long list of other possible ports, all of them much more dangerous to him.

Behind her, she heard thumps as sailors from the shoreboat swarmed up a rope ladder, then shouted orders as Roxanne directed them in hoisting the boat up the side. Norris scrambled to help, banging out the rhythm on a small drum. The crew members burst into song.

Inside her cabin, she peeled off her singlet and drawers, dropping them with a *splat* into the bucket near the door. Norris had left her favorite rough towel on the bed. She blotted water from her face and head, then wiped down her arms, enjoying the slight abrasion of the fabric against her skin.

"Don't stop on my account," Maxime said. The cabin door fell shut behind him.

Though he'd argued he should share her cabin, she'd banished him belowdecks, ignoring his complaints that the livestock in the hold disturbed his sleep. Keeping him out of her direct sight was simply easier. It had given her time to steady her emotional waves and erect a wall to block off memories of how he'd felt beneath her hands and inside her body.

She cast a glance over her shoulder. Maxime had his

own towel and was wiping himself down briskly. "Did you have a request, Your Grace?"

"Yes." He finished drying himself and tossed his towel over one shoulder. "I wanted to speak with you."

"Without clothes?" she remarked. She rummaged out her most voluminous robe and tossed it at him; he caught the silk before it floated to the deck, unfolded the robe and draped it over his shoulders. She was annoyed to find the bright blue silk looked gorgeous on him. She said, "Have a seat."

She found a dry pair of drawers and pulled them on, then added a singlet. By the time she turned to him, he was sitting in her desk chair. He appeared to be absorbed in studying one of the painted screens that were clamped to the bulkheads, though she was sure he'd been watching her dress.

She said, "The one on the left depicts my ancestor in battle. She was the first in my family to achieve the rank of admiral. If you look closely, you can see her little dog at her feet. She's rarely pictured without him." She pointed out the dog. His name, along with hers, was painted along the edge of the screen in formal characters.

"How long ago was that?"

Imena shrugged. "Three hundred years, at least. She married a foreigner, just as my mother did. Except her husband's country was conquered soon after, so he was considered an imperial from then on. It also helped that his physical type was indistinguishable from other imperials."

Maxime said, "One would think, after so many nations

were conquered by the empire, that physical appearance would matter less."

She shrugged. "If not that, some other marker of status would take its place. And skin color has the advantage of being ineradicable." She wasn't about to sit on her bunk, so she chose a trunk instead. "What may I do for you, Your Grace?"

"I was hoping—"

Imena lifted her head when he stopped speaking abruptly. Had she heard a shout?

Feet rumbled on the deck, a mass of them at once, and suddenly someone was banging on her cabin door. "Captain! Captain!"

Maxime reached the door before Imena could, and flung it open. Norris fell into the cabin, unusually disheveled. She stumbled to her feet, took a deep breath and said, "Sir. Pirates, sir. Closing fast."

Imena frowned. They were sailing well beyond the usual cruising grounds of both imperial privateers and the fringe-territory pirates whom they usually hunted. Nor were they close enough to the northern lands to encounter the barbarian pirates who sailed forth in the cold months, even had they decided to set out in the summer instead. She said, "What sort of pirates?"

Norris looked surprised at the question, but then, she had never encountered pirates, so far as Imena knew. She said, "Roxanne recognized the rigging on their mainsail. They're from the Inland Sea, she says. To the north of the Horizon Empire."

"Bloody flux in a hurricane." Imena yanked a tunic over her singlet and belted on her cutlass. "Your Grace, you'd better go below. No, go with Norris. Into the cubby, Norris."

"Sir," Norris said.

"No," Maxime said.

"Yes," Imena said.

"Pirates aren't after me in particular," he said.

"You're a valuable hostage, and you're wasting my time," she said.

"They won't have any idea who I am. I might be able to help."

And if pirates overran the ship, she wouldn't want him to be trapped and helpless. She had a moment's vision of finding his corpse, mangled and leaking blood onto the deck. Imena threw up her hands. "Fine. Don't cry to me when they slice your bollocks off and wear them for earrings. Norris, get him a cutlass. And some clothes."

"No pistols?" he asked as they hurried on deck.

"One shot and you're left with a short club. No, thank you," she said. "Stay behind me."

"What if it comes to a fight?"

"Stay behind me," she reiterated, though she wasn't sure what she would do if he refused. She wouldn't order the crew to subdue him unless his life was in immediate danger.

On deck, the crew were being issued weapons by Nabhi, the armsmaster, and by Kuan and the surgeon, who had earned her sobriquet the Knife. Chetri stood near the prow, feet braced wide, a cutlass on either hip. Imena followed the direction of his gaze and had no trouble seeing not one but two ships approaching rapidly, hull up. He said, his voice eerily calm, "They came out

of the sun. We were lucky Kiesha and Ailf had decided
to seek a little privacy in the upper nest."

Imena calculated rapidly in her head, changed a few
variables and calculated again. "It's too late to run," she
said regretfully. "Chetri? Am I wrong?"

He shook his head. "The wind is their friend today."

Roxanne slid down the rigging and trotted over. "Oars,
Captain," she said. She took a stone from her pocket and
began sharpening the tip of her hook. "They keep oars-
men down below, so there's no chance of being becalmed.
Most carry cannon."

Despite her years of privateering, Imena had never encountered the pirates of the Inland Sea; only once had
she heard of them encroaching on the empire's sea lanes,
and the single ship had been quickly routed by the navy.
The tales she'd heard about the Inland pirates had made
her glad of her escape, but now she wished she'd had
some direct experience of them. "Have you fought the
northerners before, Roxanne?"

"No, sir. I knew the look of them from my father's
tales."

"I've fought them," Chetri said. "I was a boy, but I
remember it well."

"Weaknesses?" Imena asked.

Chetri shook his head, his earrings chiming. "That
would depend on the captain. Some are no worse than
we might be. Some drink all sorts of potions before they
go into battle, so they feel nothing and fear no one. The
maddest of them build an immunity to certain poisons,
so they may hold poisoned mastic in their mouths and
thus spit poison at their enemies."

Imena said, "We'll expect the worst. Chetri, you'll take the offensive fighters, but hold them unless you see an advantage in attack. Roxanne, you'll command defense. Don't give away that His Grace has any special importance." As her first and second mates ran to assemble their crew, she called, "Norris!"

"Sir."

"The youngsters go below. All of them. Assign cutlasses, just in case. Deena can command."

"But, sir—"

Imena touched the girl's shoulder before she could protest further. "You'll run messages for me." Young as she was, Norris had hard experience behind her, and would keep her head.

Norris beamed. "Sir!" She ran to gather the rest of the adolescent crew.

Imena turned to Maxime, who was yanking on a pair of dry trousers. She averted her eyes from his bare, muscular chest. "I recall you know how to use a cutlass."

"Not as well as a straight sword, but in close fighting that won't matter much, will it?" His voice was perfectly steady. He scooped up his tunic and wriggled into it. "I might be valuable if it comes to negotiation."

Imena shook her head. "Let me do the talking. This is my ship."

To her surprise, Maxime didn't protest. He inclined his head to her. "Am I with Chetri or Roxanne?" he asked.

"With me," she said. "We stay with the ship."

"Sir."

She cast him a glance at his ready acquiescence, but he

was involved in adjusting the harness that supported his cutlass.

One-Eye, the cook, finished dousing the fires and handed out a quick meal of dried meat and cold rice balls. The Knife went below to prepare her surgery. The crew braided back each other's hair and applied paint to their faces and upper bodies, some filling in tattooed outlines, others marking themselves with vivid swaths of bloodred or cerulean. A few, mostly islanders, yanked their hair into topknots and applied paint to stiffen them. Nabhi carried around a bowl of rosin powder, to dust hands and the grips of cutlasses and knives, to ward against the slipperiness of sweat and blood.

Norris brought Imena a new jacket, a deep citrus orange with red frogging all down the front that hung to midthigh. Imena put it on, then allowed Norris to readjust her weaponry and smooth the silk over her thighs. Norris then applied kohl to Imena's eyes and stained her lips red as blood. Finally, Norris carefully shaved the stubble from Imena's head. When she'd gone, taking Imena's plain jacket with her, Maxime said, "You look absolutely deadly."

She grinned at him. "That's the idea. There will be no doubt who is the captain of this ship."

She stood near the wheel and watched the pirate ships approach, striving to learn what she could about their speed and maneuverability and, more important, the skill of their captains and crew. She forgot Maxime stood near her until he asked, "Do you have any muskets?"

She shook her head. "Too much upkeep for too little use. The humidity isn't good to bows and arrows, either, but they're still more reliable at sea, cheaper, as well, and a good archer is faster than a good musketeer. Besides, you know we don't go into battle unless attacked."

"You've trained your crew well."

"Better prepared than sorry," she pointed out. "A good captain is prepared for everything." She glanced at him. "Are you attempting to distract me?"

"You appeared tense," he said.

"I assure you, it won't affect my performance."

"It can't be pleasant, though, waiting to be attacked."

His voice was neutral, but she remembered he'd been a child when a neighboring duke had laid siege to his castle, eventually killing both his parents and making the duchy into a protectorate. How many days had that siege continued? Had he been old enough to fight?

She said, "When I served on *Sea Tiger,* the waiting was always the worst thing. I would want to crawl free of my skin, and I couldn't bear it when others coped by joking and gambling."

"Do you miss it? Being a privateer?"

She stared at him, surprised that he'd guessed. "Sometimes. I miss the camaraderie of it. Then I remind myself that those times were rare." She ran her hand over the tattoos on her scalp. "I remind myself that I'm still part of that fellowship, and will be until the day I die."

"You have your own ship now," he reminded her.

"Of course." She looked out to sea. The two ships were drawing nearer. They'd be close enough to board in minutes. "Stay behind me," she reiterated.

"I'll do my best not to have my bollocks made into

earrings," Maxime said solemnly. "I know you have use for them."

The pirate ships were similar in both hulls and rigging, but one was decorated more dramatically than the other, its hull a shiny black and its figurehead a screaming eagle, iron claws stretched out as if to seize prey. Its crew lined the rails, eerily still and silent, their weapons clearly visible. The second ship's figurehead was a more sedate bird of prey with wings outstretched along the hull, its eyes made from inset yellow stones that glowed in the midday sunlight. The crew of the second ship, she noted with surprise, were mostly women, armed with a mixture of short bows and pikes. Or—she looked more closely—*all* women.

She glanced at Maxime. "First, the show of strength. Then, the negotiation." Waving her crew aside, she strode to the rail and stood, waiting.

In seconds she knew: there would be no negotiation. The pirates did not lower boats. Instead, she saw men on the black ship swinging lines hitched to grappling hooks, ready to toss them at *Seaflower* as soon as they were close enough. She glanced at Chetri; he was already summoning a few of the crew with axes, led by Kuan, to chop at the lines and repel boarders. Roxanne assembled a company of sailors with cutlasses around the main hatches, to guard the ways below. Arionrhod, the purser, led their few archers; they had been perched in the rigging since shortly after the pirate ship was sighted.

She could not look at Maxime. She needed to keep her eyes on her business, ahead of her, and if he had decided to move away from her protection, it would really be his own fault if he got himself killed.

As if he'd heard her thoughts, he said quietly, "You may guard me, but I will also guard you."

And then the first grappling hook whined through the air and slammed into the ship, rattling and dragging along the deck. She lifted a hand, and Kuan leaped forward, hacking at the hook's rope while it snaked like a live thing across the sanded deck.

Pistols cracked, from the black ship, she thought, but she worried more about the arrows showering on them from above while her own archers remained poised, saving their arrows to defend against boarders. Someone screamed in pain, someone else in rage, then everyone was shouting, a jumbled mess of orders and battle cries from a dozen lands.

Maxime moved to her side, then attempted to step in front of her, but she warded him off with a glare as arrows rattled to the deck. They hadn't been aimed, they'd simply provided cover for more grappling hooks. Kuan, she saw, was already down. Wiscz had taken up his ax, but the grapples were too many and her crew too few.

Everyone seemed to move with slow clarity. She felt the familiar cold and lightness of battle; she scarcely noticed the weight of her cutlass in her hand. She shouted commands to her ax wielders; they shifted from attacking ropes to attacking pirates, a wave of black-clad figures who spilled over *Seaflower*'s railings like water, smashing into the ragged, fragile line of her sailors.

Her crew were not warriors, not wholly. She'd considered crewing *Seaflower* with former privateers, but she'd

gone beyond that life. She was not a brute warrior anymore. She hadn't regretted her decision, until now.

She had only a moment for regret before they were
upon her, two pirates with pikes. She topped both in
height, but was far outmatched in muscle. She sucked
in her belly to avoid a thrusting blade and felt Maxime
at her shoulder. He yelled and attacked the pirate on the
left, so she took the second, slashing low.

Sounds seemed distant, except for the clang and rasp
of blade on blade. A pike nicked her upper arm, staining
her orange jacket, another the outside of her thigh. She
stood back to back with Maxime now, fighting with
him as smoothly as if he'd been Chetri. It didn't matter,
though. The pirates were too many.

Long before she and Maxime were finally forced against
the mainmast, she knew they had lost, but she refused to
stop fighting until she could fight no more.

Her crew were being forced to lay down their weapons.
Cutlasses and pikes thudded or clanged onto a sheet of
canvas, no doubt damaging edges; she heard Nabhi spitting obscenities as she was forcibly relieved of her two
blades. Arrows and bows rattled. To the left, Roxanne
was forced to her knees and ordered in hoarse patois to
surrender her bloodied hook.

Imena strongly resented having her hands bound behind
her, but she could see the pirate captain's point: she had
not actually surrendered, and with her hands free, she
would definitely have been communicating with Chetri
and whoever else could decipher her signals. He read her
facial expressions with expertise, after so many years,

but that wasn't the same as being able to give him direct orders. She set her jaw and allowed two women, both taller than her and with arms like young trees, to tighten her bonds to their satisfaction and then propel her over the railing of *Seaflower* and onto the deck of the northern ship.

Her face itched abominably where a trickle of blood meandered down from a cut on her scalp. Deliberately, she forced the sensation away.

She hoped Maxime was keeping his mouth shut. From what she'd seen before she'd been overwhelmed, he hadn't been wounded beyond bruises and nicks. She was glad for the injuries, as they would help him blend into her crew, or the battered remnants of her crew. Hiyu, one of the topmen, had been killed, and from the glimpses she'd had, at least three more of her sailors were seriously injured.

Each of the pirate ships had a captain, and both awaited her. The woman was clearly in charge. She looked to be in her fifties or early sixties; it was difficult to tell because pale skin endured sun so badly. Her face and hands were weathered, her blond and gray-brindled hair bleached even paler by sunlight. Her bloused trousers and snug tunic, of plain linen, blended into the colors of her skin. She wore her hair swept high atop her head and clasped with a jeweled metal band that matched the bow guard she wore on her left arm and the plate belt slung low around her slim hips; those were her only adornments. She was missing the lobe of one ear and stood with commanding presence, more of a military air than Imena was used to seeing in pirates. Imena couldn't see any of the usual tattoos that would have given her more information.

The second captain was male, and looked younger, even through the smudged lines of lurid green paint streaked across his forehead and slashed across his cheeks. He dressed with a flamboyance that seemed common to all pirates, but even so, Imena had never seen a pirate who was quite so richly yet shabbily adorned.

His wore his rusty hair down his back in a messy array of asymmetrical braids, some thin and tight as tiny snakes, some thick as rope, all fraying, all of them twisted in and around with bright metal buttons and sun-faded ribbons in every color of the rainbow. His bright blue trousers fit snugly, but his purple velvet shirt flapped loose and ragged-hemmed over his waist, belted in the sort of satin cording she'd seen used to tie back curtains. Over the shirt he wore an open waistcoat, encrusted with silver lace and buttons and strings of shark teeth, and atop that a long frock coat, too large, whose snagged bloodred brocade was rubbed to white in places. Daggers sagged each of the coat's hip pockets with their weight. Another pair of crossed daggers were harnessed over the coat. Beneath all the finery, however, his feet were bare and filthy, with clawed yellow toenails.

Imena met his strangely hot gaze and had to force herself not to flinch. His silvery-gray eyes were like shallow pools with no feeling behind them, the eyes of a pitiless shark. She'd seen his type before, once, and he made her inwardly shudder as she had not done in years. As soon as her escort had propelled her within his reach, his hand snaked out and slapped her face with stunning force.

"Cassidy!" the woman snapped. "Restrain yourself."

"Venom," the pirate said, with the air of correcting a child. He licked his lips. His tongue was stained green.

Imena tried to shake off the blow; her cheekbone felt as if it still vibrated. She heard a commotion behind her, on *Seaflower,* but ignored it to focus on the woman captain. Slowly, she licked a droplet of blood from her lip.

The female pirate said, in the patois of a thousand ports, "I am Captain Svetlana Litvinova of *Riptide.* We require information."

Imena said nothing. She had been asked no question, and the blow on top of Hiyu's death had angered her sufficiently to temporarily overwhelm her good sense. She'd been too long out of the game, it seemed, spent too long covertly gathering information from the unwary. This wasn't the same, not at all. How was she to protect her crew—and Maxime—from this hostile force, without weapons, with so little to bargain? None of her valuable cargo had been loaded before her precipitate departure from the duchies.

"Give her to me," the pirate addressed as Cassidy, called Venom, said, after a few moments of chill silence. He spoke a dialect Imena recognized, from the empire's northern coast, though his accent was strange. She'd seen hair redder than his, far to the north, and had heard it was common in the barbarian islands. "My crew are thirsty for blood, and you haven't given it to us as you promised. I am thirsty, too. She looks as if she wouldn't scream for a long, long time."

Litvinova ignored him. "Do you understand me?" she asked.

"Yes," Imena said, biting back rage.

"Are you an imperial ship?"

Imena shrugged. The grips of her two captors tightened on her shoulders.

"Your ship looks imperial, but not as I'm familiar with. And though you bear the marks of a privateer, your eyes are a strange color. Do you come from the fringes of the empire?"

"Which empire would that be?" Imena asked.

Litvinova caught Venom's blow this time, blocking him with her arm. As if nothing had happened, she said, "I've never known imperials to tolerate so many mongrels for long. Your crew must be from farther south. I need to know more of those waters, and the ports you've visited in the past year."

"I'm not interested in what you need," Imena said, waiting for the threats to begin. Litvinova didn't recognize *Seaflower* as a duchy ship; she didn't seem to know what lay beyond the Horizon Empire. Which made sense, if she'd spent her life around the Inland Sea. They were isolated there, with no outlet by sea except into waters ruled by the imperial navy and, more often, imperial privateers. She wouldn't know Maxime held any importance; she might not even have heard of the duchies. That was a small relief, at least.

Litvinova gripped Imena's chin, preventing her from looking away. "Perhaps you will be interested in this. I have two ships, you have one. I carry sufficient crew to keep yours under guard for weeks on end. I have control of your ship, and I have control of you. All I am asking in return is information."

Venom smiled chillingly, and said in the northern dialect, "You promised me slaves to fuck, strong ones. This one would shriek for a long time, before I fed her to the sharks. My men are summoning them at this moment."

His statement was more in line with what Imena had been expecting. She controlled her expression so it wouldn't be obvious she understood his words. She said, "Perhaps you should have simply asked, then."

Litvinova stepped closer, pushing her face close to Imena's. "And you would have been absolutely truthful in your answers, of course."

Imena fought her instinct to step back. It would be useless, in any case, given the large hands gripping her biceps and shoulders. "You'll never know now."

Litvinova retreated abruptly. "No matter." She glanced to the side; a young woman in a snug dress and jeweled headband stepped to her other side. Venom sneered openly at her. Imena watched with interest; she would lay odds the young woman was no pirate, much less a sailor.

Litvinova's voice softened as she spoke. "Annja, did you see which it was?"

Annja's voice was low and sultry. "The big one, mistress, with the dark beard. He fought at her side and defended her to his own cost."

Maxime. He'd managed to draw attention to himself. She ought to have confined him below with the youngsters instead of letting him fight; she could have told him he was protecting them. How should she react? Dismiss him as of no importance? She didn't think they'd believe her. Her only consolation was that they could have no idea he was a valuable political hostage. She said nothing.

"Bring him here," Litvinova said. Of Imena, she asked, "Who is he? Do you own him or pay him? Or is he merely loyal?"

Imena stared back at her. Being tortured would have been fine. She could have resisted that, at least long enough for Chetri to find some advantage. But she did not think she could watch Maxime be tortured, not for long. And if she did, would it violate their contract?

At least, she thought with pained humor, she wouldn't be guilty of treason. She wasn't a citizen of the duchies.

Venom gestured sharply.

Two more large pirates, these male, vaulted the railing to *Seaflower.* They bound Maxime's arms and brought him to the pirate ship. Her crew took their cue from her and did not resist, though she could hear discontented murmuring, abruptly cut off, likely at a signal from Chetri. She knew that if it came to sacrificing Maxime for the sake of her ship and crew, she would have to do it, but the idea made her light-headed. For a moment, she fought to keep her feet.

She didn't look at Maxime as he was brought to the pirate ship, though she could feel his presence like a warmth, as if the proximity of his body to hers could raise the fine hairs all over her skin. She held Litvinova's gaze instead, deliberately loosening her muscles one by one, so if the chance occurred, she would be prepared to spring into action. This was made more difficult by Venom, who had moved close to her side. He reeked of musty fabric and long-unwashed flesh with a peculiar medicinal malodor. Laughing softly, he traced her scalp tattoos with the tip of one finger. His sharp nail sent shivers down her spine, and Imena had to fight the urge to retch, not so much from the touch but from the invasive intimacy of it, of this creature touching her where Maxime had touched her. Venom touched the cut above her temple and, to her horror, leaned forward and tasted the blood with the tip of his tongue. The cut began to itch and burn.

Litvinova abruptly shoved him back.

Was it a ploy? The "good" pirate and the "bad" pirate?

Perhaps she would not have been so immune to torture as she'd thought, if such a thing as a fingernail on her scalp could affect her so viscerally. It had been a long time since she'd been a captive, even longer since she'd suffered at the hands of captors, and she was older now, less foolhardy. She was too aware of consequences.

It took physical effort not to look at Maxime. Then he was at her side, out of arm's reach but there, accompanying his captors as if they were escorts rather than tall scarred pirates with matching broken noses and coppery hair clipped into wild cock's tails. When the pirates jerked him to a halt in front of Litvinova, he bowed, precise and respectful, and said in an appalling mixture of his own language and dockside patois, "Madame Captain. How may I serve you?"

He was fluent in patois, but after a moment she realized he'd mangled his words purposely, creating a vulnerability where none existed.

Litvinova turned to Annja. "Is this the one?"

"Yes, Captain."

Litvinova caressed Annja's cheek. "Thank you, love. You may go below now." She gently patted Annja's rear as she turned to go.

"Is she your pet?" Imena said before she could stop herself.

"You're no better, and perhaps worse, that you put him in danger," Litvinova countered, indicating Maxime with a wave of her hand. "Have you any tender feelings for him? Or perhaps, for his worth? He'd sell for a boatload of gold to a fine lady near the Inland Sea, those who have no taste for eunuchs and like them hairy and virile."

Maxime spoke up, still in the same mangled patois. "Madame Captain would allow me to demonstrate my worth? Maybe a trade?"

Imena sucked in her breath. He could not be offering to trade himself for the ship. He wouldn't be so foolish.

Litvinova addressed herself to Imena. "You should teach him to speak only when spoken to. I would have other uses for his tongue, myself."

Imena shrugged, pretending indifference. "There are men in every port, and cheaper ones, too."

"But this one is yours. You don't dress him as befits a captain's concubine, but you've brought him to sea with you, trained him in weapons and manners…of a sort." Litvinova walked over, Venom trailing her, and casually turned Maxime's face to one side, then the other. She peered at his teeth, prodded his shoulders and thighs and, more slowly, explored his crotch. Imena dared a quick glance. His jaw had set hard at the handling, even though he still forced a smile. Rage boiled in her chest. How dare this woman treat His Grace like chattel!

She reminded herself that Maxime was safer, just now, as a concubine than a duke. Too late. She felt a crawling on her skin and looked up to find Venom's eyes on her, frigid and speculative.

Venom ran his hand over Maxime's jaw, then reached down and squeezed his genitals, hard. He said to Litvinova in his own tongue, "It will be a pleasure scraping off all this hair, bit by bit. Then perhaps I could bend him over the rail, flog him and let my men screw him until he is reduced enough to amuse me with his whimpers."

It was clear to Imena that Maxime understood this vile speech, but he met Venom's sidelong sneer with an innocent smile. He inclined his head and said in patois, "Master Underling wishes his cock sucked?"

Venom slapped him. *Underling* wasn't the entire meaning of the word Maxime had used. "You will be shark food," he said, his patois the thickest Imena had ever heard.

"Gag him," Litvinova said curtly to one of Imena's guards. She meant Maxime, not Venom, but after a breath Imena realized this meant she would have only one guard. Litvinova added, "Strip him after you've gagged him and give him to Cassidy. This one can watch."

Imena's breath caught, then she sucked in air and let her cold rage flow through her veins, bringing every limb to tingling life. Her arms strained at her ropes, her wounds numbed, and the top of her head prickled as if it were about to catch fire in phosphorescence. "You will not abuse my crew," she said, biting the words off through numb lips.

Litvinova smiled with absolutely no warmth.

"He fought against us like the rest. He killed two of Cassidy's—*Venom's* sailors. I think they should be allowed a little revenge." She paused. "Unless you might be willing to help us." She paused again, and when Imena said nothing, gestured to the guard on Imena's left side.

Imena watched as Maxime was gagged with a twist of leather, covertly flexing her arm. As the guard ripped open his shirt, drawing Venom's avid gaze, she flung her weight in his direction, twisting her body and screaming with all the volume she could muster.

CHAPTER ELEVEN

MAXIME WAS DOWN.

Imena rolled to her feet, struggling wildly for Venom's dagger while his legs tangled with hers, the sharp toes of his boots digging into her flesh. The dagger's tip was smeared with a greenish oil, and whether it was poison or merely hallucinogen, she didn't dare let it brush her skin.

A flaming arrow slammed into the deck near their heads. Another landed near it, atop a coil of tarred rope, and flames burst out.

Unfortunately, despite Imena's greater weight, the pirate's wiry arms were stronger than hers, and he bared teeth in a ferocious grin as he forced her hand toward her throat.

Imena sank her teeth into the sleeve of his coat, trying to bite hard enough to break skin, clinging even as he banged her skull against a line-block and pain shot nauseatingly into her belly. Head reeling, she thrust with her knee, without leverage, and just managed to graze his privates. For a breath, his grip slackened, and she flung away his arm with all her strength.

A gust of sandalwood and Chetri was there, his hands on the shoulders of her jacket, dragging her free of Venom's scrabbling hands while she blinked away dizziness. Seretse and Wiscz leaped on Venom with all their considerable size and Imena saw Norris jump into the fray, wielding a bucket whose iron bindings might cause serious damage. Gnalam, Seretse's tiny mate, attacked a pirate with a hammer.

She saw Maxime then, tangled with his opponents on the deck, pounding his elbow into the face of one of his captors while viciously kicking the other with his heel.

She couldn't hear what Chetri was saying to her in the midst of the screaming and bellowing of a full-blown melee. Then the sound of her own retching blocked him out; he'd heaved her up and over the rail, into Roxanne's arms. Imena's weight bore them both to the deck, Roxanne shielding her from impact; she barely turned to the side before the contents of her stomach erupted.

When Imena could speak again, she asked, "Maxime?"

"Safe," Roxanne said. She'd recovered possession of her hook and began strapping it on, cursing as her fingers fumbled. Nabhi raced by her, a cutlass in one hand and a belaying pin in the other, screaming at the top of her lungs.

Imena wiped her mouth on her sleeve—Norris would weep at the state of this jacket—and discovered she had landed close to a pile of discarded weapons. She reached for a cutlass, missed, and took a breath, lowering her head.

A large hand landed on her shoulder, applying all the force of its owner's weight. "Stay down, Captain," the Knife said. "Your brain's bruised. Let Chetri earn his keep."

"Cast off the grapples," Imena said. Her stomach roiled and she swallowed hard.

"Already done." The Knife snagged Imena beneath the arms and hauled her toward a hatch. Imena felt like a child next to her powerful bulk. "You, Captain Leung, are no longer fit for duty."

Imena protested being led into her cabin, protested sitting on a trunk and protested the Knife's ministrations until she felt the ship get under way. Even then she remained tense, because she knew the pirate ships would be close in pursuit.

"We can do this on deck," she said as the Knife applied salve to a cut on her thigh, the sharp herbal tang clearing the blood and smoke from her nostrils. She breathed more deeply, hoping the scent would ease the throbbing at the base of her neck.

"You'd be in the way," the Knife said. "Also, Captain, I have taken away your trousers."

"Get Roxanne down here, to report to me."

"My love is busy," the Knife said, applying a linen bandage. She said, "If he'd got the inside of your thigh instead of nicking the outside, you'd be dead by now." She picked up another cloth, soaked it in distilled alcohol and slapped it against the cut on Imena's upper arm.

VICTORIA JANSSEN

Imena hissed. The door to her cabin swung open, and Maxime slipped in, carrying a cup. Before she could speak, he said, "We've gained a ship length. They spent time putting out the fires before they got under way."

"Who shot the arrows?" Imena demanded.

"Norris," he said.

Imena grinned. "You can tell her she's earned a bonus. Twenty gold pieces."

Maxime sat on the trunk next to her, nudging her hip aside with his. He held the cup for her and she sipped: ginger syrup, to help settle her stomach. Once she'd swallowed, he said, "Marry me. You've just demonstrated why you'd make a most excellent duchess."

Imena turned to look at him, too quickly, and had to swallow back nausea from the movement. "Because I can knee a pirate in the bollocks? I don't have to marry you, you've already given me your virtue," she said, swallowing inappropriate and slightly hysterical laughter.

Maxime only looked at her. She was surprised when he kissed her temple, gently. He said, "You've a nasty knot on the back of your head."

The Knife remarked, "There's a reason most people leave the hair on their heads where it belongs."

Imena said, "Are you finished with me?"

"No," the Knife said. "How's the nausea?"

"If you forbore from mentioning it, it would go away," she retorted. "I can puke just as well on deck as here."

Maxime leaned toward the Knife and said, "She's right, you know. I could keep an eye on her for you."

The Knife eyed him sourly. "Your charm will not work on me," she said, "but your logic will. Let me bind up your cuts and you can carry her up." She turned to Imena. "You're to stay in the pilothouse, in a chair."

Maxime smiled. "Thank you, Tessa." The Knife smiled back, without her usual sarcasm.

Imena sighed. "Fix him so I can go."

She didn't admit that it was pleasant to be held close to Maxime's chest, her face against his throat, as he carried her up the narrow stairs into the pilothouse. It would have been easy to close her eyes and drift off to sleep, had her anxiety for her ship and crew not pulsed in her chest.

The pilothouse was enclosed on three sides; the fourth side was actually a bamboo screen that could be lashed out of the way. Two chairs, both bolted to the deck, were provided for long watches. Maxime placed Imena in one of these and stood beside her. She nodded to the helmsman, Bonnevie, and breathed deeply of the clean sea breeze. She felt herself calming when she saw Roxanne approaching to report.

Aside from rope burns on her arms, Roxanne appeared unhurt. She said, "We've gained two ship lengths, Captain. The black ship is another length behind—they're sloppier sailors than the *Riptide* crew."

Imena asked, "Casualties?"

"Hiyu was killed in the first rush, and Big Wim bled out before anyone could reach him. Nevens has a gut wound, but the Knife thinks she might pull through. She's not sure about Yeadon or Donkey, and Philippe might lose an eye. Kuan's head wound wasn't as bad as it looked, but he'll be out of the rigging for a week at least."

"Keep me informed. Burials as soon as we're clear of pursuit. Send Chetri to me when he has a moment."

"Aye, Captain."

When Roxanne had gone, Imena sagged against the chair back, giving herself a few moments to mourn her lost crew. Maxime's warm hand rested atop her head for a moment, almost easing her headache, then slid down to squeeze her shoulder in a gentle rhythm. He didn't speak.

When she opened her eyes, Chetri was standing before her, and Maxime crouched unobtrusively to the side, his back against the pilothouse's bulkhead. She'd slept without realizing it. At least her head felt better. "Report," she said.

"Three ship lengths' lead," he said with satisfaction. "We can't quite smell them anymore."

"Good work," Imena said. "Keep it up." She rubbed her gritty eyes, then looked at Chetri again. "What else? Spill it."

"Captain. I took hostages."

"Pirates? On my ship? What were you *thinking?*"

"Prisoners," Chetri said. "The concubine, Annja—she wanted to go with us."

"After she betrayed Maxime to her captain," Imena said, throttling back rage.

"She had no choice," Chetri said. "The other woman, Suzela, was hostage for her good behavior, and Annja for Suzela's. They fought their way to me, Imena. Annja killed one of the pirates with a hairpin to the throat."

Imena blinked. "That was...ingenious."

"They're below. Norris took them in charge. They said they could help the Knife."

"They don't sound as if they're hostages to me," Imena said.

Chetri looked abashed. "They might as well make themselves useful."

"I will speak to them, and let them know of the penalties should they betray our trust in them. And it will be *our* trust. You will not tell them I had nothing to do with your decision and let them think to exploit the knowledge." She fixed him with her most commanding look. "Chetri, I am surprised and displeased that you did this without my permission."

Silently, he bowed to her in acknowledgment, holding the bow for long moments before he straightened. "I will accept whatever discipline you see fit to administer, Captain."

There would have to be discipline of some kind, to uphold the authority she held over the crew. Often, discipline was the only thing standing between life and death for them. She said, "When next we're in dry dock, you will take my shifts and I will take your shore leave."

"Aye, Captain." Chetri bowed again.

"You're not wounded?" she asked.

He shook his head. "I'll take good care of *Seaflower* for you, Captain, if you'd like to sleep for a while."

Maxime said, "I can help you below."

"Not yet," Imena said. "Summon the hostages. I need to speak with them."

Nabhi and Malim brought the women on deck; they were not bound, but Imena noted with approval that both her sailors carried rope at their belts, just in case. Annja, the pirate's concubine, stood just in front of the other woman, Suzela. Annja still wore the snug dress she'd had on earlier, but now the skirt was ripped up one leg and the bodice was spattered with a great quantity of drying blood. Suzela wore a shapeless, knee-length tunic that did little to disguise abundant curves; her long, glossy curls swung forward to hide her face, but the brown skin of her arms and legs was smooth and clear.

Imena did not rise from her chair, but waited until both women bowed. She said, "I am assigning your welfare to Chetri, but that's at my discretion." Neither of them spoke. Approving, Imena said, "I won't have you killed and tossed overboard. I'm allowing you to stay for now, but I expect you to earn your keep. Is that clear?"

Both women bowed.

"Good," Imena said. "You are dismissed."

Three days passed. The pirate ships remained within view, never more than six lengths behind.

Imena first felt the storm as a throbbing in her temples while she was below, holding Yeadon's gnarled hand as he drew his last breaths. When his breathing stopped, and she'd laid his payoff coins on his chest, she hurried back on deck. She could already smell the clean rush of ozone in the rapidly increasing wind, and feel the length of the heavy swell as the deck rose and fell. Clouds the purplish-black of a bruise gathered solid on the horizon.

Chetri appeared at her side before she could call for him. The long days and nights of pursuit were wearing on him; his eyes were reddened from fatigue and salt, and his frowsy hair escaped from its braid. The lines around his mouth were more marked than usual. She said, "Tie everything down, even if we lose a little of our lead. Lifelines, fore and aft, and another amidships. Bare minimum of storm canvas before the brunt of it hits." She named the sails she wanted; dangerous, but not quite so dangerous as to be foolhardy. "And extra crew to the pumps."

The light was changing already, going brassy, and thunder growled as if invisible clubs battered the sky.

"It's a bad blow," Chetri agreed. "Might give us an edge, though. It'll be harder for them to stay on us when the wind gets bad."

Imena said, "Harder if we're not trying to hold a course." She met his eyes. "Once we're out of it, I can find our way to a safe port." She was a trained starmaster. She ought to be able to get some advantage from it.

Chetri looked at her in silence for a moment, then nodded. "Aye, Captain."

The storm hit with a scream of wind and a wall of water. The few sails they couldn't haul down in time were ripped to shreds in minutes, ropes thrashing wildly, dangerously, if no one could reach to slash them loose. Even *Seaflower*'s best topmen had to rope themselves around the waist or risk being blown to the deck from a ship length's height and smashed to jelly. Imena crammed an oilcloth hat on her head and lashed herself to the mainmast until the process was complete, signaling the crew with blasts from a horn because the gale and the horrifying creak of timber whipped voices to nothing while the air churned white with rain and sleet. Soon, even hearing the horn became impossible; water flew over the rails and crashed to the decks, swimming around Imena's calves and seeping through any gap to the decks below.

She breathed a sigh of relief when the last of the hands scrambled free of the rigging. Lightning snapped, momentarily flashing the ship in negative, as if her eyes could no longer tell light from dark.

They could die at any moment, but there was a mad glory in the sting of rain on her face and the buffets of wind that nearly carried her into the air. Playful baby lightning crawled and danced through the rigging before harmlessly crackling into the sea; for a moment the beauty of it transfixed her.

Then a waterspout roared up like a legendary beast of the deep, taller than the mainmast, sucking the breath from her. She gasped and inhaled a fine salty mist instead of air; then it plunged with a perilous crash, flinging Imena nearly to the railing. For long moments the deck was so awash that the ship and the sea seemed the same; struggling fish slammed into her legs before she dragged herself upright with a lifeline, water pouring from her clothing. She'd lost her hat and the rain beat painfully on her head. Well, she thought. Their pursuers could never have predicted *this*. If she was lucky, perhaps the pirates would perish in the storm, or their ships be so damaged they could pursue no one.

She found Chetri and issued more orders, signing with her arms as well as shouting, in the hope nothing would be lost in the bellowing of the wind and thunder and the curtain of downpour. Tiny Gnalam came on deck and lashed herself to the mainmast, to be ready for emergency carpentry repairs; she and Seretse, the chief carpenter, would alternate shifts. Imena waved to her and headed for the pilothouse as lightning jagged across the sky.

The steersman Bonnevie had wedged his feet beneath iron braces and knotted himself in place with two lines, one to hold him around the waist and the other to ensure at least one of his hands remained on the wheel. Imena reeled into the partial shelter the pilothouse offered and took a moment to gasp in a breath that wasn't filled with water. She shouted, "Untie your hand! I don't want you to lose it!"

As she spoke, a wave slammed the tiller and the wheel spun to the side. With a rueful grimace, Bonnevie loosed his hand and let the wheel go, catching it again as a wave slammed into the ship's side. "Should I tie up the wheel?" he asked.

She peered at the wheel ropes. Regular maintenance ensured they weren't likely to break. "Do it, and take a rest below," Imena said. "You'll need it."

After Bonnevie vanished down the ladder, a larger figure emerged from the hatch. Maxime held out a mug to her, its top sealed with a wooden cover. "It's hot," he said, his low voice easily cutting through the surrounding noise.

Imena's oiled coat had soaked through; she took the mug gratefully, warming her icy hands on its sides. "Thank you. Now get below!"

"The Knife sent me to keep an eye on you." Bracing one hand on the bulkhead, he eased closer to her and said, "Drink the tea."

Imena thumbed aside the little hatch covering the mug's opening and tried a sip. The mint tea wasn't scalding, but the liquid heat rushed through her chilled body as if it were on fire. She drained the rest of the mug and gave it back to Maxime. "Below," she ordered. "I won't have you blown overboard."

Outside the pilothouse, the creaking grew worse; she winced and turned, trying to identify the source of the sound. Wood squealed, ripped, snapped, and the searing whine of wind in the rigging abruptly altered. The sound was familiar, a lost topmast. "Putrid melting fish guts," she swore, and dived back into the rain.

In the first onslaught of the gale, Maxime interviewed the two hostages from the pirate ship, Annja and Suzela, while pretending to allow them to interview him about conditions on *Seaflower*. They were most particularly concerned with those conditions relating to abuse of captives and concubines. Annja didn't quite believe there were no concubines aboard, and clearly expected to become Chetri's, once Maxime explained that Captain Leung preferred men. Suzela said nothing at all, but her eyes spoke volumes, most of them distrustful. She sat behind Annja, her legs curled beneath her and her arms trapping the ship's cat in her lap.

Maxime didn't push them too far. Any decisions regarding the women were Imena's to make. Besides that, remaining unmolested for a few days would no doubt reassure the two hostages more than anything he could say. He introduced them to Norris and to Deena, who would bring their food and water, and returned to Imena's cabin.

The storm lasted five days before it passed, or *Seaflower*

passed it. During the endless hours of being tossed like dice in a cup, the pirate ships fell out of sight, whether sunk or merely evaded, none could tell.

Imena ordered the lifelines taken down in the wee hours of the sixth morning. It was evening before the crew ceased the chanting that had accompanied their hours of work pumping out the hold. Maxime, who'd spelled a few of the sailors when needed, returned to Imena's cabin and rubbed his face wearily. He stripped off one shirt, sponged himself off and drew on another that wasn't soaked and encrusted with salt. He wanted a real wash, but he'd had more than enough of being doused in cold water, and it would be some time before the newly rekindled kitchen stoves could produce enough that had been warmed. He'd requested that the first available, after any needed by the Knife and her patients, be reserved for Imena.

She hadn't been to sleep in at least two days, he knew, unless she'd dozed while lashed upright on deck or, like some of the crew, slept in snatched seconds before reeling back to work again. He'd spent most of his free time in her cabin, to make sure he would see her if she ventured there, though she hadn't been below at all. Every few hours during that time, he'd gone on deck, into the maelstrom of bitter winds, freezing rain and hail to bring her tea or cold bread and salted meat, sometimes alternating with Norris, who usually had more subtlety in encouraging her to eat it.

Strange how his concerns had shrunk. He'd wanted to survive the storm, so long as Imena survived it with him. To survive, he'd wanted her to drink tea warmed painstakingly over a sealed spirit lamp, and eat a few bites, and spend a few moments out of the wind. He'd wanted to be with her, even if only for a few moments at a time.

The door slammed open and Imena staggered in. Her sopping-wet clothes were rimed with white salt and smeared with black tar. Though her wounds from the fight with the pirates were healing, her cheek bore a new bruise, her lips were chapped and split and her eyes were reddened like a lifelong smoke addict's.

"You look gorgeous," Maxime said, and meant every word.

"Don't stand in front of my bed," Imena said, taking a shaky step forward.

Maxime caught her arm and slung it around his waist. "I'll help you in," he said.

"Norris?"

"Busy." Maxime eased her atop her coverlet, then grabbed her bare feet and swung them up, as well. "Go to sleep, I'll take your clothes off."

"Promise or threat?" she asked with a weary grin. Her eyes closed. When he cut loose the wet knot at her trousers' waist, she was already limp, deeply asleep.

At least, he thought, she wouldn't notice he was washing her with cold water. She stirred only briefly when he rinsed salt from the raw scrapes on her hands and anointed them with the green salve he'd been given. His bandages, he decided, were good enough to please the Knife. When he sponged her genitals, she murmured, then subsided back to sleep.

He resisted the urge to kiss her, instead stripping off his

clothing and climbing into the bed with her. The bunk wasn't meant for two adults, especially when one was as large as Maxime, so he had to curl closely around her. He laid his palm on her belly and tugged her into the curve of his body. It was the first time, he reflected, that they'd shared a bed.

This, he thought, was what it meant to be in love.

If only she felt the same. At least she didn't snore.

He laid his cheek against the velvety stubble on her head and breathed in her scent. His muscles felt limp as soaked sails. The lamp, though dimmed, was too bright. He closed his eyes.

Someone shook his shoulder vigorously. Maxime blinked up at Imena. "You're asleep in my bed," she said.

"How long?" he mumbled.

"Four hours," she said. "I only let myself sleep the length of a watch. You'll be glad to know the ship isn't going to sink."

"Was I supposed to be worried about that?" he asked. "I don't pay you to sink my ships. Especially not with me in them."

Imena swung off the bed. "I need food," she said.

"There's—"

She swooped down upon the tray of cold rice balls, goat cheese and pickled vegetables with ginger he'd clamped to the table. "Do you want any?" she asked with her mouth full.

He shook his head. He couldn't look away from her lean naked body, the gentle curves of her hips and breasts, and the cheese crumbs she was dropping onto the deck.

There was another bruise on her tattooed thigh, about the height of one of the deck railings. When she turned away to get another slice of cheese, he slid off the bunk and poured her a cup of rice wine.

Imena took the cup in her free hand and drained it. She said, "No one knocked, or I would have woken." She set her cup aside and took another mouthful of cheese. "So you've decided to move into my cabin, have you?"

"The hostages took my space," he said. "Are you going to sleep anymore?"

"After I've eaten," she said. "I'll regret it sorely if I don't."

"Imena?" he said when she had finished chewing.

She brushed crumbs from her hands and took a step closer. She laid her hands on his chest, and his breath caught. She said, "I never meant for any of this to happen."

"Any of what?" he said. At this close range, he could see a crumb adhered to her lip. He could easily bend and kiss it free.

"The pirates. The storm. You might say I had nothing to do with either, and that would be true, but if it hadn't been for me you wouldn't have been in range of pirates, and I wouldn't have sailed into the face of a nasty gale to escape them."

Maxime brushed the crumb loose with his fingertip. "Instead, I'd likely be dead."

She said, "I owe you thanks."

"You're the one who saved me from a life as a pirate's catamite," he pointed out.

"You fought at my side, and then served with my crew

as best you could. I couldn't have asked for more even from Chetri."

"So I'm almost as good as Chetri?" Maxime slipped his arms around her waist, pulling her closer to him, trapping her hands against his chest. Her skin flowed like silk beneath his hands; he circled his palms on the small of her back, then shaped her spine and shoulders before stroking down again. He stopped himself before he grasped her rear, though his fingers strayed a little, aching to sink into her flesh. He said, "Let's cry evens, shall we? All this talk of owing makes me uncomfortable. I don't want to think of owing where you're concerned. I just want to think of you." He bent his head and brushed her mouth with his.

Imena pulled back, licking her lips. "I was hoping we'd get around to that." She laced her hands behind his neck and he shivered at the abrasion of her calluses on his nape.

"Kiss me," he said.

She didn't at first. She uncurled her fingers and scratched lightly. He shivered in pleasure and arched his back, rubbing against her.

He said, "If you like, you can even tie me up first."

Imena grinned. "I'm in too much of a rush for that." Still smiling, she kissed him.

She tasted of salt and the tang of wine. Maxime let her guide the kiss. He liked the rough press of her fingers on the back of his neck, the prickly pleasure when she gripped his hair and tugged him closer, the fervent slide of her tongue against his.

When they stopped to breathe, he said, "I'd rather do this lying down."

"I might fall asleep on you," Imena warned him. Her eyes looked dazed, her pupils huge in the dim light.

"I'll still be here when you wake," he said. He lifted her feet off the deck, just enough to make her curse him, and carried her to the bunk. Other than the cursing, she didn't fight him. He asked, "Do I really smell like a rotted jellyfish?"

She wriggled free of his arms and stretched out on the bunk, her back to the bulkhead. "Not really. You smell like something I want to devour. Come and fuck me before I fall asleep again."

Maxime crawled onto the bunk and lay on his side, facing her. "If I'd known how sweetly you would beg for my attentions, I would have attempted to seduce you long ago."

"This isn't a seduction. We're at sea."

"That makes no sense." He couldn't ask her to explain, because she kissed him again, gradually shifting until he supported almost all her weight. He shifted his hips experimentally, and groaned when she rubbed against him with intent. "Let's just do this," he said.

"You say that now, but—" she stopped and bit his shoulder, then his neck, shooting warm thrills down to his cock "—I know you want to fuck me. Be inside me. Remember how that felt?"

"I'll never, ever forget," he swore, covering her breasts with his hands and gently tugging her nipples. "Are you trying to make me go off like a badly loaded pistol?"

"I am trying to get your cock into my cunt," she said.

She reached between them and grasped his erection, sliding her thumb over the head of his cock, the rasp of her roughened skin enough to tighten his bollocks.

Maxime flinched and pushed her off him. "Turn over, I want to do it this way," he said, and when she'd turned away from him, he spooned up against her back, sliding one of his legs between hers. He was greedy for her warmth, for her scent, and could easily have spent an hour touching her, but she wanted to be fucked, so he would do it for her. He worked his cock into her from behind while massaging her breasts with his free hand. She was squashing his other arm, but he didn't care; he wanted to feel her back against his chest and rub his face against her hair and kiss and nibble her ear. He never wanted to let her go, unless he could possibly shift her even closer to him, or inside his own skin.

Imena reached back with her left hand and stroked his flank, her nails startling his hips into a sudden jerk. "I can't touch you like this," she said, gasping softly as they rocked together.

"Close your eyes and let me," Maxime said, kissing her temple. "I won't let you fall asleep until we're done."

"I need more," she said. "Harder, I need this."

He wanted to stay here forever, joined with her, their bodies sliding against each other, his world spiraling down to where his cock rubbed inside her tight grip. He caressed his way from her breast down to her belly, then into her hair and the slickness of her cunt. Her outer lips were already splayed from their position and his size. His fingertip easily found her clitoris. He stroked it once before rubbing inward, harder, to match his gentle thrusting.

Imena gasped, pressing into his hand. "More," she said. When he pressed a little harder, thrust a little faster, she moaned and twisted her neck.

He kissed the side of her face and murmured in her ear. "Feel my hand, feel it sliding on you, feel my cock stretching you inside, feel us together." He caught his breath and said, "Imena, Imena, you're holding me so tightly I can hardly breathe. I could come from just watching you, you're so lovely like this, every muscle straining toward your pleasure. You're dragging me with you."

He closed his eyes and gasped again, trying to regain control, but his hips wouldn't stop surging. He wasn't able to control his caresses very well anymore, so he simply pressed the heel of his hand into her clit, letting his thrusting motion take over. "Push into me," he said. "Rub on my hand."

She moaned, not his name but a wordless sound.

"Harder!" he said, and she obeyed, and suddenly she was convulsing around him, her cunt squeezing his cock, her legs jerking against his, her back slamming into his chest as she came on a long moan fading into a sigh.

Maxime held deathly still, letting her ride it out. He hadn't had the final, deep thrusts he craved, and he teetered on a horrible precipice, pleasure just beyond reach. As she gradually relaxed, her arms and legs falling limp, he buried his face against her and mentally counted backward in every language he knew. It didn't help. He wanted to be with her; he didn't want to resume thrusting when she had so clearly fallen asleep, but this edge was painful. He closed his eyes and withdrew from her, wincing as the tender skin of his cock slid along her leg.

"Where are you going?" Imena mumbled. Awkwardly, she reached behind her, patting at him. "Don't stop."

"You're not asleep," he said, relieved.

"Not yet. I can't sleep with you like that. Your cock, it's like a third person in my bunk, and I'd hate to disappoint him. What do you want?"

For answer, he slid his cock inside her again, groaning with relief. "I'll be quick," he said. "Then you can go to sleep."

"No wonder you're so popular," she said, pushing back against him with a satisfied noise. "Now, fuck me. Take your time."

"Funny," he gasped, but the interval had taken some of the edge off his desperation, so he experimented with a few long thrusts and slow withdrawals that caused Imena to laugh and curse him at the same time.

He reached over her hip to rub her clitoris, but found her hand already there, circling restlessly. "Don't worry about me!" she snarled.

He laid his hand atop hers and gave himself up to her and to pleasure. Three more lubricious nudges inside her and he could feel his release swell within him, inexorable, snatching his breath so he could only gasp and hold her to him.

To his shame, he immediately fell asleep, not a habit to which he was normally prone. He woke some time later when she stirred in his arms. "Four hours?" he asked muzzily.

"Yes," she said. "Let me go, I'll turn down the lamp."

When she returned to the bunk and tugged his arm

around her, he rubbed his cheek against her scalp and tightened his arm about her waist.

"Nice," she murmured.

"We're good together," he whispered close to her ear. "Aren't we? Will you marry me?"

No answer. She'd fallen back to sleep.

CHAPTER TWELVE

IMENA WOKE FEELING MUCH REFRESHED. ONCE she'd put out the lamp, she'd been able to shut down her mental clock and sleep through the equivalent of a full night's sleep. The sex hadn't hurt; after she'd come a second time, she'd barely been able to lift an eyelash.

She always slept better after sex. Most especially, she slept better after sex when her partner remained close to her throughout the night.

Maxime was gone now. She dimly recalled reaching for him when he'd slipped out of the bunk just after dawn. He'd stroked her face and she'd turned over for another hour's sleep, perfectly content.

It was a little disturbing, how well she'd slept.

Roxanne would be on deck command at this hour. Imena stretched and rolled out of her bunk before stretching again. She still ached from her exertions during the storm, and during the night, as well. She found clean clothing and went up on deck.

The full array of *Seaflower*'s canvas was hung to dry in the light, fresh breeze while various crew mended lines, stitched sails and attended to smaller tasks such as chipping rust off ironwork, scraping splintered wood and laying on fresh caulk and blacking. Norris ran up to Imena with a mug of hot tea before she could reach Roxanne, and said, "I'll have a bath ready for you, Captain, as soon as you're finished here."

Imena took a deep, refreshing sip of tea. "You are a jewel, Norris." After Norris trotted off, Imena finished her interrupted stroll to Roxanne's position at the prow, overseeing the crew's labors.

Roxanne handed over a written report. "The rudder's damaged, and the steering ropes, and we lost two topmasts. Plus, there's a leak below, and Chetri thinks there's a split from all our flailing about. We're shredding more rope for oakum, so that should help if we find additional leaks." With a grimace, she added, "We have plenty of ruined lines, after all that. I've got Kuan in charge of the pumps. Seretse and Gnalam are organizing crews to help them with the carpentry on the topmasts."

"Supplies?" Imena asked.

"The rainwater we collected is nigh undrinkable," Roxanne replied glumly. "We've no fresh fruit left, and some of the hens drowned, but the cat is in fine shape. We found him with the hostages. Arionrhod's recording the losses. Wiscz already butchered the hens, so that's some fresh food taken care of, but Tessa says everyone's in low condition after that long chase, and the gale, and that we all need a rest and some fresh vegetables."

Imena had another sip of her tea, letting it warm her all

the way down. "We need to careen the hull regardless, to take care of that split. When Chetri comes on watch, let him know. I'll see what I can find for us."

Back in her cabin, Norris brought her breakfast: rice in chicken broth, and some dried cherries and apricots. Imena ate while examining her charts against the navigational notes Roxanne had given to her, gauging their position from Chetri's star plots of the previous night and of the sun and horizon positions he'd taken at dawn. They'd been blown well off their intended course by the storm. Imena couldn't regret it, as she'd allowed it to happen, and it had enabled them to escape from their pursuers. She drew another chart from her drawer. It wasn't nearly as detailed as the charts for more trafficked lanes, but did give a few notes on favorable currents. Unfortunately, some of the notes were contradictory.

She should approach Maxime about charting some of these waters more accurately. He could afford to pay her for the service, and the charts they gained would repay him dozens of times over. She blinked and took another sip of her tea, which had gone cold. It was the first time she'd thought of Maxime in hours. What had he been doing all this time?

She wasn't worried, she realized. At some point during the storm, or perhaps before that, when he'd fought at her back, she'd begun to trust Maxime. She'd thought she'd trusted him before, but this was different. Now she trusted him to be loose aboard her ship. That was an entirely different proposition than simply trusting him to pay her wages on time.

Chetri knocked, interrupting her musings. He'd

consulted with Seretse and Gnalam already about the ship's structural state. Once he'd entered and settled next to her on a stool, they conferred over the possible landfalls Imena had identified, finally settling on an isolated island that reportedly had a wide, sandy beach that should be suitable for careening *Seaflower* and mending her bottom; regardless, they would set the crew to scraping the hull and recaulking, and carefully inspecting for any weakness they might have missed.

As he left to assume deck command, Chetri said, "His Grace is chatting with Annja and Suzela. Do you have any plans for them?"

"I've not decided. I told them to prove themselves to me first. Has Suzela said anything at all yet?"

Chetri shook his head. "If Annja hadn't reassured me otherwise, I would've thought she couldn't speak at all. Captain, I wouldn't have brought them aboard if I hadn't been worried for their fate."

"We can feed them," Imena said. She understood why he'd done it. Chetri had once been the captive of pirates, and been treated, she suspected, much worse than the two women he'd rescued. She added, "I wouldn't have put it past Captain Litvinova to have handed one or both of them over to Venom, to satisfy him after we'd escaped."

Chetri looked relieved. "The Knife said she would give them work to do."

"And she will do this for you in exchange for…?"

He grinned crookedly. "Three fine dinners of her choice, the next three times we've shore leave in a place she finds congenial." Ruefully, he added, "Once I'm allowed leave again. And it's to be dinner for her and for Roxanne, as well. She'll bankrupt me."

"You'll get to share in the food with them," Imena reassured him. She glanced down at their navigational notes. "Let's hope our island has enough fresh fruit and vegetables to satisfy the Knife, as well."

Maxime was already tired of pretending to be a concubine, but he didn't think the two women rescued from the pirate ship would believe him if he said he was really a duke. Sometimes, he didn't believe it himself, he'd spent so long as the son of a man deposed by violence.

Suzela ate a slice of dried pear, her eyes never leaving him, as if she feared he would snatch the fruit from her. She sat behind Annja on the deck, again, this time with the cat lying next to her on her discarded blanket. There weren't any bunks built into Maxime's former quarters, as normally the space was filled with cargo. Norris planned to obtain a couple of hammocks for them later today.

Maxime sat on the deck, as well, blocking the exit. He said, "So this Captain Cassidy, he's mad?"

Suzela flinched. Annja sneered. He liked that expression, twisted as it was, more than the soft acquiescence she'd demonstrated on the pirate ship. She said, "I think he's one of those who was born wrong. Belowdecks, they say his family sent him to sea to get rid of him. He killed his brother, or some say his sister or his mother, no one knows for sure. And he's killed plenty since. Has a taste for doing it slow."

Annja paused, swallowed and went on. "He likes poison. He eats it, a little bit every day, so it won't kill him. He can chew on a hunk of poison leaves and spit it at you, and it burns like fire."

"Nasty," Maxime said, disguising an inner shudder. If not for Imena, he might be in the process of dying slowly right now. "How did he end up with Captain Litvinova?"

Annja shrugged. "She hired him. They were already together when I was taken." She glanced at Suzela. "Suzela was his, but he'd tired of her. I asked for her as my maid."

"Captain Litvinova gave her to you?"

Annja hesitated. "After a while." She picked up her cup and drank, clearly considering what she planned to say. "I did some things for her first. But I don't think she wanted Venom to have Suze, anyway. She doesn't like him."

"I suspect that's an opinion shared by everyone who's ever met him," Maxime said wryly. "Do you think Captain Litvinova would turn on him, given the chance?"

Annja shrugged, but Suzela looked up at his words. Her narrow, dark eyes met Maxime's; when she seemed sure she held his attention, she nodded slowly.

A week later, long days of constant work at the pumps and endless maintenance, Imena stood against *Seaflower*'s railing, gazing over her prow at an island jewel. The sheltered anchorage, so clear one could see fish swimming below, was the bright turquoise of her favorite jacket, brilliantly contrasting with sand as white as scoured clamshells. She was relieved to note her charts had not been out of date on the depth of the beach, which was more than wide enough for their purposes.

Gulls swooped and dived and screamed. Wading birds scampered along the tide line, stopping only to stab their long beaks into the wet sand in search of food. Behind the blindingly bright sand, tall grasses waved in the breeze, gradually merging into low, darker green scrub and finally into towering, densely leaved trees. As she watched, a scarlet bird winged from the trees to a rocky outcropping that was white with guano.

Imena wondered where the people were. The chart hadn't indicated any inhabitants, but in her experience, that usually meant little. Across the island from this harbor, there might be entire villages. Though, she reasoned, the rocky terrain and dense forest made this area less suited for farming or livestock, excepting maybe pigs. There might be good reason for the silent, lonely shore.

Maxime leaned next to her, his large hands gripping the rail. "Is it full of pirates?" he asked. He didn't sound as if he was joking.

"I don't think so," Imena said slowly. "This cluster of islands—if you can call some of them islands—is marked only on my charts. There might be people here, but I don't think they're pirates. Word would have gotten out by now. It looks to be a splendid harbor, for one ship at least. The coral reefs would be a problem for more, or for anything larger than *Seaflower*."

"Then why is it on your charts?" he asked.

Imena considered lying, then reminded herself he'd be likely to keep her secret. "Some of my charts are imperial navy admiralty charts. I borrowed them from my mother."

"*Borrowed.* Hmm."

"You'd have done the same," Imena said. "In fact, compared to you conspiring with Her Grace Camille to remove her husband from power, borrowing a few charts is scarcely noticeable."

"You see, this is another reason why you would make an excellent duchess. You'd be in charge of my fleet, you know. Our fleet, that is."

Imena punched his arm. "Stop it. Why don't you go and ask Roxanne for something to do?"

"Because I'd rather stand here next to you," Maxime said in a reasonable tone.

Imena looked out to sea again. She'd been busy with the ship and crew, but she couldn't pretend she hadn't been avoiding Maxime, and the feelings he aroused in her.

Just now, she had too much to think about. After living unexpectedly through the long run from the pirates and the storm, Donkey—no one had ever learned his real name—had finally succumbed to his belly wound, and they'd buried him at sea, stitched into canvas with ballast at his feet to carry his body to the bottom. It was no consolation to her that Nevens, who had a similar wound, and Philippe were both improving. Philippe seemed likely not only to keep his eye, but to retain some vision with it.

More than usually disturbed by worries for her crew, Imena had spent the previous few nights on deck in a woven hammock, leaving her cabin to Maxime. She'd woken every few hours to take note of the stars' positions, but knew it had only been an excuse. She'd lain awake for hours, thinking on the crew who'd died on this voyage, and imagining scores of alternative actions she might have taken that would have kept them alive. In the cold dark hours of the morning, her past decisions surged and receded in her mind like surf.

Maxime said, "I know you're the captain of this ship."

"Stop reading my mind."

He grinned, that slow grin that always made her want to touch him. "Another reason you would make—"

"Stop doing that, as well." She folded her forearms and leaned on the railing. The fresh breeze tickled through her short hair and whipped her linen shirt tight against her body, pleasant contrast to the sun's warmth. She gazed at the white sand and imagined stretching out on it, letting it cradle her tired muscles, its heat seeping into her.

Minutes later, when she risked a glance at Maxime, he also was looking at the beach. She wondered what he was thinking.

The rest of the day was taken up with delicate piloting, to find their way safely into the bay through its guardian maze of coral reefs. Bonnevie took the wheel. Kuan, in one of the smaller boats, went ahead of *Seaflower* to take soundings, while Malim and Nabhi rowed and Arionrhod made notes. Imena sent the shoreboat, this one captained by Roxanne, to explore suitable inlets that might provide concealment from other ships that might approach the harbor. *Seaflower* was a large ship, and there would be no hiding it beyond a certain point, but even a few moments might be critical for their safety.

Later, she ordered the remaining boats lowered and manned by the strongest of the foremast hands, led by Wiscz. Once they were past the reef, *Seaflower* needed to be towed to shore.

Hauling the ship onto the beach lasted well into the evening, through a spectacular red-and-orange sunset and into the early, cobalt dark. Nearly all the crew, including Maxime, took turns rowing the towboats or standing in knee-deep surf, hauling on lines, while Norris led one of One-Eye's mates and the hostage Suzela in playing drums to aid in the work. One-Eye, the cook (who actually had two eyes, so his nickname, like many, was obscure), called out chants for response. They'd invented some new verses for this iteration, she realized. Some of them involved pirates and their disreputable sexual practices and terrible fates. One verse involved a sailor who was so greatly endowed that a lady whale fell in love with him as he swam.

Imena disembarked last, as was traditional. After assessing that all had gone well, and examining the split that indeed marred *Seaflower*'s bottom, she left the organization of camping arrangements to the crew chiefs. She waded a distance into the cool surf to squeeze her toes in the soft, wet sand. Later she would inspect to make sure all was happening as it should; but she counted this as being in dry dock, so Chetri would be taking the majority of her shifts as penalty for accepting hostages without Imena's permission. Tomorrow, they'd begin their work by sawing out the damaged section of the hull and fitting replacement planking from their stores.

Stars were coming out, close and touchable as salt sprinkled on a length of black silk. She inhaled the briny, fishy scent of the sea, the sharper tang of freshly kindled campfires and the flowery smell of tea brewing in a bucket. She heard splashing and glanced left—Roxanne was chasing the Knife along the tidal edge. There was enough firelight to see that neither of them wore a stitch of clothing. Roxanne had even abandoned her hook. More decorous splashing drew her attention to her right. Annja, holding her long dress carefully above her knees, was wading into the shallows. She led Suzela by the hand. The other woman wore new clothing, trousers and sleeveless tunic similar to that worn by the rest of *Seaflower*'s crew. Imena recognized the neutral colors as formerly belonging to the Knife, though there had clearly been some alterations made so the clothing would fit Suzela's much smaller frame.

Suzela glanced over at Imena and froze, dragging Annja to a halt. Imena waded over to them. "Watch for jellyfish," she said. "Some of them sting. Likely not fatally, though, this close to shore."

"Aye, Captain," Annja said after a pause. Suzela watched over her shoulder, then pointed back at the beached ship.

Possibly, she was asking a question. Imena answered, "I'd prefer you remain in sight of the others while it's dark, and in the day, make sure you only go about in groups of three or more, in case someone is hurt. That is, if the Knife doesn't have enough for you to do."

Annja said, "We're to gather plants tomorrow."

"Good. Take someone with you. Nabhi would be good protection. Or Wiscz."

Annja said, after another pause, "May we have Maxime?"

At first, Imena couldn't identify her stab of anger, then realized, to her shock, that she was jealous. Ridiculous, when she knew he'd been making efforts to gain the hostages' trust, and that they still seemed to believe his status was close to their own. Calming herself, she said, "He'll be busy tomorrow. But you can have anyone else."

Suzela bobbed, and Imena recognized the movement as an obeisance. Annja simply said, "We'll ask Chetri," and dragged Suzela away.

As if conjured by her thoughts, Maxime waded through the surf toward her. His hair was damp from spume. He wore nothing but a wrapped clout, the same as many of her crew had adopted for their long, soggy day, but she still spent several moments studying the expanse of his chest, damp from the sea, and the muscles flexing in his powerful thighs. Those thighs could hold her weight with no effort, flexing beneath her as—

"I was going for a swim," she said. "Join me?"

"I hope you aren't planning to swim in your clothes," he said. "Norris would have a fit."

Imena glanced down at her ragged knee-length trousers and salt-stained singlet. Norris likely wanted to burn these particular clothes. "If I strip, you strip."

Imena wasn't surprised when Maxime shed the clout. She'd rarely met anyone with so little modesty. Not, she mused as she followed a line of dark hair down his belly and to his prominent cock, that he had any reason to be ashamed. Any reason at all.

Sand slipped and shifted under her feet as the tide dragged in and out, lapping at her calves. She met Maxime's gaze with her own, his eyes only dark gleams in the sparse light, but his smile was much brighter as she lifted her arms and tugged her singlet over her head. She had neglected to inform him that she'd bound her breasts for the day's labors.

She dipped her singlet into the water to give it weight and flung it toward the shore, where it landed with a *splat*. She said, "What will you give me if I take off something else?"

"How many things are you wearing?" he countered, wading closer. A wave caught him off balance and he staggered, laughing as he regained his footing. "I must tell you, those wrappings are intriguing. I can clearly remember what's beneath them, and the idea of unwrapping you slowly, revealing one soft bit at a time for my tongue to appreciate, is delectable."

Imena swallowed. "You didn't say what you would give me."

"The question is, what will *you* give *me?*" Maxime stepped closer. "If you really want me to provide services for you, I ought to get something in return. A lick here and there. Perhaps a nibble."

Imena licked salt from her lips. "I definitely enjoy nibbling your shoulder."

"Where?"

She didn't normally speak of such things. But how difficult could it be? "That bit there," she said, gesturing.

"Next to your neck. The tendon along the top, there, and the muscle beneath."

His shoulder flexed, as if he imagined her teeth caressing there. "I would let you do that," he said. "I want to lick the lower edges of your rib cage. Where the skin is thin. You seem to like it when I touch you there with my fingers, so I assume—"

"I like it when you hold the back of my head in your hand," Imena confessed. She stepped toward him, then back again, as a wave pushed her off balance. "I like to hold you by the hair while I taste you."

Maxime rocked toward her. "You probably taste of salt right now."

"Yes." Without looking away from him, Imena untied the waist of her trousers and let them fall into the sea. Maxime retrieved them and heaved them to shore so they landed next to her singlet. She said, "If a jellyfish stings me in a tender place, I'm going to blame you."

He didn't appear worried. "Let me," he said, wading forward and unhooking her breast bindings. It was awkward, him unwrapping her breasts while she struggled out of her drawers, the waves and shifting sand pushing them off balance and into each other, but they managed. The noises around *Seaflower* had completely faded from her notice. She registered the campfires only as a faint scent in the air. It reminded her of camping in the highlands with her father, and later more adult excursions with the lover of her youth.

"Let's swim," she said to Maxime, though her body ached for the touch of his. Even the palms of her hands throbbed with her desire to touch him.

"Anticipation makes everything better," he said, and flung himself into the water, emerging quickly, gasping and flinging water from his shoulder-length hair. "Rat-shit! It's not deep enough here!"

Imena waded to deeper water as quickly as she could manage, but not quickly enough to avoid Maxime tackling her around the waist and bearing her down into the surf. As soon as she was soaked, he let her go, and she rose to her feet in a surge of water. "Cold as a pirate's heart!" she exclaimed. Her nipples had drawn so tight that they hurt. Maxime was beaming at her. Laughing, she lunged and easily brought him down, her limbs wrapping his like seaweed.

Together they rolled, struggled, disentangled and lunged for deeper water. Once, they stopped, treaded water and kissed, holding tight to each other's waist so they wouldn't float apart. Maxime's lips felt impossibly soft against her chapped skin; she flicked her tongue out to trace his teeth and gently met the tip of his tongue with her own before drawing back a little. She leaned in again and sucked his upper lip into her mouth, nipped lightly and then gnawed at his lower lip while he hummed with pleasure.

His hands slid lower, shaping her rear, lifting and pressing her into him. His cock was shockingly hot in contrast to the cold water. She murmured, "I thought cold water would have *some* effect," and he laughed.

"Not with a naked woman in my arms, sweet." He ran his open mouth along her neck and shoulder and then added, "Particularly one who squirms like you're doing now."

"I'm treading water." Imena bit his neck in return, hard enough to hurt a little. "I wanted to have a swim, remember? I can't swim with you hanging on to me."

"What do I get if I let go of you?"

"My continued regard," she said, rasping her nails against his lower back, and catching his gasp in her mouth. "Also, after a swim, I'll be very warm and re-laxed, and…"

Maxime bent his head and nipped at the top of her breast, then sucked gently at the spot. "And?"

"And you can have your way with me." Imena bucked against his grip, and when his arms loosened, wriggled free and set out for shore.

She liked best to swim beneath the water, her legs pressed together and beating like a dolphin's tail. The slight, persistent headache she'd had since her head injury ceased to bother her while cold water was washing over her skull. When she broke the surface to breathe, she easily spied Maxime, who swam more prosaically with his head bobbing in and out of the waves. Imena sucked in another breath and dived; the water wasn't terribly deep here, but it was enough. She swam underwater until she grew closer to shore, and the water was no longer deep enough; then she switched to Maxime's technique, her arms cutting the water while she snatched breaths.

Her headache had eased, and she felt long and loose and pleasantly warm as she coasted in to shore, but when she rose from the waves, her limbs abruptly shifted to awkward weights, and she was reminded of how tired she was. She would have to swim again tomorrow if she had time. During the day, she would be able to glide among the coral and view the colorful fish that always clustered there.

Maxime staggered out of the water a few steps behind her. "You're fast," he said admiringly. "Again tomorrow?"

She waded through the surf and grabbed his hand. "The reefs tomorrow," she promised. "Right now, I see some rocks over there. We can brush the sand off them and be perfectly comfortable. Come along, and have your way with me."

"I'd rather *you* have your way with *me*," Maxime said, his grin a flash of light in the darkness.

The next morning, Imena woke with her nose shoved firmly into Maxime's belly. Blue-green and purple light speckled over their naked forms. Sometime after they'd made the tide to the rhythm of the tide, they'd returned to *Seaflower*'s camp, where Norris had ensured Imena's tent was prepared. They lay now on piles of rugs, the tent's walls rippling from the steady breeze off the sea. Norris had to have been in and out, though Imena did not remember it; there was no sign of their sodden clothing from the evening before, and a platter sat atop an embroidered pillow near the door, filled with sticky rice balls, fresh fruit and steamed fish cakes.

Imena yawned and scrubbed at her gritty eyes. She crawled over Maxime and examined the platter more closely before selecting peeled slices of juicy marang and some acidic red limeberries, following the fruit with a rice ball. She lifted the tent flap to call for Norris and just outside found a pot of tea, still warm, with two cups.

She nudged Maxime with her foot. "Wake up! Breakfast."

"Aye, Captain," he said, knuckling his eyes. "It's been four hours, I assume. Do I smell fish cakes?"

"You do. My crew has been hard at work while we've been lying about like passengers."

"I *am* a passenger," he protested, leaning over her to grab a fish cake. Mouth full, he added, "Or maybe a prisoner. Or a concubine."

Imena poured them tea and pressed a cup into his hand. "I was willing for you to be an honored guest, but you insisted on the concubinage, if I remember correctly."

Maxime bent over the platter. "What's this?"

"Sataw, I think," she said, scooping some up with her fingers. "You can eat the seeds, too." She pressed the slippery pulp between his lips. He swept out his tongue and licked the stickiness off her fingers.

After swallowing, he said, "It's terrible. Give me some of the limeberries."

Imena shrugged. "It's supposed to be good for your stomach. I think. No doubt the Knife will be thrilled you ate some." She picked up a fish cake and then forgot it in her hand as she watched Maxime eat limeberries, then marang, the strong muscles of his jaw working beneath his close-cropped beard. Her inner thighs were scraped raw from his beard. The marang juice glistening on his lips made her want to lick it off.

"Are you going to eat that?" he asked, amused. He took more of the marang.

Imena popped the fish cake into her mouth. It was richly peppered and dusted with salt. She made a pleased sound. When she reached for another, Maxime was watching her hungrily.

Imena swallowed, nearly choked and hurriedly downed some tea. Maxime refilled her cup for her, and she smiled; it was an imperial custom to watch for your dining companion's needs. He said softly, "I could do this every morning for the rest of my life. Though I'd prefer it if you didn't look so tired. Maybe you should take the morning off and come back to bed with me."

Imena looked down at the platter in front of her. It was easy to forget the realities of life when you were trapped outside your normal time and place. She drained her teacup, hoping it would open her eyes, and held her cup out to Maxime for more.

A call from Norris, just outside the tent, saved her from making any verbal response to him other than, "You should get dressed." Her own robe was laid out near the platter. Imena slipped it on, then lifted the tent flap and gestured Norris inside.

Norris wore a matching tunic and knee-length linen pantaloons embroidered with bright flowers that made Imena squint. More flowers—scarlet, orange and purple—were pinned into the crown of hair atop her head. Their scent was thick, dizzying, almost dreamlike.

"You should have woken me earlier," Imena said.

Norris said, "It's still Roxanne's watch, Captain, and Chetri is about to take her place. They said it was all right to let you sleep. Chetri said to tell you he has your written instructions, and he'll report on those items as soon as he's completed his survey."

"Tell him I'll accompany him."

Norris's expression clearly expressed her dissatisfaction, but Imena wasn't about to let Chetri take over all the labor of inspecting the ship from hull to rigging, prioritizing repairs and assigning crews to do the labor. He hadn't worked as many hours as she had during the storm, it was true, but he was older, and she was the captain. All of it was her responsibility, weary or not. His assumption of her duty shifts would come only after she'd assured herself she truly wasn't needed.

Norris was still silent. Imena lifted her brows in query. Norris said, "Aye, Captain. Would you like anything else for breakfast?"

"No, but you may tell One-Eye or whoever made them that the fish cakes are delicious."

From the rear of the tent, Maxime said, "I thought so, too." He turned to face them while still tugging a faded red singlet over his head. His trousers were cut off at the knee, and looked as if they'd come from *Seaflower*'s slop chest.

Norris smiled. "Suzela cooked the fish. Working with the Knife made her a little green, so Chetri sent her to One-Eye. She seems much happier."

"Good," Imena said. Guiltily, she recalled that she ought to have been paying more attention to their two refugees; though Chetri had brought them on board and claimed responsibility, she was still the captain. After her initial talk with them, she'd left that duty too much to others, the previous evening notwithstanding.

It did no good to tell herself she'd had plenty more important things to occupy her. She'd been too distracted by Maxime to properly attend to her duties. She drained her teacup again and stretched while still sitting. Ligaments eased and popped in her neck, little fireworks of hot pain. She might need to indulge in a massage later if she couldn't swim the kinks out of her muscles. "Thank you, Norris. Tell Roxanne and Chetri I'll be along shortly, as soon as I've dressed."

"Do you need any hot water, Captain? We've got coppers going already, for tea and for fish soup."

Imena shook her head. "I swam last night. You needn't bother with the extra work. Go on, now."

After Norris had left, Maxime asked, "What will my duties be?"

"Toss me some clothes," she said. While pulling on ragged trousers similar to those Maxime wore, she said, "I'm afraid a great deal of what we have to do is nasty and monotonous, and the rest skilled labor. In your travels, did you ever work in a dockyard?"

"Sadly, no."

She pondered. "It's the nasty and monotonous for you, then. You've got muscle, but we won't need as much of that today. Today we'll need as many hands as we can get to shred old rope for oakum—we're going to use up every scrap we already have in the recaulking." She paused and shook her head ruefully. "That was one of the routine maintenance tasks that I normally have taken care of when we're in port, but this time—"

"This time, you fled with me in tow," Maxime finished. "I can work on oakum. And there's hot tar, as well, isn't there?"

"Wiscz is going to be in charge of that for us. He might

not want amateurs poking in his pots, but if he asks, please do help him. It's a hot and smelly task."

"Perhaps they'll let me carry heavy, stinking buckets," Maxime said in a thoughtful tone. "It will prove my devotion to my captain."

"Oh, don't be ridiculous," she said, yanking a shirt over her head.

He asked, "Will you have any free time?"

She glanced over at him. "Yes, I suppose."

"Will you do something for me?"

"Does it involve being naked?"

"I'd like you to teach me navigation."

Imena blinked. "Do you know anything of it?"

"I've read Clarence's *Basics*. And I began Huang, but I had only finished the introduction when you...rescued me."

Astonished, she said, "I have a copy of Huang. We can work through it together."

Maxime grinned, bright as midday. "I'll look forward to it."

On the beach, Kuan and his crew had already laid flat an old discarded sail and pinned its edges with rocks. Malim was brushing on hot pitch in small patches, while others followed behind him dropping handfuls of coarse oakum, and Kuan followed last, making sure it all adhered. The youngest members of the crew ferried buckets of water from the sea to splash the ship's deck planking, to prevent shrinkage and thus more work. Nevens and Philippe, who were still recovering from injuries, sat with every other spare hand on the beach or among the rocks, shredding scraps of rope into buckets or onto scraps of sail and singing a song about monsters of the deep. Roxanne had exchanged her regular hook for one with several fine claws, and shredded an old cable while she conferred with Seretse. Downwind, Wiscz slowly heated tar that would be mingled with the shreds of hemp to increase their stock of oakum. She sent Maxime to join him in the arduous task.

Imena found Gnalam standing on an overturned boat, sealing hull seams with a caulking mallet and irons; despite being such a small-framed woman, her sleeve-tattooed arms were more muscular and defined than those of many men Imena had known. Imena waited until Gnalam reached for more oakum and asked, "How much do you have left?"

Gnalam laid down her tools and stretched. "Not nearly enough. We've hopes production will keep up, but I'm afraid we might have to stop now and again."

"And putty?"

"I think we have enough, and if not we can use more pitch or fothers. Seretse is worried. But he always worries."

"Part of his job," Imena said with a rueful smile. "Thank you, Gnalam."

Later, Chetri found Imena as she scrambled crablike along a rope network, inspecting the hull close to and gently tapping it with a hammer to listen for soundness. With her free hand, she felt the vibrations of her tapping, checking for any looseness. Periodically, she dug a scrap of chalk from her pocket and marked a symbol on the planks.

"Gnalam can take care of that, Captain," Chetri

said. "In fact, it's better that she does. You know she's quicker."

"She's only quicker if she has nothing else to do," Imena called down. She shoved the grip of her hammer through her belt and flipped over, hooking an arm in the lines and taking the opportunity for a rest. In truth, she was a fraction dizzy from climbing. Her knock on the head hadn't really settled, just as the Knife had predicted.

Chetri looked at her, then scrambled up the lines to perch next to her. He laid one hand flat on *Seaflower's* hull. "I'd like to start the putty for above the waterline," he said. "One part linseed oil, five parts white lead, if that seems right to you. Nabhi in charge of it. Linseed and red lead for below the waterline. I thought Bonnevie for that."

It was the same recipes they always used. "Good," she said, and closed her eyes. "Keep the putty-makers well away from the tar fires, we don't want any accidents." The world shifted uncomfortably, and she drew a deep breath, redolent of sea breeze, wood and melting tar. "How's Norris at caulking?" she asked. "I know Gnalam and Seretse were teaching her a few months back."

Considering, Chetri said, "There's an idea. If she could take over for Gnalam, Gnalam could take over for you here, and leave you free to oversee. I could recruit Kuan to help Norris. The fothering's well in hand and Malim can handle it from here. If that's your plan?"

"Yes," Imena said. Tentatively, she opened her eyes. She didn't feel entirely steady, but she could make it down to the sand by herself. "I'm going to take a break."

"I'll report in four hours, Captain."

She would have a drink and something to eat. Then she would pull Maxime from tar and oakum, and see how well he understood the rudiments of stellar navigation.

CHAPTER THIRTEEN

THE KING HAD RETURNED TO HIS PALACE, THOUGH
Sylvie had not yet seen him. He'd been closeted with
ministers and envoys, holding private audiences, for days.
Sylvie had continued circulating among the royal courtiers and so far had little to show for it. As she strolled the
palace gardens one cool evening, pretending to admire
the relentlessly controlled flower beds, she reviewed her
progress.

She had suspicions, strong ones, but no proof of anything that she could bring to Her Grace or to Lady Gisele,
much less to the Court of Inquiry that would follow a
formal complaint of wrongdoing. After only one day at
court in the role of a lady, she had begun to realize what
Lady Gisele must already have known: no one, least of all
King Julien, would believe a mere accusation, even if it
did come from an aristocrat. Plots such as they suspected
had been aimed at Duke Maxime were as common here
as grains of sand on the beach. She'd identified several

courtiers who she was sure were spies, either for one duke or another or for the king himself. No doubt there were dozens more whom she had not detected.

She hoped nothing she did would stand out sufficiently to gain the attention of the king.

She stopped and peered at a tableau of sculptured shrubbery, lit by colored lanterns. A couple was pretending to study the topiary with great interest, but Sylvie saw clearly that the man's hand was moving inside the woman's cape, in the area of her breasts. Taking mental note of their identity, she moved on.

She had uncovered a variety of intrigues in her investigations. Two of the haughtiest ladies of the court were heavily involved in a torrid affair, which would have been of no consequence to Sylvie except that one of the ladies was also scandalously summoning one of the upstairs maids to pleasure her, as well, unbeknownst to her other partner. Anyone who knew this might have stooped to blackmail, which might have led to more serious plotting. Unfortunately, she could find no motive linking the women to Duke Maxime. With the help of Alys, she had created a master list of which footmen and upper maids visited which chambers late at night, and the same for the small squad of eunuchs who stood guard over the royal chambers; none, however, appeared especially secretive about their sexual adventures. While in other circumstances Sylvie might have applauded this, now it was a frustration. She'd expected more from the royal court.

Monsieur Raoul, she had learned, had only two servants, and one of those a groom who had nothing to say to anyone that did not involve the high-bred gelding his master rode. The other appeared to serve both as valet and general factotum, and had his own room near the other upper servants; he'd offered Alys sweets made from date sugar, but no information about Raoul or his activities in the palace.

Sylvie had been reduced to eavesdropping and discreet watching. From this, she had learned that Monsieur Raoul liked to ride and he liked to draw, and that on clear nights, he and his servant observed the stars. He danced lightly and gracefully, but only when required; he was counted an agreeable dinner companion; and he never, ever invited anyone to his suite, female or male or eunuch.

Sylvie's suspicion of Lord Odell was still the most promising, fueled by his surreptitious affair with Lady Diamanta, if one could call it an affair when Sylvie was sure they had not yet fucked. Their bodies spoke that much truth. She was not sure what Lady Diamanta's aim might be, in continually refusing his advances yet not putting an end to them for good and all. She should have the power to rid herself of him completely, so she must have some advantage in allowing him to continue pursuing her. Also, she could surely aim higher than Odell, perhaps even marry the king, except that she was Julien's first cousin and thus forbidden by laws against incest. She could marry a foreign king, however.

Did she merely toy with Odell for amusement? He was not, Sylvie thought, very amusing.

Sylvie knew that Maxime had refused to marry Diamanta, but surely that had been too recent to engender such a complex plot as this one appeared to be. Though perhaps not. Diamanta was intelligent enough to make herself rich beyond the wealth she'd inherited, and wise enough to do so despite the scorn of the rest of the court, who found such dealings crass. Sylvie could not help but respect Diamanta for that.

"Madame Sylvia."

Sylvie was glad of her immense skirts and loose cape, for they concealed her startled twitch toward the knife thrust into her bodice's decorative lacing; the knife's mother-of-pearl hilt was sufficiently artful to appear as a gaudy brooch. She patted her bosom lightly, letting her cape fall open to display herself more clearly. "Monsieur Raoul. What, no companion for the evening?"

Tonight, Raoul was dressed in full foreign regalia. His boots were encrusted with gold foil from pointed toe to calf. An abundance of matching gold buttons, shaped into individual sigils, ran down the front of his snug leather jacket and fastened the sleeves at his wrists. A hint of deep blue ruffles showed at the neck and dusted the backs of his hands. The jacket itself was so laced with gold thread as to appear luminous in the early moonlight. As always, he wore leather gloves, this pair embroidered on the backs with gold thread.

Raoul bowed to her. "I had the honor of dining with your king."

Sylvie blinked. This was unusual. Unless it was a large state dinner including most of the court, a visitor such as Raoul would not have been asked to dine with the king. "And was he in good health?" Sylvie asked.

Raoul shrugged elegantly and held out his hand to her. Sylvie took it and allowed him to draw her closer and tuck her hand into his arm. Over his usual leather, she smelled wine and cinnamon and the fresh lemon juice that would have been squeezed into each cup. She could feel the heat of his body through her dress. He said, "He was not as interested in my maps as I had hoped."

"Maps," Sylvie said. Whatever she had been expecting, it had not been maps.

Raoul began walking; Sylvie walked with him. "It's no secret any longer," he said. "I make maps. King Julien expressed an interest, after one of his courtiers brought me to his attention. I was invited by the courtier, who instructed Lord Odell to look after me. I was eager to accept. A royal commission could finance a number of journeys for me. Now, however, I am not sure a commission will be forthcoming. It's a great pity. I have no wish to return home. I am not sure they would welcome me there again."

Which courtier had invited him? Lord Odell was close to Lady Diamanta. Though Lord Odell's role at court meant he could easily have been assigned that duty by any number of people. "You *are* a merchant, then."

"I am a cartographer. That's quite a different thing. Many consider it dangerous. If not to themselves, then to their business."

"You sell maps," Sylvie pointed out. She felt foolish. She had constructed all sorts of complex explanations for his presence, but he was merely here to sell his services. Or was he? He had some secret. She knew it.

"Perhaps." Raoul covered her hand with his gloved one and gently squeezed. It was a small gesture, but his glove lent a pleasant extra layer to the sensation. She was sorry when he released his grip, using the pressure of his arm to guide her down a curving path. He said softly, "I did not mislead you about my interest in you."

"Instantly formed, I presume," she said. "You approached me before my carriage had drawn away."

He looked down at her. At last, he said, "I greeted every lady who arrived."

Unexpectedly, she felt a twinge of disappointment. Then she remembered neither she nor Alys nor her "footman" had seen Raoul with anyone else, not even anyone who might have been his court sponsor. Though she admitted to herself a strong curiosity about who that sponsor might have been. "Why are you with me now, then?"

He grinned, and she felt the same stunning effect as the first time she'd seen him smile. "You were the only lady who spoke to me in return."

"Surely not."

"I have no status here, and clearly did not travel in state," he said. "It was not only that you spoke to me. I liked the way you walked, not a frivolous court lady, but someone comfortable and honest in her body. And I enjoyed sparring with you. I…I am far from home, and I sensed that you and I, we might understand one another."

Sylvie had no answer to that.

He grinned. "Also, I have a taste for arrogant blonde women."

This path had no colored lanterns, and the pristine-white gravel gave way to hard-packed earth. Abruptly, their steps were silenced, and the evergreen hedges seemed to lean in on them, concealing them from view and softening the sounds of distant voices. To make his desires even more clear, Raoul slipped his arm around her waist.

Sylvie said, "You are confident of my interest, are you?"

She sensed rather than saw him smile. "You haven't stabbed me yet. You do carry a knife, don't you?"

"You are the one who wishes to stab me," she said with a quirked eyebrow. "Do you expect that I bestow my favors on anyone who asks?"

"Did I mention anything about *bestowing?*" he said. "As you said before, I strongly doubt I could afford you for even an hour, unless I melted all the gold off my boots."

"Not even then," she said. She leaned into his side, closely enough to feel the hard ridges of his rib cage and the swift movement of his breath. "However, I might permit you to amuse me for a time."

"In exchange for—"

Sylvie trailed her fingers over the small of his back and felt his breathing change. "There are many things about which I am curious," she said. For instance, the identity of his court sponsor.

"The land? The sea? The stars?" Raoul looked up, pointing at the sky with one gloved finger. "Did you know that the stars move?"

"We are the ones that move," she said. "Everyone knows that. Otherwise there would be no day or night."

He touched her chin with his free hand, then again

pointed upward. "The stars move, as well. Sailors know it."

"I hate the sea," Sylvie said with a little shudder. When his arm tightened about her waist, she sighed and followed his finger with her gaze. The stars weren't as bright here as in the lush pastures of her home, but still they twinkled like tiny jewels sewn into a garment. She rested her cheek on Raoul's shoulder and said, "I am more concerned with the affairs of the earth than of the sky. The sky is so far above us, you see. What we do changes nothing there."

"I had thought you might be the earthly sort," he said. He resumed walking. "There is a gazebo ahead. The roof is open to the moon. I'm told it's very lovely."

Sylvie stopped, dragging Raoul to a halt. She said, "I said nothing about accompanying you to a gazebo."

He peered down at her. In the darkness, his expression was impossible to discern, but she heard humor in his voice. "I had assumed that your hand in my trousers could be translated as acquiescence."

Abruptly, Sylvie became aware of her fingers pressed against bare skin. She had not realized her teasing had led to working her hand beneath his jacket and ruching up his shirt, until she could reach beneath his waistband. Now that she was aware, she drew deliberate lines with her nails and grinned as he shuddered. She said, "Perhaps *you* will accompany *me*. I can easily imagine what I would like to do with you." When he didn't reply, she said, "Are you worried I'll unman you?"

"Hardly that," he said. He took her free hand in his and drew it against the fall of his trousers. Sylvie opened her palm and rubbed soft linen with hard flesh beneath.

Unsteadily, Raoul said, "I must confess, I've never allowed what I think you're suggesting."

Sylvie released his cock and laid her hand on his chest. She looked up at him. "I will make sure you enjoy it," she assured him. People were always more malleable after she'd had her way with them.

He laughed, but his laughter was choked. "Lady Sylvia, I hope you cozen your clients with more reassuring words."

"Pah," she said. "Make up your mind."

He didn't speak for long moments. His fingers curled more deeply into her waist, his thumb moving in idle circles over the fabric of her dress. At last he said, "It's true I haven't mapped this experience yet. Are you willing to guide me, Madame Sylvia?"

Sylvie slipped free of his grasp and grabbed his wrist. "You will do as I say," she said.

"And if I don't?"

"I'll stop."

"A potent threat indeed," he said, allowing her to drag him down the path.

Sylvie led Raoul to the foot of the white gazebo's three steps, caressing the thin leather encasing his fingers. "You will do as I say," she repeated.

He looked back at her, solemn and intent. She could feel the tension in his tight grip on her hand. "I will do as you say, Lady Sylvia."

"Go inside, then," she said. She watched the fine view of his rear beneath his short jacket as he climbed the three low steps and went to stand inside the gazebo. Good, he was learning to obey her already. When they were done, he would answer her questions without suspicion, or at least not any suspicions that mattered.

Once inside the structure, he tipped his head back. She remembered the gazebo's roof was open to the sky. He ought to be thinking of her, not the stars, but... perhaps she was growing soft, because it pleased her that he thought of things other than the court and all its intrigues.

She entered the gazebo and removed her slippers before arranging herself comfortably on the bench that ran around the inner walls. Moonlight from the open roof, coupled with low light from a hanging lantern, created interesting shadows; it might be possible to hide against one of the walls and remain undetected by visitors, unless they listened and heard breathing. "Remove my stockings," she said. "You will have to kneel."

Raoul crouched before her, the toes of his boots just beyond her feet. He looked up and remarked, "You only command me to do what I would prefer to do."

"Remove them slowly," she said. "Use your creativity." She paused. "Keep your gloves on."

He knelt and cupped the arch of her left foot in his gloved palm. She flexed against the warm leather and he rubbed her toes between his fingers, squeezing them gently. Sylvie closed her eyes to enjoy this more fully, and was thus startled when he gripped her calf and placed her foot on his shoulder. Her skirt still covered her to the shin, but she immediately felt more exposed to him. He turned his head and kissed in the vicinity of her ankle, dragging his mouth upward and nibbling with the edges of his teeth. His beard felt softer than she'd expected, but it still rasped against her silk stocking.

He glanced up at her. Slowly, she licked her lips. He curled one hand around her calf and slid up to her thigh, seeking the top of her stocking. She closed her eyes again, holding her breath against the moment his gloves touched her. It was still a small shock when the gentle friction of leather on clocked silk changed to smooth, hot leather on her softest skin. Her eyes met his, and as he untied knots and hooked his fingers beneath the edge of her stocking, her breathing grew unsteady. *Higher,* she wanted to say. *Reach higher, and fill me with those fingers.*

He peeled the stocking down slowly and, at her nod, dropped it on the floor, leaving her garter on her leg. He didn't lift her other foot to his shoulder as she'd expected. Instead, he straddled her leg, gathering and lifting fistfuls of her skirt until he revealed the beribboned garter holding her stocking to her thigh. She lifted her foot just slightly, enough to bump between his legs. "Hold still," she said, teasing him until he could no longer control his breathing. Then she stopped and rested her foot on the floor.

He bent low and kissed her stocking, first on the embroidered band that supported the ties, then nuzzling beneath the silk, his beard prickling on her skin. She felt his tongue flick her, then he lifted his head and untied her stocking, leaving the garter still tied around her thigh. She tensed her muscle, then relaxed it, relishing the feel of the binding. Raoul pushed the stocking down her leg, both hands stroking their way to her ankle. "And now?" he asked.

Sylvie thought for a moment. "Bind your eyes," she said. "Use a stocking." With rising pleasure, she noted that his chest began to rise and fall more rapidly. "First, remove your jacket." She shrugged off her cape as he did so, then held out her hand for the jacket. Raoul drew back, until she tossed her cape aside. She filed the information away in her mind.

Beneath the jacket, he wore a ruffled blue shirt tucked into a waistcoat of blue and gold with flat buttons. His waist was trim, accentuated by his clothing's cut. She licked her lips.

His jacket was warm, and the leather scent rose up to surround her when she slid her arms into its sleeves. No blades were concealed within, she noted with surprise. "Bind your eyes," she said again, and this time he picked up her stocking from the floor, straightening and folding it between his hands.

"I will tie it on," Sylvie decided. "Remain kneeling."

The wood floor was cool on her bare feet, but smooth and well polished. She noted that fact absently while she picked up her other stocking from the floor, took the folded stocking from Raoul, and then laid her free hand atop his head. His short hair felt crisp and springy. She tangled her fingers among his curls and lightly scratched his scalp. He pushed into her touch like a cat and reached up. "Hold still," she said. "Arms down." She padded his eyes with the folded stocking, then used the other to tie the pad snugly to his head. Then she waited.

Raoul could not remain silent for long. "What next?" he said.

"So impatient," she answered. She paced around him in a circle, her skirts rustling across the floor. Now that he couldn't see her, she glanced up and saw stars thickly clustered above their heads. It was indeed beautiful. But beauty was easily found. The man kneeling before her was just as lovely, and much more pleasing to the touch.

Decision made, she returned to the bench and sat. "I require you to please me with your mouth," she said. "You will not touch yourself. I will take care of that later. Tell me you understand."

He was breathing faster again. He touched his lips with the tip of his tongue. "Is there a trick?"

Sylvie shrugged, then remembered he couldn't see her. "Being blindfolded isn't enough for you?"

He bowed slightly, like a swordsman in acknowledgment of a hit. "My gloves?"

"You will wear them."

She sat mere steps away from him. He rose to his feet and swayed for a moment before reaching one hand in her direction. "I'm here," she said. He stepped once, twice, three times. She dodged to avoid fingers in the face and his hand landed instead on her shoulder.

His fingers trailed down her arm as he slowly crouched beside her, leather on leather; she couldn't feel very much, but the sound was evocative. He hadn't approached her mouth or neck, and seemed likely to bypass her breasts, as well. Her respect for him rose. He was taking her at her word, and approaching her pleasure by the most direct route.

She pulled his jacket closed around her, and deeply inhaled the scent of leather.

Raoul opened his hands and traced them just above the floor. "I can feel where the floor is located," he said. "As if it presses up against my hands. It's just—" he lowered his gloved hands "—just there." He tapped his fingers against the wood in a dull, rapid tattoo. "And you, Lady Sylvia, you're there." He slid his hands along the floor until his fingertips encountered the hem of her skirt.

"It's not entirely silk," he said, rubbing the fabric between his fingers. He brought it to his lips; his tongue darted out to touch and savor. Arousal bloomed in Sylvie's belly. "If it were entirely silk, it would be more slippery."

"It's silk and fine goat's wool," she said, astonished that he'd been able to tell through his gloves. "It wears better. Also, the cost is less." She paused. "Are you finished being astonished by all you can sense without your eyes?"

He grinned. "Surely you appreciate sensuality."

"I am not sitting here to be admired like a porcelain shepherdess," she noted.

"I'm not fond of porcelain shepherdesses," he said. "Too finicky and easily broken." He gathered up fistfuls of her skirt hem. "I want to give all I have. I want you to be able to take it." Sylvie waited to see if he would thrust it upward, or venture to her waist to unhook her skirt from her bodice. Instead, he lifted her skirt and her layers of petticoats and dragged the mass of fabric slowly over his face, then his head, before letting it fall. Abruptly, Sylvie couldn't see him, either.

But she could feel him. The heat of his body scorched her thighs. She felt his gloved hands taking hold of her chemise. It wasn't as full as her skirts. She wouldn't be able to spread her legs very far apart while wearing it. She reached out and touched the mound of his shoulder; then she heard a ripping sound, and felt it, as well, deep in her cunt.

Raoul's gloved hands gripped her bare thighs, squeezing gently. He crouched lower, and she felt his hot breath on her inner thighs and on her mound. He inhaled deeply, and she felt coolness before a thin stream of warm air teased through her pubic hair. She closed her eyes at the wash of sensation.

His hands crept higher, pressing her thighs apart. Sylvie did not resist; she leaned back against the wall, letting her legs fall open more widely.

Time passed.

"I do not have all night," she snapped.

Raoul laughed. He turned his face into her thigh and laughed some more. "I see you are overcome with pleasure."

"Not *yet*," she said bitterly. "And after such a promising beginning, too."

"Promising, am I?" One of his gloved hands landed atop her mound, pressing in lightly. The leather pulled at her hair, almost uncomfortable, but her sensations were confused at the moment. With his other hand, he followed her thigh to her abdomen, and from there found her lower lips. Delicately, he spread them with opened fingers, and Sylvie bit back a whimper.

Another stream of air hit her inner heat, and she gasped and grabbed his shoulder through layers of skirts. "Kiss me," she demanded.

He understood; he leaned forward and pressed his open

mouth to her cunt, his upper teeth rubbing at her clit. She cried out, then swiftly muffled her voice with her hand. She had no desire to accidentally summon royal guardsmen.

Raoul's lips felt impossibly soft against her soft inner tissues. His tongue probed, sharp but delicate, finding the narrowest folds to explore. And all the while his gloved hands gripped and released, gripped and released, in constant underlying sensation.

She wasn't sure how long it continued. She wished she could reach through her skirt and guide his head, force him to more intensity, more of the occasional delicious nudges of his teeth behind the softness of his lips. "Your hand," she gasped. "Your finger."

His right hand shifted, and then his gloved finger had breached the entrance to her passage, thicker and less slippery than a finger. The abrupt stretching almost hurt, and she laughed and gasped at the same time. "More!" she demanded. "Fuck me." To convince him, she braced her hands against the wall and shoved herself toward his hand.

He pushed back with a hand on her stomach, and she would have protested, except his finger entered her more fully. The leather of his glove was slippery with her fluids, but even so, as he thrust his finger in and out, leather dragged at her skin in a way that ought to have been uncomfortable but instead excited her more. She threw back her head, her mouth working with sounds she could not utter.

Raoul's mouth returned to her cunt. He tongued along the edges of his finger where it vanished into her flesh, outlining the extent of his penetration, making her all the more aware of how lusciously he stretched her. "More," she said. She lifted her hands to grab his head, then let them fall, frustrated by the interference of her skirt. She would not be able to feel him through the fabric. She could only feel him beneath it, intensely and unmistakably fucking her with finger and mouth. She seized the lapels of his leather jacket and twisted them in her hands, desperately resisting the need to cry out, and cry out loudly.

Raoul's lips closed around her clit, soft, so soft. No hint of teeth now. She needed more intensity than that, and then he gave it to her, thrusting harder with his finger, turning his hand so his thumb could rub against her outer lips, adding another layer of sensation. She clenched her inner muscles on his hand, in a hard rhythm with his fucking, and immediately shuddered with a small climax, then another, then another. His gloved finger was much slicker now, moving quickly, almost too quickly for her to grasp with her cunt. She tightened on him and gasped; he sucked hard on her clit; and then spasms rent her apart, her legs shuddering, her belly twitching, and deep inside, her cunt pulsing with long throbs of release.

She fell back against the wall with half-closed eyes, gasping when he withdrew his hand and a residual orgasmic shudder passed through her. Raoul lifted her skirt and backed out from beneath it, dropping to a crouch in front of her. As she watched, he lifted his gloved hand to his mouth and thoroughly sucked each finger clean.

Her eyes drifted down and noted his state of readiness. "You may remove the blindfold," she said, taking care not to let her voice slur. She could easily have fallen asleep. She had not, she remembered, had sex in more than a week because she'd been busy pursuing information. Though she could view this, too, as being in the line of duty.

Sylvie rose to her feet and shook out her skirts. Raoul, also now standing, was having difficulty with her knots; she took over and untied the blindfold herself, dropping her stockings on the floor.

His eyes met hers. He didn't speak, but his lips parted slightly.

"What is it?" she asked.

He drew one finger along her cheekbone. "You look even more lovely than you did before, Madame Sylvia."

"How so?" He didn't need to flatter her, and she wasn't sure she liked that he had bothered. She was about to give him what he wanted, after all.

His finger left a warm tingle in its wake as he traced the short length of her nose and shaped the corners of her mouth. "Relaxed," he said at last. "Did we do that together?"

Of course she was relaxed. That was one of the purposes of sex, after all. She reached down and cupped his genitals, to remind him what they were about. A gentle squeeze and caress told her his interest was still high. "I need to know something," she said.

"Yes, I enjoyed that," he said. "I didn't think I would do so, but...the blindfold forced me to concentrate on you even more." She squeezed him more firmly in an irregular rhythm, and he gasped with each constriction.

"Oh! The softness of your…skin and…your scent and all the…shapes inside your petals."

"Petals," Sylvie repeated. She restrained a laugh, but barely.

"Does it matter what I call them?" he asked tartly, pulling free of her grip. "Your language is sadly deficient, you know."

"My questions have nothing to do with what you thought of my petals," she said. "If you would be quiet and listen and do as I say, you, too, could be relaxed very soon." She cast her eyes about the gazebo's interior. Except for the benches along the walls, it was regrettably bare. Unless—she inspected beneath one of the benches and found recessed handles. She tugged and out fell a drawer, stuffed full of rugs. "Take some of these out and spread them on the floor," she said.

"May I—" Raoul indicated his trousers. The fall drew tight across his bulge, and surely the buttons were digging into his flesh.

"No," Sylvie said. She didn't carry a cock ring with her, so the trousers would have to do. While Raoul gingerly bent and tugged out small carpets, she extracted her knife and swiftly unlaced her bodice, taking a grateful breath once she was done. "When did you come to court?" she asked. She knew, but wished to establish his capacity for truth.

"Two months ago," he said, then stopped when he saw her open bodice, rugs falling from his hands. Sylvie cupped her breasts and eased them free of the top of her dress, lightly massaging them.

"Keep working," she said. "Unless you wish to have

splinters." She stripped off her loosened bodice and dropped it on the floor. The cool air felt good on her bare breasts. Her nipples drew pleasantly tight. "How long was your journey?"

"Eight months," he said. "As I told you, I am a cartographer. There were side trips."

"And your sponsor allowed this?"

"I wasn't being paid very much. It seemed only fair to me. If I arrived and received no commission, I would at least have new measurements and drawings."

Sylvie watched him spreading rugs on the floor. Rather than a messy pile, he arranged several edge to edge before spreading additional rugs on top, overlapping them in a geometrical pattern. She untied the inner lacings of her skirt and let it fall around her feet. Her petticoat strings had been knotted too tightly, the fault of Alys. She worked them loose as she asked, "Where did you go?"

Raoul froze for a moment, staring at her disrobing, then tossed another rug haphazardly onto the pile. "North," he said, another rug dangling forgotten from his fingertips. "By sea. She—my sponsor—hired a ship for me. A northern woman was the captain. There were two ships, really. The second was escort to my ship. I think. I didn't go aboard. No one spoke of it much, or of its captain. It was painted black. Your petticoats are red."

"They are," Sylvie agreed. She let all of them fall at once, then stepped free of them. "Get more rugs."

"Your garters," Raoul said in a choked voice when he turned again. His arms tightened on the rugs in his arms.

"I will leave them where they are for now," she said. "Are you finished with the rugs?"

"Yes," he said. After a moment, he threw the rest of his armload onto the pallet he'd made. "Why—"

Amused, Sylvie waited for him to finish, while she stretched, readying herself for exertion and providing him with a distracting sight. "Why what?"

"Why are you asking—"

"I am curious as to the identity of your sponsor," she said. "That's all."

"And you'd make love to me to find out?"

Sylvie shrugged, and grinned when his eyes followed her bosom's movement. "I'd fuck you anyway," she said. "You are a very beautiful man. Who is your mysterious court sponsor?"

"Lady Diamanta," he said. "I suppose it doesn't matter now if I tell you. Did I mention I had a weakness for blondes? Her first, then you."

She breathed out slowly. Puzzle pieces came together in her mind, *click, click, click.* She realized she wasn't surprised by this information in the least. But she was, just a little, jealous. "What need could she have for a maker of maps?"

"Money, she said," Raoul said. He looked at her hungrily, but his mind was clearly working at the problem. "She was interested in certain spices of which I know the origins. Also in trade routes by sea, and then ports into inland cities. What anyone would find interesting, if they wanted to parlay a small fortune into a large one. I appreciated the chance to visit and explore so many seaports and river systems in so little time."

"Lady Diamanta already has a large fortune."

"Maybe she wants something else, then." He took a step closer. "I almost forgot. Do I have permission to come closer?"

Sylvie considered. Best to distract him now. "Be silent and remove your shirt," she said. "Leave the gloves for now."

He closed his mouth and toyed with the top button of his shirt. There were only two, so far as she could see, before the shirt disappeared into his embroidered waist-coat, which had its own row of buttons. She could dip her hand into his waistcoat, and tease apart his shirt to reach his belly. Except she didn't want to prolong their play too much longer before she took his cock inside her. The fun was to torment him, not herself.

"Waistcoat first," she amended.

His fingers flew down the front, flicking buttons open with practiced ease, despite the awkwardness of his gloves. His shirt wasn't ruffled at the bottom, and it easily fell open. "Untuck it," she said. "Take it off."

He did so, letting shirt and waistcoat both fall to the floor.

The semidarkness was a hindrance to fully examining his chest, but she had a good view of the essentials. He was wider and more muscled than she would have suspected from his wiry appearance. Tight dark curls clustered in the middle of his chest and laid a trail down his belly. His nipples appeared firm and succulent atop pronounced pectorals. She would lick them, she decided, lick and suckle them until he could bear no more.

"Stop," she said. "Hands at your sides."

His chest lifted, then fell. The cool air tightened his nipples; she felt her own crinkling as if in sympathy. She padded forward on bare feet and laid her hands on his chest, circling in random patterns with her nails, imagining the currents of sensation she was building across his skin, deepening the pressure whenever she heard his breath catch. She leaned forward and licked his right nipple, letting her hair brush against his chest, nudging him with the tip of her nose as she settled in to nip at him and suck his skin between her teeth.

Her hands drifted down to his hips as she tormented him with her mouth. One of her favorite parts of a man was where the soft flesh of the abdomen yielded to hard hip bones. The skin was thinner over the bones, far more sensitive than elsewhere. She prepared him with slow passes of her thumbs, warming his skin, then dug in with her nails. He made a sound, his hips jolting forward, and she felt an answering jolt deep inside her. "Yes," she said against his chest. She took his right nipple in her mouth and suckled it, occasionally flicking it with her tongue. His hands lifted, then fell when he remembered her command.

"Good," she said, rewarding him with another scrape of her nails. She continued to torment his nipples and chest until he moaned. Then she slid one hand around him and massaged his buttocks, pulling him closer to her. "Now you may touch me."

His gloved hands landed on her waist and she shuddered at the smooth feel of the leather on her skin. She grabbed his head and yanked him to her for a long, luscious kiss. His lips were as scrumptious as she'd imagined, and as she'd felt caressing the folds of her cunt. She tasted him thoroughly as her hands returned to their gentle scratching all along his torso. She pressed her belly into his erect cock, rubbing him through his trousers, and savored his groaning response, a mixture of pleasure and pain.

She pulled away and said, "Take your cock out. Keep the gloves on."

Even in the dark, she could see the desperation in his face. He fumbled with the fall of his trousers as if her direct gaze physically impeded him; at last he ripped it open without grace and moaned in the back of his throat as he freed his cock, one gloved hand curling around his length.

"Don't stroke yourself," Sylvie said. Did she want to taste him first? Lick the head, rub his foreskin against the silky hardness beneath? Or she could have him stroke himself after all, his glove separating his own skin from that on his cock; the friction would be different, and the feel.

No; he could try that on his own time. Her cunt throbbed, and she clenched her inner muscles. She wanted him inside her, now. Whatever relaxation she'd enjoyed from coming earlier in the evening had long vanished.

"Lie down on the rug," she said. "I want to take you there." Her throat felt thick.

"I want to touch you," Raoul said.

"Make me come and then you can touch me," she said. "On your back."

She didn't allow him to get too comfortable on the pile of rugs. Straddling his hips, she plunged down on his cock as a guardsman might stab a target. Panting, she rolled her hips, savoring the sleek feel of him inside her. She bent low and let her hair slap his chest. "Good," she said.

Raoul gripped her hip with one hand, almost but not quite stilling her movement. He slid his other hand between their bodies and plucked her clitoris, so harshly that Sylvie cried out. "Yes, yes!" She clenched her inner muscles around him. "Harder!"

His thumb dug into her flesh and she let out a small scream, convulsing hard around his cock, lost in the effort and sweetness of the release. When next she was aware of her surroundings, heat branded her hips: the bare skin of his hands. She covered his hands with hers, her sweaty palms sliding on his smooth skin. "Fuck me," she said. "Quickly."

He thrust upward, forcefully. "Oh, yes," he said. Sylvie closed her eyes, sinking deeply into her body's sensations—hard, wet, hot, jolting fucking. She came twice more, smaller than before, but she knew a greater climax was within reach; she bent low, changing the angle of his penetration, and gripped his shoulders hard as she moved on him.

Her climax built slowly, deep inside her belly, tightening her muscles so she could hardly breathe, but she had to breathe so her moans of pleasure could escape. Raoul's nails buried in her shoulders, the small of her back, her buttocks, but she hardly felt it, she needed more sensation so acutely. His deep groan as his strokes turned short and rapid sent her over the edge. She shuddered in slow, heavy waves as he frantically thrust inside her, fighting the current of her clenching muscles. She bit his shoulder and he came with a shout, his body quivering beneath her. His hands fell limp on her back, fingers splayed. "I think you've killed me," he slurred.

Sylvie shifted until she lay fully stretched down the length of his body. His hands moved, lightly caressing her back. She felt a slight difference in texture, as of scarring, but it wasn't on his fingertips. She turned her cheek to rest on his shoulder and said, "It's only a little death. I find I have a taste for it."

"I suspected you might," he murmured, his hands moving absently. He nuzzled the top of her head, a pleasing sensation. "Your body is soft, gloriously so—" his arms squeezed her, then relaxed "—but you are not soft in the least. I could see it in your bearing, in your eyes."

"Sentiment has little place in my life," she admitted, despite feeling a distinct sentimentality about the attractive man she lay upon. That was the problem with sex. If the experience was too good, if the participants were too much in tune, it led almost inevitably into sentiment, and the only escape was physical escape. She was lucky that she only lived close to one or two of her favored partners. Otherwise, her life might become impossibly complicated.

Also, curiosity was a problem. Once she'd fucked someone, man or woman, she often found herself wondering why they'd acted as they had. Why did they let her torment them, or refuse to do so? Why did they want uncomplicated sex, or why was such a thing anathema to them, yet they went through with the act anyway?

"Why do you wear gloves?" she asked.

A long pause. "My fingers are stained with ink. I've left marks on your hips."

"And the scars? Let me see."

She both heard and felt his breath catch. He didn't speak or move.

Sylvie poked him hard in the ribs. "Don't be ridiculous. Let me see." Reluctantly, she rolled off him and captured his hands before he could pull away. She didn't see any ink on his dark skin, not in the gazebo's darkness, but she did see the lighter scarring around his wrists, patches of smooth pinkish skin over the prominent bones of his wrists. "Ah," she said. "Shackle galls. Best to keep those hidden here, I agree."

He pulled his hands from her grip. "I don't wish to discuss this."

"I may discuss whatever I like," she said. She straddled him again, then squirmed into a more comfortable position. "I would like your arms around me again. It is disagreeably chilly in this garden." After his arms came around her again, albeit slowly, she added, "If you didn't wish to discuss it, you would not have removed your gloves." She rubbed her cheek against him. "I had no objection to them. The feel of the leather, the idea that your hands could not quite touch me while I enjoyed all the pleasures of your touch—all of that was most inspiring."

In a low voice, he said, "You can speak of it like that. As if, as if I had done this for the sake of titillation."

"Why not take advantage?" she said. "It's clear you would not enjoy the gloves all the time, but for an occasional savor...oh, yes. It matters nothing to me if you

THE DUKE & THE PIRATE QUEEN

were once imprisoned. By your own government, were
you?"

"Yes," he growled. "I told you cartographers are considered dangerous."

"Only to the wrong people," Sylvie said contentedly.
The crook of his neck was a lovely place to press her nose.
"The right people would not care if your government
betrayed you."

Raoul was silent for a long time. At last, he said, "I
have not removed the gloves with a woman since I was
released from prison."

"Did you have many women?"

"One or two," he said. "Shortly after my release."
He grinned. "I wanted…release. The ladies of my local
brothel did not require me to strip off my gloves."

"They probably liked it," Sylvie said, idly tracing a rib
with the edge of her thumb. "Lady Diamanta was a fool
not to take advantage of your many talents."

"She might yet," Raoul said. "I haven't given up.
Quite."

Sylvie didn't chastise him for speaking of it while in the
arms of another woman. She herself had already begun
pondering how she might take advantage of Lady Diamanta with Raoul's help. If, that was, she was complicit
in the threat against Maxime's life. Was she? Would she
go that far, and risk her own status? Anyone she asked
to do murder for her would no doubt report the connection as soon as they were caught. How arrogant was
Diamanta?

What role did Lord Odell play in all this, the man who

wanted Diamanta, but had been scorned? Did he bear any past grudge against Maxime?

Sylvie resolved to find out. And Raoul...perhaps she would enlist his help. If he continued to please her with such honesty, perhaps she might even tell him the truth.

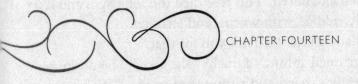

CHAPTER FOURTEEN

AFTER SEVERAL DAYS OF HARD WORK INTER-
spersed with long swims, Maxime and Imena took the
smallest boat and journeyed to one of the other islands in
the archipelago; Imena because she chafed at remaining,
essentially, docked, and Maxime in the hope of having
a little more privacy with her. He'd enjoyed their navigation lessons, particularly the silent moments in which
they worked equations or charted theoretical courses,
but there was always the possibility of interruption by
one of her crew.

The forest here was dense. Maxime used the excuse of
a massive fallen tree trunk to grasp Imena's long-fingered
hand in his and haul her up to join him. No new sap-
ling reached very high yet, so the clearing was pleasantly
sunny and free of annoying insects. "What kind of tree
was this?" he asked.

Imena reclaimed her hand once she'd scrambled up the

tree's side and settled next to him, letting her legs dangle. "It's difficult to tell, with no leaves or bark left."

He ran his hand over the smooth, sun-bleached wood. "Is it any good for ships?"

Imena considered, touching the wood herself, then tapping it with her knife. "Maybe, if it had been properly felled and cured. This tree died too long ago, and is probably riddled with worms and termites."

He made a face. "Thank you for that."

She grinned at him. "Lunch?" she asked. She unslung the bag she carried and rummaged inside. "We've got fruit and fish rolled up in flatbread, and a flask of lemon water, and a green coconut."

Imena used her cutlass to open the coconut and they shared the thin milk between bites of fish roll. Neither of them had thought to bring a spoon, so Maxime used his knife to scoop out bite-size portions of the coconut's gelid meat, delighting in how casually Imena ate them straight off his blade.

After only a few days wandering the reef island and its neighbors, she already looked much better, the dark stains beneath her eyes nearly erased and, even more reassuring, the dreadful tightness gone from her expression. She hadn't shown signs of dizziness or confusion since shortly after they'd made landfall. He hoped her injury had completely healed.

Maxime leaned over and kissed Imena's forehead, and nuzzled in the soft fuzz of hair just above. He drew back and said, "Shall we save the lemon water for later?"

She looked at him, her face soft with puzzlement. "What was that for?"

"Well, we had the coconut juice already. We might want the water later on."

She shook her head. "I've been thinking about our hostages. Why didn't you take Annja up on her offer?"

"What offer?" Maxime said. Now he was the one confused. He trailed his fingers along her thigh.

"I am the captain. I know everything," Imena said. "She offered herself to you."

Maxime shrugged. "You know why I have no interest in Annja."

"She's warm and willing. And you might have been able to get a little more information from her if you'd fucked her."

He hadn't expected her to put it so coldly. He withdrew his hand from her leg. "Is that what you think of me?"

"Am I wrong?" she asked.

Their eyes met and held.

Maxime looked away first. "If I was sure she had information that we needed to protect ourselves, and there wasn't any other way of getting it…yes, I would fuck her." He paused. "But if you told me you didn't want me to do it, then I wouldn't."

Imena blinked. "What if I ordered you to do it?"

"That would be different." Her steady gaze and her questions were making him uncomfortable. It was clear where all this was leading. He drew up his legs and wrapped his arms around them. "I would do that for you, if you needed me to."

"Would you enjoy it?"

He wanted to give a flippant response. To anyone else, he would have done. Imena wouldn't have asked if she hadn't really wanted to know; and if he wanted to move forward with her, if he wanted to convince her of his feelings for her, he had to be truthful.

If she didn't like his answers, he might lose her.

He swallowed down his terror at the thought and said, "I enjoy sex under most circumstances. So I suppose I would feel physical enjoyment. It would be stupid to suffer through something I had to do if I could feel pleasure instead. And I find it easy to enjoy sex. That's the way I'm made. But afterward...no. I wouldn't like that. I truly *dislike* dishonest sex. And it would be dishonest. To question her afterward, I would be pretending to feel more for her than was true. I would do it, if you asked, or if I felt it necessary, but I wouldn't enjoy it."

Imena was still watching him when he glanced at her. She said, "Why do you think Annja propositioned you?"

Not a word about what he'd just said. Maxime reined in his emotions with a sharp jerk. Perhaps this wasn't about him and Imena at all, but about Annja. He said, "She wants security. A place in the crew. I am becoming convinced she wants to stay on *Seaflower*."

Imena said, "Why not approach Chetri, then?"

"She considers me lower status. A stepping stone, perhaps."

"And now?"

"Perhaps now she'll speak to Chetri. He wants her, you know."

"I suspected that." Finally, she looked away from his face for a moment, and he could breathe again. The change of subject relieved him. She wasn't going to stop speaking to him. She wouldn't have, not entirely, but he realized he'd feared she would treat him differently after hearing how he felt about sex as an interrogation technique.

Maxime unfolded his legs and slid off the log, wincing when sticks crackled sharply beneath his feet. He held up his arms.

She checked to be sure her bag was slung properly, then slid off the tree trunk into his arms. Maxime held on to her for a moment, then another and another, treasuring each breath. Imena leaned into him, resting her forehead against his cheek. She lifted one hand and rubbed his chest, a gesture more soothing than erotic. She said, "Thank you."

"For?"

"Being honest with me. I value that in you."

"I'm always honest with you." He'd been more honest with her than with anyone he'd known in his life.

Imena lightly slapped his chest. "Let's walk. We're meant to be gathering fruit."

As they walked, Maxime stripped off his shirt and tied it around his waist. The tall trees blocked most of the sunlight from above, but the air was still warm, and here, away from the sea breeze, humid. He was glad the Knife had given them both an anti-insect salve to smear onto their skins, as, besides the usual gnats and flies, the occasional large wasp buzzed past.

Flower-laden vines crawled among the decaying leaves beneath their feet, taking advantage of every tiny patch of sunlight in their climb up the trunks of the giant trees. In this part of the forest, most of the flowers were a deep

orange red, the color of the silk jacket Imena had worn
the first time he'd seen her. She'd carried a sailcloth port-
folio beneath her arm, bearing trade agreements from one
of the smaller island nations on the fringes of the empire;
she'd promised to deliver them to his duchy, along with a
cargo of rice and spices. He remembered how Roxanne
and Chetri had flanked her, aloof and protective, but he'd
barely noticed them, his gaze devoured by the strong
bones of her face and her steady confidence.

"Maxime!"

Imena shoved a handful of green fruit into his arms.
She'd collected it while he daydreamed. Reflexively, he
grabbed and promptly regretted the action as sticky juice
adhered to his chest. "What is this?"

"Jubo," she said. "Don't eat the skins. I need to climb
that tree." She removed her cutlass from her belt, bent
and swiftly roped her ankles together.

Maxime looked up, and up, and up. The coconut tree
wasn't as tall as *Seaflower*'s mainmast, but devoid of rigging or footropes. "Are you going to throw them down
on my head?"

"I'll lower a net," she said, bracing one hand against
the tree and giving it an experimental push. He'd scarcely
drawn a breath before she grasped the narrow trunk firmly
and leaped, gripping with her roped feet. She hitched her
way upward, not as quickly as a monkey, but deftly. The
view of her back and rear and long legs was spectacular.

"I'll just sit down here," he called.

"Keep your eyes open," Imena replied. "Snakes and
such."

He looked down at his bare feet. Perhaps if he was

lucky, snakes wouldn't want flesh that had been smeared with insect repellent. He began retrieving the coconuts Imena sent down from the tree, then another tree and two more after that. He unfolded a tattered piece of canvas, cut from a retired sail, and laid it out on the ground, tossing the coconuts onto it along with the jubo. A few coarse stitches and the bundle would be easy to drag back to shore. He and Imena together would be able to lift it when needed.

As she shimmied her way down the last tree, he eyed the second piece of canvas they'd brought. It wouldn't be needed to carry supplies; they wouldn't be able to carry any more than they already had. He tugged the bundle of coconuts out of the way and spread the doubled canvas over the clearing. It wasn't a soft bed, but it would do. It would take a while for ants to find their way onto it to bite his ankles.

Imena's feet met the ground and she bent to slide the looped rope from her feet. Then she straightened, brushing scraps of bark from her singlet and worn trousers. "I should have known you had other motives for helping me," she said. She indicated the spread canvas with her chin.

"You're surprised?" Maxime dusted the soles of his feet against his calves. He untied his shirt from his waist and tossed it down before he settled cross-legged on the canvas pallet. "If you have no interest—"

"Oh, enough of all that," she said, sitting down next to him. She smiled, and cupped his cheek in the palm of her hand. "I'm not sorry I questioned you earlier."

"It's your right," he said. "You're the captain of the ship, not me."

"It isn't so much that as…" Imena's hand dropped to his bare shoulder and caressed him idly. "It bothers me."

Maxime pulled away from her. "What does?"

"That you're so free with your affections."

His stomach felt cold and he had to resist pulling away from her. "You mean I'll fuck anything that moves. Isn't that what you really mean?"

"Not *anything*," she said, but her smile at the attempted joke faded when he didn't reply in kind.

He said, "I thought you knew me better than that."

Imena drew her knife from its sheath and stared down at it as she rolled it back and forth across her palm. "I'm not sure what I think," she said.

"About me, or about your ideas of me?" he asked. Then he looked away. He hadn't meant the words to come out so harshly.

"We shouldn't talk," she said in a rush. She turned away from him and flung her knife. It stuck in a tree, quivering.

"Yes, we do get on a lot better when we're just making the tide," he noted bitterly. He straightened his legs and pulled her down to the pallet with him. Her singlet came off easily enough when she lifted her arms to help him remove it. While she braced above him on bent arms, he wriggled lower, splayed his hands on her smooth, muscled back and settled in to tease her breasts, using his beard as much as his lips and tongue. Her skin tasted of sweat and herbal insect repellent, and he hoped it wasn't poisonous to humans, because nothing was going to make him stop.

After a few moments, she used one hand to plunge her fingers into his hair, holding his head to her.

He lifted his head slightly. "Oh, I'm forgiven, am I?"

"There was nothing to forgive," she said.

"I feel as though there was," he said. He rested his forehead against her sternum. "Were you hoping I would say no? That I never would have fucked Annja for any reason, because I only want you?"

"That doesn't make any sense," she said, bending her head closer to his. "If it got us information we needed…" She blew out her breath. "Yes. All right, yes. It's entirely an emotional reaction, but I wanted you to say no."

"I know you did," he said. "But I wouldn't lie. Not to you." He tugged her closer and pressed the flat of his tongue to her nipple. Her breath came faster and she shifted slightly, releasing his head. He turned his face to rub the side of her breast with his cheek. Despite all the noise of the forest, the buzzing and burring of insects, the cries and calls of birds, he could clearly hear the soft rasp of his beard against her skin, and felt the sound down to his own skin. "Can't you tell what I think? How I feel? Our bodies don't lie," he said. "Not nearly as much as our mouths can do." He kissed her breast, this time drawing her nipple full between his lips. "My mouth wants you," he said. "You're like food to me."

Imena said, "Like meat? Or vegetables? Or rice?"

"The food I must have, and that I need the most," he said. "What is that food to you?"

She arched her back, brushing his face with the tips of her breasts. "Why must you always talk so much?"

"Don't you want to know who's with you?" he asked.

He dug his fingers into her muscular shoulders, pressing in with the tips of his nails. She made a gratifying noise but then wrenched herself free.

"Imena—"

She was already on her feet, reaching for the cutlass at her side, the cutlass that she had set aside to lie down with him. Maxime sat up slowly. He, too, now saw the five men standing at the edge of the clearing, and the brutal short spears they held steady and level.

She should have attacked instantly. Chance might have made her lucky, except she'd feared Maxime, dazed by arousal, would not react quickly enough, and be speared in the melee. Now it was too late and she would have to wait for another opportunity to attempt flight. At least their captors had let them put their clothing back on.

They were forced to walk at spearpoint through the forest toward an unknown destination. Imena glanced at Maxime, then indicated the man in front of them with the barest inclination of her chin. Another wary glance told her Maxime was now watching the man, too, and his slightly unsteady gait; he walked as if his feet were numb, or not attached to the ends of his legs. He smiled widely and incessantly, which she found disturbing. He still carried a spear, though; all five of the islanders did, in menacing contrast to the crowns and streamers of pink-and-orange flowers they wore tangled in their long hair. She wished she could see the other four men, who walked behind them and to the side, occasionally prodding her and Maxime with the butts of the spears.

Sunlight filtered down through the trees where the heat

was trapped. She felt it more powerfully with her clothing on. Sweat had begun to trickle down her back, mingling with tiny fragments of bark from her tree-climbing and the sticky residue from the Knife's insect-repelling balm. She was going mad with the urge to scratch. Finally, she gave in. Aside from a brief poke from a spear butt, their captors allowed the movement.

Maxime eased over, his hand lifted to scratch for her, but a spear promptly shoved them apart.

She waited a few minutes, then asked, in patois, "Where are we going?"

One of the men behind her spoke. His tone was slow, measured. "Don't worry, beautiful lady. We won't kill you. Unless you do something we don't want you to do."

She and Maxime exchanged a glance, ripe with irony. She said, "What don't you want us to do?"

Another of the men began to sing. It wasn't any song she'd ever heard, and it didn't seem to have any words, only vowel sounds. She didn't think it was a language. The pitch wavered gently up and down long stair steps. Mostly, it was loud. Soon, one of the other men joined in, and the first man, the one who'd spoken, began mumbling to himself. She couldn't catch any individual words. Some sort of ritual?

She didn't like not knowing who had taken them captive. She didn't like not knowing what purpose their captivity would serve. She concentrated on trying to identify their origins.

All but one of the men were medium brown in skin color. The outlier was dark brown. His skin was a shade lighter than her crewman Seretse's, though his features were similar, especially his broad nose. The others, despite similarity of skin color, had a wide range of facial features. The mixture made her think the men were, or had been, sailors. She guessed some were from the edges of the Horizon Empire, others possibly from the duchies; the darkest man likely came from farther south.

She shifted her weight, so she was walking a little closer to Maxime. In a low voice she hoped the singing would cover, she said, "I don't smell alcohol, but…"

"They do seem a bit to the wind," Maxime agreed.

She waited to see if any of their captors would react to their conversation. None of them displayed any reaction; they continued their strange song and mumbling. She murmured, "I don't like unpredictable people with spears."

"They haven't harmed us yet."

"Unless you count my bleeding ears," Imena remarked.

Maxime hid his laughter in his fist.

They walked through the afternoon. When the singing finally died out, Imena didn't risk speaking again, but she and Maxime communicated their feelings with eloquent glances, until it began to grow dark. As the stars began to be visible, Imena smelled a hint of smoke. Soon, she was sure the smoke was from campfires, some of them being used to grill fish on flat rocks. Her stomach growled. Maxime shifted closer and bumped her shoulder with his, suffering a punch from a spear butt without complaint.

The camp was substantial, with at least three hearths and numerous shelters leaning against the trunks of the towering trees. Perhaps fifteen men and women were in easy view, though she couldn't be sure of that, outside the flickering firelight.

An old man with matted hair came forward and, smiling broadly, gestured for them to sit. Under guard from their original five captors, plus five more who ambled forward, the old man bound Imena and Maxime, both wrists to opposite elbows across their chests, and ankles to knees, and their ankles then bound to each other. He smiled all the while, his hands as swift as birds. Imena's mood plummeted just as swiftly.

She could recognize the knots' origins, an effective blending of peninsular and imperial styles. The rope stretched between their ankles was no more than the length of her forearm. They might manage to walk a little, with coordination, if their lower legs weren't bound, and if they, perhaps, had their hands free to help them balance. They weren't tied as uncomfortably as they could have been. It was still enough to prevent them getting very far.

Maxime spoke up just as half the spearmen wandered away, muttering among themselves. "What's your name? Are you going to feed us?"

The old man looked puzzled for a moment, then said, "I'm Sheng. Would you like some flowers? You don't have any."

"I'd prefer some fish," Imena said.

After a long pause Sheng said, "Oh. Yes. I suppose I can get you some. It helps the stomach." He went to one of the campfires.

Maxime said to their remaining guards, "We're tied

very tightly. I don't think you'll need to harm us with those spears, do you? We aren't going anywhere."

To Imena's surprise, two of the men considered silently for a time, then ambled away. The last three remained, but one of those leaned on his spear.

Maxime glanced at Imena. He lifted his brows. Imena nodded, to let him know she understood. These men weren't drunk, but they did seem to be suggestible. Did it have something to do with the pink-and-orange flowers?

She and Maxime were only outnumbered by one man now. She wished she could see where her cutlass and their knives had been taken. Perhaps their situation was better than she'd supposed.

"Some of them speak imperial," Maxime murmured.

"I noticed," she said. "The dialect is southeastern, for the most part."

"Are they any danger to you?"

"To me?"

"Yes, to you," he said. "You're the one with the… family," he said discreetly. "And the former career."

"My hair has grown over the only tattoos that truly mark me," she said. "There's a reason we put them on our scalps, you know."

"Hard luck if you go bald," he said, grinning.

Sheng returned then, carrying green leaves stuffed with flaky cooked fish. He knelt before them and Imena barely had time to open her mouth before he shoved fish into it. The meat was slightly burned and tasted of no spice other than smoke. She didn't care. It was food. She ate all she was offered.

Maxime reminded Sheng he was hungry, too.

Sheng smiled. "Oh, yes. It will be a long time before the others arrive. I should feed you, too." The old man returned to the cluster of campfires to obtain more fish.

Others? Imena concentrated on the activity in the clearing. A small group of islanders had begun assembling an open-sided hut on the edge of their camp, bamboo framework roofed in palm mats. The builders were women. They wore minimal waist wraps, strings of shells that dangled on their bare breasts and the inevitable flowers in their hair. Two women wound flowering vines around the support poles while two more fetched armloads of blankets. Imena recognized the type of blanket; they were woven from beaten and shredded plant fibers, and very soft, surely too luxurious for prisoners. When Sheng returned, she asked, "What are they doing? Over there, with that hut."

Sheng pushed fish into Maxime's mouth and said, "Oh, that's for you."

"For me? Or both of us?"

"Oh, for both of you. It's beautiful, isn't it?" Sheng glanced at the hut, seemingly transfixed for a time by its beauty. Maxime cleared his throat. Sheng fed him more fish and said, "You can smell the flowers while you perform for us."

Was it the smell alone that drugged the people here? How close did you have to be to that scent? Were they too close already? Belatedly, what Sheng had said caught up with her. "Perform?"

Sheng beamed. "Oh, yes. You'll love the smell of the flowers. But you have to wait until the others get here."

He gave Maxime more fish and told him, "You'll need your strength. We haven't had anyone new in a very long time. I'm looking forward to it. These days, I enjoy watching quite a bit."

Imena swallowed. "Tell me more about this performing."

Sheng didn't seem to be listening to her questions anymore. He nudged Maxime's leg with his foot. Maxime didn't react, didn't even blink. "Does he need any rest first? Your man? He's a big one, they tire out more quickly in my experience. I heard you were at it before Waitimu found you. Did they get to you before he spilled himself? Waitimu wasn't sure. He can't remember."

Imena looked at Maxime, horrified. He looked back without speaking, his gaze heavy with irony and something else she couldn't quite identify. He didn't say it, but in her mind she heard, "*You're* the captain."

Sheng ran his bare foot along Maxime's calf, then drew it back hastily at Imena's glare. It was interesting information that her glare would be respected. She decided against demanding more information and, since Maxime hadn't spoken, decided to try a more diplomatic approach herself. Forcibly steadying her breathing, she said, "He'll last longer than you think, for such an old man."

"He's not too old, is he? He's not nearly as old as I am, and I can still—"

"Oh, no, no," Imena reassured him. "He's very— Do you want to give him a try?"

The smallest of choked sounds escaped Maxime, but Sheng didn't hear; he was backing away too quickly. "Oh, no, ma'am, of course not. Not before the performance. I can't damage your chances at winning the competition with the others. That wouldn't be fair at all. Captain Pauk would be very disappointed in me if I did that." Then, to Imena's immense frustration, Sheng wandered away.

She subsided to the sandy dirt, uselessly shifting against her bonds. The rope was old. Given enough time, and a little more freedom to move, and a sharp edge, she might eventually work herself free, but she doubted she would be given any of those commodities. And what would happen if the islanders forced the drugging flowers on them? "Well?" she murmured. "What do you think?"

Maxime's voice was tight as he muttered back, "He treated us well, you notice. Not really like prisoners. He might have kicked us, or dumped our food on the ground. He asked after my, um, stamina."

"Maxime! They want to watch us fuck!"

"I had gathered that," he said. "It's not a form of sailors' entertainment, is it? Public fucking? If it is, I can't believe how I missed it."

"Not normally," she replied, offended. "Maybe among pirates. I wouldn't put it past Venom. But on shipboard, that sort of thing is frowned on. It makes others jealous. It can lead to all sorts of dissent among the crew. Even the newest common sailors on *Seaflower* have somewhere private to go. I learned that much from serving on a privateer. It's a better solution than the navy, which simply denies the problem and punishes the offenders." She wondered what kind of ship Captain Pauk had commanded.

"I didn't think it was common," he said, "but one never knows everything that goes on. So other ships, not navy ships, it's the same?" His question seemed uninterested.

Imena glanced sharply at him, wondering what he was hiding beneath the bland tone. "It's not a ship game," she said slowly, "but it might be an islanders' game. I think I've heard of such. Small islands, not many resources. They're easily controlled when the empire controls their trade. They can't waste what they have in making war over disagreements, and the people here don't seem inclined to make war, anyway. So…"

Maxime's tone remained distant as he replied, "And perhaps they get some new blood into their groups that way. Small islands don't take well to a steady population. They need new blood. I'm sure whatever they do with those flowers encourages them, as well."

"That makes sense," she agreed. She glanced apprehensively at the pavilion. The women were now busily shredding the pink-and-orange flowers down to petals, and flinging them all over the mats. Imena could smell the sugary fragrance from where she sat.

Maxime bumped his shoulder against hers, offering comfort she could pretend she didn't need. Just for a moment, she leaned into him. He said, "Not to worry."

She said, "I can't make the tide in front of people. You might enjoy it, but I—" She looked away. Suddenly, she could see her cutlass and their knives away across the camp. They were laid out on a mat in the firelight, ready for her to snatch them up, if she could only reach them.

"There's nothing to fear, Imena. Odds are, if we do as they ask, they'll let us go." He bumped his shoulder against hers again, and smiled at her. Deliberately, he fluttered his eyelashes in a parody of flirting.

She couldn't laugh, not quite. "My crew," she said,

though at this moment she was worried for herself, as well. What if the islanders drugged her, and Maxime? What would that be like? What might she reveal to him?

"If we do well in their competition, we might be able to come to some arrangement," Maxime pointed out. "We're not even sure they know or care about *Seaflower*. This is a different island, after all, and they don't seem very aware of their surroundings."

Do well, Sheng had said. She wasn't sure she liked the implications of that. "I don't see how they could have missed us, drugged or not," she said bitterly. "We have no idea, Maxime, no idea at all, how many islanders there might be, or what their intentions truly are. The people you're responsible for—they aren't here."

"Chetri and Roxanne aren't useless," he pointed out. "They're your officers for a reason, aren't they?"

"Don't tell me my business," she snapped.

Maxime, wisely, kept his mouth shut.

The women at the pavilion were sitting on the ground now. They didn't appear to be doing anything except sitting. She would have expected them to eat, chat, begin working on small tasks. They did nothing. She watched closely, wondering if she would see any coded gestures, or any new activity. They appeared to be breathing deeply. Preparing to sing or chant? Or inhaling the flowers' scent or pollen?

The youngest of the women scooped up a handful of the flower petals and stuffed them into her mouth. The woman next to her slapped her hand, not quickly or very hard. None of them spoke. The one who'd eaten the flower petals slowly sagged to the ground. Soon, Imena heard her begin to snore.

"Soporific flowers?" Maxime murmured. He'd been watching, too. "That could go along with the suggestibility and the odd things they've said."

"The others aren't asleep, so it might not always be a soporific," Imena said. "We can't assume they'll all eat the flowers and fall unconscious." In fact, two of the women, then three, had begun to caress each other, their carnal intent clear.

"That would leave us still tied, anyway," Maxime said. He sounded abruptly weary, more so than she'd ever heard him sound before. He closed his eyes and dropped his forehead to his updrawn knees. Given that their ankles were tied together, she could feel his beard against her leg; she shifted slightly, caressing him as best she could.

She said, "We'll get out of this."

His cheek still resting on his knees, he turned his head to look at her. "That was unconvincing, Imena."

She wasn't sure what had led to his change of mood, but it was clear to her that he needed a distraction. She made a decision. "You do the talking. When they come to us again."

"You're the captain."

"And you're the diplomat."

Maxime sat up and brushed her cheek with his, a momentary shivery pleasure. "Imena, I think we'll have to do what they ask. We could refuse, but—do you want me to tell them we refuse?"

She swallowed. "You're better at this sort of thing. Do what you think is best. I trust you."

Maxime breathed out slowly, and leaned his shoulder into hers. "Thank you," he said. "I'll get you through it."

He sounded sure of himself, but something in his tone betrayed him. Attempting humor, Imena said, "And you'd better make me like it."

 CHAPTER FIFTEEN

NOTHING ELSE HAPPENED FOR THE REMAINDER
of the night. Imena watched the islanders as closely as she
could while they ate fish and sometimes flowers, copu-
lated, sang badly and eventually fell to sleep punctuated
with quantities of loud snoring, like a houseful of drunks.
She was grateful for their physical distance from these
activities. She would also have welcomed a blindfold. She
wasn't sorry when, eventually, the untended campfires
went out.

She and Maxime weren't expected back to *Seaflower*
until the following day. There might be a chance of rescue
after that. She didn't plan to wait that long, and felt sure
Maxime didn't, either. She utterly hated being helpless.
Even worse, being helpless on land. On a ship, there was
always something to be done, even if it was only polish-
ing the brightwork. Here, she could do nothing.

Maxime leaned into her shoulder. "Stop thinking about
it," he said.

She supposed if she could have an extra sense about his feelings, he could have the same. She gave in, leaning back into him. Their ropes rasped together. "We're going to be cramped in the morning," she said.

"We'll be better for some sleep," Maxime said. "We can lie down here. Close your eyes. I'll watch."

"You need sleep, too. Wake me in a while."

"Maybe I will, maybe I won't."

"I'm the captain."

"You said I was in charge." He kissed her temple. "Now, go to sleep."

Imena wanted to continue arguing—anything to keep back her thoughts and his—but for his sake, she curled uncomfortably on her side, Maxime at her back. She closed her eyes, listening to the soft sound of his breath. Eventually, she slept.

Just past dawn, a dozen new people arrived at the camp, nine men and three women. Ignoring the islanders still sleeping around the dead campfires, the visitors marched into a pattern, an arched grouping that opened to briefly reveal a litter and its occupants, two more men. The litter was then transformed into a shelter similar to the one built for Imena and Maxime; two women lifted poles and spread woven palm leaves, obscuring Imena's view of the people inside.

"Ratshit," she said, straining to see.

Maxime's voice in her ear startled her. "Pretend they're officious customs agents."

"This situation is *not* the same. Though…either way, we're going to get fucked."

Laughter burst out of him. Imena relaxed a little.

Perhaps he was feeling better than he had the previous night.

Several of the visiting islanders turned to them, and she finally had a glimpse of their opponents: two men, both burly as foremast hands, both naked except for crowns of flowering vines. One of them stepped from beneath the shelter and stretched upward, showing an impressive array of muscle and, on his lower belly, a tattoo of an octopus.

"Maxime!" she hissed.

"A very nice specimen," he said approvingly.

"His tattoo!" The octopus was a symbol of Maxime's duchy, and tattoos of the animal were common among a range of professions, including soldiers, sailors and prostitutes. If the man was a prostitute, who knew what range of special skills he might possess?

She, too, had a tattoo of an octopus, nearly hidden among the designs on her thigh.

"I see it," Maxime said. "He's proud of himself, isn't he?" The man was now stretching downward, his back to his audience, showing off his long, lean legs and powerful buttocks tattooed with sharks. The sharks' jaws moved with each flex of muscle. "The sharks are far too showy. More traveling fair than brothel."

"I appreciate that you're trying to distract me, but that wasn't what I meant. Do you think it will help, that he likely came from your duchy?"

"Not a bit. He probably doesn't even know the duchy is a duchy again. None of these people look like recent arrivals. Their clothing would be in better condition if they were."

The other man had emerged from the shelter to join his partner. His buttocks tattoos were snakes, writhing with each clench of his muscles. He bore no octopus, but a more ordinary sailors' anchor decorated one shoulder blade. When she looked up at his face, she realized he was staring at them, his expression revealing only vague disinterest. Imena bared her teeth at him; he reared back. At her shoulder, Maxime snorted appreciatively. "That's the way." Pointedly, he smiled at their competition, a patently false smile demonstrating defiance more than friendliness.

She swallowed hard. "How are we going to do this?"

"I'm not sure yet. I do hope they untie us first."

She hadn't considered that. "If they untie us, I could cause a distraction, and you could flee."

"I won't leave you."

"If there's a chance—"

"I won't leave you, Imena. You told me I could lead, remember?"

"I'm in charge of escape attempts."

"And I say we won't make one. This will work out better if we don't."

Their opponents were standing, arms outstretched, before their audience while attendants fed them flower petals and massaged them lightly with coconut oil, the smell strong even this far away. The sleeping islanders had begun to wake and stumble about their morning routines. Someone out of her line of vision had begun playing a drum desultorily, and a bamboo pipe joined in, preparatory short flutters of sound.

Imena breathed out slowly, and paused before she spoke again. "I wish I hadn't said you could lead."

His voice full of mock hurt, Maxime said, "You don't trust me?"

Looking at the sand, she said, "I do. Truly, I do."

Maxime nuzzled her shoulder, his beard prickling pleasantly against her skin. "You wish you'd had more choices," he murmured. "You dislike handing over command, but it was the best thing to do here. That doesn't mean you have to like it."

"Yes," she said, relieved he understood. She took a deep breath. "I'll try to remember what it was like being a starmaster's mate, and how to take orders."

"Suggestions," he murmured. "Orders would be another type of encounter altogether. Entertaining, but not as useful for our purpose today."

Copying his lighter tone, she said, "If it seems otherwise, feel free."

"Really?"

"Only this once," she said. She leaned against him.

Sheng walked over to them, trailed by a much older man who leaned on a tall, carved stick decorated with flowering vines. Maxime whispered in her ear, "Don't forget to express the proper awe when my cock reaches its full glory."

While she sputtered with laughter at his deadpan tone, she missed the first words the old man said. Maxime answered, "If we win, Captain Pauk, you will of course free us."

Imena straightened her spine at the authority in his tone. She blanked her expression and eyed Pauk. He didn't look like a pirate to her eyes, but that proved nothing. She was fairly sure he was not drugged; his eyes were too bright, his expression too sharp. In appearance, he might have been an imperial, from one of the western provinces, or just as likely from one of the more mixed populations on the empire's fringes. His white hair hung straight nearly to his waist, and his withered chest was tattooed with faded blue fish in a mass of waves. Around his hips, he wore a length of bright indigo silk that hung to his knees.

Pauk said, in imperial-accented patois, "We will discuss your freedom once you've done what I ask. You will perform to the best of your ability and make sure all those watching enjoy themselves. No tools are permitted beyond your own bodies. You will have one hour and one hour only, by hourglass."

"Is anything forbidden?" Maxime asked. "What if we offend one of those watching?"

Pauk chuckled. "I doubt that's possible. Nothing is forbidden here." He glanced back at the group of islanders preparing the visitors' shelter. "We have few other entertainments available to us here, you see."

"And if we lose?"

Pauk looked down his nose at them. "We'll keep you for a while. We need a pair of champions. But you must realize my folks' approval is fickle. I can't speak for how they might react if you…disappointed them too many times."

Maxime said, "We won't lose. After we've won your battle for you, you will set us free." His gaze didn't waver from Pauk's. "Or we will not win for you."

"There's nowhere else you can go on this island. We are your only hope of survival, and it's not a bad fate, not at all. The flowers make everything bearable. Or I could simply have you killed, to save us trouble." Imena tensed at the old man's casual tone. Perhaps he was a pirate, after all.

Maxime didn't look or sound rattled. "And then where would you be? You obviously haven't been able to defeat your opponents with the people you have. We're your only hope. You're lucky to have found us. I can assure you, you won't suffer from setting us free. The contrary, in fact."

"And what does your companion say? She's no concubine." Pauk's dark gaze fixed on Imena. She bared her teeth at him.

"My companion is united with me in this."

"What do you have to say for yourself, girl?"

Imena met his gaze and said in her own language, "I say you're very lucky he's in charge just now, and not me. Or you would be short a testicle."

Pauk chortled. "I hope those knots are tight enough," he remarked. He turned back to Maxime, but included Imena in his gaze. "So what's to guarantee I will set you free after you've won?"

Maxime smiled. "Why, your word. Because if you don't announce our prize before the competition begins, we will not compete. I suspect the people here won't think to protest if we entertain them first."

"What if you lose?"

"I already told you that we would not." Maxime beck-

oned one of the nearby women with his chin. "Untie
us," he said.

Despite herself, Imena was impressed at the ring of authority in his voice, and the woman had already stepped
forward before Pauk nodded to her.

The woman loosened the knot tying Imena to Maxime
first, then the ropes binding their lower legs together.
Imena swung her legs beneath her and stood, cautiously
flexing her muscles to send blood through her cramped
limbs. Maxime stood with her, a little more awkwardly.
In other circumstances, she might have remarked on his
increasing age, but for now she only caught his eye and
gave him a significant look. In return, he wrinkled his
nose at her. He didn't appear worried. Imena glanced back
at their opponents, but was unable to see them anymore,
they'd been surrounded by so many islanders.

As soon as the ropes fell away from her arms, Imena
stretched them, shaking out her arms until her fingers
returned to life.

"No coconut oil for us?" Maxime inquired.

"That was not part of our agreement," Pauk said. "Besides, we don't pamper our warriors. Not like some." He
cast a contemptuous glance at their opponents.

Longingly, Imena thought of running. It would be
awkward in the sand, but if she caused enough upset,
Maxime might slip away unnoticed. Belatedly, she remembered she wasn't escaping. She glanced bitterly at
Maxime, who shrugged and smiled ruefully as if he'd
read her mind.

The islanders brought forward whisks made of leaves
to brush the sand and dirt from them. Two women then

attempted to remove their clothing. Imena balked at the hands on the hem of her singlet, drew a deep breath, then took her cue from Maxime, who stood, arms outstretched until his shirt was taken, staring into space. Probably she was the only one who detected the faint tightness of his jaw, his lowered eyelids that shuttered his gaze from their captors. She felt a little better that he wasn't as insouciant about this process as he'd appeared. They were together in that.

When the islanders laid hands on her clothing again, she reminded herself she was about to expose herself considerably more in front of these people than a mere lack of clothing. She stared at the forest and submitted. When two men arrived and began massaging her shoulders and Maxime's, she didn't acknowledge them, either, even though she couldn't help but appreciate the service. Being tied all night had been a miserable experience.

Maxime's hand closed over her elbow. He said to Pauk, "We need a moment to discuss our strategies."

Imena was astonished when she and Maxime were actually allowed to wander a short distance away, until she saw two men with spears just at the forest's edge. "They haven't said a word about *Seaflower,* and Pauk told us we had nowhere to go," she murmured. "Surely they would have mentioned it by now if they'd found it. What's our strategy going to be?" After they won, if they won, they would have to find a way to return to the ship without revealing its position.

Maxime rested his hands on her shoulders, reminding her anew of his size and strength. He studied her face for long moments, then finally murmured, "I need you to get me through this."

"What?" That was the last thing she'd expected him to say. Except…he had been acting strangely ever since he'd heard about the public competition. Was he truly nervous about it? Maxime?

He said, "I'm trying to make it my choice to do this, our choice, but it's difficult. I know you hate the idea of performing in public. I don't want to burden you with my feelings, as well. But…" He looked at the ground, then back into her eyes. "Imena, I don't want to do this, either. I know I've had dozens of lovers, I've even had three partners at once, but that's not the same thing at all, nothing like being forced to show yourself and watched by strangers."

At first, Imena had thought he was cleverly distracting her by focusing her attention on him instead of her own fears. The more he spoke, the more she realized he was speaking truth; his eyes told her, and his voice, and the faintest trembling in his hands. She touched his face, stroking his bearded cheek with her thumb. His eyes closed, and he drew a shaky breath. Her heart twisted.

She said, so he would not have to, "That happened to you. You were forced to perform for strangers."

He opened his eyes, looking into hers. He didn't speak. He inclined his head just a fraction in affirmation.

Imena felt the pain like a stab in the belly. She said, "You'll look at me, not at them. That's an order."

"Thank you, Captain," he said. He leaned forward, pressed a kiss to her brow, then let go of her shoulders, clasping his hands behind his back. "Order me again if that's what's necessary." He drew a deep breath and began speaking again, quickly. "I think all we need to do is seem more sympathetic than our opponents. They seem to be taking too much advantage of their status, and likely that's resented."

She noted his advice, but the competition had receded in importance. "Maxime—who—" Then she guessed. "When you were young, and a hostage for your duchy— did Camille's father—"

Maxime said, the words clipped, "I was of age, and he never touched me himself. That would have been illegal, as I still might be considered a peer under the law, and besides, I don't think he had a taste for men." He took a deep breath and spoke faster. "He only made me perform for his closest cronies, usually with one of the servants. I grew used to it. At least the servants were well paid for their extra duties." He swallowed. "He did it because my distress amused him. I think, also, he wished to remind me of my status and prevent me from aspiring to his daughter."

Understanding the reasons behind his abuse clearly didn't matter much to his emotions. "I'm sorry," Imena said, though she was more angry than sorry. She slid her arms around his waist, pressing close to him. "I'm sorry that I…" She burst out, "I wish I could have killed him for you."

"That would have been too much honor for the duke," he said, kissing her temple just as four large islanders dragged them apart.

Imena struggled in her captors' grips, more as a matter of form than a real attempt at escape. She had no desire to make this easy for them. Her thoughts focused more on Maxime's revelations. How had she not known this? Did Camille know? Imena didn't think so. The more she thought about it, the more she realized it was likely Maxime had told no one. No one but her.

She could only see glimpses of him now; they were led in opposite directions, to make some sort of grand entrance. The drum had begun again, playing a fanfare rhythm she recognized from the peninsula. The flute soared above it, swooping intervals like the tavern music of the empire. She tried to estimate how many islanders were present. Movement among them, plus new arrivals, meant she lost count after about thirty individuals. How had so many people been stranded here? She was sure there were not as many as a hundred from the two cadres combined, but perhaps there were sixty islanders, total. Surely there were no fewer than fifty.

Some of the islanders were short enough for Imena to see over their heads. She peered toward the pavilion built for their opponents, but the crowd standing close around it obscured all but glimpses of flesh. She needed a few moments to discern that the two men seemed to be engaged in an unusually acrobatic position, making flamboyant use of upper-body strength. After a moment, she realized one man was holding the other upside down so he could suck cock in midair.

Over the sound of the flute and drum, and the conversation of the crowd, she could only barely hear effortful grunts. She could easily ignore the sounds, so she did, bringing an image of *Seaflower* to mind instead, and carefully reviewing each repair task that remained, and the state of those already begun.

When a spear butt prodded her, Imena blinked back to knowledge of her surroundings. She found Maxime. He was watching her. His usual expressions in uncertain situations, she'd learned, were either of affable charm or calm authority. She'd never seen this look on his face before: tightly controlled desperation, visible only in the tense wrinkle between his brows and the firm set of his lips.

Even given those hints only, she knew this expression. Dozens of young sailors had passed beneath her command as a privateer and, later, as a semirespectable merchant captain. Maxime wore the face of someone about to enter a fight he wasn't sure he could win. Someone who looked to his captain to lead him through.

Imena caught his gaze with hers, and smiled.

Tentatively, he smiled back, and in one breath more, his affable mask slid into place. But his eyes still sought hers repeatedly, even as they walked toward each other, while the islanders split apart to make an aisle for them.

Pauk offered them flowers to eat. Maxime shook his head. Imena refused, as well. The crowd murmured at this, but the sound soon faded.

Within a few steps she could smell the heaps of torn flower petals. She drew the sweet scent deep into her lungs, attempting to shut out everything else but the pavilion, and Maxime. Another step, and another. It was not at all like going into battle, as she'd feared. Maxime's revelation to her meant it was like going to lie with a lover for the first time, when they would both see each other truly bare: a moment of breath-stopping decision, and then the leap.

Just before she stepped beneath the pavilion's shelter, her guards released her. She took a moment to rub her arms and rid them of the memory of those strangers' touches, breathing deeply. She smiled at Maxime once more. Slowly, he rubbed his arms, as well, mirroring her action. She stooped and grabbed a handful of pink-and-orange petals, rolling them slightly between her palms. She rubbed them over Maxime's chest and arms, then down his thighs and the tops of his feet, finishing by standing and stroking the petals lightly over his face, while he closed his eyes and inhaled the fragrance. After she opened her hands and let the crushed petals fall to the ground, he again mirrored her actions, though he let petals drift to the ground the entire time he stroked her body with them; she felt them like phantom touches that trailed his large, warm hands. He gathered new petals for her face, two large handfuls of them, and rubbed them over her short hair until sweetness filled her lungs. She closed her eyes and he crushed flowers against her forehead, her eyelids, her cheekbones, her lips.

She was careful not to take any of the petals into her mouth, but even so, languor seeped through her body, loosening her muscles. She hoped the same was happening to Maxime. This would be easier for him if the edges of the experience were dulled.

Pauk stood in front of the pavilion, ritually repeating to the islanders the same rules he'd told them already: the competitors would perform to the best of their ability. No tools were permitted beyond their own bodies.

Competitors were given one hour, by hourglass. Imena barely listened. She breathed in flowers, and opened her eyes to Maxime, his expression unusually solemn. An orange flower petal clung to his beard. She brushed it away.

Maxime turned more fully toward the crowd, and by that motion, drew all eyes. His eyes on Pauk, he lifted a brow. Pauk looked at Imena. She crossed her arms over her chest and leveled a privateer's battle stare at him.

Pauk turned back to the crowd. "If our champions are chosen the victors, they will be freed."

Noise erupted. Practiced at judging the tone of shouting crew, Imena thought most of the noise was protests, albeit slow ones. This might take some time. She went into the shady pavilion and sat down on the flower petals. They were soft and damp. After what they'd just done with the petals, they felt disturbingly erotic.

Maxime sat next to her, his feet kicking a small cloud of petals into the air. He tugged on her arm and she leaned close, to hear him over the noise.

"Sit on my lap," he said. "I want to hold you. I feel as if I might float off."

She almost protested, before she remembered yet again what their purpose here was to be. She glanced out; several older islanders, from both groups, were clustered about Pauk, shouting. She turned her back on them and straddled Maxime's lap. She'd done this once before, in her cabin, with his feet hitched to the deck, and their bodies roped together. This time, his arms roped her to him, and he buried his face in her neck.

Imena shifted to be more comfortable, and to rub a

little harder against his cock. She felt his hum of pleasure against her throat, followed by the soft touch of his tongue, then velvety hot breath and a slow, gentle pressure of his teeth as he bit a fold of skin.

"Mmm," she said, letting herself drape over him. Loosely, she clasped her hands at the small of his back. She couldn't comfortably nibble his ear while he was biting her neck, so she settled for kissing whatever she could reach and rubbing her breasts against his chest hair.

The sound of voices receded from her consciousness; she was reminded of a portside pirate tavern of her youth, where sailors with only a single night's leave had fondled their partners in plain view, some of them even coupling in the darker corners. She'd been disturbed but aroused, as well, though at the time, she'd departed as soon as she'd realized everyone in the tavern was occupied with activities other than drinking.

She could feel Maxime's arousal tentatively growing and shifted her weight again to push against his cock. His breath stuttered and he bit the top of her shoulder, where she so often liked to bite him; she shuddered deep inside at the soft pressure. "A little harder," he said in her ear, and tightened his arms around her. "I need the distraction."

"Kiss me," she said. "I want your tongue in my mouth."

Maxime groaned, then chuckled breathlessly. "Oh, such words of devotion!" His mouth met hers, slanting and rubbing, before he pressed harder, opening her to him. Imena bit his tongue, but gently; his hands crawled up her back and splayed, as if trying to pull her completely within his body.

Imena clenched her thighs around him as best she could, though she hadn't intended to go so far, so fast. She remembered suddenly why: the competition. It hadn't yet begun for them.

She pulled her mouth away from Maxime's and gasped for breath, only to realize that the crowd had fallen utterly silent.

Maxime's body tensed against hers. She leaned close to his ear and murmured, "No one can see you. I'm guarding you."

His hands moved, sliding up and down on her back, and she mirrored the action. "This is nothing," he said in a low voice, as if reassuring himself.

"Nothing at all. I'll feed you a flower if you like."

"No," he said. "I want to know what we're doing. I want to know it's you."

His direct words were like a sharp pain in her throat. She began feathering kisses on his face: the bridge of his nose, the sharp cheekbones above his beard, the corners of his mouth. For good measure, she pressed against his erection again, and was relieved to feel his breath gust out. "We're doing this for diplomatic reasons," she prompted.

"And think of the advantages to be gained. New trade goods or…or…a fine duke *I* am. I need help. Tell me something else."

"New allies," she said, nuzzling his ear. "Will you lie down for me?"

"It's begun, hasn't it?"

"I think so." She kissed him briefly, hard. "I want to ravish you."

"That's the sort of thing I like to hear. Anything you want," he said. He kept his arms around her as they shifted and stretched out on the bed of flower petals.

Maxime lay beneath her, his chest rising and falling with the nervous breaths he hadn't been able to control. His eyes fixed on her, large and dark. They were such a soft hue, like well-steeped black tea, with a ring of cinnamon color around the outer edges of the iris. As she bent low over him, she could feel his panting breath on her skin. Supporting herself on her arms, she bent closer to his mouth, brushing her breasts against his chin.

If she'd been less aroused, his beard might have been too prickly, but his quick breaths, his focused gaze, had made her skin ache to be touched all over. She shifted again and his mouth closed over her right nipple, drawing it out with his lips, then suckling, then drawing out again. She choked back a cry at the intense sensations that shot down her torso and twisted inside her womb. "Yes," she whispered to him, unable to stop the words. "Please, don't stop."

His hands lifted, cupping the sides of her breasts and holding them more closely to his mouth so he could easily tease one nipple and then the other. His thumbs brushed against her skin, maddening extra flickers of sensation that drove her arousal higher still. There was some noise behind her now, low voices in commentary, but she couldn't discern what they were saying and really didn't want to know. She shut the voices out and stared into Maxime's eyes. She couldn't remember if she had ever done that for so long a time before. She felt suddenly afraid, and to break the intensity bent to kiss his forehead and the corners of his eyes.

Maxime paused, slid one hand around the back of her neck and said softly, "I need you on my cock."

The bluntness of his need tightened her belly. "Do you want to be inside me?" she asked.

He shook his head, his fingers brushing restlessly over her skin. "Your hands, your cunt, it doesn't matter. Just, just be close. Please."

She kissed his mouth, deeply, messily. She let her arms collapse, let herself fall atop the solid support of his body. His cock felt rigid and hot against her thigh; still kissing him, she squirmed until his erection nestled between her thighs. He moaned softly and she pressed against him, harder.

Maxime stroked his hands down the length of her back, then gripped and kneaded her rear. "So good," he said. "You feel so good to me, Imena. I wish we could stay like this for days on end." He laid kisses on the side of her head, warm echoes of the damp throbbing inside her cunt.

"Maxime," she murmured, letting her lips brush his ear as she spoke. "I could take you like this."

"I would like that," he murmured back. "I like to watch your breasts. I like to watch your face when you're close to coming, and when you're trying to fight it off."

"Or," she said, quickly licking his ear and undulating against him, "I would like you to be deeper inside me." She hadn't said enough. He wouldn't understand. She drew in a deep breath, closed her eyes and spoke quickly, the words pouring forth like water. "So deep I can't sense anything but you against me, in me. I want you to come into me from behind, your hands grabbing my hips, squeezing my breasts, your chest rubbing against my back, your mouth at my ear, saying my name."

Maxime's fingers were going to leave bruises on her buttocks. After a long, gasping pause, he said, "You are going to kill me, sweeting."

"Will you do that for me?"

"I'd fuck you in front of the whole of Julien's court if you asked it of me," he said and half chuckled, half groaned. "Let's turn away from our audience, though, shall we? If you can't see my face, I don't want anyone else to see it, either."

Behind their pavilion lay trees. Imena stared at them with inner relief. She could lose herself in the forest, find distance from all observation. Except for Maxime. As he knelt behind her, leaned over her, wrapped one muscular arm around her waist and pressed his cock so slowly, so deliciously, into her cunt and against the walls of her inner passage, she could not see the trees and the freedom they offered. She closed her eyes and gave herself up to the feel of his skin against hers, inside and out, as he pushed deeper, deeper and deeper still.

She couldn't quite catch her breath; she needed all her air and strength to bear down on his cock with every inner muscle she possessed, and to thrust back against him so he would not withdraw from her, would not separate them. Maxime's belly heaved on her back, little sobbing breaths as his hips jerked against her, as sweat sprang between his chest and her back, his hand slipping in sweat over her taut abdomen, her breasts, and down into the upper folds of her cunt where she lay stretched wide open to his touch.

She was barely conscious of anything beyond the slick rubbing of his cock within her, every fraction of movement nearly unbearable against her swollen flesh that wanted nothing except more friction, deeper, faster, more. She let her head fall forward, cushioned by flower petals, and arched her back, working herself against him with blind fervor, each breath a sob of effort that squeezed her ever higher.

Maxime suddenly froze, his arm clenching her hard around the belly. "Imena," he said in her ear, his voice desperate. "Oh, Imena. I love you so much."

His hot breath scorched her ear and she cried out, bucking against him, writhing, her climax spilling out from her cunt in stormy waves, jerking her body against his belly, yanking crying sounds from her throat. As her convulsions slowed, she fell slack against his restraining arm and felt, impossibly, his cock swelling inside her.

He'd said something. He'd spoken her name, and—

She arched back against him, and with a cry he drove into her, deeper and faster than before, until he, too, came hard, his semen flooding down her thighs.

It was some time before Imena realized that their opponents had never reached climax, and that she and Maxime had won.

The most embarrassing thing about the whole experience, for Imena, was cleaning up afterward. Imena had to fight off the help of any number of jubilant islanders who wished to pamper their winners with all manner of locally manufactured unguents and intimate personal services. No doubt Maxime was more used to such things than she was; he at least had a personal servant who saw to his clothing and grooming, and a bevy of additional body servants for formal occasions requiring complex clothing and preparations. She knew for a fact he'd had casual sex with at least three of them, male and female alike. She preferred Norris, who would never intrude as they were being intruded upon now.

Maxime captured her hand and led her behind the pavilion, shouldering aside dozens of grasping hands. It wasn't much better, given that the pavilion had no sides, but after a few stern glances, their would-be helpers retreated, leaving a woven basket and a pile of clothing behind.

The music still played, and islanders mingled and danced in the clearing where before they'd argued. No one could hear them if they spoke in low voices. Imena found a towel in the basket and said, "If they follow us back to the boat they will recognize it comes from a larger ship." Briskly, she wiped herself down, beginning with her thighs and cunt.

"Then we won't let them follow us." After a brief hesitation, Maxime reached into the basket and removed a cloth for himself.

"If I were in command here," she said, "I would wonder where two such well-nourished castaways had sprung from. I'm not sure if Pauk or anyone else has begun to wonder." She grabbed her clothing, ragged and dirty as it was, and shimmied into it, breathing a sigh of relief once she was clothed. She'd feel better with the addition of her cutlass, but this would do for now.

"Then we'll get away from here quickly," Maxime said, tossing his used cloth onto the ground. "Should we slip away now? Most of them already seem to be involved in postcompetition celebratory flower-eating."

Imena thought, then shook her head. "I don't want any pursuit."

"I'll speak to Pauk, if you permit."

"I was hoping you'd be willing."

"Imena! Diplomacy is my second most valuable skill!"

Before negotiations began, Maxime demanded their knives and her cutlass back. Being granted her own weapon went a long way toward improving Imena's mood. She kept the cutlass in her hand while the two men spoke.

Pauk said, "And what of our usual prize? You seem like a man who would appreciate having his pick of our most attractive women, and I'm sure they'd appreciate you." Pauk smiled significantly. "Or you may have men, if that's your preference, though we have none to match those." He waved a hand toward their competition.

Maxime cast a glance at Imena, his eyes alight. "Do we have time, do you think?"

Imena scowled, only then noticing the naughty light in his eyes. "I think we have what we need," she said.

Maxime bowed to Pauk, short and formal. "Then we'd like to depart. If you've left our boat?"

"I offer escort, one of our young men."

"No need." Maxime paused and then said casually, "If

we should return. Could we claim our prizes then? Or perhaps some other services of commensurate value?"

Imena recognized the commanding tone in his voice, but she didn't think Pauk did. Pauk merely nodded, as if it were of no consequence, and popped a flower into his mouth. "I am sure we could come to some arrangement."

CHAPTER SIXTEEN

ONCE CLEAR OF THE BREAKERS, IMENA STOPPED rowing. "Hold on a moment," she said.

Maxime pulled in his oar and leaned back, stretching. Before he could ask why they were stopping, Imena slid over the side, clothes and all.

Washing off the experience? Or washing off *him?*

It was difficult not to feel hurt, even after she surfaced and, in her normal tones, said she'd be glad to mind the boat while he had his own dip.

He made a point of holding out his hand to help her climb over the boat's side. Her grip was firm, her hand cold from the sea; once she was back in the boat, she rubbed her head dry with a cloth and then busied herself with the oars.

Maxime yanked his shirt over his head and scrambled out of his trousers. There wasn't much room for dressing and undressing in the boat, but swimming in his clothes would be far too much like being in a shipwreck.

If only that had happened. He would have been content for quite some time as a castaway with her.

He slid into the water, sighing as it lapped at his shoulders, then kicked his feet up and floated. Salty seawater cleared the musty scent of flower petals from his nostrils, and it felt good to expose his flesh to nothing but the vast stretch of empty sky.

His earlier feeling of hurt washed away as waves lapped at his skin. Imena understood what it was to be in command, to always be watched. She had been right to give them this little time before they returned to her crew.

Maxime swam back to the boat and rested his forearms on the side, lazily treading water. "What are we going to say?"

Imena wasn't looking at him, but she rested her hand near his elbow. "I'm not sure," she said. "We can't leave yet. *Seaflower* isn't quite ready. We can't depend on avoiding the islanders for the rest of our stay, even if they are on another island."

"And if we encounter them? And they inform your crew that we're their champions?"

Imena shrugged.

"You're not worried for your dignity?"

"I'm the captain," she said. "My dignity is implicit."

Maxime grinned. "Even naked."

"Especially then." Slowly, she smiled back. "Are you planning to swim all the way back?"

"That depends on if you let me back into the boat."

She chewed her lip, pretending thoughtfulness. "I don't really want to row this boat by myself. You have quite a few more muscles than I."

"Showier ones, anyway," he said. Once back in the boat, he took a cloth from her and scrubbed at his hair and beard. "I have another question for you," he said after he'd struggled to pull his clothing back over his damp skin.

Imena found their water flask in the bottom of the boat and drank from it. "Another question about my dignity?"

"The islanders," he said, accepting the flask. "Is the location of these islands widely known? Are they charted?"

"It depends on one's charts," she said.

"Ah. For example, is this group of islands closer to the duchies, or to the Horizon Empire?" Her gaze flicked to him. He added, "I haven't thought this through yet. But it's best to be prepared for the future, isn't it? And wouldn't this make a lovely anchorage for certain times when you needed just that? Completely aside from possible benefit to the islanders. I don't think they can survive here indefinitely, not without outside help."

Imena pushed an oar into his hand. "We need to row."

A few minutes later, she said, "I had forgotten you were a duke."

"I forget quite frequently," he said.

"If you weren't a duke, or...if you wanted to give it up, would you have stayed? With the islanders?"

He answered without hesitation. "No." Then wondered why she'd asked.

Imena sounded thoughtful as she continued. "They

offered quite a few incentives. And I think you could have helped them."

"I could have. I've been trained to be a leader. That doesn't mean I want to lead every person I meet." And Imena would not have stayed with him. Would she?

"You might be safe there, in hiding," she said, and he realized the direction of her thoughts.

"I'm not going to hide, not like that. Would you?"

Imena sighed. "No. I wouldn't, either." Clearly changing the subject, she asked, "What if these islands are closer to the empire?"

That was easy enough. "Then you can tell your mother about the islanders if you wish. Or do nothing if you think that's better."

Leaning into her oar, Imena said, "We can decide later. I'll need to think on it."

"It's not as urgent as all that," he said. "But…they did treat us honorably. By their standards. They set us free in the end."

Her expression was eloquent, but she didn't argue. "Put your back into it," she said. "We can worry about the islanders once my ship is repaired, and we've figured out who's trying to kill you. And the pirates. I confess I'm a little worried about pirates just now."

He admitted that she did have a point.

CHAPTER SEVENTEEN

ONCE THEY'D SAFELY RETURNED TO CAMP, MAXIME decided he would see what he could do about Imena's worry. They had a source of information on the pirates ready to hand, thanks to Chetri. He spent the next two days observing Annja and Suzela as they went about their tasks: Suzela collecting fruit, shellfish and turtle eggs, and Annja working in turn with Kuan, Nabhi and then Seretse, the carpenter.

On the second morning, in a temporary lull in his ship work, Seretse set a blanket on the beach. Next to it, he laid out his tattooing tools, wooden handles with clusters of needles at one end. He'd recruited Annja to keep water boiling over a small fire, to supply him with a stream of clean cloths, which he used throughout the process to wipe blood and excess ink from his client's skin. Annja would also clean the needled tools of blood after they were used. Maxime thus had an excellent excuse to wander over and chat with her. He wasn't the only one who found the prospect of watching Seretse pound colored ink into people's skins fascinating.

Most of the time was spent on Kuan, whose back was already covered with outlines of fish; Seretse was coloring in a section of the outlines with soft, steady strokes. While he worked, Maxime asked Annja, "Where is Suzela?"

"She didn't want to watch this," Annja said. She, however, was watching avidly as she spoke. "Haven't you noticed that by now? She's soft as a jellyfish about some things."

"And you?"

Annja shrugged. "Kuan is willing to have this done to him, and Seretse is only hurting him as much as is necessary. I don't mind the blood, either." She grinned briefly at Maxime, and he blinked, startled. "We women, we bleed every month, and if we do it's a wonderful thing."

"I hadn't thought of it that way," he said. He rested his chin on his updrawn knees and watched as Seretse wiped blood and ink from Kuan's lower back. "Are you going to ask for a tattoo?"

Annja shrugged again, but her indifference seemed feigned. "I might." She sat for a time, watching, then added, "I like the ones Chetri has."

"Perhaps you could ask him about them," Maxime suggested.

"Hmmph." Annja lifted the lid of her water pot and peered inside. "Fetch me another bucket of water, will you?"

That afternoon, Maxime discreetly trailed Annja as she collected Suzela and Chetri and headed to a quiet inlet.

I'm not a voyeur, Maxime reassured himself, stretching out more comfortably on a warm rock. It overlooked the beach. *Chetri is too sympathetic to those women by far. Imena needs an objective opinion on them.*

In the tiny cove below him, the rock's shadow stretched on the sand, where Chetri had spread an array of woven blankets in bright colors. Chetri leaned over the edge of a blanket, using the shells of recently devoured mussels to scrape sand into a small mountain range. His hair was loose, drying slowly in the sun, and he wore only tattered trousers and one of his necklaces, and the earrings and brow ring he never removed. Annja and Suzela, in patterned linen wraps, sat near him, sucking the last scraps of freshly caught, freshly cooked flatfish from bones. It was a good thing Maxime had eaten before ensconcing himself on the rock.

Chetri abandoned his mountain range and leaned back on his elbows, closing his eyes against the late-afternoon sun, which glinted from his silver jewelry. Maxime noted with interest that neither of the women moved away from him, though there was plenty of room for them to do so. Suzela braided Annja's hair, then twisted her own river of curls into a loose knot, securing it with an eating utensil, or perhaps some device Maxime hadn't seen from above.

A few minutes later, Annja rose to bury fish bones in the sand. Chetri glanced at Suzela. "You've had enough to eat?" he asked.

Maxime noted he'd given her a question she could answer by a nod or a shake of the head. But Suzela, astonishing him, responded verbally. "Yes, thank you."

Annja looked up sharply. She stood and brushed sand off her knees. "We're going to talk?" she said.

Suzela nodded. "I think it's all right."

Chetri was staring at her, astonished. "You've never spoken before. I was beginning to think you couldn't."

Annja snorted. "She speaks when she needs to do so."

Suzela drew her feet beneath her before she continued. "Norris said…she said she had a secret, and that no one on the ship, no one, had ever betrayed that secret to anyone. She's been on the *Seaflower* four years, since she was twelve." Suzela's voice was rough, vibrant, the sort of voice that grabbed a man by the bollocks. It was almost, Maxime thought, as attractive as Imena's voice.

Chetri asked, his curiosity evident, "Did Norris share her secret with you?"

"No," Suzela said. "Was she telling the truth?"

"She was."

Annja sat next to Suzela and wrapped a protective arm around her shoulders. "We don't have to talk to them at all. We can leave if you want. I'll go with you. What kind of secrets could a twelve-year-old have?"

Suzela touched Annja's face. "It doesn't matter what sort of secret it is. If it's a small secret, then even better. I think we can trust them." She paused. "And you said I could be the one to choose."

"So I did," Annja said, her tone grudging. "This one did rescue us, after all. Not like that useless concubine."

It took Maxime a moment to realize she meant him. He bit his lip hard to keep from laughing.

Annja withdrew her arm from Suzela's shoulders and

resettled herself, arms crossed over her chest. "Go on, then. Tell him."

"And—" Suzela said.

Annja grinned. "Oh, yes, afterward, certainly that."

"Certainly *what?*" Chetri asked. "You can't simply run off. You have nowhere to go."

"We weren't talking about leaving," Annja said.

Suzela said quickly, "You wanted to know Captain Cassidy and Captain Litvinova."

Chetri turned slightly to face the women directly. "We do. It's true we've escaped them for now, but it's not unlikely we'll encounter them again. It's to your advantage to tell me what you know. We'll protect you. My captain will not give you back to them, after they treated you so poorly."

Suzela and Annja both nodded. Maxime was interested to note that Annja did so more emphatically; Suzela's nod was merely a confirmation. Suzela, it appeared, had made her decision based on other factors than her own immediate safety. She might, he thought, value loyalty, the loyalty that Imena's crew possessed and the pirates apparently did not.

Suzela said, "Would you like to tell him, Annja?"

Annja shrugged. "You wanted to know what Captain Litvinova was after, didn't you?"

"Among other things," Chetri said solemnly.

"Well, she wasn't sailing those waters by chance. She was looking for your ship, I think, or one like it."

"Looking for *us?* Why?"

Suzela said, "She talked of trading ships. Ships that had been to certain ports."

Chetri asked, "In the duchies, or the empire, or elsewhere?"

Good question, Maxime thought approvingly.

"Other ports," Suzela said. "I had never been to any of them, nor Annja."

Annja said, "She was interested in a kind of balsam. I'm afraid I don't know its name. It was new to her, and to her employer, and apparently very valuable."

Maxime had already guessed to which balsam they referred; he was interested to note that Chetri apparently had done the same, for he didn't mention it, neatly deflecting the conversation. "Her employer? I wasn't aware pirates had employers," he said.

Annja shrugged again. "Captain Litvinova needed funds. To get them, she had to look for this balsam. Captain Litvinova hired Venom to help her in case there was a fight, but she regretted it later."

"Who paid Captain Litvinova?" Chetri asked.

"It was a woman in the duchies. I had never heard of her before. She called herself a lady, though, as if she had status."

"The lady Diamanta," Suzela said.

Maxime was hard put not to exclaim aloud. He bent closer to the colloquy below. It was clear from the expression on Chetri's face that he had no idea who Diamanta might be.

Annja helped him. "Lady Diamanta said she was from the court of King Julien of the duchies."

"Ah," Chetri said. "Do you know if she was interested in anything aside from this balsam? Did she say anything more about the duchies? About anyone in particular from there?"

Suzela shook her head. Annja shrugged. "No, no one else. It was all for money, as usual. Everything comes down to payment in the end."

"Not everything," Suzela said. "There's giving."

Annja's expression softened, and she brushed her fingers down Suzela's arm. "For you, maybe there is." She turned to Chetri again. "We know more, but none of it is quite as important, I think."

"Will you speak to the captain about this? And answer all her questions?"

"We will," Suzela said. "Both of us."

"Then I thank you," Chetri said.

Suzela said, "If she will permit, we will swear our loyalty. I'll stand surety for Annja."

"We all stand surety for ourselves," Chetri said. He looked at Annja, his expression solemn. "If you didn't want to do that, we wouldn't abandon you. We'd take you to the nearest port, make sure you could get to a safe place. The captain's employer would insist upon it. To him it's a small expense."

Annja shrugged. "I'll do what's necessary to stay with Suzela. I have no plans to betray your ship to pirates. I hardly want to return to them, do I?"

"Good," Chetri said. "Then perhaps we should return to the camp."

"Not yet," Suzela said. Sudden silence fell. Maxime, who'd been about to slide discreetly off his rock, froze. When he dared to peer over the edge of the rocks again,

Suzela was kissing Chetri, both her hands gripped in his long hair.

Maxime could hardly depart after *that*. If they heard or saw him, they would be embarrassed, and what if the women refused to share any more information?

His conscience twinged. He and Imena certainly hadn't liked being watched. But that had been different, much different. This was an accident, and also he would apologize later, if it seemed the right thing to do. And also…

Chetri was grinning and looking dazed. Maxime recalled that shore leave had been curtailed on his own behalf. Chetri didn't have a regular partner aboard *Seaflower* and Maxime didn't think he had an occasional partner, either. Chetri would not thank him if he interrupted.

Chetri was stroking Suzela's cheek; then he turned just slightly and wrapped his free arm around Annja's shoulders, holding her close. Annja ducked her head and hid her face in his neck.

Maxime swallowed. He would wait a few moments, that was all, until the trio became too involved to pay attention to their surroundings, and then he would slide off the rock and return to camp. He needed to see Imena, to pass on what he'd learned.

Maxime found Imena in their tent, reading through long lists and making occasional notes. She must have tucked her pen behind her ear at some point, because a smudge of ink marked her temple. He let the tent flap fall shut behind him and knelt beside her.

She looked up, clearly abstracted, and smiled at him.

He couldn't help but smile back. He kissed her. "I have information from Annja and Suzela."

She stiffened, but only for an instant. Wondering, he realized with anger that swiftly turned to sadness, how he'd obtained this information. "I didn't," he said. "Imena, I don't think I could."

She lowered her gaze, then looked up again, her eyes meeting his. "I'm sorry, Maxime. I don't think that anymore, not really."

If she didn't think that of him, she would not have stiffened, but he accepted the apology, not wanting to argue with her, not now. "Thank you."

"The information?" she asked, clearly not wanting to argue, either.

"Suzela can speak, did you know?"

Imena shook her head. "I'm glad."

"She's a cautious woman, and from what I overheard, I think she's the true leader of that pair."

"Tell me."

Maxime related how he'd seen the two women with Chetri, skipping over the more intimate aspects of the conversation. He finished by telling her, "So the pirates weren't sent after me. Captain Litvinova never mentioned anyone from the duchies, except for Diamanta."

Imena stretched her neck first to one side, then to the other. "So someone else entirely is trying to kill you. Someone tied to Lady Diamanta."

"Yes, the pirates were only trying to kill *you*. Well, not trying to *kill* you exactly, but pursuing you and your knowledge. I feel much better now."

Imena snorted a laugh, then said, "We still don't know who's plotting against you in the duchies."

"But now we have enough information to begin a few inquiries. We need to visit a port, Imena."

"Yes. We need current news. Yes, I think we must take the risk."

CHAPTER EIGHTEEN

SYLVIE SHARPENED HER KNIFE WHILE ALYS OPENED the letter. "It's from— Oh," she said, abruptly disappointed. "I can't read it." Then she looked over at Sylvie, eyes shining. "It's ciphered!"

Sylvie put aside her knife and wiped oil from her hands on a clean rag. "Give it to me."

"If you show me the cipher, I could—"

Sylvie gestured. Alys handed over the letter, then gathered up the sharpening stone and the little flask of oil while trying to look over Sylvie's shoulder.

The cipher was a variant on one Sylvie had been taught by the eunuch Kaspar, who was Duchess Camille's chief guard. Sylvie had used the cipher often enough with her sometime lover, a brothel owner called Karl Fouet, that she could read it easily without recourse to pen and paper.

My lioness: Our conspirator is not wise. My first inquiries among the usual suspects led to tales of rewards offered for secret entry to the ducal castle. I enlisted our friends Kaspar and Arno to gently question those who'd spread the tales. Two of them were in port on the night in question, and were the originators. They were paid by a courtier who attempted to dress as a merchant. I recognized their description easily enough. The man has a mole high on his left cheekbone and blue eyes. He's visited my brothel. He will do so no more. It was Lord Odell. I've retained the witnesses until Lady Gisele can send an escort for them.

Scribbled at the bottom, in a more private cipher, he'd added:

It has been too long, my lioness. You must come and visit me when this is concluded, and I will entertain you to the best of my ability. I've created a new room in the lower levels that is completely dark and lined entirely in silk velvet. I am sure you will make use of it most creatively.
Your Karl

Once the delicious ideas for Karl's new room had finished swirling through her mind, Sylvie said, "So."

Alys stopped what she was doing in midmotion. If she'd been a puppy, her ears would have pricked. Sylvie considered withholding the information, but it would be unnecessarily cruel, and she needed Alys to help her.

"My contacts have identified our culprit."

"Not the mysterious Raoul," Alys said. She had formed

her own theories, and shared them with Sylvie whenever she was allowed. Sylvie forgave her for it, because Alys's well-practiced look of stupid innocence had been so successful among the palace servants.

She said, "No. The culprit is lord high steward of the Duke's Council."

"Odell!" Alys bounced on her toes. "The man Her Grace Camille did not like!"

"Madame is very astute," Sylvie agreed. "Now we must prove his motive."

"Money," Alys said.

"That is no doubt part of it. It's clear he's ambitious. But I suspect something more is at the heart of it. He's been too reckless for it to be otherwise."

"Tell me what I'm to find out next."

Sylvie tapped the letter against her leg. "First, I will destroy this letter. Second, I will write a note to Odell, which you will deliver."

Alys curtsied. "Yes, madame."

Sylvie decided that Raoul could be trusted with at least some of the truth. After leaving Alys to deliver the forged note, she found him in his chambers and invited him for a stroll in the gardens, where she outlined her investigation and requested his aid. And accompanied him to the gazebo afterward.

She had the key to the plot, she knew it through intuition. If Sylvie waited a little longer, to see the outcome of her forged note, she would have proof.

The following day, she and Raoul sat together at an outdoor table in the palace garden. Courtiers circled the white-graveled paths, chatting and eating and drinking hot sweet mead, seemingly aimless. Sylvie knew better. Intrigue scented the air more richly than the roses. She forked a bite of cake into her mouth and murmured to Raoul, "Stare into my eyes."

"What?" Raoul said. His mouth was full of cake, and a crumb of almond icing clung to the corner of his lips. She brushed it off with her thumb.

"Yes, like that. I'm watching Lord Odell, but I wish to appear as if I'm completely involved with you."

Raoul finished his mead. A liveried servant instantly appeared to pour him more from a silver pot with a long spout. Steam rose from his goblet as the servant retreated. When they were private once more, he said, "I've told you, Lady Diamanta won't have him. I've been watching these past three days."

"And that is the answer," Sylvie said. She took another leisurely bite of cake, licking every scrap of icing from the silver tines of her fork. "She won't have him. He is angry."

"That has nothing to do with your duke."

"Not my duke," she reminded him. "It doesn't matter. He can be blamed."

Raoul sipped more mead. "When she wouldn't have *me,* I found the next beautiful woman and gave her free use of my person." He grinned.

"Not all men are as wise as you are," Sylvie noted. She laid her hand atop his gloved one. "Hush. There she is."

Lady Diamanta appeared from behind a bush cut into the shape of a stag. Her long blond hair was dressed atop her head in pinned curls adorned with fuchsia ribbons; her pale pink gown, of thin wool with a slight sheen, began high on her throat and cascaded to the pointed toes of her boots. A chain around her neck suspended an enamel pendant against her large, shapely breasts; Sylvie appreciated her bosom for a few moments, then blinked and peered more closely when she recognized the pendant's shape. It was one of Captain Leung's recent imports from the western lands. She'd seen that pendant, or one very like it, when last she'd visited Maxime's duchy. His aunt Gisele had demonstrated how the top slid to one side, revealing a tiny casket of rare balsam mixed with purified sheep fat, which sounded revolting but smelled divine. Gisele had said the concoction faded all sorts of imperfections of the skin, bumps and scars alike.

A valuable item, and rare. Maxime must have given the balsam to Diamanta as a gift when he'd rejected her as his bride. It was a motive. Not for murder, but instead a motive that implied Diamanta had an interest in Maxime's survival, even if he would not marry her. Diamanta might even be better off without a husband, as she would not have to share her monetary gains.

It came down to money. There would be more money to be made if Diamanta could deal with Maxime and his fleet of trading ships. With Maxime dead, who knew what the king would do, and whether Diamanta would have any chance to insinuate herself?

Raoul squeezed her hand hard. Sylvie blinked at him. He murmured, "You were staring. I'm the one who's supposed to stare at her."

"She does have a most impressive bosom," Sylvie noted.

"I don't think you were looking at her bosom. What do you suspect? I still don't think she would involve herself in an assassination plot."

"But a plot involving commerce?" she asked.

Raoul nodded. "Oh, yes." He grinned. "She is amazing. Before I took her contract, I read some of her previous contracts with importers in the peninsula. She took every legal advantage."

Sylvie said, "I think her greed marks her innocence."

Raoul frowned. "I'm not sure I see your logic."

"In the matter of assassination," she clarified. Movement caught her eye, and she said, "Hush. There he is."

Lord Odell was a tall man, elegantly dressed, with long wavy hair he habitually wore loose. His sideburns emphasized the jut of his cheekbones and the mole on the left one. At the moment, he was striding rapidly toward Lady Diamanta, who'd just accepted a goblet of spiced mead from a servitor.

Sylvie murmured, "Watch her. I will watch him."

Odell did not speak to Diamanta as far as Sylvie could see; he simply strode to her side, seized her upper arm and kissed her.

A moment later, he flew backward amid a spray of hot mead. His velvet-covered rear skidded along the fine white gravel.

Conversations ceased abruptly.

Then a crisp, authoritative voice snapped, "What's going on here?" and the silent onlookers froze in place, some with goblets half lifted.

King Julien had made an appearance.

He was flanked by two guards, enormous men carrying swords who wore leather jerkins and vambraces. The leather had been dyed purple and inset with silver in the royal crest, an eagle bearing a sword and a scroll in its talons. The crest also adorned each guard's helmet.

Julien himself was, Sylvie noted with surprise, not overly tall or muscular, and he wore spectacles like a clerk. When she'd last seen him, at Maxime's ascension to duke, he'd seemed much larger in his formal robes and headgear. His face had been bare. Seen close to, she might not have recognized him except for his guards. Julien's tunic and trousers fit him beautifully, and his tall boots gleamed in the way only extremely expensive boots could gleam, but he wore no jewelry save a signet ring, and his plain brown hair had been cropped almost as short as a soldier's. It stuck out at undignified angles.

Sylvie remembered she had intended to watch Odell, and looked back at him just as he scrambled to his feet, his expression blank. Diamanta scowled. When Julien's gaze found her, she tossed her empty goblet to the ground near Odell's feet. "You've interrupted the entertainment, cousin," she said.

Julien's gaze snapped to Odell. "Why are you here, Odell? I left you preparing letters." He turned away briefly, and addressed the courtiers. "Get back to enjoying yourselves!"

Amid the rising hum of movement and conversation, Sylvie realized she might not be able to hear what transpired. She slid from her seat, stopping Raoul's similar movement with a glance. Carrying her goblet, she ducked behind a bush cut into the shape of a hound, close to the king. One of Julien's guards stared at her, easily able to see her over the top of the branches. She smiled flirtatiously, licking her lips. The guard scowled, but did not ask her to move away.

Odell stepped closer to the king, bowed deeply then straightened again, clasping his hands behind his back. Diamanta seemed about to move off, but was summoned closer, as well, with one glance from Julien. The guards turned their backs on the small group, effectively shutting away outsiders.

Odell said, "I received an urgent note, Your Majesty. Lady Diamanta summoned me here."

"I did not," she said.

Sylvie waited, breathless, for more, but Diamanta was silent and proud. She could easily begin to admire Diamanta, as well as her bosom.

Julien said, "Odell, this must stop. Diamanta, you must stop him. It's beneath my dignity to curate my courtiers' affairs. You will settle this now."

"Very well," Diamanta said. Turning to Odell, she said briefly, "You're a toad. Never speak to me again."

While Odell goggled and Sylvie held in a delighted *whoop,* Diamanta turned to Julien and said, "Is that sufficient, cousin?"

"Your Majesty—"

"No more, Odell. Attend to your duties. No more trips to the coast, no more unsavory visitors to my palace late at night. I've had enough of your romantic intrigues."

Blanched white as a peeled almond, Odell bowed. "Your Majesty," he said in a choked voice.

"Leave us."

"Your Majesty."

When Odell had gone, Julien said, "Diamanta?"

"He was persistent," she said with a cold dignity that reminded Sylvie, suddenly and forcefully, of Duchess Camille.

"I have never known you to hesitate in expressing your preferences."

"I did not hesitate. He was persistent."

Julien waited. When she said nothing further, he nodded. "Very well. We will meet in my office in three hours by the clock. We have much to discuss."

Diamanta dipped her head in acknowledgment of the command. "Your Majesty."

Sylvie was not pleased. She had never planned to eavesdrop in the private office of the king. There were no handy nearby rooms or corridors where one might loiter unobserved; footmen lined the approach and guards were posted at the doors. There were no windows. Not even servants were permitted into the room when the king was present.

Therefore, she would not try to eavesdrop on that meeting. She would simply request an appointment beforehand.

From what she'd overheard, she suspected the king did not know the full extent of Odell's machinations. He might have been concealing all he knew, but she could not count on that. She needed to speak with him; it would be the quickest and most effective way to ensure Duke Maxime's safety, and beyond that, Duchess Camille's, as she might be blamed for Sylvie's actions should anything go wrong. And aside from that, Sylvie now feared for Lady Diamanta's safety. She did not think Odell would admire Diamanta's public rejection in the way Sylvie had done. And that...had been brought about by Sylvie herself. It had needed to be done, but she wished...she was not sure what she wished. For the world to be different, perhaps, but she knew that was foolishness.

She found Alys in their chambers, exuberant from the success of the note she'd delivered. Raoul was also there, lounging in a padded armchair with his booted feet on a stool. He slid catlike to his feet when she strode into the room, all in one motion. "What shall we do next?" he said.

Sylvie caught Alys's arm and held her still. "Tidy yourself and go to the king's secretary. Request an urgent meeting with Duchess Camille's envoy." She reached into her bosom and produced a small silken bag that contained one of the duchess's seals. She placed it in Alys's hand.

Eyes shining, Alys bounced a curtsy. "Yes, Sylvie!"

When the girl had gone, Sylvie turned to Raoul. "I will need your help to get out of this dress."

He smiled. "I am, of course, willing to oblige you."

"Quickly," she amended. "I need to appear with the utmost dignity and probity."

Wisely, Raoul did not comment on this. He helped Sylvie out of her garden-party garb and into a sober gown of blue wool. In the process, she divested herself of a knife in a thigh harness, a knife concealed in her busk and a miniature pistol that normally resided in a snug pocket at her hip.

Raoul said, "If I'd known you were armed so heavily, I might never have approached you."

"You were not meant to know," she replied tartly. "The king's guards, however, will not hesitate to search me with great thoroughness."

While kneeling at her feet to lace up her boots, he asked, "What will you do if he refuses to speak with you?"

"He will not."

Raoul caressed her calf. "And once you've met with the king? What then?"

Sylvie shrugged. "I will likely travel to the coastal duchy, to relate what I've done here."

He patted her leg and sat back on his heels. "Would you be distressed if I accompanied you? I'd like to visit there, and perhaps find a new commission."

Sylvie studied his lithely handsome form. "I would not be averse. For a time."

Sylvie was relieved when Alys brought word that the king would see her. While dressing, she'd mentally placed all her discoveries in logical order, all the while aware that when she presented them to the king, he might listen or he might throw her into a cell.

As she'd expected, a female guard, one of the few in the royal palace, searched her thoroughly before her appointment. Then a discreet servant tidied Sylvie's hair, a service which she found ludicrous but also reassuring; she would not go before the king without dignity.

She was escorted into the royal presence by two guards, both of whom remained in the room with their backs to the two doors. King Julien did not sit behind the massive polished desk that filled a third of his private office. Instead, he'd chosen a corner of a small sofa, one arm flung along its back, one booted foot curled beneath him. Sylvie was sure he knew how disturbing his informal pose was to her. She did not believe for a moment she would be allowed so much as a slouch. Not when his eyes, behind their spectacles, were so intense. She curtsied deeply, her head dipping and her full skirts pooling on the polished hardwood floor. He indicated with a wave of his hand that she should sit on the sofa with him.

Julien dug into his trouser's pocket and produced Duchess Camille's gold seal. He held it out to Sylvie without speaking, so she took it. It was warm, which should not have disconcerted her but did. He said, "I remember you. You're Camille's chief maid."

"Yes, Your Majesty."

"And her bodyguard, and her spy. I imagine she relied on you to help her get rid of her husband. That might have ended badly for her and for you. You were lucky I didn't have your head lopped off for treason." It was a statement. He quirked a questioning brow.

"Yes, Your Majesty." She curled her fingers more tightly around the gold seal. If he meant to destroy her composure, he was fast succeeding.

"Through her, you owe loyalty to me, as well."

"I am your subject," Sylvie said cautiously. For the first time in her life, she was confident that flattery and promises of sexual favors would get her nowhere. She was not entirely sure what the king expected of her. But she had to do this. Her mistress relied upon her. She opened her mouth, then closed it. Julien had not given her leave.

He sat silently staring at her. She didn't know how, but his spectacles made it worse. Sylvie fought the desire to close her eyes. She could hear breathing, and the ticking of the immense ormolu clock on the mantel. One of the guards shifted his weight, and she tensed.

At last, Julien said, "Tell me what you're doing here. Did Maxime ask Camille for your help?"

"No, Your Majesty."

He quirked a brow. "It is because of His Grace Maxime that I am here, however," she said. "There was a plot to assassinate him…" She began at the beginning, giving credit to Captain Leung for ensuring Maxime's safety. Julien did not stop her at any point. When she paused to breathe, he again lifted a brow, encouraging her to go on.

She left out most of the mundane details of her investigation. If any were of concern to him, no doubt his own spies would have reported her activities, and those of Alys. But she did include the report she'd had from Karl Fouet. The king would know of Karl, as he'd also assisted in bringing Duchess Camille to power. Whether the king trusted Karl or not was another thing entirely.

When she'd finished speaking, Julien said, "Ah."

Sylvie waited for an additional question. Instead, he said, "Marco."

One of the guards said, "Your Majesty."

"Send two of your men to fetch Lord Odell. No explanations. Put him in a cell."

Marco nodded and stepped outside the door. Within

moments, he returned, resuming his stance as if nothing had happened.

Julien said to Sylvie, "You will accompany me to Maxime's duchy. Marco."

"Yes, Your Majesty."

"Inform Lady Diamanta that I wish to speak with her. And have her maid pack for her. She will accompany us also."

CHAPTER NINETEEN

"I AM SO HAPPY TO BE BACK AT SEA," IMENA SAID. She was leaning on the rail at *Seaflower*'s bow, a fine salty mist blowing against her face and beading on the long woolen coat she'd buttoned on against the evening's chill. "Let's hope we're finished with pirates and storms for now."

Maxime stood at her shoulder, his arms bared to the breeze. She might easily have leaned over and licked salty droplets from his shoulder, but refrained, given that they'd spent most of the night, their last on land, making the tide with silent urgency. They'd barely had a chance for a quick dip in the sea before it had been time to tow *Seaflower* past the reef.

The rest of the day, for her, had been satisfyingly full of hard work. All the rigging had needed to be tested and adjusted to peak efficiency, and every inch of the ship inspected to make sure the stresses of sailing had not revealed any weakness in their repairs. She'd been on her feet all day, except when she hung by her knees.

She realized she'd covered Maxime's hand on the railing with her own, was rubbing his skin with her thumb. "Let's go below," she said.

"More inspections?" he asked. The corner of his mouth lifted slightly, making it clear he wasn't referring to her work.

"Of a sort," she said, returning an arch look. "Roxanne is on duty now. I don't need to be on deck."

"It's lovely up here, if you want to stay," Maxime said. "I would stay with you."

"You'd rather that than go below with me?"

"Only if it's what you would prefer," he said. "You don't have to cater to my wants, Imena."

She grinned. "Oh, I have wants, as well. Surely last night taught you that, if you didn't know it already."

Maxime shrugged. "For you, I am always willing," he said.

She looked at him closely, to see if he was joking. He appeared solemn, too solemn. She wondered if he was still upset that she'd doubted him about Annja and Suzela.

She turned back to the sea, though she could sense him watching her. Without looking at him, she reached out her hand. He took it in his, and she twined their fingers together.

Music swirled up from the stern, pipes and single-string and drumming, soon joined by voices raised in song and the syncopated thump of feet on the deck. "Or we could dance," she said. "For a while."

He grinned and gripped her waist, momentarily lifting

her off her feet. "One dance, and then another," he said. "That's what this evening has been missing. Shall we head sternward?"

"Here," she said. "We can hear the music perfectly well." And she wanted him all to herself. If they joined the celebrating crew, he would feel obliged to talk and dance with anyone who asked, and she could not be an anonymous reveler, either.

Without further discussion, Maxime swept her into a swirling couples pattern that she recognized from the duchies. The bounds of the deck weren't calibrated for dances that traveled, but they made do, adding breath-stealing twirls and the occasional impromptu hop over a bollard. For a few steps, Maxime even lifted her, swinging her feet on empty air until she couldn't stop laughing.

The music slowed and stopped. Gasping, she leaned on Maxime, her arms looped around his waist. He kissed her somewhere near her ear and lifted her off the ground once more, squeezing her tightly before he set her down again.

From the stern, she heard the clink of mugs as the frolicking crew refreshed themselves. "Let's go below," she said. "We can have a drink in our cabin."

"*Our* cabin, is it?" he asked as they went below.

She hadn't realized she'd said it until he repeated her words. "You'd prefer me to say *your* cabin?" she asked.

Maxime chortled, and held the door open for her. "What do you have to drink?"

Imena took off her coat before she went to the relevant trunk, removed its covering and flipped up the lid. A third of the space was taken up by a wooden rack that supported an assortment of bottles, some made from glass, some from ceramic. Maxime peered around her shoulder. "Is that the stuff made from cactus?" he asked incredulously, pointing out a round ceramic jar wrapped in rope. It was shoved in atop some extra blankets.

"I think so," she said. "Yes. I remember. It tastes like green fire, and the morning after…ugh. Do you want any?"

"Definitely not," he said, "if, that is, you expect me to do any more dancing."

She pulled out a clear, golden honey wine and a murkier, somewhat stronger wine made from rice. "One of these?"

"The honey wine," he said. "I haven't had that in years."

They sat cross-legged on her bunk to sip the wine from tiny blue glasses. Imena looked up to find Maxime watching her. He didn't say anything immediately, only held her gaze for several breaths, her heartbeat quickening with each breath. She reached over and placed the glass into its niche, then leaned forward and laid her palms against his cheeks.

Maxime lifted his glass and pressed it to her lips. The rim was warm from his mouth. He tipped the glass and she drank, then kissed him, pushing a little of the wine into his mouth. He sipped from his glass and did the same, and they continued until both glasses were empty and her head swam with timeless desire.

Maxime's hands loosely encompassed her forearms, sliding from wrist to elbow and back again in a gesture that was both soothing and inflaming. "Shall we have another night like the last?" he asked. "We don't have to talk."

He sounded...wistful. "I thought you liked what we did," she said. To her, it had been reassuring to be private, to know no one was watching them, and to have the freedom to go completely within herself for long minutes at a time without worrying that some disaster might befall them, outside of her attention.

"I always like sex with you," Maxime said. He tugged her toward him and kissed the end of her nose. "I also like to talk with you."

Imena pulled out of his grip. "What's the matter?" she asked. "What are you trying to tell me? Stop being diplomatic and just tell me."

For a moment, Maxime looked as uncomfortable as she'd ever seen him. "You don't love me, do you?"

Imena couldn't catch her breath. When she didn't immediately reply, he looked away from her, lashes lowered to protect his eyes, arms curling to protect his upper body. From her.

He said, his voice low, "I love you, Imena." She tensed, waiting for more, but for the first time in her experience, he stopped speaking and simply looked at her.

She slid off the bunk and paced to the porthole. "You did say it, back on the island, didn't you?" she said. "I wasn't sure. And then I thought I'd imagined it."

He gave a short, harsh laugh. "The first time in my life I tell a person I love them, and they're not listening."

She whirled on him. "The situation was considerably distracting."

His mouth twisted. "You had my prodigious cock to

distract you." He caught his breath. "Ah, Imena. I'm sorry. I didn't mean that. I'm just a little upset. I had planned that this would be slow, romantic, tender, elegant. Me on my knees before you. You smiling down at me. I've been dreaming, haven't I? Making stories in my head."

Her throat tightened, as if he'd yanked on a knot. "You can't love me," she said. "You just can't."

"I can do what I like," he said. "You might not want to marry me, but that won't change my feelings for you."

"I can't marry you," she said desperately. "I can't. You're my employer, and you're a duke, and you need to marry someone else." She said the words, already knowing he didn't want to marry someone else, or he would have said so; that his position and hers meant nothing to him; and that their employment relationship could easily change. Easily. So easily, she could have him, have a partner and a life in the duchies, perhaps even children, and all she had to do was hold out her hands to accept it. Accept him.

She couldn't hold out her hands. Couldn't take that risk.

He said, "I meant it, you know, when I asked you to marry me. If you married me, and didn't love me, I would understand. I would do that for you. But I love you. When I told you so back on the island, I had hoped you would tell me yes or no. But you said nothing. And when it comes to you, Imena, I want you so badly I can't trust my own instincts. So I'm asking if you'll tell me. If you love me. If you think you might one day. If you would truly and honestly consider marrying me."

She fancied she could hear his heart beating in concert with hers, but it was her own heart, pounding doubly hard in her ears as she closed her eyes and tried to say the words she knew must be said.

Maxime's hand slid around her waist, then he pulled her against him, all warm flesh against her back, his cheek pressed to the side of her head, his arms holding her upright, warming her, steadying her.

He was always there for her, just like that: a solid, warm presence guarding her back.

She swallowed the lump in her throat. "I was wrong the last time," she said.

"On the island?" he murmured.

"No. The last time I thought I could have a relationship with my employer."

His hands stroked her, soothing rather than arousing. "It wasn't just that he was your employer, was it? Tell me."

"I should," she said. "After what you told me back on the island."

"You don't have to unless you want to," he said. He took a breath and said, "I'm not sure I would have told you those things if I had been able to hide them from you." He paused again, then said, "You don't have to tell me. I won't think less of you."

"Hold me tighter," she said.

This time she did hear his heartbeat; she could feel it against her back. Deliberately, she slowed her breathing to match his, and gradually she relaxed against him. He shifted his weight until they were even closer than before, in body at least.

"After I left off being a privateer," she began, "it wasn't easy to find another ship. Even in the empire. There's always a suspicion of piracy, even when you've spent years fighting piracy. I suppose you know not all privateers are as scrupulous as we were."

She opened her eyes and stared out the porthole into the darkness. "I didn't want to be dependent on my mother. It seems ridiculous, when she could easily, willingly, have found me some sort of position, but I'd been on my own for several years by then. The things she expected of me… it was like wearing an anchor around my neck, growing heavier each time she told me I should apply for an exemption to enter the navy, should enter the civil service and work unpaid in the hope of an honorary position, or that I should marry. Going back would have been horrible, and I would have felt a failure."

She turned in Maxime's embrace and wrapped her arms around his waist, pillowing her cheek against his chest. "I went to the borders of the empire, and beyond. I was running out of money when I found a ship that would take me as its starmaster."

"You trained as a starmaster," he said. "I remember."

"I never imagined I would find something as good as that, not at first. I was willing to sail as a common sailor. I thought…my hair had grown back by then. My tattoos weren't visible. I thought that was the reason I was hired this time, when all the times before I'd been denied. But it wasn't the reason."

Maxime's hands slid up and down her back, pressing softly. She continued, "Even though I needed money desperately, I considered refusing the position. Privateers have honor, you know. We have to. Otherwise, it's too easy to slip, to become like the pirates we hunt. I went back the next day to tell the captain I'd been a privateer. But he already knew. He said he'd seen me in the port and been smitten by me, that he'd been driven to find out more. That the offer of a berth came after he knew I had the skills he needed, but that wasn't his first interest in me."

She paused, gathering herself. "He was charming, amusing. I liked him. We were good together. He spoke of a partnership. I began to imagine marriage. It was the first time I'd allowed myself to think of marrying. I was drunk with the idea. It seemed like a freedom I'd never before known."

She stopped, and swallowed. "I think I need more of the wine," she said.

"I'll pour," Maxime said. He brought a single glass back to the porthole and they drank one after the other. She sat on one of her padded trunks and he sat next to her, holding her close to his side.

She took another tingling swallow of the wine, and said, "I thought I loved him. I did love him."

She fell silent. After he'd finished the wine, Maxime said, "But?"

"He was a pirate."

"Ah. Surreptitious, I take it."

"Yes. Otherwise I would have known immediately. But he was mostly opportunistic. Called it salvage. Even when crew was still aboard a damaged ship. I wouldn't have learned of it at all, except…the purser was ill. I helped her with her inventory. I knew our ship had never legally taken on some of the cargo I found."

"And you confronted him?"

She nodded. Her throat drew tight, preventing her from speaking. Maxime rubbed his hand over her back and kissed the top of her head. When she could speak again, she said, "I thought I was pregnant."

"Were you?"

"No. I think—I think now that I was late because I was so upset about what I'd discovered. I made sure of the piracy before I said anything to him. I spoke to the other officers, I spoke to the crew. I was very careful not to let them know my opinion on the matter. I wanted to have all the evidence before...before—" She stopped. She didn't want to relive those days, not now.

"What happened?"

"What do you think?"

"He betrayed you," Maxime said softly, squeezing her against him.

"He had me tossed over the side," she said. "If I hadn't made friends with the purser, and she'd sent one of the boats down to me, I would have died. I nearly died anyway." She stopped, swallowed. "When I reached land, I reported him. He was caught later, and executed. Do you see? You understand why I can't just—" Unable to continue, she laid her hand on his thigh and held it tightly.

"Let's go to bed," Maxime said. "You need sleep."

"I'm not finished," she said. "When he was caught. There was a reward. A substantial reward. And I was still licensed as a privateer, though without a ship. So the reward went to me. All of it, since I had no shipmates with whom to share it. I used the money to buy *Seaflower*. I took his betrayal, and I bought myself a life with it."

Maxime said, "Good."

"It was blood money," she said.

"The knothole-fucker threw you overboard," Maxime snarled. "He said he loved you, and then he threw you overboard." He cupped her face in his palms, his expression fierce. "You had no choice but to turn him in. You did your job, and you did it well. He was no different from any of the others, except in the way you felt about him. But that can't change what he was."

"I know that," she said. "I know."

"Believe it, then. You earned this ship. Every plank and peg." He kissed her, lingering. "Come to bed, Imena. I'll make you forget it all for a while. We can talk more in the morning."

"I want you to make me forget, but it's wrong. Wrong of me to want that."

He smiled gently. "Not if I say it isn't. Not if I want to do this for you."

"Take your clothes off," she said, stripping off hers with shaking hands. "I want to touch you all over."

When they were both naked, Maxime caught her up in his arms and laid her in the bunk. "Lie down," he said. "Let me massage your shoulders. I don't want your head to snap off while we're making the tide."

She tried to laugh, but only managed a croak. "Don't put me to sleep."

"I wouldn't dare," he said. He put his hand on the back of her head and pressed down. "Lie still. Breathe."

"I don't know," she said after she'd turned her head to the side. His large hands closed over her shoulders and squeezed. It felt so wonderful that tears sprang to her eyes. "I don't know if I can marry you, Maxime. I don't want to marry a stranger whom my parents have chosen, but I don't know if I can marry you. What if it all goes wrong?"

He sighed. "We could talk about this in the morning."

"I have to do it now, before I lose my courage."

"You, lose your courage," he said, with heavy irony. He leaned down and kissed her ear before resuming his massage.

"Yes, me," she said. "You don't know that about me. You think you can depend on me, that I'm never afraid."

"I can depend on you. Because you *are* afraid." The manipulations of his fingers crushed out any reply she might have made into a soft moan. "If you're saying I don't know your faults, then please, tell me them. I can refute you for hours on end. It'll be great fun."

"Maxime!"

"I'm sorry," he said.

"Listen to me. I don't know if you can trust me. I don't know how to mingle work with emotions, and I might betray you."

Maxime's hands stilled. "Betray me. How? By discovering I'm a pirate?"

Imena rolled onto her back and glared up at him. "That is not what I meant."

"Isn't it?"

"Answering questions with questions infuriates me," she growled.

"It's effective," he said. "If I was a pirate or, for example, someone in my employ turned to piracy, I would want to know. You know that. Don't you?"

"Yes." She paused, and amended. "My mind knows it."

Maxime sat on the edge of the bed. He rested one hand flat on her belly. "We aren't going to solve this tonight."

"I'm afraid."

"I'm pretending I'm not," he said.

"Pretending very well."

"I have years of practice." He leaned down and kissed her belly, then her breast. "If you won't let me massage you, then perhaps we should make the tide." His hand slid down her thighs. He brushed between them with his thumb, a pang of pleasure. Imena sighed and eased her thighs apart.

"No more. Just come into me, please."

Maxime looked at her, seemed about to speak, but then didn't. He climbed into her bunk and pushed her knees apart with his hands before entering her.

"More," Imena whispered into his ear.

He nuzzled her cheek and throat. His hips nudged at her gently. "In time. It's low tide, not a squall." His mouth closed over hers, and she shut her eyes, losing herself in the hot wetness of his kiss and the steady pressure of his chest on hers.

Gradually, he eased his cock inside her, each increment a new hint of pleasure. She wasn't sure how much time had passed. She rubbed her cheek against his braced forearm. "Deeper," she said.

"Breathe," he said. "Open for me. Think of water dragging against the beach."

Imena's hands slid in the sweat on his back. She scratched him lightly with her nails, to hear his breath catch, to feel his uncontrolled jerk that seated him more deeply inside her. She braced her heels and thrust up against him. He grunted. "What are you thinking?"

He rubbed fiercely against her, pushing her into the bunk. "I'm thinking it would feel really good to—" He thrust hard, seating himself fully.

Imena gasped, then laughed. She squeezed his hips with her thighs and rocked. "It does," she said. "Now, where is this tide you said we would make?"

"If you'd let me go I could move," he pointed out. When she loosened her grip, both hips and arms, he reared back and plunged his cock deeply into her, reseating at a slightly different angle, simultaneously higher and pressing more deliciously inside her. "Better?"

"Oh," she moaned. "Oh, Maxime, fuck me now."

"Be with me," he said. "Imena—" He kissed the side of her mouth, and after that they didn't speak, only gasped for breath.

She came first, pressing her mouth hard against his shoulder and trembling helplessly from scalp to toes. He coaxed her into another orgasm with his hand as he continued to seek his own pleasure, rocking her against the bunk. Weakly, she lifted a hand and scraped her nails over his belly; he moaned and his head drooped as he thrust faster, harder. "Come," she said. "Come for me."

"Not yet," he said through clenched teeth. "I never want this to end."

She summoned all her remaining strength and pushed back at him, grinding hard, little sobs of effort escaping her lips.

"Fuck," he said, and lost control. At the last moment, his ragged thrusts shoved Imena over the edge once more, and she jerked in helpless ecstasy beneath his weight.

Unusually for him, Maxime immediately fell asleep. Though Imena had craved just that result for herself, instead she lay entangled with him far into the night, listening to his steady breathing, inhaling their mingled scents and staring into the dark.

Maxime was nothing like Ying. She'd had opportunity to observe how Maxime worked with his captains, and some of how he ruled his duchy. She'd had a much closer view of his aunt Gisele, who served as his chief minister in matters of bureaucracy. He respected women; not just Imena and his aunt, but Duchess Camille, and Sylvie, and even the woman he'd refused to marry. All her instincts said he was honorable, thoughtful and trustworthy. He hadn't been unfaithful to her. She was sure he loved her. But she was too afraid to explore whether the caring she felt for him was love.

Why did she resist? Why was she still so afraid?

She knew Maxime would not betray her as Ying had. It didn't seem to help. There was no chart for emotion that could guide her.

Perhaps she should do what she'd done at the very beginning: forget that marriage to Maxime might lie in the future. Forget that there was a future.

Maxime had said he was willing to give more than he took. It wasn't fair to him, but…she was too afraid to be the woman he truly wanted her to be. And too weak to give him up.

The next morning, when he woke smiling into her eyes, his smile warmed her whole body with pleasure so intense it burned. She slid down his body and pleasured his cock with her mouth. That way, she didn't have to speak. And while he still basked in relaxation, afterward, she made sure to remember an important ship duty to which she was required to attend.

Maxime found her on deck as the sun was sinking. He had washed his hair, she noted, and tied it back with a blue silk ribbon; he wore a clean pair of sailcloth trousers and a new linen tunic.

Her heart thudded painfully against her ribs as she awaited confrontation; the feeling was all the worse because during the day she'd been able to subsume her worries in her role as captain, and almost forget her tortured nighttime thoughts.

Maxime stood next to her, mirroring her pose, with hands clasped behind her back, gazing out to sea. She could feel his warmth on her arm. He said, "If you don't want to talk about it now, just tell me."

At first she couldn't make sense of his words, then she was overpowered with a rush of relief. She said, "I don't want to talk about it now."

"May I inquire when the right time would be?" he asked, distantly polite.

She could not be cruel and tell him she didn't know. "After this is over," she said.

Whatever *over* might mean.

CHAPTER TWENTY

TWO WEEKS PASSED, DURING WHICH IMENA RISKED a brief stop at a peninsular port; they remained anchored overnight while she sent Chetri ashore with a letter to Lady Gisele, informing her that *Seaflower* would be returning to the duchies, and giving an approximate date. Once there, Imena would again send a messenger ashore to find out if it was safe for Maxime to return home.

Maxime did not argue with this plan.

He continued to share her cabin, but they rarely spoke, rarely joked. He saw to her pleasure with scrupulous care, but only once, in desperation, did she force him to forget himself and fuck her with abandon. After that one occasion, he rose and departed the cabin, not returning until the morning, while she sat awake and steadily drank rice wine in the hope of an oblivion that never came.

She found that what she missed the most were their hours with the charts and tools of navigation; not only the satisfaction when he grasped a concept, but the quiet times as they watched each other record angles, compute azimuths and calculate lunar distances. When she woke in the night and ventured topside, she still took pleasure in the cool silences, but missed his warm presence at her side.

Delaying discussion of their relationship wasn't the wisest choice she'd ever made. Fear was a terrible guide. She was angry with herself for succumbing to it, and a little angry at Maxime for accepting her choice.

Thus she welcomed the chance of action. They'd made landfall in the hope of obtaining news of the duchies. It might already be safe for Maxime to return home. She didn't think on what she would do then.

The port was small and limewashed, its income reliant on an odd mixture of summer visitors and a brisk export trade in both pickled eels and the distinctive blue-trimmed barrels in which to store them. It was a good place to buy small, pretty gifts, eat freshly fried eel with mugs of foaming ale and gather information.

As Imena wandered the streets with Norris, she began to have second thoughts about sending Maxime with Chetri. It wasn't that she didn't trust Maxime to be discreet, because she did; it was only that he didn't have the skills she did as a spy. Chetri would have done well enough on his own, or with Norris. No one was after Chetri, so far as she knew, and he had only been intending to speak to some of their usual contacts, people who had never realized *Seaflower* had more purpose to her journeys than mere trade. And buying pickled eels.

"You're worried about him, aren't you, Captain?" Norris said. "His Grace, I mean." Norris had long legs, but Imena realized the girl was skipping a little, to keep up with her headlong strides.

Imena slowed, pretending to look into a shop window. The shop was full of millinery, ornate constructions of straw and netting and beads and feathers, many of them accessorized with enormous beaded pins that resembled stilettos more than a lady's decoration. Perhaps that was the true purpose of the pins—weapons. Imena tried to imagine herself wearing one of the bonnets, even to conceal weapons, and almost laughed at her mental picture. No, she could not redesign herself.

Maxime had not asked that of her.

Norris stopped short and began examining the merchandise with great interest, her breath leaving a cloud on the wavy glass. Imena admitted, "I would feel better if I had my eyes on him."

"Chetri can protect His Grace," Norris said loyally. She shifted from foot to foot and said after a few moments, "Do you think it would be all right if I— It's not a dress, it's just a bonnet. Do you think it would be all right if I wore a hat like one of those? Sometimes?"

Norris was skittish about her female clothing; Imena had learned that, growing up, she had suffered greatly for being born a boy who nonetheless wished to live as a girl, and had only truly been able to dress as she liked after she went to sea, where strange customs abounded. Norris knew she didn't care what her crew wore, but still felt the need to seek reassurance on occasion.

"I think," Imena said, "that one of those bonnets probably costs a great deal, and wouldn't be very practical aboard ship. But if you wore it many times, say, every

shore leave for six months, the value per wearing—"
Casually, she laid her hand on her knife. "Pretend nothing is wrong," she said.

"What is it?" Norris asked.

"I thought I recognized someone. There, across the street. One of Venom's sailors."

Norris's breath caught. "I see her. She's the one who made Roxanne take her hook off. I recognize her scar, there, by her ear. You can see it when she turns her head."

"She's seen us," Imena said. "Let's walk, shall we? Easy. Think about bonnets."

"There's no joy in hats for me just now," Norris said, her breathing a little rushed.

"Stay calm," Imena said. "Pretend you're about to shoot someone, and need to have steady hands."

"That is *completely different* from this, Captain," she said. "We're not in the middle of a battle, when you expect such things. Any minute now, she's going to throw a knife at us, or shoot, and next thing, we'll be running down the street with a troop of filthy pirates chasing us. I thought I was *done* with that sort of thing. I thought I only had to keep your clothes clean and pressed. And take a turn in the rigging now and again. Do you know how many times I've been chased in my life?"

"No, I don't," Imena said, slowing before another shop window. The glass was poor quality, but good enough to see that their follower had been joined by a companion.

"I don't, either. It was too many times to count. I don't want to die now. I'm too young. I haven't even—"

"You're armed," Imena reminded her. "Use your cutlass

if you have to. I know you can do it. If you lose your cutlass, use your knife."

"Aye, Captain," Norris said. She sounded a little calmer.

"Is your pistol loaded? Don't put your hand on it."

"Yes, sir."

"The next time I chaff you about carrying that thing, remind me of this day."

"Aye, Captain."

Deliberately, Imena slowed her pace. She hooked her arm casually through Norris's and led her down a narrow, angled street. "I've spotted another one," she said, keeping her voice low and steady. When she was sure Norris had regained her equilibrium, she released the girl's arm and slipped her hand into her trouser's pocket. She carried a knuckle protector there, on some occasions, and was pleased that this was one of them.

Imena said, "If we're attacked, and there's an opening, you're to run. That's an order."

"Aye, Captain." Norris did not sound pleased.

"You're to run and fetch help. Don't bother hunting for Chetri in particular, it's numbers I'll likely need. Use your judgment."

"Sir." Norris's voice squeaked slightly on the word, but Imena didn't remark on it.

She'd spotted a third pirate, and a fourth. These were less concerned with discretion than the others. One of them, a brawny man with waist-length braids, elbowed aside an innocent pedestrian, who nearly complained before taking a good look and retreating hastily.

Norris squeezed a little more closely to Imena's side

and said, "I saw another one, Captain. Do you think if we went into one of these shops, we could—"

"No. We don't want them to follow us in, and perhaps harm people who have nothing to do with this." She paused. "You could do that alone, perhaps. I could cause a distraction, and you could escape out the back, and bring back reinforcements."

"I don't want to leave you, Captain," Norris said.

"You will if I order you. But all right. You may stay with me a little longer."

Imena walked more quickly. In her peripheral vision, she saw another pair of pirates, easily recognizable in their black garb as two of Venom's crew. One of them braced a halberd against his shoulder, and she caught a glimpse of a cutlass at his side. The other's torso was wound with chains; spiked metal balls dangled against his ribs. She'd never seen anything exactly like it, but it was clearly a weapon. The scars on his face indicated he'd fought often and bloodily.

"We'll avoid those two," she murmured to Norris. "Don't look! We're probably faster, but that won't help against that much upper-body strength, and their weapons look as if they have reach. We'll aim for the women we saw first. They were only armed with cutlasses, that I saw."

"Aye, Captain." Norris's voice trembled slightly. Imena squeezed her arm, and her shaking eased. Norris said, "They're herding us back to the docks."

"Yes."

"We might find help there."

"Very good," Imena said. "Don't forget the water as an

escape route, and the ships and docks as protection. Just be careful where you jump."

"I grew up portside," Norris said, now sounding more miffed than afraid. "I know not to bash my head on a piling."

Imena grinned. "Good, then you'll jump right in as soon as you're clear. Look, you can hide behind that heap of nets and then make a dash for it."

"Captain!"

"You will fetch help," Imena said, implacable. "On my mark. One, two, go!"

A small shove helped Norris on her way. To Imena's satisfaction, the girl darted swiftly into concealment for a short distance before appearing only briefly at the end of a dock. She plunged into the water like a thrown harpoon.

Imena's breath rushed out of her, then she drew it in again, deeply, preparing for a fight. The pirates didn't rush her as she'd expected. All six of them approached her slowly, closing in, forcing her toward a long pier.

She glanced left; she was at the far end of the docks, well out of range of *Seaflower*. She glanced right and saw Venom's black pirate ship, its paint and rigging altered to look more innocuous. At the end of a nearby pier stood Cassidy himself, a cutlass balanced on one shoulder, his poisoned dagger in his free hand. He was smiling at her, well pleased with himself. He spat on the dock.

If he'd been smart, he would have simply shot her. Imena bitterly regretted not borrowing Norris's pistol.

She glanced around. This far-flung area of the docks was nearly clear of ships and their accompanying cargo,

fishing gear and other detritus. There was little concealment. She glanced over the side. Along with the usual
flotsam, something white and red bobbed in the water,
jerked, was dragged and once again bobbed to the surface. Another—they were the corpses of goats or sheep,
she couldn't quite tell—slammed into a piling and was
swiftly dragged under, streaming red into the murky
water. Snouts and fins surged, white and gray. Heavy
jaws seized and mauled; the sun gleamed off flashes of
razor-sharp teeth.

"Fuck him with a brittle bowsprit," she muttered,
drawing her cutlass. The cup-guard hilt curved over her
bare hand. She drew her knife with her other hand, glad
she'd carried the longer one today. Its prominent cross-
guard would help her to keep Venom's poisoned blade
from her.

She wasn't sure when or if help would arrive. Regardless, she was equal to this type of fight, and angry enough
that she didn't want to draw it out. Taking another deep
breath, deliberately emptying her mind, she strode to
meet her opponent.

She stopped just out of lunging reach, her weapons at
the ready. "Where's your mistress, Captain Cassidy?" she
asked.

"Otherwise occupied," Venom said, again flashing his
unsettling, empty smile. "My name is Venom." He lifted
his cutlass from his shoulder and spun it in his hand, the
blade flashing in the afternoon sun.

"I'm surprised she let you out on your own."

Venom took a step closer, and she retreated the same
distance. He said, "Litvinova is no longer my concern."

She hadn't succeeded in luring him into a rage. Imena shifted her balance, watching Venom's every twitch and hoping for a momentary advantage. If she was quick, and lucky, she might be able to end this before it really began. She eased closer, close enough for their blades to engage. "Does that mean she didn't provide you with a reference?"

"I've taken my payment and have no more need of that old cow. She did not amuse me." He licked his lips. For a moment, they gleamed. "After I've killed you, I'll take your ship."

Imena laughed. "Feel free to try."

Venom spat. Green liquid pooled on the wood near Imena's foot. She sucked in a breath and he attacked, a straightforward lunge.

She flung up her blade to parry his. Steel rang. She withdrew a step, then attacked.

She didn't think. Her feet moved, her arms swung her blades, all too fast for thought. His longer blade clashed against hers, skidded, clanged into her cup guard. The shock reverberated up her arm. His teeth flashed, bubbling with poisoned spit. She reared back and he lunged with his poisoned dagger. She barely managed to trap its blade with her own knife. When he spat, she ducked sideways, eyes closed; poison landed on her tunic. She wasn't sure if it would burn through the cloth, wasn't sure of its effects. She had to finish this quickly.

Using all the strength of her back, she shoved him away from her, at the same time thrusting and twisting her knife in a sharp move that flipped Venom's dagger out of his grip.

He staggered backward and she lunged, her cutlass meeting his in a flurry of noise and numbing impacts. She risked a glance to see where the poisoned dagger had landed; it wouldn't do to step on it with her bare foot. In that instant, another dagger shot into Venom's hand from a concealed harness she should have been expecting.

He forced his blade to scrape along hers, pushing with his superior strength to get close enough to use the dagger. One touch of its poisoned tip and she likely wouldn't last long. Panting, she used leverage to thrust him away from her again and attack in a shower of blows, forcing him to engage at greater distance.

When she began to tire, Venom attacked vigorously, grinning each time his heavier strikes knocked back her blade.

She could sense the end of the pier to her left, the sides of it before her and behind. Unless they changed direction, one of them would be forced off the pier, into the roiling mass of blood-crazed sharks. Which was Venom's intent, she assumed. She roared out a battle cry and attacked again, trying to force him back, her breath sawing in her chest.

She stumbled. Venom yelled in triumph. She twisted her body, turning her lurch to momentum, to a lunge that slapped her cutlass flat against his body and shoved him off the edge of the pier.

First she heard only her own sobbing breath; then splashing; a wild, unrestrained screech; and then footsteps, slapping against the wood of the pier, rushing toward her. She turned and Maxime stumbled into her, seizing her arms.

His voice cut through the horrible gurgling and occasional shrieks coming from the water. He said, "Are you all right?" Looking her up and down, he yanked off his tunic and used the fabric to scrub at the blob of green poison on her chest. "Did it burn through?"

Imena looked. "No." She took the shirt from him and tossed it into the water just in case, following it with her stained tunic.

Maxime wore a pistol tucked into his belt. She took it, checked to be sure it was loaded and walked over to the pier's edge. She waited a few moments until Venom, or his remains, surfaced, took careful aim and shot. She gave the pistol back to Maxime. "I wasn't sure if he was dead yet," she explained.

Maxime swept her into his arms, squeezing her so tightly she couldn't move. Over his shoulder, she saw Chetri and a group of her crew, armed but milling uncertainly on the dock. The other pirates were either being pursued by Roxanne and her group, or they'd already fled. She could take a moment, and if she didn't, she thought she might collapse. She wriggled free of Maxime's embrace and trapped his face between her hands to kiss him.

It felt like more than a kiss. It felt as if time stopped. She only released him when she had to breathe. She didn't resist when he trapped her in his arms again, his breathing rough against her ear, his beard prickling her neck. Without willing it, she relaxed and let him hold her.

Maxime's arms felt like safety. She knew it wasn't true. But her feeling would not be denied.

If she'd died instead of Venom…she might never have known this.

Would giving up Maxime be worse than death?

For this, she would give up a great deal.

"Will you marry me?" he murmured at last.

"I'll think about it," she said.

Several hours later, Imena and Maxime were ensconced in the port master's cozy office, eating buttered bread and drinking hot tea. They'd both refused the pickled eels. "I appreciate your help with capturing Venom's crew," Imena said.

The port master sipped his tea. He was a heavyset man, wrinkled like dried fruit and bald as an egg. He said blandly, "I appreciate you feeding a pirate to the sharks. That crew has been quite troublesome in the past week."

"Norris was very pleased with her reward." She'd purchased a special basket just to hold her new hat. Imena decided not to wonder aloud where the port master's guards had been while she'd been battling a pirate for her life. She said casually, "I assume I have the right of salvage for the pirate's ship? My first mate, Chetri, can take it over. He's a sailor of great skill and many years' experience." She smiled.

Looking only slightly disgruntled, the port master nodded. "I'll have the papers drawn up immediately."

Maxime poured more tea into Imena's cup. He looked about to speak, when a furious pounding began on the door.

"Master Chandler! Master Chandler! Pirates!"

★ ★ ★

This time, the pirate was Captain Litvinova. Even in the darkness, the bright lanterns hung on her ship made it clear she'd anchored a short distance out from Venom's ship, currently occupied by a mixed crew of locals and sailors from *Seaflower*. Sound carried easily over water, and Imena heard nothing from the ship that sounded like preparations for battle.

Shortly, a boat launched. The lamps hung fore and aft signaled its ostensibly peaceful intentions. It contained only two figures, one rowing and the other sitting upright in the bow. It was easy to see her crested hairstyle even at this distance.

On the dock, Maxime stood at Imena's shoulder. There were people nearby, but he spoke close to her ear so no one would overhear. "We know now it's you they want," he said. "But perhaps I can negotiate for your ship's safety. Offer her more money than Diamanta, at least."

"Which you are carrying…" At the moment, Maxime looked like a sailor cleaned up for shore leave, not a duke. He didn't even have any jewelry, except the gold earrings she'd lent to him. True, there was easy authority in his posture, but that might not be enough.

"The promise of money, then."

"What if she just prefers Diamanta?" Imena shook her head. "I think she came here after Venom, not me. We defeated her crew once, and now she's lost both her allies and the element of surprise. It would be madness to attack us when we're in a friendly port."

"Could she have come for Annja and Suzela?"

"Perhaps."

Maxime said, "I'm more neutral in this matter. Would you like me to speak for you?"

Imena pondered. At last she said, "I'll speak for *Seaflower*. But be ready if I should need you."

"Always," he said.

Imena met his eyes. "Don't."

He flinched. "I thought you'd reconsidered my offer."

"I did. I am reconsidering. It's just…difficult. I've stopped worrying so much about how it would be between us. Now I've moved on to my parents, and your king, and the world."

He put his arm around her and squeezed, following with a rough shake. "Small matters, then."

Imena resisted the urge to lay her head on his shoulder and close her eyes. "Come. We need to return to Master Chandler's office."

CHAPTER TWENTY-ONE

IMENA FOUND THAT SHE COULD NOT QUITE LOOK at Captain Litvinova without anger. The woman had been responsible for the deaths of *Seaflower* crew members, and indirectly for damage to the ship itself. Unimaginable horrors might have resulted from Venom's cruelties if they had not promptly escaped, and any number of other crimes might be laid to her account. Imena had fought pirates for too many years and seen too many atrocities to trust a pirate to tell the truth.

She did, however, believe that Captain Litvinova had not been entirely pleased with Venom's actions. The stories she'd been told by Annja and Suzela, in addition to what she'd witnessed with her own eyes, convinced her of that. Thus, she *could* believe that Captain Litvinova had a shred of conscience, and was willing to listen to her, while maintaining a healthy level of skepticism.

Maxime and Imena concealed themselves in a curtained alcove while Captain Litvinova faced the port master.

After an initial exchange of stiff pleasantries, Litvinova said, "None of my crew will come ashore."

Master Chandler said, "My men will be keeping watch."

Litvinova said, "I would like to request information of you."

Master Chandler looked at her for a long moment, then sat. He indicated the chair across his desk. Looking surprised, Captain Litvinova sat, as well. He asked, "What sort of information?"

"We intend you no harm. Neither your people nor your port."

"Yes, yes. What did you want to know?"

Litvinova shifted in her seat. "The ship that now flies a salvage flag. I was searching for its captain."

"Dead, I'm afraid," Master Chandler said. He did not bother to affect sorrow.

Imena noted with interest that Captain Litvinova's posture visibly eased. "And his crew?"

"In custody. We cannot charge most of them, as their names and descriptions are not all on record. We will wait weeks or months for a reply from the imperial authorities regarding those men. Perhaps you would like to take custody of a few?"

"No. Thank you. We do not have sufficient supplies…"

Master Chandler sighed. "A pity. But if you would care to give evidence…"

There was a long silence. Imena, watching closely, did not see Captain Litvinova's expression change at all, but her hands tightened their grip on the arms of her chair. After nearly a minute had passed, she said, "I fear I cannot. I hired their captain, though I did not know enough of him. I regret it now. But they were under my command, regardless. I cannot speak against them, and I haven't the knowledge of their activities to speak for them, either."

It clearly wasn't the answer the port master had hoped for, but it was an answer Imena could respect. It might be possible to obtain a few truthful answers from the pirate, after all. First, she would confirm the information she'd received from Annja and Suzela.

Maxime suggested they take a walk along the docks before Imena spoke to Captain Litvinova. It would be best, he thought, if the conversation took place on *Seaflower*. Imena had the power there, and Litvinova would know it. "And," he added, "it will shock her when your concubine speaks."

Imena changed direction, so they were walking toward *Seaflower* instead of back to Master Chandler's office. "Tell me what you plan to say to her. You're sure she isn't involved in the plot against you?"

"No, I don't think so. I'm not sure what I plan to say," Maxime said. "It will depend on her, somewhat. What she says and how she holds herself."

"You won't offer her any kind of ducal pardon."

"No," he said. "Members of your crew died."

She looked away, out to sea, and walked a little faster.

He lengthened his stride to catch up. "I try to imagine how that feels for you, and can only think of when

I've sent out a courier and the courier never returns. My couriers aren't as close to me as your crew is to you, far from it. But I think I have an inkling of what it means to lose someone whom you've vowed to protect."

"Just tell me what you want from her, Maxime." Imena stopped abruptly and turned to face him, arms crossed over her chest. Maxime recognized the posture and the tone of her voice. She was annoyed. "Now is not the time for us to discuss…the other thing."

She was worse at discussing her feelings than many men he'd known. Maxime mentally rolled his eyes and said, "I thought I might see if she was willing to visit the islanders."

"I won't give her my charts," Imena said. "Would you give away a safe harbor to a known pirate?"

"She might be trustworthy if she's paid enough," Maxime said. "Assuming Diamanta truly did hire her, then I would wager she has some honor. Diamanta has a difficult personality, but she's one of the shrewdest people I know, particularly where business is concerned. She wouldn't waste her money on someone who would cheat her."

"No, only on someone who would hire a spitting madman."

Maxime chuckled. Imena threw up her hands. "All right," she said. "You're a shrewd man, yourself. I concede that you might have a good idea."

"Thank you," he said, absurdly pleased.

"Besides that, you pay me."

"Not enough, I suspect." He leaned forward; she didn't draw back. He kissed her lightly, not touching her except with his lips. "I concede that giving Litvinova the location of that safe harbor might not be the best idea. Perhaps Chetri could take on that task."

"That's a better idea," Imena said. "And Litvinova?"

"My other idea, if she seems canny enough, is to employ her temporarily. It bothers me a great deal that we know so little about the northern lands. Unless the Horizon Empire regularly sends envoys?"

Imena shook her head. "They don't. The northern barbarians aren't rich enough to make good vassals, and their climate is horrific."

"So you wouldn't be interested in visiting there, yourself."

"Not in the wintertime, that's for sure," she said. She began walking again.

Maxime caught her hand in his. "We work well together," he said with satisfaction.

"So long as you do as I tell you," she said, but she didn't let go of his hand, and she smiled at him sidelong.

Imena had chairs brought to the rear deck and shaded with an awning for their discussion with Captain Litvinova. Chetri would command the crew while Nabhi stood guard over their visitor. Maxime stood behind Imena's chair. Imena instructed Suzela and Annja to remain below throughout the meeting.

Captain Litvinova again had only a single sailor to row her over from her ship. Roxanne tossed down a ladder and then escorted her over to Imena.

Litvinova bowed low. She was not wearing a cutlass.

Imena wasn't sure if that was a sign of goodwill or if she merely wished to avoid handing it over.

Imena said, "Sit, please."

Litvinova gave Nabhi a glance before sitting, probably remembering her savagery in battle. Nabhi bared her teeth.

"I'll talk, you'll listen," Imena said. Litvinova nodded, her face impassive. Imena continued, "I killed Venom. If you cross me, I will kill you."

"Fair enough."

"I need to know who hired you."

"Lady Diamanta Picot."

"For what purpose?"

"I was to find the source of a certain balsam, learn all I could of how it could be purchased and shipped, and report back."

Imena swiftly confirmed the remaining details and at last said, "Why did you allow Diamanta to hire you?"

Litvinova cocked her head to one side. "I needed the money. My crew depend on me to provide for them. None of them have homes to which they can return, and our navy does not accept women as sailors, more fools them."

"Why did you hire Captain Cassidy?"

Litvinova glanced at Nabhi again. "I was told you were dangerous. That you'd killed dozens of pirates before you reached the age of twenty-five. That you'd betrayed your own lover after serving on his ship, and he was beheaded. It seemed only prudent to find additional support."

"Those things are true," Imena said.

Litvinova waited a moment, then said, "I wish now

I'd chosen someone other than Captain Cassidy. He was the most violent man I ever had the misfortune to meet. I'm pleased you killed him, and I owe you my thanks."

"Instead of your thanks, I would like his ship," Imena said.

"I have no rights to it. I think it's fair salvage."

"And his crew? Should any of them be remanded into your custody?"

"*My* custody?"

"Yes." Imena had decided, at some point during the past few minutes, that Litvinova should go free. She possessed some honor and, if she had honest employment, she would likely behave honestly. "Venom's crew?"

Litvinova shook her head. "Only if the two concubines were among them. Annja and Suzela. I had hoped they fled to you and not to Cassidy, but—"

"They fled to me," Imena said. "Maxime?"

And then Maxime took over. Imena blinked as he proceeded, swiftly and almost undetectably, to first convince Captain Litvinova that he was in fact a duke, then to make her loyal to him, or at least to the duchies. Starting with her crew and the problems of keeping them employed and fed, moving on to the reasons this was so difficult in the northern lands, he then subtly led her to realize the duchies, in particular his, might be a better refuge.

Imena had known, she thought, how good Maxime was at talking people into doing things. He was a duke, after all, and before that he'd been a protectorate lord, a position which required even more diplomacy. She'd thought she'd known all his different techniques: simple authority, quiet sympathetic listening followed by a predatory pounce, relentless logic and smiling charm. This was something else entirely, a seamless aggregation of all those methods. Without apparent effort, he was extracting every pin's worth of the pirate's personal feelings and opinions. From there, he was no doubt forming an array of plans for how to bend her to his will, now and in the future.

Imena remembered her initial, drunken interview with him and winced. Except, after the formal interview, they'd *both* been drunk. That wasn't logical. He'd gotten drunk with her, something she had never experienced again.

It was amusing that she could cling to the fact that they'd gotten rolling, jelly-brained drunk together, as a sign that he really did care for her.

In the end, Litvinova agreed to sail to the duchy, where Maxime would find her employment. As an added incentive for good behavior, Venom's ship would accompany her, commanded by Chetri. Litvinova's contract with Diamanta was at an end. They would discuss terms for a new contract with—Imena admired this touch—his aunt Gisele. Litvinova agreed to all of it.

All that remained for Imena was to inform Chetri of his good fortune.

The evening included an endless obligatory formal dinner with Master Chandler and various other worthies of the port. Late that night, back on *Seaflower* at last, she lay half asleep while Maxime massaged her feet. "Are you attempting to bribe me?" she slurred.

"You aren't susceptible to bribes," he said. "Unless there

is some bribe of which I am unaware that would tempt you?"

"You already did that thing," she said, smiling dreamily. "I will look favorably upon your advances tomorrow, though."

"And when we return to the duchies?" His tone was idle.

She said, "I don't know yet."

Imena spent the next morning closeted with Chetri in his cabin, then later with both Chetri and Roxanne, discussing how their duties would alter. Roxanne would be promoted to first mate. She and Imena would hire the new second mate together. In the meantime, Nabhi, the armsmaster, would take on that role. Nabhi's master's mate, Kuan, would go with Chetri to be trained as his first mate. Annja and Suzela would also accompany him, Suzela as cook and Annja for Kuan to train as armsmaster. Also, Suzela had insisted she be allowed to take the cat.

Maxime spent most of the morning in Imena's cabin, writing to his aunt Gisele. Imena stopped in periodically to read over his report and offer additional details, or suggest avenues for obtaining further information on the pirates. As they ate a midday meal together, she said, "I suppose I could write to my mother. She might have reports from any naval expeditions that have ventured farther north."

Maxime beamed. "You would do that for me? Petition an admiral of the Horizon Empire's fleet for aid?"

"She's my mother." Imena set down her cup, struck. Her mother was an admiral of the fleet, but she didn't command Imena. She couldn't force Imena to marry. She couldn't choose Imena's husband unless Imena allowed her to do so. Her mother was not the empress. Imena was a competent adult who could make her own decisions.

It was much easier to remember that fact when she was far away from her parents.

She added, "It might not be necessary to bring her into it. First, I'll send letters to some of my old mates from *Sea Tiger*."

They remained in port for over a week, resupplying and performing maintenance that was easier in a shipyard than careened on an island. Imena gave her crew shore leave, as well.

Chetri reminded her he was supposed to give up his shore leave this trip. He didn't seem disappointed to instead spend the time aboard his new ship, which he had named *Highest Mountain*. He would need to remain in port for at least a week beyond Imena's departure. He'd already had some success in hiring additional crew, and in giving the ship itself a thorough going-over. He also planned to have his new crew run sail drills together.

Imena hadn't realized his happiness would make her so painfully happy, as well. Chetri was no child, in fact he was older than she was, but she still felt responsible for launching him into freedom.

When it was time for *Seaflower* to depart, Imena wasn't sure she could say goodbye to him. Chetri stood before her, gleaming with silver jewelry on his ears and brow as well as around his wrists and neck. He wore his best silks, the ones adorned with silver embroidery he'd purchased for Maxime's accession ceremony. And he looked about to weep.

"Don't be foolish," Imena said, though he hadn't spoken. "You've been able to command a ship on your own for decades."

Chetri smiled even as a tear found its way down his cheek. "It's not that. It's the honor you've done me, Imena."

She shifted uneasily. "Someone has to take *Highest Mountain* in. I trust you to do it, that's all." When he didn't reply, she added, "You're not obligated to work for Maxime, you know. You could make a few voyages on your own if you like. I know there are places you'd like to see, or revisit."

Chetri nodded. "Aye, Captain." He sniffed, then clapped her shoulder hard enough to hurt. "Enough of all this sentiment. I'll meet you in the duchy, hopefully only a few days behind you."

"Take care of my crew," Imena said. "I'll be wanting them returned to me, except for Kuan, since I can't leave you without a mate. You'll have to spend your own time recruiting more."

"I recruited at least six of them myself," he mock protested. "Not counting Suzela and Annja."

Imena grinned. "Then you should have found your own ship before now. Fair sailing, Captain." She gave in to impulse and hugged him before kissing his forehead.

"And to you."

Home at last. It felt as if years had gone by. The weather had changed while he'd been gone. He felt auguries of autumn in the breeze.

The pier heaved beneath Maxime's feet. He grabbed Imena's arm for balance, hoping he hadn't drawn any extra attention to them.

He felt strange, a different person than before.

"Careful," Imena said as she steadied him. She hadn't shaved her head as she usually did for dockside visits, and had shielded her features with a broad-brimmed hat nearly identical to the one she'd crammed on Maxime's head. They both wore long, loose coats that didn't seem out of place because of the brisk seaside breeze. He'd gone along with the rudimentary disguises. There was no sense in taking unnecessary risks, even though he was home.

He said, "We'd better get started."

Imena shook her head. "I'll get us a cart. You don't want to climb the whole way, do you?"

No, he didn't. He'd done it before, but it was an arduous climb, and he didn't want to arrive at his castle puffing and red-faced and undignified.

While Imena went in search of transport, he wandered a little, breathed in the scents of home and swallowed down unexpected emotion. He could see his castle, its green-and-white stripes clean and bright against the vivid blue sky. Down here in the port, the duchy's citizens hurried past, carrying bundles or babies, leading animals, talking and laughing, completely unaware of him as he loitered along the dock. Competing scents of salt and fish and cooking food assaulted him with a hunger that lived in his heart, not his belly. He would have stopped to buy fried dough, but he didn't have any money, so he stopped near a stand instead and deeply inhaled the sugary perfume.

"I told you to wait over there," Imena said with mock irritation, appearing in front of him. "I've found us a pony cab."

At the castle, Maxime had the driver bring them to a side entrance. The guard recognized both him and Imena, and bowed deeply as she held the door open for them.

Though the ground had stopped shifting beneath him, the marble floor felt much different than usual to his bare feet, smooth and cool and luxurious. Imena chuckled.

"What's funny?"

"The guard. You might as well have put on a coronet and had someone blow a trumpet," she commented, following him to Gisele's office.

Business had to wait while Maxime allowed his aunt to hug him, kiss him, exclaim over him and hug him again. At last Gisele pushed him away, only to hug a startled Imena.

Maxime fell into his favorite armchair, suddenly exhausted. He hadn't slept much the previous night, while he thought about Imena and how he might convince her to marry him, once and for all. She was close to accepting him. She'd said so herself. But there were outside obstacles in the way. He could do something about that. He would go to the king. He'd even go to her parents if nothing else worked. He'd marshal his arguments first, and—

"Maxime!" Gisele said. He became aware she'd said his name more than once. "Out of that chair. You have to get a bath and get dressed."

"I am dressed," he said. "I'd really like a bath and a

nap, though. Imena, would you be interested in a bath and a nap?"

"You weren't listening," Imena said. "Your king is here. In your castle. Today."

It took a moment for her words to make sense. "Bloody dripping weaselshit!"

The door swung open and a slender figure stepped in. "Oh, is that how you think of me?" Julien asked. He wore riding leathers and boots, and looked distinctly dusty, except on the lenses of his spectacles.

When in doubt, bow. "Your Majesty," Maxime said.

Julien waved a hand. "Never mind all that. Maxime, why didn't you tell me someone was trying to kill you?"

"I was wrapped in a carpet, Your Majesty."

"And you must be Captain Leung."

Imena nodded. Maxime was startled at her informality before remembering she wasn't actually a citizen of the duchies. She said, "Time was of the essence."

The door opened again and Sylvie slipped into the room, also clad in riding gear, a pistol at each hip. "So," she said, "you were not killed by pirates, after all."

Maxime crossed his arms over his chest and glowered. "Enough. Your Majesty, may we reconvene in an hour, perhaps in my library?"

"Two hours would be preferable. I think we'd all appreciate a chance to clean up," Julien said. "I, for example, am going to take advantage of your fine hot springs. Sylvie, you'll accompany me."

Any plans Maxime might have had for a private bath with Imena were dashed by the presence of his king.

Giving in to the inevitable, he summoned servants to provide scrubbing and massage for himself and his three guests, then was unable to properly enjoy being scrubbed because he couldn't help but remember the last time he'd been here with Imena. It was agony to see Sera, one of the servants, massaging her naked skin mere feet away. Even the skilled hands of his favorite body servant, Stefan, couldn't ease his longing for Imena.

Stefan trimmed his beard, mustache and hair, then washed everything. A subtle pressure of his smooth hands on Maxime's chest let him know that other services were also on offer today. Maxime sighed and murmured, "I'm sorry, Stefan. I'm afraid I've become staid in my old age."

Stefan smiled as he smoothed an unguent through Maxime's hair. "It was just a thought, Your Grace. Is it your captain?"

Maxime, to his horror, blushed. He could feel the heat up to his hairline. Stefan chortled and used his hand to tip back Maxime's head. "I'm very pleased for you, Your Grace. Now, close your eyes, I need to rinse your hair."

Maxime noted that Stefan and Sera left together, exchanging gossip in voices too low for him to hear. Deliberately, he chose a different soaking pool to the others, one too small for anyone else to join him, and slid beneath the water until the two servants had departed.

After he surfaced, Maxime couldn't stop himself from watching the king in his peripheral vision, hoping to discern his intentions; but Julien, bred and trained to the throne, was as unreadable as a handful of sand.

CHAPTER TWENTY-TWO

IN THE SPACIOUS READING ROOM ON THE CASTLE'S first floor, Maxime finally learned the full extent of the plot against him. He sat on a small sofa, one arm flung along the back. Julien took the largest armchair (Maxime's favorite), and Sylvie, now divested of pistols, was unusually demure in another armchair near him. Imena didn't sit next to Maxime as he'd hoped; she stood somewhere behind him, outside the circle of seats.

Gisele also stood, because she only remained long enough to give an account of events that had transpired during Maxime's absence. She paced back and forth as she related how tavern tales had surfaced about Maxime's fitness to be duke. Some of them were familiar, from before his accession. Every duke had detractors, whether they took measures to stop the dissent or not. But there were new tales that arose suspiciously soon after Imena had learned of the plot against Maxime's life, tales that implied serious wrongdoing. Gisele had immediately begun to send her couriers out to find the sources of sudden rumors that Maxime had committed disturbing sexual crimes, or stolen a large shipment of jewels from the king, or plotted with foreign powers to overthrow other duchies. At the same time, printed broadsides had mysteriously appeared on the doorsteps of a large list of dissenters, and been posted on trees and walls about the university.

Maxime hadn't heard Gisele's full report before this. The more he heard, the more enraged he became. He set his jaw while she explained how the duchy's courier network had painstakingly tracked down the printer of the broadsides, who worked in the royal city, and from him obtained a list of runners who'd distributed the new tales, both print and verbal. The printer, who was very organized, had obtained a written contract from Lord Odell. The contract didn't give specific details of what was printed, but Gisele considered it to be enough evidence against him.

She'd spent quite some time investigating and quashing the rumors, time she was very irritated to have lost. Julien seemed to take the hint, and dismissed her after only one or two questions.

Sylvie spoke next. Maxime recovered his temper somewhat as she spoke of her work with his young cousin Alys and of how she'd obtained information from Raoul. It was clear to him that Raoul was her lover. Trust Sylvie to find any opportunity to bang bodies.

Sylvie finished her report by saying, "Odell did want money and position, but more than that, he wanted Lady Diamanta. He only needed money in order to convince her to marry him." She shook her head, looking bemused. "He could have had any number of women. It was foolish to risk his position by attempting assassination." She selected a sesame candy from the tray in front of her and popped it in her mouth.

Maxime smiled ruefully. "I can understand why he did it."

"No matter his motives, he won't be remaining in my country," Julien said, and sipped his lemon sherbet. "He would have killed you, Maxime, and shown not a moment's remorse. If he'd succeeded, he would already have lost his head. He's no better than the pirate Captain Leung fed to the sharks."

Maxime glanced at Imena. She'd continued to stand for the entire discussion, half turned toward a window, staring out at the harbor. At *Seaflower,* he was sure. He said, "Venom deserved it. Besides, she's licensed to kill pirates."

Imena said, "So, did Lady Diamanta hire other pirates to search for other captains?"

"No," Julien said, addressing her directly. "Your reputation preceded you, and she had the advantage of several visits to Maxime's duchy. She knew your ship was the source of the balsam." He took another sip of his sherbet and added, "I questioned her myself. I can always tell when she's lying."

"You're sure?"

Julien didn't express any outrage at being questioned by a mere ship's captain. "Yes. She'd exhausted other avenues. She'd even hired a foreign cartographer in the hope of learning more about the overland trade routes.

That was perfectly legal. In hiring Captain Litvinova, she only skirted the law. Diamanta did not instruct her captain to use violence."

"I lost crew to the pirates," Imena said. She turned to face Julien. She wore one of Maxime's long silken robes over a plain tunic and trousers, her feet bare, the beautiful curve of her skull still visible beneath her short hair. Maxime's heart hurt from the suppressed emotion in her voice. "Four people died as a result of her greed. Two of them died slowly from their wounds."

"Indirectly," Julien said. "Outside of the bounds of the duchies. The pirates were also hired outside the duchies."

That was all true, but it wasn't right. Maxime hadn't known any of the sailors who'd died. If he had—if Chetri had died, or Tessa, or Norris—he would not have let mere law stop him from seeking some form of justice for their deaths. He could only imagine how Imena felt. If Julien did nothing, then Maxime would.

Power could be a good thing if he wielded it with justice and conscience, remembering the individuals who made up his duchy.

"Hiyu," Imena said. "Big Wim, Donkey and Yeadon." She drew a deep breath after naming the dead sailors, and Maxime's heart broke for her. She said, "Lady Diamanta will pay the expense of pensioning their heirs. Otherwise, it might appear that you and your country condone the use of pirates as part of your business dealings, and your ships might become prey for privateers."

Maxime blinked, impressed. Given that she had contacts among the privateers of the Horizon Empire, she'd made a serious threat. He didn't think she would actually carry out the threat because almost all of the ships in the duchies belonged to Maxime, but it would impress her serious intent upon Julien where it would hurt most, in his treasure vault.

Maxime tensed when Julien shifted in his seat and relaxed when Julien inclined his head to Imena, a remarkable gesture of respect. "Very well. Send the names to my chamberlain. Or you may give them to me personally, and I will convey the information when I return to the palace. Their direct heirs will receive the same pension as a member of my personal guard, and additional help if it's needed."

Imena nodded once, decisively. "That's satisfactory. Thank you."

Julien said, "Now, the other matter. Sylvie, you're no longer needed. You may go."

As Sylvie, uncharacteristically silent, left the room, Maxime asked, "What other matter?"

"The matter of your marriage," Julien said pointedly.

"Ah. I'd hoped you'd forgotten about that." Maxime shifted in his seat.

Imena said, "I should also take my leave. I have duties on *Seaflower* to which I must attend."

Maxime cast her a desperate glance, but she was looking at Julien. He pushed his spectacles higher on his nose and said, "Captain Leung, I'd like you to remain a little longer. Maxime, perhaps we might have tea brought? Or would you prefer wine?"

Imena said, her gaze steady on Julien, "I'm not your

subject, and I don't think I need to remain for this discussion."

"Would you be interested in changing your affiliation?" Julien asked. "Please sit, Captain. If you so desire. It would make me happy."

"Do I want to make you happy?" she asked. To Maxime's gratification, she sat next to him on the sofa, crossing her legs and flinging her arms along the sofa's back so their forearms touched. "What do you have to say to me, Your Majesty?"

Julien said, "It's what I have to say to both of you that will be of interest."

Maxime shifted his leg a little closer to Imena's. He couldn't quite touch her, not without being obvious. "I trust Diamanta's plotting has convinced you she isn't suited to be my duchess. Or anyone's duchess."

Julien countered, "You might have made a good pair if you hadn't treated each other as obstacles to be overcome."

"You can't overcome a lifetime of antipathy so easily," Maxime said.

"Put her to work," Imena said, interrupting. "At least give her the choice. If I were in her position, I might have killed you all before now, out of frustration."

Julien was silent. Maxime cleared his throat. "Actually, I'd hoped to send her off with Captain Litvinova, if they'd both agree."

Imena smiled at him. "I approve. I'd prefer not to see either one of them for quite some time."

"It was because of you that I thought of it."

Julien rose from his chair, forcing them both to look

up at him. "Sylvie was right. You two are besotted with each other."

Maxime saw red. "That squeaking rat! That's none of her business!"

Imena said drily, "There's a reason Her Grace Camille employs her." Then she caressed his arm and took his hand. Maxime was absurdly pleased by her public gesture.

Julien stared down his nose at Maxime, something he couldn't do when both of them were standing. "Every aspect of my dukes' lives is my business. I questioned Sylvie thoroughly before we arrived here."

Maxime said, "Your Majesty, if you know that, then you know that I would prefer to marry Captain Leung."

"I had suspected it," Julien said.

"I understand it's out of the question," Imena said. Her fingers tightened on Maxime's. "I assume you know I'm of mixed blood. Hardly fit to marry into your aristocracy."

Maxime felt a pang in his chest. He leaned over and kissed her cheek, not caring if Julien saw.

Julien dropped back into his chair, suddenly more casual, one leg flung over the chair's arm, hands loosely clasped on his belly. "Is that what you think, Captain Leung? Daughter of Admiral Leung?"

"Yes, it is," she said. "Do you think my mother's position gives her special privilege? Because it does not. She herself suffers politically from her youthful indiscretion."

"Which was marrying your father?"

"Yes."

"So there would be no additional harm to her if you, too, married outside the empire."

"I can't see the future," she said.

Maxime couldn't remain silent any longer. "Your mother isn't the most important person involved here. You are. You'd have me, wouldn't you, if His Majesty endorsed our marriage?"

"He won't," Imena said.

Julien pinched the bridge of his nose between finger and thumb. "I am weary of people assuming they know what's in my mind."

Maxime said tartly, "You can hardly blame us, when our lives might depend on your thoughts."

"Maxime," Julien said, "I didn't know you cared so much."

Maxime would have hit him if he hadn't been the king. "Well, what do you think, Your Majesty? Wouldn't Captain Leung make an admirable duchess? She's intelligent, brave, a leader, a warrior. She might even make a better duke than me."

"No, thank you," she said.

"I think," Julien said, "that you're right."

"But," Imena said, prompting.

"But she might be too good for you."

Imena laughed. Maxime didn't. He said, "I know that, Your Majesty. Yet I continue to hope."

"She does have *some* assets," Julien said.

As if she were a horse he planned to buy. Maxime thought about hitting him, right in his patronizing mouth. There weren't any guards in this room. He stood a reasonable chance of survival.

Imena said in a dangerous tone, "Please, enlighten us about my assets."

Julien stared at them both for long, uncomfortable moments. Then he smiled. "Indeed. For instance, Captain Leung is *not* part of my aristocracy. She is not and never has been a courtier. After recent events, I find that most refreshing. She's not involved in the intrigues of the empire. And I needn't fear ridiculous, convoluted plots against me. Captain Leung would simply kill me without fuss."

Imena was silent. Her fingers squeezed Maxime's until they began to grow numb.

Julien spooned up more of his lemon sherbet. He stared at Imena over the tops of his spectacles as he said, "Also, despite her assessments of her social rank, she is still linked to a powerful family in the Horizon Empire. The empire which never hesitates to inform me they are the most powerful in the world. The captain might say I am unimportant to *them,* but that sort of connection is important to *me* and to the duchies. You have *enough* social rank, Captain Leung. And *not* enough social rank to be potentially troublesome to me." He paused. "You do understand me."

Maxime's heart began to pound. Deliberately, he pried his fingers free of Imena's and tugged her close to him. She didn't resist, too occupied with staring at Julien.

Julien leaned back in his chair and crossed his legs. "Aside from all that, Her Grace Camille has been pestering me about the women of the court. She's done good work for me since her accession, so I am inclined to indulge her. Putting you in a position of power might please her for a time, and reduce the number of letters she sends me."

Maxime stifled a chuckle. If he allowed himself to laugh, he was sure he wouldn't be able to stop.

Julien continued, "Not to mention that I'm sure a number of my courtiers will be afraid of you, Captain Leung, particularly if you visit court with those tattoos blazoned all over. If you'd be willing to intimidate one or two of them for me every now and then, I would be grateful." He smiled at her. It was a charming smile, which always surprised Maxime, though it shouldn't have. "In short, you'd make a perfect duchess." Julien turned to Maxime. "If you don't marry her, I'll be sorely disappointed."

Maxime grabbed Imena's head and kissed her. "Marry me," he said. He kissed her again. To his surprise, his hands shook. "Please."

Dazed, she stared at him, then tipped their foreheads together. "Can it be so easy?"

"Yes," Julien interjected.

"Please," Maxime murmured. "I would love you if you were the lowliest sailor, you know. Do you love me?"

She lifted her hand and laid it against his cheek. "I do. I'll marry you." She kissed him softly, briefly. Then she turned to Julien. "I'm not marrying him because of you," she said. "I won't be bought in that way."

The king was finishing his lemon sherbet. "It was melting," he explained, staring into his goblet. "Captain Leung, I didn't intend to buy anyone. That never works out well. Would you accept an offer of citizenship? In the ordinary way of things, you'd get that simply by marrying, but since Maxime is a duke and you're a foreigner, I must grant you citizenship first."

Maxime took a deep breath, trying to calm himself. He was still in too much shock to feel happy yet. He couldn't let go of Imena. He said wryly, "I assume there's a fee involved?"

"Naturally," Julien said. "Which you will pay." He named the sum. Imena's eyes widened.

"Done," Maxime said.

Imena gave him a look. "I didn't accept the offer of citizenship yet." His panic must have shown because then she grinned and said, "I accept, Your Majesty. If you will excuse us?" She climbed into Maxime's lap. "We'd like to celebrate our engagement."

Maxime met with Diamanta in Gisele's office. Imena had gone back to *Seaflower* to speak to her crew and have Norris pack her things for an extended stay ashore. Norris would accompany her to the castle along with Roxanne and Tessa, who would be Maxime's guests.

As they'd discussed ahead of time, Gisele did most of the talking, while Maxime sat at his ease. Diamanta wore a traveling gown in charcoal gray with a high collar that nonetheless managed to show off her bosom through the judicious use of decorative seams. Maxime was unmoved. With every word Diamanta spoke, he became more grateful that he had not agreed to marry her.

They were far too much alike. He would have spent all his days looking for double and triple and quadruple meanings in every minor comment and gesture. He admitted privately to himself that she ought to have been a duke, or a duchess who ruled her own duchy, like Camille. If she had been, he might have been afraid of her. Of course, if she'd had such power in the first place, a great deal of her scheming might not have been required.

Gisele said, "I have a contract here. You would be officially in the employ of Duke Maxime. In all matters save those of the ship's business, you would be in command of Captain Litvinova."

That was chancy, but Maxime thought it would work. Diamanta would not risk her life by allowing Captain Litvinova to commit piracy.

Diamanta uncrossed her legs and leaned forward in her chair. "I have changes to make to the subsections." She glanced at Maxime. "However, the basic structure of the agreement is sound. I infinitely prefer this contract to the marriage my cousin originally suggested."

"Thank you," Maxime said with heavy irony to match hers. "If, later on, you'd like to allow Julien to pay your considerable salary, I wouldn't take it amiss."

Diamanta smiled. "Oh, I don't think so. Not just yet. You will not regret your investment in me, Maxime." Then she turned back to Gisele, who'd watched the whole exchange with amusement. "Shall we move to the table, to look over the papers?"

Maxime said, "It seems I'm not needed any longer. I'll be in my office."

Sylvie found Raoul in the baths. Except for him, they were deserted at this hour of the morning. He looked up at the sound of her boots ringing on the stone and blinked lazily at her. His svelte dark form was ensconced in one of the hot soaking pools; a silver pitcher and goblet stood near to hand. The scars on his wrists gleamed with ointment.

Sylvie stripped off her jacket, then her boots. "I'll join you shortly," she said. "Unless you would like to scrub me." She shucked off her riding leathers, then her lacy bodice.

Raoul said, "It wouldn't be a hardship." He turned fully, braced his arms on the side of the pool and lifted himself out. Sylvie watched with appreciation as water coursed down his sleek skin. As he walked over to her, he asked, "Are you going to instruct me?"

Sylvie finished undressing and picked up a cloth and soap while Raoul filled a bucket. The past few days in the company of King Julien had temporarily cured her of the desire for play with authority. "Take all the time you like," she said. "I trust you'll be creative."

Raoul would have made an excellent bath servant, if he ever tired of cartography. He mapped every arch and crevice of her body with first his tongue, then a soapy cloth. Sylvie was near delirium by the time he'd washed her hair and was massaging her scalp; he'd licked her to orgasm once, but his slow attentions afterward made her feel as if she hadn't come for weeks.

"Hurry," she said. "I want you to fuck me."

Raoul roared with laughter, collapsing onto her shoulder and gasping into her neck. "I knew it! I knew you wouldn't be able to last without ordering me!"

"Well, if you'd been quicker about it I wouldn't have

had to order you," she said crossly. "There are chambers next door. With beds."

Some hours later, after a long interlude in bed followed by another bath, she and Raoul lolled in the soaking pools, speaking softly so as not be overheard by Lady Gisele, who was being tended by one of the servants on the other side of the room. Raoul said, "I've enjoyed our time together."

Sylvie stared up at the ceiling. Some new tiles had been mosaicked into an underwater scene, and the swirl of octopus tentacles in cobalt water made her contemplative. She said, "You can't resist traveling, can you?"

"No," he said. "Even as a boy, I regularly packed food and books and wandered off into the mountains. I was the despair of my mother."

Sylvie said, "When you return, you may visit me if you like."

"I would like that," he said.

"Where will you go?"

He pressed a kiss to her temple. "I spoke with King Julien yesterday. I would like to travel with Diamanta."

Sylvie realized she didn't mind. It wouldn't do to grow too attached. She rolled her head to the side and smiled slyly at him. "You still have hopes, do you?"

"Yes." He grinned back at her. "If I fail, the whole ship is full of women. Perhaps I'll be luckier than I imagine."

"I wish you all the luck you can sustain," Sylvie said. Then she closed her eyes. She would seek out luck for herself, as well. After Maxime's wedding to Captain Leung, perhaps she would go to visit Karl Fouet. It would be good to renew their friendship, and perhaps explore what could be done in a darkened room lined with velvet.

Imena didn't get a chance to return to her cabin until the evening watch. She didn't expect to find Maxime lounging on her bunk, reading a book.

On second thought, she shouldn't have been surprised. She hadn't seen him in two days. If he felt as she did, the separation must have seemed interminable. She'd grown accustomed to having him near enough to touch.

Maxime dropped his book onto his chest. He was nude, so it made an odd picture. "I've missed my navigation lessons," he said.

"The azimuth doesn't alter if you're naked," Imena remarked. "You could have summoned me to the castle if you wanted to see me."

"Everyone's looking at me in the castle," he confessed. "Especially Julien. And everyone in the castle whom I've ever fucked has made a point of congratulating me and offering me a celebratory goodbye."

Jealousy stabbed her stomach, but she would not ask. "Oh?"

He stretched like a cat. "Don't look at me like that. I refused them all. I think they were testing me. You'd think they'd feel a proper decorum toward their duke."

Imena didn't say they might feel more proper decorum if he hadn't fucked most of them. She sat on the edge of the bunk. "I didn't ask."

"Well, you should have." He nudged her with his shin. "You won't hurt me if you ask. I've decided I need the reminder now and again. I plan to be faithful to you,

Imena. I've never tried that for any length of time, and I worry it might be difficult. I don't want to hurt you, ever. So if you ask me when you think I might need to be asked, you'll help me." She turned to face him. He looked uncertain. He said, "You'll do that for me, won't you?"

He planned to be faithful to her. Imena laid her hand on his thigh and rubbed it. "I don't know what to say," she said. She hadn't even known she needed to hear his words until they'd tumbled from his mouth.

"Tell me you love me," he said.

"I do love you," she said. "I'm going to marry you. And I'll kick you in the bollocks if you need it."

Maxime laughed. "That's what I want our marriage to be like. Not kicking me in the bollocks. Helping each other. Supporting each other as we try to overcome our worst qualities."

She chuckled, feeling teary-eyed at the same time. "And me? What will you support for me?"

"Sexual satisfaction," he said, his tongue curling lovingly around the words. "And…sometimes I fear you're a bit too…"

"Demanding? Commanding?"

"Alone," he said. "Wait! Stop! Don't weep!"

"I'm not weeping, you fish-brained fool!" she said. She sniffed hard, and stood up. She began stripping off her clothes.

"So it's all right, then? If I tell you that you can come to me always? Even if you want to tie me up?"

"Yes," she sniffed. She tossed her clothes over her chair and stretched out next to him, snuggling her face into his beard. "I expect the same of you. Except for the tying up. I'll need to think about that."

"And teach me knots." Maxime kissed the top of her head. "I spoke to my aunt, you see."

"About?"

"About marriage. It will take practice. We'll have to work hard."

"I know. I've watched my parents my whole life. If they can manage, so can I," she said. "We can talk about it more later. You know I can't think when I'm naked with you. Now kiss me."

Maxime kissed the tip of her nose. "Those are the words I was waiting for."

Imena fitted herself to him, sliding her leg between his, touching her cheek to his bearded one, pressing her breasts against his chest. He spread one hand wide over her rear and stroked the other down and up her back. Imena closed her eyes to better appreciate the sensation of her nipples being abraded by the scruff on his chest, and the friction of the coarse hair on his legs.

They shifted position until she lay beneath him. "Am I too heavy?"

Imena spread her hands over his rear, massaging gently. "Not yet," she said.

He sighed against her cheek and began to work his way down her jawline to her neck, kissing and nipping. Imena shifted beneath him restlessly and ran her nails over his rear, then his lower back, then his rear again.

"More?" he murmured into her ear, his warm breath sending a pleasurable chill down her spine.

"I want to suck your cock," Imena confessed. She

arched her back, pressing against his erection, and he moaned, pressing back.

"Right now?" he said. "Because I really want to be inside you. So close that we couldn't possibly be any closer."

"I can wait," she said. "You see, we're already helping each other to make decisions."

Maxime stifled his laughter against her breasts, then sucked her nipple into his mouth. "So long as we're negotiating, what are your views on—"

"Remember, I said we'd talk about it later," she said. She reached down and found his cock. She used her thumb to find his most sensitive spot and grinned when he moaned and melted into her. She murmured, "Except for this one thing. Your cock is mine. Is that fair?" She squeezed, pulled.

"Very fair," he gasped. "If I get your cunt. Including your clit, mind." She felt his hand wiggling its way between them, gently pressing her lower lips apart and sliding inside her.

"What's yours is mine," Imena said. "I'm going to put mine into yours."

"I can agree with that," Maxime said. "Collaborative effort."

Much, much later, Imena woke to darkness. She'd trapped Maxime beneath her outflung arm and leg. He was awake, watching her.

In the dark and silence and gentle rocking of her ship, it was easier to speak. "I'm afraid," she said. "What if we can't do it?"

"We'll work at it," Maxime said. "You watched your

parents. Until they were killed, I watched mine. We can do this. I won't let you fail."

"Then I won't let you fail, either."

Imena didn't so much chafe at being landside as at the fact that while she was staying in the castle, everyone wished to consult with her about plans for her wedding. She would rather have jumped the cutlass and been done with it. If only they'd thought to do that back on the island. Life would be much simpler if they'd just stayed on the island. Well, aside from the occasional sex competition.

She wanted this marriage. She wanted a life together with Maxime. The idea of being called Your Grace frightened her a little, but she imagined she would grow used to it, as she'd grown used to being called Captain. When she thought of the challenges ahead, she welcomed them.

It was only the wedding she dreaded.

Today, she was discussing mechanics with her officers and Maxime. She sorely missed Chetri, who had a gift for cutting to the heart of matters and hauling everyone else along with him. The rest of her crew seemed determined to drag the discussions out for months.

"Why can't we have the wedding on the ship?" the Knife asked.

"Too small for all the guests," Imena said.

"We could have a smaller ceremony of our own," Maxime said. "We could take a small cruise, perhaps an island idyll."

"That would require even more planning," Imena

grumbled. "Roxanne, that will be your duty. As if you didn't already have enough to do."

Roxanne looked grim, the Knife delighted. Norris entered the room, followed by Alys and several more of Maxime's young female cousins. Every one of them had a cascading armful of bright silks.

Imena held up her hand. "No."

"But, Captain, this blackberry-juice purple—"

"No." Imena sighed. "My mother is providing the silks. In fact, Norris, you had better go and consult with her courier."

Maxime said, "The rest of you, too. Out!"

Imena grabbed Roxanne's arm. "Can you go to the docks today? See if the repainting is complete? And I'll need a report on the shore-leave rotations."

Roxanne grinned down at her. "Naturally, Captain. You know, you should have just jumped the cutlass, like I did with Tessa."

"Do you think I don't know that?" She let Roxanne go.

The Knife said, "Am I dismissed also, Captain? I'd like to catch Norris before she goes too far. Your crew would look stunning in some of those silks."

"Fine, fine."

Alone at last. The room seemed unnaturally silent.

Maxime closed his hands over Imena's shoulders and massaged. She moaned and let her head fall forward. "The protocol is killing me, Maxime."

"Luckily, you don't have to do it all yourself, as I have tried to impress upon you before this. I have a staff. A large staff."

"A very long, thick staff," she said, then laughed until she snorted.

Maxime dragged her over to a sofa, pulled her onto his lap and proceeded to kiss her witless. She retaliated. Sometime later, they curled together on the rug, leaning their backs against the sofa. Imena said, "Sylvie carried the invitations to Her Grace Camille and Henri, didn't she?"

"She left yesterday."

"Do you think they'll arrive before my mother and father?"

"It seems likely. You did instruct Chetri to take his time about fetching them." Maxime nuzzled her neck.

"He can only dawdle on the way there. Coming back to the duchies, he'll have my mother staring at every move he makes." Imena was extremely grateful she wasn't transporting her parents herself.

"I still think Camille and Henri and the baby will be here first."

"Good." Imena relaxed against Maxime's shoulder. "Do you think Camille would be willing to take charge of my mother?"

Maxime kissed her with enthusiasm. "You see! You're already a diplomat! I told you what a wonderful duchess you would make!"

Imena patted his chest. "Well. Then in return, I'll make a sailor out of you." She grinned. "Perhaps we'll start with the basics of scrubbing the captain. What do you think?"

★ ★ ★ ★ ★

ACKNOWLEDGMENTS

Ann, Ef, John, Judith, Steve and Ricardo, of the Nameless Workshop, critiqued for me, and their comments helped me make this novel a good deal more coherent and complex than it might have been were I left to my own devices. Lorrie, as always, provided sanity, small monkeys and pie. Charlotte brainstormed with her usual brilliance. Sherwood told me about invaluable research books, and I was further inspired by the sea-battle scenes in her *Inda* series. Arionrhod and Kyle Cassidy contributed their names in support of charitable causes. Nif and Jen patiently listened to me relate the entire plot when this novel was still nascent. Special thanks go to Lara Hyde for okaying the pirate-eating sharks (and for the ice cream) and to Susan Swinwood for her insightful revision notes. And finally, thanks to the production folks at Harlequin for yet another beautiful book.

Further information may be found at my website, www.victoriajanssen.com.

the LOVERS
Eden Bradley

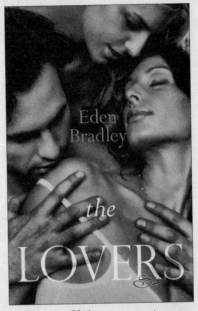

I had long dreamed of having a single experience that would change me forever. Who knew the one to change me would be a woman? But the story doesn't end there. No, that in itself is a whole new beginning.

It seemed ideal—two months at a charming writers' retreat, surrounded by kindred souls. But Bettina Boothe wasn't prepared for just how long eight weeks truly was. Or that in the process she would have to open up and reveal the most secret places in her body and soul.

Fortunately, her fellow authors do not share Bettina's self-consciousness and begin to draw her out of her self-imposed shell. One in particular—Audrey LeClaire—seems to ooze confidence and self-assuredness. Dark and petite, Audrey possesses a potent sensuality that draws the men *and* women in the workshop to her like flies to honey. Bettina is just as vulnerable, finding herself overwhelmed by a very unexpected attraction to Audrey, who makes Bettina her special project.

But when Jack Curran arrives at the retreat, everything changes. Jack is tall, beautiful, masculine. A writer of dark thrillers, he is as mysterious and alluring as his books. He and Audrey are obviously an item, but they eagerly welcome Bettina into their bed. Suddenly Bettina finds herself swept up in a maelstrom of lust, obsession and jealousy, torn between her need for two very different people in a love triangle where she will either be cherished…or consumed.

Available wherever books are sold!

A Hell's Eight erotic adventure from national bestselling author

SARAH McCARTY

Before his trade became his name, "Tracker" Ochoa was a scrawny Mestizo runaway. Now as fearsome as he once was frightened, he's joined the notorious Hell's Eight… and they have a job for him.

He must rescue kidnapped heiress Ari Blake and deliver her safely to the Hell's Eight compound—by any means necessary. Turns out that includes marrying her if he means to escort her and her infant daughter across the Texas Territory. Tracker hadn't bargained on a wife— especially such a fair, blue-eyed beauty. But the pleasures of the marriage bed more than make up for the surprise.

Tracker's well-muscled bronze skin and dark, dangerous eyes are far more exciting than any of Ari's former debutante dreams. In the light of day, though, his deep scars and brooding intensity terrify her. But he's her husband and she's at his mercy. With the frontier against them and mercenary bandits at their heels, Ari fears she'll never feel safe again.

Tracker, too, remembers what fear feels like. Though he burns to protect Ari, to keep her for himself always, he knows that money, history—and especially the truth—can tear them apart.

"If you like your historicals packed with emotion, excitement and heat, you can never go wrong with a book by Sarah McCarty."—*Romance Junkies*

Available wherever books are sold!

www.Spice-Books.com

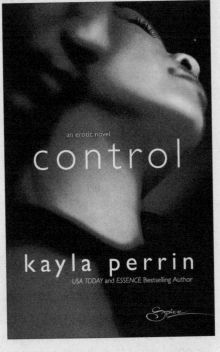

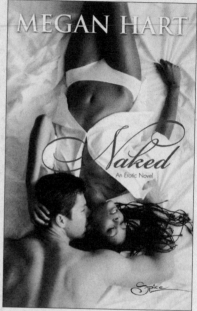

ALISON's WONDERLAND

ALISON TYLER

Over the past fifteen years, Alison Tyler has curated some of the genre's most sizzling collections of erotic fiction, proving herself to be the ultimate naughty librarian. With *Alison's Wonderland,* she has compiled a treasury of naughty tales based on fable and fairy tale, myth and legend: some ubiquitous, some obscure—all of them delightfully dirty.

From a perverse prince to a vampire-esque Sleeping Beauty, the stars of these reimagined tales are—like the original protagonists—chafing at unfulfilled desire. From Cinderella to Sisyphus, mermaids to werewolves, this realm of fantasy is limitless and so *very* satisfying.

Penned by such erotica luminaries as Shanna Germain, Rachel Kramer Bussel, N.T. Morley, Elspeth Potter, T.C. Calligari, D.L. King, Portia Da Costa and Tsaurah Litzsky, these bawdy bedtime stories are sure to bring you (and a friend) to your own happily-ever-after.

"Alison Tyler has introduced readers to some of the hottest contemporary erotica around."—*Clean Sheets*

www.Spice-Books.com

SAT60545TR